Penguin Book 2865
Stepping Westward

KU-780-067

Malcolm Bradbury was born in Sheffield in
1932 and read English at University College,
Leicester. He has studied and taught at various
universities in England and the United States and
is now Senior Lecturer in English and American
Literature at the University of East Anglia.
He has contributed regularly to many magazines,
including *Punch* and the *New Yorker*, and has
been active as a literary critic. He is the author
of one other novel, *Eating People Is Wrong*
(1959), also available in Penguins; two collections
of humorous articles, *Phogey!* and *All Dressed
Up and Nowhere to Go*; a critical book on Evelyn
Waugh; and a small volume of poems. He has
edited a collection of essays on E. M. Forster,
is co-editor of the forthcoming *Penguin
Companion to American Literature*, and author of a
study of the social context of modern English
literature which is to appear shortly. He is
struggling, against overwhelming odds, to
complete a third novel.

Malcolm Bradbury

Stepping Westward

Penguin Books
in association
with Secker & Warburg

Penguin Books Ltd, Harmondsworth,
Middlesex, England
Penguin Books Australia Ltd, Ringwood,
Victoria, Australia

First published by Secker & Warburg 1965
Published in Penguin Books 1968
Copyright © Malcolm Bradbury, 1965

Made and printed in Great Britain by
Hunt Barnard & Co. Ltd, Aylesbury
Set in Monotype Imprint

To Bet with all my love

The flute is not a moral instrument; it is too exciting

Aristotle

Prologue

The small town of Party lies in the American heartland some-where near the point where the various wests collide – where the middle west meets the far west and the southwest the northwest. That long, slowly uptilting cornfield that begins in Ohio turns to shortgrass plain, to gullies, gulches and parched mineral-bearing soil, just before it reaches the Rockies, which burst forth in a wild, pushing mass of jagged peaks. In this parched section, short of water, lacking in trees, lies Party – a town reclaimed from nothing, captured from one of the least desirable sections of the frontier. It has the air of being settled by those pioneers who were too tired to go on, who said, on sighting ahead of them the magnificent range of the Rockies, that they could take no more. The Indians who preceded them in the section were tired and debilitated, horseless cowardly braves with holes in their moccasins, without an art, without hogans, lax even in their production of arrowheads, a bore to anthropologists. The town itself has an unfinished look. A mass of trees, carefully planted, shade it from the sun in the summer and hang with snow in the winter. Its lawns, sprinkled daily during the growing season, are unnaturally green, bursting with chlorophyll, save when they disappear all winter under a cloak of snowdrift and icesheet. All these things look as if they could die at any moment. Party is a marginal sort of town, unlikely to win any contests or orbit its own satellite or be featured in *Life* magazine. What small reputation it does possess derives from two things – its annual rodeo, an important tourist occasion, when the motels and tourist cabins fill and cowboys lope the sidewalks; and a college called Benedict Arnold University, a curious founda-tion, half private, half state-owned, whose battlemented walls and gothic buildings rise up on the edge of Party's best residential district, a ziggurat of culture, noble above the arid shortgrass plain.

The frontier is not forgotten in Party. The new crematorium, which advertises ashes to ashes in easy payments, was designed by a devout Miesian; but the tourist bus takes summer visitors to the old graveyard, just beyond the town limits, all of whose inhabitants seem to have met a violent death before they reached thirty. Though the obituaries in the *Party Bugle* record modern bourgeois deaths from coronaries, ulcers and drunken driving, the stones and crosses in the old graveyard – which say 'shot', 'murdered', 'hanged', 'lynched' and 'died of plague' – recall a world that some Party citizens can remember, and quite a lot of others think they can. Even today covered wagons pass through Party's streets, bearing members of the Junior Chamber of Commerce advertising the rodeo. The Wigwam Motel consists entirely of wigwams – each containing box-spring beds and television. The banks, whose tellers wear Stackolee vests and string ties, pay out in silver dollars, in western style. With a ten-dollar order, the Piggly Wiggly supermarket regularly gives away a small bag of gold dust. For rodeo time the regular inhabitants grow prospectors' beards to celebrate their frontier heritage, causing enormous problems of conscience to the beatniks at Benedict Arnold, who, caught between two kinds of conformity, never know whether they should shave their beards or not. Last year there was an unhappy moment over rodeo time when a dope-pusher from Berkeley who was trying to make a connexion with the guitar-player at Lucky's Place found himself offering a fix to the newly-bearded president of the First National Bank, a leading rightist who had once tried to have Benedict Arnold closed down on the grounds that education was by its very nature subversive. This did nothing to improve relations between college and town. But then, nothing ever did. Steady warfare engaged the columns of the *Party Bugle* as the citizens tried to drive the college away from the town and the students tried to drive the town away from the college.

But if the town, with its low buildings and, in places, its old wooden sidewalks, gives the impression of impermanence, the campus gives the opposite feeling – of too much solidity. Its buildings are so very ponderous, so ungraciously traditional, that Dr Styliapolis, head of the Department of Architecture, told his students, shortly after arriving in Party from an eastern, Ivy League school, that he had written direct to the Kremlin to ask that they be included in their list of strategic targets. Thrump Hall, the biggest girl's dormitory, is modelled externally on Hampton Court, with green bronzed caps on the towers, but, as the President points out, 'not so gloomy'; panties hang out of the arrow slits on the days of the big football games. The Student Union, on the other hand, is a direct imitation of King's College Chapel, Cambridge, though exigencies of the site made it rather narrower and twice as long. Ye Bookshoppe is an enlarged version of Anne Hathaway's Cottage. Most striking of all, though, is the Administration Building, provided by an eclectic, cosmopolitan architect with a tower from a French château, a bastion from a German schloss, a turret from an Italian castello, and a minaret from the Taj Mahal. Dr Styliapolis habitually takes his students on a tour of these buildings, pointing out the contrast of terrain and style, commenting on the way in which they symbolize the American capacity to draw upon world thought; then he goes into a lather of rage and describes them as 'a triumph of the spoiler's art, notice, a manifestation of architectural lunacy. Beware, beware.' He does, on the other hand, praise another kind of architecture which has more recently made its mark on campus, the mark of international modernismus. There is an auditorium, built in the shape of a hamburger, which can be totally dismantled for change of needs and re-built in the shape of a hot-dog. There is the chapel, which is bell-shaped, and, being suspended from a gantry, does not touch the ground at all, except when it goes into orbit in times of high wind. Each kind of building has its own adherents among the faculty, which, like all faculties, is divided between conservatives and radicals, and which, like all faculties, comes to the boil at least once a year in a spate of petitions and accusations and calumny.

But there is one man to whom every brick, in every style, is dear; there is one man who can embrace all causes and faiths and styles of heart and stay sane and comfortable. The name of this man is President Coolidge – Ralph Zugsmith Coolidge, president of Benedict Arnold these last five years. A craggy, heavy-browed, middle-aged man with the brightness and innocence and spirit of the very young, President Coolidge is that rare thing, a totally eclectic human being. That is why he is here, that is why he succeeds. If the tradition of Whitman-esque acceptance seems to be dying, Coolidge proves in person that it is not yet dead. One scathing faculty member, an urbane man named Dean French, said of Coolidge once, on the only occasion when the President was late for a meeting (he had just broken his arm testing some physical education equipment), that Coolidge's moral powers had shrivelled at the age of six and all that remained was sheer verbal fluency; he was no thoughts and all words. But even Dean French knew this was unfair; it was clear that Coolidge was a man who loves. He had come to his post from an executive position with one of the big insur-ance companies, came, saw, and was conquered; his heart had leapt and he proposed marriage on the spot. He came at a time of troubles, when the previous president had resigned and no one seemed minded to take on a job which involved him in immediate hostilities with the state and the faculty. Coolidge had taken it all in his stride; the university had wowed him. All that lay within it won his care and attention; he appointed his janitors with the same attentiveness, and the same depend-ence on the fashionable insights of personal analysis, as he did his professors. The colour of every new garbage can was as much an issue with him as the installation of the new cyclotron. He was bland with the faculty, bland with the state, bland with the world. In any disinterested evaluative scale of American colleges, Benedict Arnold hardly ranks top; to Coolidge it was more scholarly than Harvard, better built than Yale, socially more attractive than Princeton, and with better parking facilities than all of them. The student body, as it teemed about campus – very much body, the girls in their shorts, the boys in theirs – he saw from his window as young America, the best of all possible young Americans. No possible evidence of ignorance or of vice could disillusion him. Responsibility to them and to the world weighed on his head, like an over-large hat. He was totally serious; he groaned in the night; he cared and worried. He ran advertisements in the quality monthlies: 'For the future! A B.A. from B.A.' He shivered when Harvard got Riesman or Toronto Frye, shivered because he saw a prospective Benedict Arnold man drawn off into false paths.

The absence of any previous university experience whatsoever prevented him from being embarrassed by standards. Yet even so, Benedict Arnold managed to grow and thrive. It was, perhaps, because the region had a highly regenerative climate, and because the ski-slopes of the Rockies were only four hours' drive away, rather than because of Coolidge's efforts; but Benedict Arnold continued to attract a large and reasonably good staff and student body. It managed to hold concurrently the reputation of 'a play school' and a good place to be. A lot of students came to Benedict Arnold because they were weakly, and their doctors recommended it (Coolidge had the wit to advertise also in medical journals). Similar reasons of health and geography, together with a high salary scale, enabled it to claim some good faculty talent. Tubercular biologists, rheumatic physicists, asthmatic sociologists and rickety soil-mechanics men abounded in its departments, coughing their way through the laboratories or limping down the corridors. But as President Coolidge often said, looking out of the window of his suite at the campus spectacle, a lot of intellectuals have been sick.

Then there were other attractions. The excellence of the Physics Department is supposedly accounted for by the fact that, during one short-lived phase in post-war history, Party was outside missile-range. Even the English Department, in a state not noticeably teeming with literacy, had a high reputation, firstly because an enterprising member of that faculty, since gone into the advertising business, conceived the idea of approaching living poets and novelists and asking them, not for their cast-off manuscripts, which came expensive, but for their cast-off clothes, which are to be seen, displayed on facsimile dummies, in a small museum in the library; and secondly because it is in the custom of taking on, each year, a writer-in-residence – a young poet or novelist, who usually, after or even before the expiration of his term of duty, writes a novel in which the university and many of its faculty appear in print under only the faintest of disguises. This has resulted in enormous publicity for the college, and President Coolidge keeps a collection of these works in his office and sends out to his friends cyclostyled excerpts of passages which refer, usually unfavourably, to himself. 'I think we're making our mark with this little experiment, you know,' he would say. 'My guess is that it's boosted enrollment around twenty per cent. Kids like coming here after reading those books. It's like visiting Dove Cottage in Wordsworth's Lake District.'

This year, the meeting that was convened to appoint the new creative writing fellow took place, in one of the conference rooms in the Taj Mahal wing of the Administration Building, over a lunch hour toward the end of March. The lunch-hour conference was one of President Coolidge's innovations; it had hotted up the pace of faculty life considerably. The previous president, an easy, rotund spirit who had reached the post internally through a simple willingness to take on any administrative duties enabling him not to teach, had always spoken of the great virtue of a university as being the context of leisure it provided – for thought, for disinterested study, for afternoon naps. But Coolidge . . . well, Coolidge was reputed not to sleep at all. Late-night travellers crossing the campus saw the lights in his study burning and a hunched figure leaning across the desk and, though some said he employed a man to play the part, the work he did was phenomenal. When there was none, he invented some. His régime had multiplied problems and decisions and the need for dealing with them. In addition to lunch-time conferences, there were weekend study conferences in wooden cabins up in the Rockies, and seven-day conferences in Reno or Denver.

The committee concerned with the new writing fellow convened just before one. When they arrived, one of Coolidge's many secretaries was setting up the large tape-recorder with which he liked to enshrine all proceedings. 'Come right in, we're all set,' said the girl. 'And talk good.' They gathered round the shiny conference table; there were several members of the English Department, with whom the writer was officially connected: there was the present writing fellow, a humble creature in spectacles and string tie; there was Dean French, who never spoke, and Dr Wink from Business Administration, who always raised difficult objections; and there was an assistant professor from Physical Education named Selena May Sugar. They gathered together at the table, spreading out their cartons of milk, their hot-dogs and their chicken salad sandwiches. Some, not familiar with the experience, insisted on gazing through the window with white faces at the students making their way across campus to the delights of the cafeteria.

'They don't know how lucky they are,' said Dr Hamish Wagner of the English Department. 'Boy, could I just eat a steak in the Faculty Club right now. I just hope to God my belly won't rumble and get on to that tape.'

'Take it easy, Hamish,' said Selena May Sugar. 'Let's don't drive ourselves out of our minds.'

Outside it was a beautiful day, and the sun tinged the snow with red; in it, through it, the students walked, in bright winter clothes, the occasional plaster cast, from a skiing accident, adding a further glow of colour to the scene (decorating plaster casts was a local student folk-art). A small scampering horde of German shepherd dogs worried the frigid, iced trees and were chased in their turn by the uniformed figures of the campus policemen, always poised against anarchy. You could almost hear the spring cascading down the Rockies, stood off there on the horizon. Insects buzzed over the campus and peered in the windows at the committee. 'It's beautiful out there,' said Selena May Sugar. The campanile, an immense phallic object set directly in the middle of the campus and worshipped nightly in its dells, grottoes and parking lots, began to shake as it rang out one o'clock and followed it, as for dessert, with the state song.

As the hour struck, the door opened and President Coolidge came in. He wore a distinctive after-shave lotion which penetrated the whole room; one always knew where he had been. He sat down at the head of the table and called the meeting to order by rapping on the wood with a large Phi Beta Kappa key he carried for this purpose. 'Okay,' he said. 'Well, this meeting is to consider who, whom, I don't know which, we should appoint to next year's writing fellowship. Present at the meeting, oh hell, everybody, I guess. Now just a minimal point before we start talking this one out and I hand over to Harris; remember if you don't speak right there into the mike Rosemary in the stenographic pool ain't going to hear a single goddam word you say and you'll be out of the record. Well, okay, I'll pass the buck right to Harris Bourbon. Hey, where is he?'

'I think he went over to the student cafeteria to get a chocolate shake,' said an associate professor in the English Department named Bernard Froelich.

President Coolidge looked petulant: 'I just want to remind you all that all these meetings are scheduled for me in a very tight schedule and I have to depend on your punctuality,' he said. Then the door was pushed open and Dr Harris Bourbon, the head of the English Department, stumbled in. The chocolate shake he had just imbibed had left its traces on his grey moustache. He was a big and totally unimpressive man who had been raised locally on a farm and had risen in the academic world through sheer endurance. He always wore, in the snowy American winter, a fantastic headpiece, a kind of Eskimo flying helmet; he took it off slowly now, shaking a flake or two of new snow from the furry earflaps, and set it on the table in front of him, while the tape-recorder recorded this piece of business.

'Hit's real cold still,' said Bourbon, sitting down, and taking some tattered notes from his pocket. 'Want me to give them the poop?'

'If you'd do that, Har,' said Coolidge.

Harris Bourbon gave them the poop, while the rest sat silently round the table. He pointed out that your aim in founding your creative writing fellowship was that of conveying to your student the high ideals and distinctive standards of your creative life. But there was a problem. Writers were not what they used to be. In fact, this was an age in which the literary life was a form of delinquency and all kinds of questions had to be asked about the way writers acted. Bernard Froelich, unwrapping a hamburger from its waxed paper, recalled that Bourbon had not done very well out of the few representations of him that had appeared in the fiction of the creative writing fellows; his unimpressive demeanour and his instinctive conservatism had been pinned down for posterity rather too neatly to please. Another problem, said Bourbon, was that Benedict Arnold was not one of the best known of your American colleges, and. . . . 'That may have been true a few years back, Har, but I wouldn't like to think that was the situation now,' said President Coolidge. Bourbon realized he had made a slip and tried to backtrack. The real point, he said, was that it was difficult to find anyone who was sufficiently unsuccessful to take a fellowship so remote from New York, and publishers, and the big TV networks, and yet was good enough. All the leading neglected writers had been snatched up long before by Wellesley and Bennington and Kenyon and Hillesley. The only poets and novelists who were neglected were so goddam bad they had to be, and those who wouldn't have taken the appointment at any price because they believed that success was the mark of failure, or that to live on campus was a fate worse than death.

'Well, okay, fine,' said President Coolidge, when Bourbon's drawling western voice had stopped, 'but I thought you painted the picture a little black, Har. I should have thought this country was full of fine young writing men just waiting for an opportunity like the one Benedict Arnold has pledged itself to give them.'

The present writing fellow, clearly depressed to see his sands running out, looked up and said, 'Why, I'm sure there are a whole lot of writers who'd be mighty glad to be here.'

'Well,' said President Coolidge, 'this is a man who should know, and I think while he's here we should just give Mr Turk a little round of applause for the work he's put in this year.' Mr Turk bowed his head as the committee clapped him.

'Waal,' said Harris Bourbon, stubbornly, when this was over, 'we already made a whole lot of approaches.'

'In the circumstances,' said Dr Wink from Business Administration ('Take a B.A. in B.A. from B.A.' Coolidge had advertised in the business journals), 'I'd like to propose to this meeting that we abolish the writing fellowship completely and put these funds to another use. I have no complaint against the present fellow, Mr Turk, and I'm pleased to see him here today, but not all his predecessors have been particularly desirable men. In many cases, Mr President, their politics and values have been so undesirable as to be a menace to security. One man used to lie naked on the front lawn of a house he'd rented in a first-class section of town. My wife pointed him out to me several times. It was said that realty prices dropped substantially the whole year he was in that section. And I'm told that the man before him was not heterosexual.'

'Is this an ethical objection to the fellowship, Dr Wink?' asked Coolidge from the chair.

'No, what I'm talking about is the overall failure of this project. Almost none of these writers we've had has been an asset to the university.'

'They wrote about it.'

'Not very favourably – and most of them never bothered to meet the classes allocated to them. The influence they've exerted over the students here doesn't seem to be exactly the kind of thing we had in mind. One man boasted to me in the Faculty Club that he'd spent three weeks living in a closet in Thrump Hall. We have enough difficulty graduating the occasional virgin without that kind of person around.'

'Well, that sounds to me like an ethical objection,' said Coolidge. 'Not that I've any objection to ethical objections, but have you any objection beside the ethical one?'

'All this seems enough for me, Mr President.'

'Rosemary, make a note of that ethical objection by Dr Wink, will ya? Yes, right, well, thank you. Any other objections that aren't ethical?'

Bernard Froelich, who had spent the last few minutes trying to get the noise of his mastication of the hamburger on to the tape, leaned to Selena May Sugar and whispered, ' Neat.'

'Ah, Coolidge is all right.'

'Oh, Bernard, Selena, there's nothing we have to say at these meetings we don't want the whole group to hear,' said Coolidge. 'We're trying to think in a group because we know we think best in a group. Can we have that again?'

'I was asking Selena if she wanted some of my onions,' said Froelich.

'I said I had sufficient onions,' said Selena.

'Rosemary, forget all that in the transcript,' said Coolidge. 'Okay, well, has anyone else here a suggestion he wants to put into space and see if it orbits? Looks like we're waiting for a breakthrough on this one.'

'I'd just like to ask Dr Bourbon,' said Bernard Froelich, 'whether he thinks that it's necessary for a writer to be a conformist before we ask him to this campus. Seems to me that could be a very dangerous policy.'

'Well,' said Bourbon, 'I think we're talking about a real problem here. I mean, it's right, we want someone who's goin' to behave right and git on well with the students and all, carry a portion of the teachin' load. Hit just ain't easy.'

'Perhaps that's because we're looking for the wrong kind of person? I should have thought that most of the major writers of our time would miss out on that definition.'

'I don't see why we shouldn't look for a feller of this kind. We done well for ourselves this year. Hen Turk's been teachin' six hours and he's got one boy written a novel about Madison Avenue that he's sent off to his own publisher and is expectin' a favourable report on.'

Froelich looked across at the present incumbent, a depressed, elderly person who wrote novels about the Old West, careful historical novels in which every trace in a set of harness, every knot in a cowboy's string tie, was there because it had been found in the records. It was well known that he bored his creative writing classes by giving two-hour talks on researching the frontier. He sat across the table, dry and speculative, his Stetson in front of him, his gold-rimmed spectacles shining green in the glare, exactly the kind of person that Froelich hoped never to see again in the fellowship. 'Well,' he said, 'I think that kind of demand is a mistake, but it's your department, Harris. Still, since we've not been successful, maybe there's something else we can do. I'd like to make a proposal, President Coolidge.'

'Sure, Bern, yes, lay it on the table.'

'Well, my thought is, why don't we approach a foreign writer? This kind of fellowship isn't very common over in Europe, say, and the students would learn a lot if we got someone from abroad.'

President Coolidge nodded and said, 'Well, that's a nice idea, Bern, really. We can look it up, but I think I'm right in ad-libbing that there's nothing in the statutes that limits this appointment to an American citizen, and, well, as we all know, Europe has produced one hell of a lot of great writers. . . . '

'I don't see why we can't find some American boy just starting out in the writing business who'd come to this campus and do what we tell him to,' said Dr Wink.

'I thought it had been said that all the genuine possibilities of that kind had been exhausted,' said Froelich. 'What I'd say about this is that the Europeans have lived with the arts a good deal longer than we have on this side. They've got a style to the literary life over there, and I think it might be a lesson to some of our students on this campus if we did tempt over someone like that.' President Coolidge nodded approvingly, and Froelich found that he was growing excited. He was a complicated, ambitious person who took rather a different view of the function of the creative writing fellow from his colleagues. He thought these writers proved the superiority of creation over criticism, a thing that English Departments quickly forget about, and every excess they achieved, every shock they gave to Bourbon, provided Froelich with a peculiar pleasure. When they took off their clothes at freshmen mixers and seduced the wives of the faculty members down by the lake on campus, Froelich could do nothing but rejoice; this was the lesson of the wildness of the world in a community that believed in reducing art to simple order.

And Froelich felt indignant for another reason; he discerned a flavour of nervousness and conservatism in the protests that had been brought up at the meeting, and his liberal hackles were rising. Froelich, educated in the east, was perpetually amazed by the note of caution that kept being sounded in this pioneer section of the west. And also, because he was from the east, the word 'Europe' sounded sweetly on his tongue; he liked to repeat it among people who had dismissed that place long ago, or thought it had been abolished. So, looking round the room, shining white from the reflected snow, he went on to point out how successful European writers had always been when they had visited the campus to lecture. He recalled some of the speakers who in recent years had stirred the campus to excitement – Auden, Simone de Beauvoir, Dylan Thomas. At the mention of the last name Bourbon visibly shuddered, and Froelich, who was not only a partisan but a politician, realized he might have been running ahead rather too fast. Not all the campus had been ready for Thomas yet, and some had been too ready; he had come and gone, leaving the place in a state of disorder, a state, indeed, of oestrus.

'He was a very interestin' man, but I don't think he'd fit in for a whole year, Bernard,' said Bourbon.

'I thought he was dead now,' said Selena May Sugar.

'That's right,' said Froelich. 'No, I was just using him as an example. But if someone like that seems too far out, well, there's no race like the English for producing respectable writers.'

'Well, yes, Bern, that's right,' said President Coolidge. 'There are other European writers. I've met quite a number of them myself, I might say, and mighty nice polite people a lot of them were, too. A lot of people think of Europeans as immoral, but I found a lot of them over there were as moral as you or I. What do you say on this one, Har?'

Bourbon was obviously very doubtful; Froelich, who knew all the flaws and uncertainties in his department head, and had long ago learned the art of exploiting them, knew he would be. But he always gave in to the sense of a meeting, lacking any positive principles of his own, and Froelich knew that his cause was as good as won. This gave him considerable pleasure, because he always liked winning causes, but also because he had further ends in view. His efforts were not over yet, and he poised himself for the second part of his campaign.

'Waal,' said Bourbon, 'if there ain't no limitations in the terms of the fellowship. . . . '

'No, we're quite free on this one, Har, I just looked it up, we can play it by ear,' said President Coolidge.

' . . . Waal then, darn it, I think I'm in favour. We're takin' a hell of a chance, but why not? One thing I'd like to say right now, though. I think we oughta try to find an Englishman, and I'll give you my reasons for that. A Frenchman or a German or someone of that kind would be nice, and I don't want to sound prejudiced, but if we picked someone from those areas there's a grave risk the freshmen wouldn't understand 'em.'

Froelich saw that Bourbon's manner had brightened, and he realized why. Surely, Bourbon was thinking, surely in England, if anywhere, the old gentlemanly idea of the man of letters still reigned. A Gosse, a Saintsbury, even a Forster, seemed to him the kind of thing that Benedict Arnold needed most, a man of culture, a stabilizing influence. Froelich, who felt he had fed the crumbs of these thoughts to Bourbon's imagination, knew intimately what kind of pleasure he was getting. Coolidge asked for some suggested names, and Froelich, looking around at the sense of the meeting, played his next card. He proposed the name of James Walker.

It was a name that rang no bells. Harris Bourbon, a farmer but a gentleman, read nothing after 1895, and regarded *Jude the Obscure* as the ultimate in literary daring. He had said as much in his book *The Bucket of Tragedy* (1947), in which his concern with the Jacobean dramatists, who now occupied all his time, provoked him into condemning all literature not formally tragic in structure. Dr Hamish Wagner, another representative of the English Department, was an Auden expert who had recently taken charge of the day-to-day direction of the Freshman Composition programme. This had happened in 1955, and since that year his reading, apart from Auden, had stopped completely. All he thought about now was the Unattached or Dangling Modifier, the Gross Illiteracy, and Manuscript Mechanics, the basic principles of Comp. . . . His red moustache shone bright in the snow-glare; he wanted to say something, to express approval or disapproval, but nothing came to mind, for he was irrevocably out of touch, an academic casualty. Dean French, a big urbane man, said he approved of the principle; Dr Wink said he didn't. Selena May Sugar, who was interested in anger, seemed to recognize the name when it was put. President Coolidge nodded sagely at it.

'This,' said Froelich, 'is the James Walker who wrote *The Last of the Old Lords*. He's a youngish man, very promising. There was a story on him in *Time* magazine about two months back. . . . ' Froelich did not know Walker, and he had picked the name fairly casually. But though he didn't know him, he liked his general context and spirit. His name had appeared in literary magazines and little reviews in connexion with Amis's, Wain's, Murdoch's. At the same time he was thought rather more provincial; he was a regional man, a man who wrote about sensitives who live away from the places where things happen. In the new version of this familiar kind of English novel, the heroes are demoted half a class, rebellion is increased proportionately, significance ensues. But Walker did it all very vigorously; he had a stylish way of exposing just that very gentlemanliness and culture that Bourbon admired which made him, here and now, of special interest to Froelich. Froelich wanted a rebel, but he wanted an interesting one. Like so many Americans, Froelich was a devout democrat who was charmed by the English class-system. And Walker, he had sensed, was a man who was in much the same position – a man poised between an old order and a new one, looking forward, looking back, hung between revolution and restoration. At any rate, he was likely enough to cause confusion and to take to him, Bernard Froelich. So Froelich went on to stress the advantages of his proposal, tuning his words to Coolidge, and Bourbon, and the whole committee. Walker was sufficiently well known to be meaningful to the right people, but not sufficiently well known to be cavalier. There were honours being done on both sides, and Benedict Arnold could restrain him if he proved very difficult.

'Would he come out here to this savagery?' asked Dean French, straightening his already neat necktie.

'I think he would,' said Froelich. 'We're offering him a real chance. That's why it's all so smart.'

'Look, Bern, just brief me some more about this man,' said Coolidge.

Bourbon intervened to ask if he were 'considerable enough'.

'Well,' said Froelich, 'let's put it this way. He's not a book, but he's a chapter.' The remark came to mind because this, to Froelich, was exactly what James Walker was. Froelich was writing a book; it was on Plight, Twentieth-Century Plight, with special reference to Post-War Plight. It was a long and wide-ranging book (there is plenty of plight in the twentieth century) and Froelich was covering all there was to cover – Alienation, the Existential Dilemma, Rebellion and *Angst*, in their American and their English manifestations. It was a book that was important to Froelich because his chances of promotion lay in it. And of the many long chapters one of them, entitled 'Anomie Versus Bonhomie in Contemporary British Fiction', was to be largely concerned with the novels – so splendidly typical, so socially representative, so aptly full of The Liberal Dilemma, Loss of Self, and Us Versus Them – of James Walker. This was yet another reason for wanting the man; he could feed his life into Froelich's book, he could be kept perpetually under observation. The pattern seemed so neat – Walker's liberalism, his Englishness, and his very existence, ready for the observant biographer – that Froelich grew quite excited. 'He stands for something,' said he. 'The new English writing at its best. Form *and* matter. Style *and* content. I'm sure we'd all learn a lot. He's neither proletarian nor dilettante. He's riding all the contemporary storms. He's, well, I'd say he's a snip.'

'For forty-nine cents he's a steal,' said Selena May Sugar, 'so okay, let's steal him.'

Dr Wink protested vigorously, but the tape-recorder flapped at the end of the reel and President Coolidge, already thinking about a meeting with the Alumni Friends of Football Committee, said, 'Well, fine, Bern, let's say we'll try him. Will you get his address and write me out some kind of letter, Har, and I'll sign it?'

Froelich sat back with a sense of pleasure and achievement. A few alternative names were suggested and then President Coolidge brought the meeting to a close. Froelich left the room with a strange, intuitive feeling that he *knew* that Walker would come, that the next year would be a good one, that his own future, and his own plans for the liberalization of the campus, were already set well into motion. A mental picture of the fiery English genius, so different from Henry Turk, filled his mind. 'You're so smart,' he said to himself.

The committee meeting was held in late March, when the snowploughs were still scraping up a late new fall from the campus paths and the cracking of ice on the streams presaged the sudden outburst of spring. Two days later, President Coolidge, pausing on his way to a ten-dollar-a-plate banquet of the Faculty Wives for Chopin, signed the letter Harris Bourbon had drafted, and soon winged messengers sped it across the Atlantic to England and James Walker, for whom the year was turning, too.

(*Benedictus Benedice*) in a delicate grey. He took it upstairs and got back into bed with it, pulling the covers over himself to keep warm. Elaine always left him a flask of coffee; he poured some out into the beaker, took a sip to bring freshness, and then slit the envelope with his thumb and took out the inside sheet. It was a sheet of expensive ripple paper, typed in that strange new typeface that only very modern typewriters affect, and it told him, in short, that he was wanted. A request from the world! He sat up in bed and cried, 'My God!' He felt warmed, excited, because though he had long held to one of the most fundamental of all literary convictions, that the world owed him a living, he felt curiously disturbed now that it seemed to be offering him one. He got out of bed again, hair tousled, and lit a cigarette, wondering what he should do. It seemed to him, at first thought, that he was ready for this. A break in the universal silence, an opportunity! Here was an invitation to be what he secretly had been for so long, a writer. Though a far from diligent creature, he had now written three novels, all of them described by the weekend reviewers as promising. He had been mentioned in a few articles, and it was evident that there must be a small audience for whom he stood for something. The problem was that he had no idea who this audience was; he had never been clearly accosted by it before. His novels had made him a little money; more than enough to cover the costs of the paper he typed them on and the cigarettes he smoked while he wrote them. They dealt with heroes like himself, sensitive provincial types to whom fate had dealt a cruel blow, for whom life was too plain and ordinary to be worth much at all. In the last pages, the heroes, trapped by their remoteness from history, died or made loud perorations about social corruption. They spoke of the impulse to be better, to lead meaningful lives and, written at the kitchen table he used as a desk, as he looked out at a bored tree, they came out of his heart.

These books had appeared in the United States as well as in England, and it had often struck him as odd that it was from America that most of the few letters he received, most of the invitations to write on his theories of literature or the personal misfortunes that had made him as he was, should come. American glossy magazines with large circulations and advertisements for very complicated corsets printed, between the corsets, the short stories that in England no one would look at; and college text-books with titles like *The Ten Best English Stories About Class* reprinted them and sent fees. The American (but not the English) edition of *Vogue* had mentioned him in their 'People are Talking About . . . ' column, and he had come to believe that in that foreign land (but not in England) people were. What did they say? It didn't matter; they spoke. *Time* had written him up, printed his photograph, called him 'bird-eyed, balding'. The Buffalo Public Library had bought his manuscripts, which he rewrote for the occasion, since he had destroyed them. Girls wrote him letters, and one ambitious youth in Idaho had proposed to write a thesis on him. Editors and publishers, wrote his American agent, Ellis Tilly, were dying to meet him. And this is me, he used to think, as he carried coal up two flights of stairs, really me. The letter now converted all these hints and promises into something larger, an offer. It said, You count, you exist. It came at the right time; he knew, as he lay in bed in the morning, that he had to stop being promising pretty soon, and become important, or all the fire would go out. He had to flower, to burgeon.

The time was in all ways ripe. The two part-time jobs with which he had until lately filled out his life were coming to an unexpected end. For two years he had been teaching, in the Georgian premises of the Adult Education Centre on Shakespeare Street, an ambling, inconsequential class on modern literature to a group of day-release clergymen. Across the road was the now emptied University College where Lawrence had gone; he could see it from the window as he debated on the disease-imagery of *Women in Love*. But the group had dwindled, out of boredom or offence, and had now gone. He also used to wear, for a pittance, experimental socks for a local knitwear firm, but a scientific advance had ousted him. Now all he did was to write, alone in the flat, until Elaine came home in the later afternoon, bringing Amanda with her. When he thought about his life, it seemed to him resourceless and minute. The realities he lived among gave nothing back, and he imagined a universe of energy in which he might find himself at home. Now he stood at the window and looked down, through the steaming city, and he felt that its provincial mist had seeped into his soul and stayed there, a standing, always forecast fog. The rain blew in his heart as well as outside the windows. A blackbird, wedged in the budding tree in front of him, sang a spring song; he felt his own need for new leaves. He took the letter and went through into the living-room, dense with last night's cigarette smoke. Here they were – his radio, his table-lamps, his coal-bucket, his armchair, the sum total of his visible achievement. A toy panda lay on its face on the hearthrug, as if it was being sick. He recalled an old vitality and felt that environment had squeezed it from him; he seemed to suffer from sleeping sickness or, like the potted plants on the windowsill, from wilt.

But by contrast the letter in his hand wriggled with life. Ah an envoy! It offered a promise of esteem, a taste of freedom, and a passable salary for being free. And freedom – *that* meant something to Walker. He shared in his heart, and with energy, the intellectual conviction that tells us we have a big debt to pay off to anarchy for all the civilization we have gathered around us. Disorder he willingly waved forward. For he felt not only bored by what he did, but guilty for it too. Art was life; it was written out of growth, and he had none. And didn't freedom and anarchy and growth cluster together when the word America was mentioned? A lot of young writers went to America now; in fact, all of them did; it was a necessary apprenticeship. Ought one to reject possibility, or even resist the trend? He belonged, after all, to a generation of literary men all of whom, thanks to a common educational system and a common social experience, had exactly the same head, buzzing with exactly the same thoughts. It was a virtual guarantee of success, then, that others had been. He dropped the letter on his desk, piled with five first chapters of an evidently unworkable novel, and walked round the room in a burst of excitement, seeing new landscapes in which mesas and skyscrapers mingled together in improbable confusion. Give yourself, said his heart, spend some spirit. But what was there to spend? And how, day-to-day, would it be? No, he was lost; he would have to ask Elaine.

The thought, once thought of, complicated the matter. It was known, even to him, that he was a married man. And Elaine, who had a sick mother to whom she dutifully fed Brand's Essence, would not leave her; that he knew. Intellectual temptations were not the stuff of her world. And Walker hardly felt that he could manage without her; on the other hand, he realized, with some suddenness, that he wanted to try. The eight years of his marriage had been exactly like the life of a foreigner in England; everything had been comfortable, domestic, snug, but kicking and screaming of the spirit occurred regularly as one thought of the real world outside. Walker had, in his young days, been something of a wild young man; he used to sit in coffee bars, wearing a small, dissident beard, and occasionally he would meet and seduce young groping girls whose parents had annoyed them. He would go to wild parties and walk home late at night through the suburbs, kicking over milk bottles. That was all gone but not forgotten. He had met Elaine about three years after he had taken his degree at the university, met her at a dance. At this time he was still leading a life of furtive studenthood; he had found out that one of the things about a university was that no one stopped you going in, so even then he had gone on attending, playing bridge with the students, using the library, often sleeping in the university grounds. It had been the ideal creative life, though at that time he had not actually written anything; just being a writer was enough.

The writing itself came later, with respectability, after he had met Elaine. She was a big unexpected girl who had been imported in a busload from a nurses' home to attend a student dance. She wore a dress of some thick material and heavily patterned design like a sofa fabric. He didn't know why he had chosen her that evening, but within days she was expressing a deep proprietorial interest in him. She took him out to parties, bought him drinks in pubs, made him shave. Her friends, people who played tennis and drove sports cars, were his enemies; her taste for expensive drinks and travelling in taxis made him furious; he was bored and frightened by the trips she took him on into the countryside, she carrying great furry handbags that looked like folded-over foxes. He always felt that one day she would pick him up, shove him in her handbag, and click the fastening to. So she had; that was his wedding day. For their honeymoon, Walker had rented a cottage in Cornwall. Here, amid post-marital struggle and sexual euphoria, he had begun his first novel and evolved an effective method of supporting them both without income; he used to go out each night into the countryside with a long knife and reappear with a broccoli, a turnip, a cabbage. But gradually the old marginal Walker, the professional student, was converted into a new figure, Walker paterfamilias, fatter, more adjusted, the owner of his own ton of coal. In bed erotic spontaneity seemed to fade under the professional demands of hygiene. 'Have you washed your hands and face?' Elaine began murmuring on the first night. 'Have you cut your nails? You're not coming to me with your socks on.' The train journey back from Cornwall advanced the process further. They sat in an open coach, near the lavatory, the door of which would not stay shut. 'Go and shut it,' said Elaine. He did so. The door swung open again. 'It's open again,' said Elaine. From Truro to London Walker tried to find a way of keeping the door shut, until finally he completed the journey in the stifling toilet with his foot against the door. 'We can't go on like this,' he said when he emerged. But it seemed to him that they had.

Now the possibility of redeeming this man, in one simple gesture, went to Walker's head; he got out his raincoat, put it over his pyjamas, and ran downstairs. In the street, trolley-buses swished by in the rain. He went to the callbox, down past the greengrocer's; liberal housewives from all the other top-floor flats looked up from buying green peppers to stare at his pyjama legs, multicoloured below the gabardine, as if they represented some bawdy invitation. The telephone booth smelled of something very nasty. Walker found four pennies in his raincoat and dialled the hospital switchboard. 'I'd like to speak to Sister Walker, on Maternity; it's urgent,' he said when they answered, putting a note of pleading into his voice; you practically had to say you were giving birth in the callbox before they would connect you. There was a pause and then Elaine's voice, as professionally stiff and starchy as the uniform she wore, came on to the line. 'Maternity ward, what is it?' she said. Walker could imagine her, breathing hard, a dragon in her uniform; she still, after eight years, made him nervous. 'It's me, Jim,' he said.

'What's up?' said Elaine.

'Well,' said Walker, 'there's a letter in this morning's post.'

'Really?' said Elaine.

'I've been asked to go to America.'

'Have you?' said Elaine, 'and who by?'

'Well, some university over there is looking for a creative writing fellow and they naturally thought of me.'

'What does it mean?' said Elaine after a pause.

'Oh, I go and sit around and write creatively and they pay me seven thousand dollars for doing it.'

'I thought you always said that creative writing was ridiculous,' said Elaine.

'Well, okay, yes, I do,' said Walker. 'Still, every man has his price. Mine happens to be six thousand nine hundred dollars.'

'They just topped it,' said Elaine.

'It looks like it,' said Walker.

'Do you want to go?' Elaine then said.

This was it, and Walker knew it was; he said, 'Do I?' and then realized he was being irritating. But how did he know? He tried it another way. 'Do *you*?' he said. Elaine didn't speak for a moment. Walker felt his ankles getting cold.

Elaine said, 'No, I couldn't possibly, could I? You'd have to go on your own.'

'Think about it,' said Walker.

'No,' said Elaine, 'you're the one who has to think about it. I *can't* go, but you mustn't let it stop you, if this really is what you want. Would it help your writing?' Elaine always said 'your writing' as other wives of generous character might have said 'your drinking'. He said slowly, 'It might.'

35

'Well, you must consider it seriously, then.'

'Without you?'

'How long is it for?' inquired Elaine.

'A year. An academic year.'

'Well, a year away from home would probably do you a lot of good,' said Elaine. 'Perhaps you'd learn to take care of yourself a bit.'

Walker said hopefully, 'Could I manage then?'

Elaine replied, 'You could learn to try.' Then there were noises at the other end, and Elaine seemed to be shouting something in a voice that boomed off the ceiling. Presently her voice came back on the line: 'Look, ducks, must go,' she said. 'Doctor's rounds. Did you put a clean shirt on this morning?'

'I'm not dressed yet,' said Walker. As he spoke, he realized he had made a fatal move.

'You're standing naked in the phone-box?' demanded Elaine.

Walker said, 'I've got my pyjamas on.'

'In the phone-box?'

'I'm wearing my raincoat on top,' said Walker.

'You're a hopeless case, Jim,' said Elaine.

'I thought,' said Walker, 'that medical rule said there were no hopeless cases.'

'I thought so too, before I met you. Well, go home, you nit, before you starve to death. And put a clean shirt on.'

Walker said, 'You're trying to make me middle class.'

'I thought you were middle class,' said Elaine.

Walker, who knew he was, knew it bitterly, said, 'No, I'm not.'

'Well,' said Elaine, 'whatever class you are today, go home before you freeze.'

'See you at four,' said Walker.

'In a clean shirt,' said Elaine.

Going back home, the rain wetting the bottoms of his pyjama trousers, Walker tried to imagine what it would be like to be wifeless. Nothing came to mind. But ambition and hope flourished in his heart, and the need to break this static peace became positive. He smelled the polish in the hall, and disliked it. Back upstairs on his desk the letter sat, calling him to America, as once American writers had been called to Europe. There were paperback copies of Henry James and Henry Adams, dusty in the bookcase, to remind him that there was a tradition in this sort of going, to remind him that there were men who had seen the gangplank of the Cunard steamer as the gateway to new pastures of mind. The market-town world that had fed his last books, the world of Dolcis and Marks and Spencer and the primary school on the corner, could only look thin; and thin, too, was the bland, uncreative British liberalism that gave him his perspective on life. Away, I'm bound away, said his spirit. He ate a peanut and groaned at himself. He stood in the room and felt at odds with it. There was no place in it for growth, for more understanding, for higher sympathies. A vision, please, he cried, a vision! He looked again at the letter and sat down at the desk. Hurriedly, before Elaine came home from the hospital with a changed mind, he sat down at the typewriter which she had bought him as a wedding present and pecked out his note of acceptance. Then he dressed, picking out a clean shirt, and went downstairs again to take the letter to the little post office at the back of the greengrocer's. Here he watched while it was weighed, stamped, decked out with a blue airmail sticker. Then he went outside to the red English post-box and dropped the letter into it with a hand that visibly vibrated with guilt and excitement.

The actual day of departure came, a bright day in late August when Nottingham sat in comfortable sunlight and the chimes of the Council House clock rang out nine as he arrived at the Midland Station with his departure committee, composed of wife and child.

'You know,' said Elaine, 'I shall miss you. All that time.'

Walker, full of doubts now, trying hard to avoid sentiments of guilt at his leaving, said cheerily, 'It's only for nine months.'

'A lot can happen in nine months,' said Elaine.

Walker refused to be sad. 'I hope it doesn't,' he said, trotting down the steps of the overbridge, a suitcase hung with ship's labels suspended from each hand. Twirls of train smoke blew across the platforms into their noses, and people hurrying to work locally jostled by them to pile into little green diesel trains. Further down the London platform black-suited businessmen, holding leather briefcases, stood exactly at the point where the first-class carriages would halt. He put down his suitcases and wiped his brow with his sleeve, while two neglected porters watched and sniggered.

'Well, this is it, I suppose,' he said. 'I hope I'm doing the right thing.'

'You always have,' said Elaine, '– hoped, I mean.' There was a bookstall behind them, laden with westerns and other people's novels; Elaine went and bought a *Guardian*, to push into his jacket pocket. 'For your lively mind,' she said. 'You mustn't forget to take your values with you.'

Feelings of departure hung over them. They stood in silence for a moment, Walker, Elaine and their daughter Amanda, a podgy, puritan, bespectacled creature, carrying his portable typewriter.

'Now be polite to America, you hear me?' said Elaine. 'Think before you speak. Don't forget you're an ambassador.'

Walker smiled and said, 'Some ambassador!'

'People will judge England by what you say and do,' said Elaine, looking at him sceptically. 'Some of them over there will never have seen an Englishman before. Act sensibly. Don't get in any fights. Don't join any processions, you know how you do.'

'I can only be myself,' said Walker, conscious he was offering the world a valuable commodity.

'Oh, Jim,' said Elaine, 'the flat will seem quite empty when you're away.'

Walker was fearful of the pressure of sentiment, for there was no confidence in him that all this was proper and right, and so he said, 'Oh, you'll get used to it, you'll enjoy it for a change. And besides,' he went on, beaming forcedly at Amanda, 'Amanda will take care of her mummy, won't you?'

'No,' said Amanda, flashing her spectacles, ' 'cause I'm going to America with Daddy.'

38

'Oh no you're not,' said Walker, looking at the child, the fruit of his loins, with the terror that from time to time she inspired in him, 'you're staying here.'

Amanda was firm: 'Oh yes I am,' she said. Walker suddenly saw his future threatened, saw an ignominious return home to the flat to sort out this crisis.

He was essentially a rational man and he brought reason to the fore. 'Come here,' he said, crouching down, 'and Daddy'll explain to you the difference between wants that can be fulfilled and those which can't.'

'I don't like being explained to,' said Amanda, dropping the typewriter, which hit the ground with a rattle of keys, 'I'm going to America with Daddy.'

Walker gazed hopelessly at his daughter, a folly of the first year of their marriage, conceived when he was more prone to gestures towards posterity and society than he was now; he now had another response to offer to the future. He tried to go on being reasonable. 'You can't go,' he said, 'and for three reasons: one, Daddy hasn't got enough money to take Mummy and Amanda with him; two, Mummy and Gran need their Amanda to look after them while Daddy's away; three, Peter Panda is waiting at home for Amanda to go and put him to bed in his cot.'

'How old do you think I am?' said Amanda. 'I'm seven and I'm going to America.'

'You talk to her, Elaine,' he said.

'Out of the way, Jim,' said Elaine. 'Come here, Amanda, and shut up, for goodness' sake.'

'All right,' said Amanda.

'Let's let Daddy go off and leave us,' said Elaine. 'He'll learn to appreciate us more. He doesn't know how much he needs us, does he?'

'No,' said Amanda.

'So you tell him to be good while he's away, and not be lascivious. Tell him that.'

'Be good, Daddy,' said Amanda, 'and don't be sivious.'

'I'll do my best,' said Walker, wondering whether he would. He felt, as usual, defeated by this female conspiracy, but it was the last defeat in that line he would suffer for some time.

'And write to us, won't you?' said Elaine. 'Tell us about all the fun you're having. I know if you aren't having fun you'll write, but try and report the good things as well.'

'All right,' said Walker.

The London train came in, drawn by a black engine, blustering smoke beneath the overbridge. It travelled down the platform and stopped at the far end of it. 'Come on, you'll have to run,' said Elaine. Walker picked up the suitcases and the typewriter and broke into a trot. There was an empty second-class compartment in the last coach, tricked out with maroon upholstery and sepia photographs of winds blowing over the Gleneagles Hotel. Elaine opened the door and he got in and heaved his luggage up on to the rack. Elaine stood outside and watched him; then, as he came back to the door, she reached out and delicately, with two fingers, lifted up the bottom of his trouser leg and exposed him to the knee. 'I thought as much,' she said. 'What socks have you got on?'

'You can see which socks I've got on,' said Walker, 'so can everybody.'

'Amanda,' said Elaine, 'can you smell Daddy's feet?'

'Yes,' said Amanda, 'they're terrible.'

Elaine opened her foxy handbag and pulled out a little pair of rolled socks. 'Put these on,' said Elaine. 'You're disgusting.'

'Yes, all right,' said Walker. The guard's whistle blew and Elaine pushed the door shut.

'Make sure it's properly fastened before you lean on it,' said Elaine. 'You'd look a fool if you fell out at this stage.' The engine blew off steam; the wheels gripped; the train began to move. Walker stuck his head out of the window, feeling the sun beat upon it, and felt a great sense of release.

'Say good-bye to Daddy,' said Elaine to their daughter as they trotted lightly to keep up with the moving train.

'Good-bye, Daddy,' said Amanda. 'And Peter Panda says good-bye too.'

A seed that had been growing within Walker germinated suddenly, and he tore the veil from unreality in a phrase: 'No, he doesn't,' he cried, 'because he can't bloody well talk.' He looked at Elaine and added, 'And I'll change my socks when I like.'

'God bless you, Jim,' shouted Elaine, stopping moving.

'Good-bye, darlings,' shouted Walker, full of guilt for what he had done, and what he was doing, and the irresponsibility he was performing in leaving like this. He blew a few kisses and then the train took a curve and they were gone from view. The sun shone into the coach. He sat down and felt the train moving through the Nottingham back streets, with their grey midland mist, past the cattle market, the wood-yard, the Co-operative bakery. Now, suddenly, there was a blurred mass of metal, all angles and fury, like a wild abstract sculpture; the train was crossing the heavy iron bridge over the River Trent, which marked for Walker the boundary between the north of England and the south. Behind him, now, lay decency, plain speaking, good feeling; ahead lay the southern counties, all suède shoes and Babycham. A strange queasy sensation, as if two holes had been bored into the lower part of his stomach, letting the contents flow into his legs, came to him. He was alone; his wife and child were gone; two suitcases and an old typewriter were all there was of him. The cases, which he had bought for their honeymoon, looked unprepossessing; the typewriter, a tired and elderly machine with a black rexine case, added a final parochial touch. Already he felt a foreigner in the world. The fine Midland countryside, with its valleys and long scarps of land, its brick cottages and sharp church spires, sat peacefully and domestically in the heat haze; but already signs of disjunction and southerliness were evident. The architecture was altering faintly; the names of unknown foreign villages showed on signposts; the people began to look different.

Piety filled Walker, a sense of hearth and home, and he went down the swaying corridor to the cubicle at the end of his coach. Here, dutifully, he stripped off the old socks and flushed them down the toilet. He imagined them blowing away, scaring rabbits, confusing chaffinches. Then he put on the new pair and, rising, caught sight of his face in the mirror. 'Who is this handsome, well-dressed stranger?' he said, looking uneasily at the ghostly lugubrious face that stared back at him, that domed head, that exportable commodity, that kernel of wisdom he was ferrying across the seas. It looked conspicuously unconfident. The upper part of his features were bony, intelligent-seeming, with bright round eyes and receding hair. Lower down, though, things went rather to pieces; here were jowly northern cheeks, like a spaniel's, which made him appear to be eating all the time and contributed to an expression both perplexed and sad. 'You're off,' he said, 'going to the States.' The face refused to be pleased; it simply looked darkly forward into a future of lost luggage, missed trains, incorrect papers, unbooked hotel rooms, and perpetual loneliness. Walker, shaken, turned away and walked back along the corridor to his compartment, eyeing the girls in the other compartments as he passed. Domesticity, clearly, had softened him, weakened him, left him ill-equipped for this kind of pilgrimage.

London's suburbs were upon him before he realized it. The train was flashing through commuter stations whose walls bore advertisements recommending those three great urban luxuries, theatre visits, evening newspapers, and corsets. Red London omnibuses filled the roads. Then the train slowed and they were into St Pancras, a great gothic cathedral of a station, testament to the conjunction of travel and moral seriousness. He got out of the train and went along the platform to the taxi rank, where he found a cab to take him across the river to Waterloo. Here the atmosphere was lighter, more disturbing. The style of the station, vain and cosmopolitan, spoke of another and more whimsical kind of travelling. The loudspeakers were playing music; the roof-pillars were slender and gracious; the whole place smelled of cigars and chorus girls and afternoon adulteries. Walker gave up his ticket and went down the platform beside the Pullman coaches, conscious of his own inadequate elegance. A stout predatory station pigeon came waddling up to him, getting under his feet; then it dissolved into a flutter of wings and took clumsily into the air; the heavy creature, rather like Walker in appearance, became light, enjoyed itself in the air for a moment, and came to ground farther along in front of a group of young expensive-looking American girls, who reached into their purses and began to scatter bread for it. Foreign aid, thought Walker, and wondered how he would fare. He looked curiously at the girls, neat, fresh, delectable, chattering and shining against the Pullman. They were avaricious internationalists, evidently, their legs turned nutmeg by a sun that had come to find them daily in different places; their airlite luggage, which the conductors were carrying aboard the train, was garish with the labels of hotels in Vienna and Rome, Brussels and Paris, places he scarcely knew at all. Their polaroid anti-glare sunglasses had consumed all their European sights. I dreamt I did Europe in ten days in my Maidenform bra, thought Walker, finding the very sight of these international creatures tantalizing and enlarging. They made him feel that he was, after all, in motion, going somewhere, that he was of their band and their temper.

He found the coach that corresponded to his seat reservation and handed over his ticket. The conductor picked up his suitcases and typewriter and led him aboard. Inside, the white tablecloths shone, the pink-shaded lamps on the separate tables cast a saucy boudoir light. The other passengers, of all nationalities, sat in their places, leaning on their elbows, smoking urbane cigarettes, watching him join them on their journey. They all seemed entirely and perfectly at home; they evidently sensed and understood the ship, drifting on her ropes at the Ocean Terminal away in Southampton, knew by experience the six days of travel, the clicking open of suitcases at the customs, the sending of telegrams; they even understood America, big and awful and inviting to the west. Because he didn't know these things, because he couldn't predict his future, because he was an innocent at voyaging, Walker grew even more nervous and concerned. He followed the steward down the car, his feet sinking into the thick carpet between the tables. The train, indulging all his English nostalgia for the plushy and the genteel, seemed to him a deceit. It spoke of a time when you could travel over Europe, every signal off, and find the whole world not, as you might terrifyingly suppose, all different, but all the same – all service and respect and three-star comfort. Since the world wasn't safe and secure, and since Walker knew he was a voyager into insecurity, he felt troubled. It only postponed the moment when the difficulties would begin, when he would start to suffer and be hurt. Walker pitched his mind to meet that moment. 'Here we are, sir,' said the white-coated steward, pulling back a deep chair at one of the tables so that he could get in. In the facing seat, at the table for two, sat a German newspaper with large heavy type, held by two hairy hands on which gold rings gleamed. Walker tried to sit down and kicked a foot. The paper collapsed, to reveal one of those wise, heavy, experienced faces that Europe has always been so good at producing; sad faces that make all Englishmen look un-tutored. Two serious eyes regarded Walker curiously. 'I'm sorry,' said Walker. 'Oh, please, it is nothing,' said the face, and Walker said 'sorry' again and thrust his buttocks into the plush.

The man with the German newspaper suddenly folded it decisively. 'Vell, here we all are, the Fulbright generation,' he said. 'So when does the seminar start?'

'Pardon?' asked Walker.

'Oh, these summer liners, they are always full of scholars. I suppose you are one?'

'In a sort of a way,' said Walker.

'I too,' said the man. 'It is always the same: Americans studying in Europe, Europeans studying in America. Why we do this I do not know. After all, all the world is the same now. What we have at home is what we vill get everywhere. All societies are the same; all libraries are the same; what do we think we get out of it?'

This was a depressing thought to Walker, and he said, 'Oh, we get a lot.'

'Vell,' said the man, 'six years ago, maybe seven, I visited your city here. Then it was called London. Now I have visited again and it is called Nowhere. They have pulled half of it down, and what they have not pulled down they have dwarfed to make it count less. The people, well, they have lost their

44

style, they don't know how to be English, and even the food is hamburgers.'

'Progress,' said Walker.

'Progress,' said the man, 'that is the optimist's word for change. However, it is always pleasant to meet an idealist.'

'Well,' said Walker, 'things have got better in England in lots of ways. People have more money and expect more of life.'

'So it is all for the best?' asked the man.

'Some of it,' said Walker.

'Vell, I am an old man, so I will give you some advice for living in this world. I will tell you the best profession for a man to enter today. I will tell you how to answer when they come to you and say, you have been a most splendid fellow, so here is a prize, your life over again, what will you do with it? My friend, pick the demolition business. Those men up there on those cranes, hitting down those buildings, they are heroes, kings, gods.'

The train jerked and began to move gently along the platform. There was an explosion of light; they were out from under the protective dome of Waterloo. Great towers of apartment blocks, with knickers flapping on high balconies, stood out against the sky. Green caterpillar-like electric trains flipped by; steam engines with military names stood in sidings. Through a gap in the towers of flats Walker could see the Houses of Parliament, where they governed him from. But whatever they had for him today they could, he thought, keep, for he had done it now, cut the umbilical cord, moved into a new regimen. A tug lowered its funnel to pass under Westminster Bridge. The back streets came into view, with small dirty children playing on pavements, electric milk-carts navigating brick-strewn roads, babies and prams crying outside shops. On a bombed site a group of youths in deviant clothes and hostile shoes stood smoking; Walker felt for them that slight flicker of respect his time had taught him to feel at the sight of the disorderly. The sadder parts of London unfolded further. Someone had painted on a railway wall *Ban the bum*. Walker turned his attention within the coach, where the waiters were moving along the tables disseminating afternoon tea. 'Of course we must celebrate this English rite,' said the foreigner, straightening his tie, which had a streak of lightning down it. 'That is the England we come here for.' Across the aisle an austere, dowagerly-looking lady, with a lot of gauzy veils wrapped about a swan's neck, an apotheosis woman, an English type, rang the bell marked *Attendant* imperiously. There was a lot of grandeur about, and Walker took his pleasure in it – in the walnut and the brocade, the pink lamps and the brass fittings, the foreign newspaper opposite, the party of American girls chattering somewhere back down the car. It gave him a sense of his own importance, made him feel his situation was enviable. It seemed to him right that travel should not be ordinary, that it should be attended by this kind of special richness.

Two of the American girls came down the car, talking together. He watched them with curiosity. One of them was big and blonde, with a finely cantilevered bosom, and the other was dark and rather morose. The blonde one said: 'I guess the fountain's up this way some place.' A real fountain, tridents, dolphins, high spouts of water, and the conceit, on this train, seemed almost probable. But it was just drinking water they wanted; the man opposite, who had been equally attentive to the pair, rose dramatically to his feet, dropping his newspaper on his shoes, and said, 'Attention please; I recommend not to drink the water.'

The two girls paused and looked down at the foreigner and Walker. 'They told us we could drink the water in Britain,' said the blonde girl. 'They gave us this orientation course and they said Britain was one of the countries it was okay to drink the water in.'

'Oh, in hotels, but the train is a different matter. But let us consult a citizen. Our friend here will tell us.'

Walker became embarrassed and looked at the tablecloth. 'Well,' he said, 'I don't really know. I never tried drinking water on trains, but I imagine it's all right. I never heard of anyone catching anything. I suppose the safest thing would be to stick to the tea, though.'

'Oh, Jesus,' said the dark girl, 'not more tea. I just don't

46

know how you people can go on drinking the stuff the way you do. I'd like to see inside your stomachs.'

'Oh yes, you must take tea,' said the foreigner, 'it is a custom, something to tell them in Oshkosh.' He clicked his fingers and waved to the attendant. 'Please, these girls would like some of that splendid English tea you are serving there.'

The attendant looked at him and said, 'All right, all right, we'll get to everyone in due course, sir.'

Walker looked up and smiled a little at the girl with the cantilevered bosom. 'I guess if you're brought up on it you get inured to the stuff,' she said to Walker.

'I suppose we do,' said Walker.

'You sell a lot of these fine teas?' the foreigner was asking the attendant in great amiability.

'Quite a number, sir,' said the man.

'Such cakes, such sandwiches, it will put pounds on the bottoms of these girls,' said the foreigner.

'They look as though they can stand it,' said the attendant.

'They are Americans, you understand, these things are an experience for them.'

'Quite,' said the attendant.

'Well, thanks a lot,' said the girl with the bosom, and the two of them went back down the car to their seats. 'If we die we'll hold you responsible.'

Walker turned in his chair to watch them go. Their buttocks curved the fabric of their tight twill skirts. It was all very splendid, and brought back into Walker's heart an old instinct which eight years of marriage had kept dormant. Walker rationalized it; it was a necessary curiosity about the world. There was nothing like sexuality to keep a man interested in other people; and since in the modern world there was little other approved relationship available he felt he was growing back into life.

'Nice girls,' said the foreigner, sitting down again. The encounter seemed to have excited him rather, and the little performance he had put on had clearly given him a great deal of pleasure.

'They are,' said Walker.

'I have pursued a lot of interests in my time,' said the man, 'but there is no doubt of one thing: vomen are the most interesting interest of all. And most of all American vomen. You know, those girls are not just *girls*. They are central figures in the American mythology. They are charismatic leaders in their society.'

'I see,' said Walker.

The man leaned forward, bending his neck over his firm, formal collar. He smelled of after-shave lotion. 'You see, every country cares for something. In Germany, it is veal and *gemütlich*. In England it is, vell, dogs and diplomats. In America, it is girls. Young girls, of course. That is why those there are so well endowed, why they have money to travel and dress so vell. All the energy of their fatherland goes into producing them. That is why you must take care.'

'I will,' said Walker.

'And it is not that they are just girls. Of course that is important. But sociology tells us, well, it tells us everything, but one of its discoveries is that in America the voman is powerful. So, sex is all different. It is necessary to know this before you appear in bed with one of these ladies. Which is vot all Europeans wish to do.'

'Naturally,' said Walker, 'if they all look like that.'

'Ah, but beware!' said the man, shaking his finger like a rather dangerous father, like a Marx or a Freud, 'this America is a matriarchal society. That means it is better to be a voman than a man. Anxious fathers in the maternity hospitals always are praying, "Let the child please be a girl." '

'Women to be frightened of,' said Walker.

'Yes, they will eat you up for their dinner,' said the foreigner. 'In America Little Red Riding Hood is a man.'

'But they're sexually very lively, I'm told,' said Walker.

'Vell,' said the man, 'in this modern world we are short of good reasons for relationships. Friendship is now abolished. No groups are secure. Sex is a good basis for human contact; in America it is the only one.'

'Well, it has its limitations, but it's nice,' said Walker.

'Nice?' said the man. 'Oh, there is much more to say about

it than that. It is carrying now all the burden that religions and gods carried before. In the bedroom man is worshipping himself. That is why in America it is not only necessary to be a girl but a young girl. In England a voman looks best and dresses best when she is over forty. That is because the English respect experience and thought. In America boties are respected. . . .'

'Boties . . . ?' asked Walker.

'Yes, the human boty. All the best clothes go to the young. In the street where I live there is an old American lady who always dresses in bermuda shorts. In Vienna or Paris she would look a noble woman, or like so.' The man gestured at the dowagerly lady across the aisle. 'In America she looks perfectly gross. But the young girls, there is another kettle of fish.'

Walker began to feel a new kind of hope, a new region for deconstriction emerged; he said, 'It sounds very attractive to me.'

'Sure,' said the man, 'but it is only unstable societies that believe so in the very young. In old China, when you wanted to flirt a young lady, you told, "How very charmingly old you are looking today!" In America, you must always tell, "How young you are looking, my dear!" '

'Tea, gentlemen?' The waiter had reached their table.

'Ah, yes, that is why we are here!' said the foreigner. Walker, being a provincial, was impressed by cosmopolitanism; and his companion seemed a man perfectly at home in these plushy surroundings of travel. He reminded Walker of those courtly sinister foreigners who, in old British films, frequented the Orient Expresses, diamond-headed pins in their dark cravats, murmuring, 'We are taking your frendt away with us for a pairfectly simple brain operation.' The accent of Mittel-Europa gave him an automatic air of wisdom. Now, as the waiter began to serve plates of sandwiches, their crusts cut off, he took up his napkin and tucked one corner into the collar of his formal shirt. An adequate Virgil. His expression was one of bonhomie. When the rest of the tea came he attacked it with energy; his long hands flitted over the table like a card-player's, dealing cress sandwiches here, currant cake there. 'In England,' he said, 'the afternoon tea. In America the martini. Why is this difference?'

'A difference in temperament,' said Walker.

'Of course,' said the man, eating a sandwich, 'but why? I will tell you my theory, I always have a theory. It deals not only with this question but also with another – why the Americans believe in progress and why the English believe in things as they are. Is it not because in England, for reasons of weather and that national temperament we are talking of, it is necessary to make the days seem shorter? One serves tea and fruit-cake and what is the consequence? One goes to sleep. In America it is necessary, for the obverse reasons, to make the days seem longer. One serves martinis, and the consequence is, one starts on another day, at night. You drink this thing and at once you want to go out dancing, or sleep with a girl, or paint the town red, as is said. The English give tranquillizers, the Americans give pep-pills. So, what is produced? According to my theory, every American has the sensation that his life lasts exactly four times as long as an Englishman thinks.' The foreigner cut a cream cake and stuck one piece between his lips. 'What is produced, the American starts to change the world, because he must live in it for so long. He wants many things of it. When he dies, he is very pleased with himself, except that the world is now so changed he does not understand it in the least. In the meantime, the English keep changing the guard only and make the best of a bad job. When they die, the world may have changed, but they blame others for it.'

He said, 'Well, at least it all sounds exciting,' and knew he was expressing a profound hope.

'Exciting?' said the foreigner. 'Ah, you want excitement. Well, you will find it. America has always been a place for starting again.'

'That's what I hoped,' said Walker.

'Ah, you are Henry James in reverse. European experience coming to seek American innocence.'

'I'm not sure *I'm* the experienced one,' said Walker.

'Ah yes, that is true,' said the man. 'It is now a case of

European innocence coming to seek American experience. Today it is the young people, the young countries, who have the experience. Only the old are innocent. That is what the Victorians understood, and the Christians. Original sin is a property of the young. The old grow beyond corruption very quickly.'

'Are those girls corrupt?' asked Walker, looking back down the car.

'Of course,' said the man, 'they have had Europe terrified for three months.'

'Why?' asked Walker, 'what have they been doing?'

'I will tell you,' said the man, 'they are bagpipers.'

The waiter came by to clear the tables, and the man said, 'Wait please. More tea here to be drunk.'

'What did you say they were?' asked Walker.

'Bagpipers. You do not believe me? Well, it is true. There are forty of these girls, and they are a bagpipe band from Hillesley. You have heard of Hillesley?' Walker shook his head. 'Vell, Hillesley is a very expensive girls' college in New England where good, rich American girls go, to learn how to be more good and more rich and more American.'

'Why do they play the bagpipes?' asked Walker.

'They play them because it brings prestige,' said the man. 'In colleges of that kind, prestige is of importance, and at Hillesley the most exclusive thing there is the bagpipe band. For many years this has been one of the cultural treasures of America, this band. And now they have gathered up some money and showed it all to Europe.'

'You know a lot about them,' said Walker, 'and about America.'

'Of course, I have looked at the Americans very closely. In fact . . . I am one myself.'

'You surprise me,' said Walker.

'Oh, there are a lot of surprises with America. Yes, I am an American citizen. Of course I did not always live there. When Europe was better I lived in Europe. Now I come and visit it. Like the bagpipers.'

'How did the tour go?' asked Walker.

'Mine or theirs?' said the man. 'I will tell you about theirs. It was a great success. They have had enormous audiences in Paris and Rome and Salzburg and Vienna and London. Europe is fascinated by American girls playing the bag-pipes.'

'Scotland too?' asked Walker.

'Of course, Scotland,' said the man. 'In Scotland there is great interest in the bagpipes.'

'But they do have their own pipers,' said Walker.

'Yes, men with bare knees, but these are pretty girls, with bare knees and rich fathers, playing the bagpipes. These girls have done for the bagpipes what I think was never done for the bagpipes before.'

The waiters made another attempt to clear the table. The sugar bowls rattled on their trays as they gathered up the last crockery and silver and collected up the cloths. Walker looked out of the window, and found countryside. The man opposite put his head against the bulge of the seat and was evidently lapsing into sleep. Soon they would be in Southampton, where the real voyaging would begin. Walker turned for solace to the *Guardian*, which called up an old familiar world of Scandinavian furniture, car seat-belts, and amiable liberal-ism, his own intellectual milieu. His unassuming faith in the faint but gradual betterment of the world was supported here; when experience seemed sombre, and the bland egalitarianism of the new Britain began to jar, he could turn here to find that it was, after all, for the best. But there were times, yes, there were times, when another vision of the situation intruded; when he felt that he was living in the midst of a vast degenera-tion, a major abnegation of any regard for the quality of human life. All the social forms which had kept intellectual and moral and spiritual aspiration alive somehow seemed to have lapsed; they seemed to have lapsed in the years since he was born. When he thought this, Walker saw his life as a kind of impatient time-serving, an empty performance composed of aimless doing without end in view, without future. Then the impulse towards giving meaning came to him, and sent him forth on pilgrimages. But what if there could, now, be no meaningful pilgrimage? What if voyaging was just events and not lessons? If that were true, it would be the darkest discovery of all. Perhaps, though, one never made it; perhaps such searches were real and false at the same time. Perhaps one amassed facts, made comparisons, but could not judge, could not learn any truth that helped the heart. Then all the choices one made, all the deeds one performed, were whimsical. They served only the day and the hour, the things that Walker had been serving for too long. Walker finished the paper and then, seeing that his travelling companion was awake, he offered it to him.

'Very kind,' said the man, 'but no, thank you. I always believe that reading someone else's newspaper is like sleeping with someone else's wife. Nothing seems to be precisely in the right place, and when you find what you are looking for, it is not clear then how to respond to it. But you may read my newspaper if you care.'

'I have no foreign languages,' said Walker.

'Of course,' said the man, 'I forgot, you are English, we all speak yours. Vell, you will not need to worry about that in America.'

'No,' said Walker, looking out of the window; the train was going through back-yards and suburbs where people took dogs for walks. They slid past level-crossings, signal boxes, goods-yards.

'I suppose this is Southampton,' said Walker, looking for a glimpse of the sea. 'Now the ship.' But there was only town, sitting toad-like and sombre; then, suddenly, he noticed a glimpse of water where spidery cranes hung like rudimentary wings in the air. Gulls flapped over an estuary. Now he could smell the sea and hear it. By the line-side, goods in boxes were labelled to exotic ports. His throat went dry, the quiver in his stomach returned, he felt all the menace that the Englishman feels when he steps off his island into the void. Now it would begin. The great cavern of the terminal station suddenly swallowed them. They sat in the half-dark until the train stopped.

'Vell, no doubt we shall meet again on the ship,' said the

man. 'Tourist class is a very small society. Oh, please, introductions. My name is Dr Jochum.'

'Mine's Walker.'

'How do you do?' said Jochum, rising and shaking hands. The train gave a final rock as they nodded to one another across the handshake. There was a gaggle of noise along the car. 'And I will introduce you to those bagpipers,' said Jochum.

'All of them?' asked Walker.

'As many as you can manage.'

'Ah, that's the problem,' said Walker, 'where to start and where to stop.'

He went along the car and got off the train, tipping the conductor who had put his luggage out on the platform. In the line at the immigration desk, someone behind him was talking in a supercilious accent about the provinciality of modern Cambridge: 'Actually the only way I got anything out of university at all was talking to the girls on the tinned goods counter at Sainsbury's.' A man rushed by with a porter. 'Be careful, that's a double bass,' he cried. A notice said: *Keep ceaseless watch for Colorado Beetle.* The immigration man spared Walker from England very easily; he thumbed his passport, checked the contents of his wallet, and then he was beyond his own shore, officially in passage. A moment later he was walking up the gangplank and into a maw giving on to a passenger concourse. Wooden walls shone and white-coated stewards bustled; a chalked notice told him to book his dinner place in the Winter Garden Lounge. A steward took the enormous paper ticket he had been instructed to hold in his hand. Then he led him through dark wooden-walled passageways and down innumerable staircases. On the walls, arrows pointed disturbingly toward the lifeboat stations. After a long walk, the steward dived into a tiny narrow passage, pulled a curtain aside, and revealed his cabin – a small square box with four bunks, three of them already claimed, presumably by persons with more rapid forms of transport. On the wall was a large picture of a healthy-looking girl strapping round her bosom a lifejacket she did not appear to need; it was captioned: *Directions for Adjustment.* 'Don't open the porthole, sir, or you'll sink the ship. We're below sea-level down here.' 'All right,' said Walker, but it was a thought to keep in store for the bad days ahead.

He waited until the steward had gone and then began to look around. There was little to see. The bunks were set on either side of a narrow strip of floor, two on each side, one above the other; the central space was so tiny that two persons dressing at the same time would probably end up in each other's trousers. There was a tiny washbasin, about the size of a big girl's navel. It contained a small bunch of white heather, and, looking at it, he discovered that the message on it read 'Bon voyage and all my love, darling, Elaine.' This was very touching, and he squeezed the bunch into one of the four toothglasses and managed to make space for this on top of the chest of drawers. Then he got up, with the aid of a ladder, on to the top bunk on the seaward side, which was the only one left and was slightly curved to allow the ship to come to a point at both ends. Above him, for he was close to the ceiling, he could hear a scampering noise – other passengers, perhaps rats. The ship swayed slightly and he felt more uneasy than ever. He put his head on the pillow and went to sleep.

When he woke up some time had gone by, but the ship still seemed to be relatively still. He climbed down the ladder and went to book his place for dinner. Outside the cabin, the ship was confusing – little passageways, little cabins, little bathrooms, led in all directions. In front of him two Americans walked down the corridor; one, with a cropped poll, said, 'Yeah, I grant you, he's very civilized, but deep down don't you think he's sick sick sick?'

'Well, right, so Mozart's sick,' said the other. 'Who isn't?' He followed them and they brought him up to the next level. Inside a cabin a group of old English ladies were guffawing and one said, 'Fancy, isn't it a big ship? Think of all the dusting!'

Walker realized that he had committed himself to an institution. Like most young Englishmen, he was used to this; he had been to school, university, hospital. He found it, indeed, a natural situation; there were times when marriage seemed to him unnecessarily small as a unit; it was very nice, but why only two or three or four of you? He was accustomed to giving up the right amount of individuality, of retaining just sufficient selfhood to get by in a crowd without producing such an excess as to clog the system. These were simple modern arts, and he had grown up in their service. But they had their delicacies and complications. He remembered this when he got up on the main deck and looked at all the notices telling of the coming delights on ship-board – bingo, cinema shows, fancy-dress dances, get-together balls, competitions for the most original headdress, the most original footwear, and the like. Such societies were competitive. Built into the pattern of them was the assumption that one had to capture the best-looking girl, the best-placed deckchair, the best seat in the dining-room; in these systems prestige all went that way. Skill and perpetual alertness for every advantage were required; one's social antennae had to be out all the time. But what with the retreat into the privacy of marriage, and that lethargy which had let him go to sleep exactly at the crucial moment, he had destroyed himself, certainly diminished his chances. He would be lucky if he didn't spend the rest of the voyage as outsider and outcast.

Walker looked into the tea-lounge. Padded chairs with wooden arms were fixed to the floor; in them were seated middle-aged English aunties who looked triumphant because they had found out how to get tea. 'It's very nice here, but it's not like your own home,' one of them was saying, standing up and shaking out her dress. In a corner by the door a bald American was apparently holding an informal seminar on Pasternak; he could be heard saying, 'It may be panoramic, but the basic structure is a set of symbol-clusters or rather central events or discoveries around which the characters are drawn together in an unrealistic and stylized way. No?'

The whole ship, though, seemed somehow reassuring – with its bulky décor, its fitting of inlaid wood, the dedicated effort of tasteless craftsmen, the solemn commitment to tea, the small orchestras and the bridge, the vestigial displays of deference and service from rubber-lipped stewards. It was a failing reassurance, of course; like a country house made over into a lunatic asylum, it presupposed more grace and quality in its inhabitants than in fact they had. It promised the grand voyage, if people were prepared to voyage grandly, but what Walker had learned in one afternoon was that this was an illusion. He walked around some more and at last came to the Winter Garden Lounge, where the places for dinner were being issued. There was a long queue, of which Walker discovered himself to be the perpetual tail; he was, presumably, the last person in tourist class to realize what was happening. In this room, the décor was slightly more heady; the chairs were of green wicker, the mural displayed a scene of pastoral licentiousness, and there were a few carnivorous-looking flowers set in tubs. The radio was playing Children's Hour; a pop group, called the Haters, were tunelessly celebrating dim proletarian adolescent oestrus. He stood in line, wondering how in this world he was going to manage. It struck him that one of the main reasons for his attentive concern with sex and marriage and individual people was that he had always felt at odds with this kind of mass situation. It brought out the Shelley in him, seeking the single meaningful soul who could lead him through the mob chaos. How would he manage here? What about the get-together dance, this night? Would persuasive patter come to his lips, would his one dance-step, which he used like a skeleton key for every ballroom situation, fit the case and bring him companionship and escape? The curse of solitude, the one flaw in his argument for leaving home, sat heavy on him. He began mentally to prospect, not for infidelity, but for some nice girl who would understand, hide with him in some dark, quiet place behind the funnel, sit out the journey. But even finding so much required a rare energy and facility, and the lethargy of the last eight years had left him rusty even in those skills. He saw that he was back, a damaged creature, with the old familiar problems of the world.

The queue moved onward and he reached the table at which the uniformed purser sat, fair-haired and amiable. 'I'm afraid there's not much left, sir,' he said. 'We've got some places at the children's sitting; the only thing for second sitting is one place at a table for six.' 'Oh well, I'll take that,' said Walker.

He placed the ticket he was given carefully in his wallet. Going out of the lounge, he had a vision; he caught sight of himself in a dolphin-etched, full-length mirror. In his brown, fibrous, hard-wearing suit, with its large lapels and wide-bottomed trousers, he looked like a little ghost from the provincial past, tired, deeply out of touch. It didn't bode well for his chances; it showed him wan, wind-blown, incomplete. He looked for a moment; he flattened a violent spurt of hair on his head, pulled in his stomach, pushed the knot of his handwoven tie so that it covered the collar-button. It didn't do much.

The ship's hooter sounded. He found the door that led to the deck and pulled it open. Outside he was violently pinned by the wind and struck by the cold. Salt air blew up in his face; the wind slapped off the waves to hit him; the black curdy water floated below; the tugs were on; the sun was lighting the bottom of the sky. It was a confused, undesigned seascape, too much tinged with business and industry, cranes and dockers, to be romantic, too dirty and impersonal and vast for Walker to feel that it was his. Suddenly there came a little lurch; he looked down again to see the tugs pulling, churning a great vortex in the sea. The wild suction, the tossing of dirty waters, whirled violently in his head. 'Call me Ishmael!' he cried. A siren roared over him, rattling his eardrums, and grit from the funnel fell on him. On the other side, on the roof of the Ocean Terminal, a small band boomed martial music, and people were waving and shouting. He could see Southampton untying itself and beginning to float away. His sensations reached the full; a multiplicity of allegiances left him confused. He felt doses of guilt for leaving his wife, his child, his home; he felt little spurts of pride at being able to do it; he felt little throbs of queasiness at the awareness of the risks that there were in the doing. It was all a mystery beyond him; he was at the centre of a vast web of forces, but he was bare, forked Walker, alone in the universe, with nothing to claim of it, nothing he knew he ought to do. Yet expectation remained.

When early summer with its bright clear days has brought the academic year to a close, emptying chalky classrooms and leaving books at rest on library shelves, then academic folk long to go on pilgrimages. On both sides of the Atlantic they gather on the piers; their baggage is around them, their typewriters are handy, their card index is carefully packed in their stateroom luggage. They are off on mythological journeys in both directions. Floating in the harbours of New York and Southampton and Cherbourg, American professors going east stare across their ships' rails at European professors going west. Learning and wisdom lie before them, isolated on the other side of the Atlantic. In America the numbers are large, the grants are generous. They go aboard the fat liners, their prows hard against the riverside expressways. The tugs go on, and they ease out, down past the Battery. Give us your poor, your tired, your huddled masses, says the Statue of Liberty as they pass it, and we will give them homogenized milk, send them to college, and return them to you on a Fulbright. They line the rail until, Nantucket light once past, they go below and the social life of liners gets under way. There are girls to pinch and write stories about, there are short-term acquaintances to be made in the lounge, there is orientation for wives and new boys. How many raincoats does one need for England? Is the milk safe in Paris? Does one need typhoid shots for the Edinburgh Festival, and are the mosquitoes in Vienna malarial? Thus, with a certain nervousness about prophylactics, and even greater nervousness about the prime European terror, servility, and sense of acting in the great tradition of Franklin and Jefferson and James, the New World, clean, fresh, and decent, comes to captivate the Old.

It is a little later in the summer that the voyagers in the reverse direction convene, a smaller and altogether seedier band of pilgrims, altogether too few in number for the historians of race-migration to notice. They are worried about their errand, doubtful about the misfortunes that will befall them. Suppose they get ill in America, outside the sphere of the maternal National Health Service? Will the dog be all right with mother? And does the milkman really understand that he isn't to call for a whole year (think of all the bottles if he did)? Their clothes, on the whole, are thick and woolly; their suitcases have been in the family for twenty years. They tingle with silent, unassertive patriotism and with doubts about the value of what they are doing. Chance, new alignments of wealth and power, have pushed their journey in this direction, but they can't help wondering whether they haven't set a foot wrong and blighted their careers, their morals, their gastro-intestinal tracts. So they gather in the bright light of the Ocean Terminal and then go abroad – professors and lecturers who have fought all year for sabbaticals no one felt they deserved (surely going to America is a holiday?), bright young men fresh from graduation ceremonies carrying mint theses and X-ray photographs of their chests, and writers and editors hoping to produce another book about America without leaving the apartment they have borrowed in Greenwich Village. They compare notes, studying the relative merits of their scholarships (English-Speaking Union fellows get met on the boat; but Harkness fellows get the use of a rented car); they compare destinations and lists of exploitable friends. They are painfully aware that there is no real tradition in what they are doing, except that tradition, set up by Dickens and Matthew Arnold and Mrs Trollope, of going to America and disliking it.

It pleased Bernard Froelich, sitting on his patio in Party, drinking iced drinks and watching the sprinklers fizzing on his dried-out lawn, to consider that this year he was promoting a voyage in reverse. Party's contribution to the Sabbatical Generation had already left town, but Froelich was not miserable to remain. For what he saw ahead of him was a good year, his year, the year when Europe came to America. He had lost to Europe the men he had wished to lose; he had gained from Europe the man he had wished to gain. It was a balance of power ideal enough to console him for the fact that his sabbatical wasn't due for two more years, that the British

Museum and the all-night Boots in Piccadilly were still twenty-four months ahead. The boats to Europe had taken away two of the men he had most detested in the faculty; the boat from Europe was now on the water bringing him the man he really wanted to meet. The heat sang on the house-roofs, he felt the sweat in his sneakers. The future bloomed.

He happily spared his enemies. Dr Wink, the man from Business Administration who had opposed Walker's appointment ('Our aim in this business school is not to produce a narrow academic guy but to well-round his personality so he can sell himself to everyone he meets'), was off on a Guggenheim to Perugia, where he was loaned to well-round the Latin personality for a year. S. Leonov, another of Froelich's *bêtes noires*, was also en route, leaving Froelich with a zestful sense of freedom. Leonov was a large, square-faced old man who had skilfully escaped Russia before the Bolshevik revolution and now graced Benedict Arnold, where he had charge of Russian History, teaching the only course in the university in which J. Edgar Hoover's *Masters of Deceit* was a set text. He was an implacable enemy of Froelich, whom he had once denounced as a one-man protest movement undermining the fabric of this our life academical. He lived in a decaying house in Party where he gathered together a small émigré circle which met for pre-revolutionary evenings; they began (Froelich had been invited there in the early days of his tenure in Party, before hostilities began) with a dull two hours devoted to the eating of blinis and the telling of stories about Tolstoy talking to clods of earth, and ended with the condemnation of America's softness toward present-day Russia. During the McCarthy period Leonov had helped to bring about the departure from the university of three men who had been members of timid left-wing groups in the thirties, though he had missed the one active communist on the staff, a man so cunning in concealment that it was virtually impossible for him actually to be actively active, so well camouflaged that he had been approached for funds by the John Birch Society (he had paid, of course). Yet another enemy of Froelich's, Henry Leibtraub, a Jewish intellectual in the department of Theater Arts and Communication Skills, who took the advanced stand that what modern liberals had most to beware of was the compulsions in themselves that made them modern liberals, was off to England for one semester to supply one of his famous static productions of *Hamlet in Reverse*, which begins with the killing of Claudius and then goes backwards through the text looking for a motive. All that remained was to await the arrival of the man who was to be ally and admirer, the man who would understand and applaud, the man who had taken the Creative Writing Fellowship. Froelich drank his gin and tonic and looked across at his wife. 'Hurry up, James Walker,' he said.

'It seems a very intellectual ship,' said James Walker, as his three cabin-mates introduced themselves to him that evening just before dinner. He washed his face and watched them in the mirror, Julian, Richard, and Dr Millingham. They were bright, classless youths in tab-collars and suède jackets, with short hair and well-scrubbed faces. 'I'm surprised they let anyone aboard with less than a first,' he said, squeezing through as he made for the dining-room. There he found his table for six and sat in lonely state, the first arrival, listening to two youths at the next table talking about *The Faerie Queene*. I never thought I'd be embarrassed about my ignorance on a *ship*, he thought.

'Hullo then,' said a grey-skinned, demoralized-looking steward who appeared from behind a pillar to flick away some crumbs from the table with a dirty cloth, 'aren't you going to put on the paper hat?'

'Is it compulsory?' asked Walker, noticing the party items that lay beside each plate.

'We always do this on the first night,' said the steward. 'Fun, you know. Be a sport, go on.' Walker picked up a tiny black cardboard bowler, which stuck raffishly on his head, giving him the look, he could see in the pink wall mirror, of a rather tipsy civil servant. He sat like this for ten minutes, while nobody came. Finally a small round Indian appeared and sat at the far end of the table.

'Good evening,' he said, 'I see you are having a party.'

'Yes.'

'It is always pleasant to wear such hats and enjoy oneself enormously,' said the Indian, putting on a false nose. 'I have met these customs before on P and O. That is Pacific and Orient. It is the ships that cross to India. India is my native land.'

'Really?' said Walker.

'Hoho!' said the Indian, pulling at his false nose to speak more clearly, 'already I am excited. I am looking at the menu for smoked salmon. That is a very fine dish. However, there does not appear to be any.'

'Smoked salmon is first-class hors d'œuvre,' said the steward. 'Down here it's pickled herrings.'

'Alas,' said the Indian.

'I say! Hats!' said a voice at Walker's side, and a girl of about thirty, with frizzy red hair and a large figure, attempted to sit down. She wore a black suit with an astrakhan collar.

'Oh, please be careful,' said the Indian, rising. 'These chairs are fastened with hooks to the floor. It is a precaution against big gales. If you do not take your seat carefully you will certainly fall down. Has anyone here listened to the weather report?'

'I'll put mine on,' said the girl, donning a tarboosh. 'Why, is the weather going to be bad? I thought these ships were too big to be affected anyway.'

'Oh, no,' said the Indian, 'sometimes the big ships are wery wery bad indeed.'

'Lavender's blue, dilly dilly, lavender's green,' said a croaking old voice on the opposite side of the table; the dowagerly lady Walker had noticed on the train was taking the seat opposite him.

'Anybody here play shuffleboard?' cried a man with a Brigade tie, sitting down across from the Indian. The sixth place, between the old lady and the Indian, opposite the frizzy-haired girl, remained vacant a moment longer, and then there came to it Dr Jochum, the European-American Walker had travelled down with in the Pullman, fully changed, dressed in dinner jacket.

'Ah, hello there, my young friend!' he cried.

'Good evening,' said Walker.

'I say, that's not fair,' said the old lady. 'Some people know people already.'

'Are you, er, going to a university?' Walker asked the frizzy-haired girl next to him.

'Oh no, nothing so grand. I'm going to be a secretary in St Louis. That's in Mo.'

'I am going to a university,' said the Indian. 'It's a wery big university. It is called Harward.'

'All this education's getting out of hand, isn't it?' said the old lady to no one in particular.

'I suppose we are moving,' said the frizzy-haired girl.

'Yoho for the life of a tar,' said the old lady.

'You know,' said Dr Jochum, 'my experience of ships is that on them one makes an interesting discovery about the world. One finds one can do without it completely. Here we are, away from land, and we are totally content with ourselves. I have a theory, a very whimsical theory, that sea-voyages are the only part of eighteenth-century life which has survived into the present. Here we have servants, we have leisure, we can cultivate conversation, we even have cheap gin. I want to go to the captain and say, Stop the ship! This is all we need for the rest of our lives!'

'Mind,' said the steward behind Walker, poking a bowl of soup at him, 'or you'll get this all over you.'

'I am liking it all wery much,' said the Indian.

'You play it with a sort of long stick and those round wooden counters, I suppose you might call them,' said the shuffleboard man.

'Talk, talk, talk,' said the old lady.

The ship suddenly dipped and trembled a little in the open sea. Laughing screams came from other tables, and the steward spilled a bowl of soup in the lap of the shuffleboard man. 'Good God, man!' he cried.

'Oh lord,' said the steward, 'look at me.'

'It's going to be rough,' said the girl next to Walker, looking at him with fright.

'Please do not be afraid,' said the Indian. 'That was really not at all bad. I have been in a ship that turned itself over. But I do not think this ship will turn itself over.'

'A good wipe and you won't know there's been anything spilled at all,' said the steward, wiping the lap of the shuffleboard man with his cloth.

'The crew are all drunk,' said the old lady, leaning forward and looking at Walker. 'Let's all pray.'

'And it is so very much safer here than to fly,' said the Indian. 'I have been on an airplane that crashed and burned many people to death on the side of a mountain.'

'I bet you have,' said the old lady.

The ship seemed to have steadied again, but it had disquieted all the less sophisticated passengers, of whom Walker was one.

'I don't know, I think I'd rather fly,' said the girl next to him, turning to face him, 'wouldn't you?'

'My dear,' said the dowagerly lady, 'if God had intended people to fly, he would have given them wings, you know.' She turned her stony blue eyes to look at Walker and added, 'Isn't that so, Mr Bigears?'

Walker said rather boldly, 'Well, by that rule, if God had intended people to go from England to America at all, he would have joined the two continents together.'

The dowagerly lady became haughty and declared to the shuffleboard man, 'Mr Bigears knows no fear. Mr Bigears is absolutely fearless.'

'My name isn't Mr Bigears,' said Walker delicately.

'That's my name for you,' said the old lady, snatching up a cardboard dunce's hat from beside her plate and putting it on her head. 'I always have my own names for people. I call all my friends the most atrocious names. They hate me for it.'

At the other end of the table, Dr Jochum, who had donned a scholar's cardboard mortar-board, was talking to the Indian about American schools. 'Such places!' he cried. 'There are in existence many records of feral children, children who are abandoned in woods and parented by wolves or bears; of course they cannot write or talk or reason logically but they are capable to catch a rabbit. So it is with these places, these high-schools. We abandon our children there and when they grow up they cannot write or talk or reason logically but they know how to dance the quickstep. Always the minimum necessary for survival.'

'I hope America's nice,' said the girl next to Walker. 'Have you been there?'

'No,' said Walker. 'I hope it is too.'

'They all smoke between courses,' said the old lady.

'I never expected to go,' said the girl. 'It seems amazing, somehow, me here. I live in Rickmansworth, and I taught in a private school. Nothing ever happened to me. Then suddenly a friend of my father's, who happens to be a London business-man, had to go over to America and he found they were terribly keen on having English secretaries over there. Appar-ently it's a great status symbol to have people with English voices answering the telephone. So, well, this friend of my father's told an industrialist in St Louis, Mo., that I had secretarial qualifications. And the next thing was, right out of the blue, such a surprise, I got a letter from him asking me to be his private secretary. Well, I weighed it up this way, and I weighed it up that way, and finally I decided to go. But I don't know, I'm afraid it's going to be very different over there, different from everything.'

'I suppose it will be,' said Walker.

'I suppose that's why people like us come. You can get so terribly bored with yourself, can't you?'

'Yes, indeed,' said Walker.

'I never do,' said the old lady. 'I find myself endlessly fascinating.'

Walker found himself gradually tempted to withdraw from the conversation. The gay concourse with wonderful people that he had rather expected on the voyage was hardly what he was getting, and in addition the swaying of the sea was up-setting him rather badly. The food struck him as rather less than magnificent, too, and all in all the bright light of new experience and great discoveries that he had expected to shine here on the ship was far from present. Some of his fellow-travellers struck him as even duller people than himself.

Then, suddenly, the old lady tapped on the table with a knife. 'No more private talking please,' she said. 'This is not a good conversation. Not what I'm used to. We must have a simply brilliant conversation. Like people used to do. My mother used to say, No talking between meals. People thought she was terribly dull; then she would come down and be absolutely brilliant all through dinner. She was saving it up, you see; we must all save things up. As my mother said, the dinner table is for conversation: one can always snatch a scrap of something to eat between meals.'

'Oh, very fine,' said the Indian.

'You push them along the deck into some marked squares, and that gives you your score,' said the shuffleboard man.

The old lady looked at him indignantly, and then turned to Walker. 'Think of something for us to talk about, Mr Bigears,' she said. Walker felt uneasy, as victims who know they are in for misfortune often do, and he blushed and straightened his bowler hat.

'I know,' said the old lady, 'let's play "Who said it?" '

'Oho! Is this a game?' cried the Indian. 'I am always delighted by games.'

'Yes, well, it's a game about poetry. I don't suppose you have any poetry in India.'

'Oh, there you are quite wrong, there is much poetry in India.'

'Well, don't tell us any. I'll start. Who said, who said, who said "They also serve who only stand and wait"?' There was a pause. 'Do you know, Mr Bigears?'

Walker said grudgingly, 'Well, yes I do, as a matter of fact.'

'Well, say then. If you win it's your go.'

'Well, it was Milton.'

'NO!' cried the old lady. 'You lose, I win. Now it's my go again. Who said, who said . . . ?'

'It was Milton,' said Walker.

'Mr Bigears, it was Shakespeare.'

'Well,' said Walker, 'we can look it up in the ship's library after dinner. It's the sonnet "When I consider how my light is spent. . . . " '

'Shakespeare.'

'I think you'll find . . . '

'Temper, Mr Bigears, temper,' said the old lady. 'Who said, who said . . . ?'

The girl beside Walker had been growing bright red, and now she leaned forward and said, 'But Mr Bigear . . . this gentleman's quite right actually. It *was* Milton.'

'My dear,' said the old lady. 'Don't take so many potatoes, they're bad for your spots.'

'I learned that poem at school.'

'My dear, of course it was Milton. But it's my game. I want to win it.'

'Oh, my word,' said the Indian.

'So let's get on. Who said, "Shall I compare thee to a summer's day?" '

'Ah well, by the same logic,' said Dr Jochum, 'this must be Milton.'

'No, you lose.'

'Who did say it?' asked the girl.

'Omar Khayyám,' said the old lady. 'Well, now I've won twice, that's enough of that game, isn't it, Mr Bigears? Now you think of one.'

'I suppose there will be many games at the Dance tonight,' said the Indian. 'Also I am anticipating balloons.'

'Fun and games,' said the old lady. 'I love them. At home I have little parties when my friends come and dust. We play dusting games. It's terribly popular, quite a thing in the village.'

'Do people dress up very much?' asked the girl. 'I mean, for these dances on the ship.'

'I hope so,' said Jochum.

'The Get-Together Dance,' said the girl. 'It sounds great fun.'

'Ah yes, getting together is great fun, but I have always found that the great difficulty is getting apart again. What impossible friendships one makes on these ships! What hateful people one loves! After all it is only for six days, so one doesn't need to be so selective. It is all splendid at the time, but a year later the telephone is ringing and a voice tells, "Hello, you remember me on that ship; you promised to be my host for three months in your house." We must not take these things too seriously.'

'I should never dream of doing so,' said the old lady.

'Cheese or fruit?' said the steward breathing hard into the exposed entrance of Walker's ear.

'What kind of cheese?' he asked.

'Well, now,' said the steward, 'there's ordinary, and what's that one that begins with a g? We've got that.'

The old lady suddenly leaned forward and waved her purse.

'Oh, Mr Steward,' she said, 'be a nice man and get me some figs, will you?'

'Gorgonzola?' asked Walker.

'Figs is first-class fruit, madam,' said the steward, putting his hand on Walker's shoulder to lean over.

'Oh come on, Mr Vasco da Gama, you go and tell the Chief Steward that Lady Hunt-Francis would like a few figs.'

'Gouda?' asked Walker.

'I'll see what I can do, my lady,' said the steward, going off. Defeated by privilege, reduced by this apotheosis of England, Walker looked across at the old lady, tying a scarf across her pinched and ancient breast. He felt that he and she were participants in some old war which he was always in the habit of losing.

'See you at the dance then,' said the girl next to him.

'I insist you don't dance with me, Mr Bigears,' said the old lady. 'I looked under the table at your feet. They're as big as your ears.' The steward came back and set down two plates: for Walker a piece of ancient mousehole cheese, and for Lady Hunt-Francis a large plateful of gaily arranged figs.

'Thank you,' said Lady Hunt-Francis, and then looked up across the table to catch Walker's eye. 'Shakespeare,' she murmured, as she tackled a fig.

Why voyage? thought Walker, standing on deck after dinner, a sadly aggrieved man. Such things are never what they are said to be. The water whirled, the thought of the Get-Together

Dance saddened him, and the prospect of dancing with the red-haired girl, who before they had left table had secured a promise of several dances, was as exciting as going to the dentist's. Why did I come? he wondered, looking down over the side. Detritus poured out of a hole in the ship into the water. I've condemned myself to miseries I could get more cheaply at home, he thought. He went inside and stumbled, in the rock of the ship, downstairs to his cabin. Richard, Julian and Dr Millingham were getting ready for the dance, taking up all the available space. They stood in line in front of the mirror, tying their ties and discussing whether Wordsworth's 'Immortality Ode' was his farewell to departing powers or his invocation to new ones.

'I thought you'd got lost,' said Dr Millingham, surveying him through the mirror. 'Nearly sent out the lifeboat.'

'I just went out on deck for a minute.'

'Going to the dance?' asked Dr Millingham.

'I was thinking I'd go to bed, I don't fancy it very much.'

'Oh, come on, it's going to be utterly wild. To my knowledge there are thirty balloons up there. And a banner saying "Welcome Aboard." I'm expecting an orgy.'

'Anybody seen my heather?' asked Walker. 'I left some heather in a toothglass on that chest of drawers, and it's gone.'

'Oh, was that yours?' asked Millingham. 'I put it out in the passageway. Actually it was eating all the oxygen in here.'

Walker went outside and brought it back in again. 'It was from my wife,' he said.

'Oh, very sorry,' said Dr Millingham. 'Far be it from me to intervene between man and wife. Look, shove a bit of it in your lapel and then you'll look a real cut.'

Walker stood passively while Millingham inserted the heather in his buttonhole. 'Now you're all set,' said Millingham. 'Come on, I'll take you up there and buy you a drink.' They went out into the passageway. 'Look, everyone's going,' said Millingham. 'Just listen to all those lavatories flushing. All getting ready to get together. Where did you say this dance was?'

'In the bar on the sports deck.'

As they went up the next staircase the sound of the Hokey-Cokey grew audible. 'You put your left ear out,' said Dr Millingham. 'All the modern dances.'

The bar was a small room, mildly decorated with streamers, and some of the tables had been moved for dancing. A few people, mostly English girls with round blunt bosoms, sweatily danced the Hokey-Cokey to the music of Jack Wilks and His Trio, a group of elderly patriarchs trapped together with their instruments in one corner. Along the bar sat a row of Australians, men and women, all over six feet tall. The men wore black shoes, the women white gloves. As they arrived, the man at the end flicked the ear of the girl next to him and said, 'Pass it on.'

It was all rather like the public houses Walker went to in Nottingham, and 'When will this sameness cease?' he sighed to himself.

'What's it to be?' asked Millingham, pushing up to the bar.

'I'll have a stout,' said Walker, looking around and noting that the red-haired girl was not yet in sight.

'That's not drink, that's food. No, come on, try something American, one of these Tom Collins things. They even give you a stick to poke people with.'

When they had been served, Millingham picked up the drinks and made for the tables. 'This is the really nice thing about these ships, the cheap booze,' he said. 'That's why people sentimentalize about travel. They do it in a permanent alcoholic haze.' They passed a table where a group of English youths sat, throwing potato chips in the air and catching them in their mouths as they came down, and another where three close-cropped American boys in tennis shoes wooed a French girl with a high hairdo by mentioning in rapid succession the titles of books they had read. The third table was empty and they sat.

'Well, here's to God's Own Country,' said Millingham, raising his drink, 'where the Elk and the Buffalo roam. Not to mention Rotary.'

'Cheers!' said Walker, tasting the concoction; it was nice, but not like stout.

'Where are you going?' asked Millingham.

'I'm going to a university called Benedict Arnold University.'

'Never heard of it. And I've heard of most of them.'

'I hadn't actually, until they wrote to me. It was headed writing paper, so I thought they must really exist.'

'Where is it?' asked Millingham.

'I forgot to look, exactly. Somewhere in the middle.'

'The cow country, the Bible belt. Where raiding parties from the *Chicago Tribune* kill off Englishmen travelling alone. You're a brave man, Mr Walker. I'm playing it safe, going to Yale. They've got a lot of books at Yale.'

There was a stir in the doorway. Smart, looking as though they had just been unwrapped from cellophane, in came seven or eight of the American girls Walker had seen on the Pullman. 'What's this?' said Millingham.

'Oh, they're bagpipers,' said Walker. 'There's a party of girls who have been touring Europe playing the bagpipes on board. From a girls' college in New England.'

'Why the bagpipes when they could squeeze *me* against their chests?' said Millingham.

The girls, wearing either neat black dresses or cashmere sweaters and pleated skirts, sat down; one of them called over a steward and ordered drinks. 'You know, it's funny,' said Millingham, 'American girls always look like English men. Neat hair, suits, white raincoats, very straight bodies. I'm fascinated by them. Do you think that makes me a fairy?'

'I don't think so,' said Walker. 'I'm fascinated by them too.'

'Salt of the earth, American girls,' said Millingham. 'The only thing is, it's like shopping in a supermarket. There are so many good brands with only marginal differences that you never know which to pick. An embarrassment of riches, that's what that lot is.'

'I know,' said Walker. 'At one time, there were only a few beautiful girls. Think of all the expense of spirit you went to to get near them. Pushing other people out of the way, stamping on their fingers. Now there are so many it's enough to turn men passive. Not like it was in my day. I sometimes think I missed out on all the good things. I was a bohemian when the world was against them; I was a lecher when it was frowned upon. It makes me feel like a tired old pioneer.'

'Well, speak for yourself,' said Millingham. 'It still is *my* day.'

'I blame it on the orange juice,' said Walker.

'Of course these American girls are very demanding,' said Millingham. 'The thing is, they're so inexhaustibly verbal. Take an English girl out and if she's said "Ooo" three times that's a good conversational evening. But American girls talk about everything. They're like these American sports cars with a hundred clocks on the dashboard. They have to have a report on every area of sensation. And they want pleasure at all times. Stop amusing them for a minute and you've taken away one of their inalienable rights, the pursuit of happiness.'

'Ah, my old friend!' Dr Jochum, still in his dinner jacket, but now with a small scarlet cummerbund, stood over Walker.

'Ah, join us,' said Walker. 'This is Dr Jochum, I met him on the train. Dr Millingham, my cabin-mate.'

'We sound like a medical conference,' said Jochum.

'Oh well,' said Millingham, 'if this ship should sink, the world of learning would be set back two hundred years. Let me buy you a cheap drink.'

'No, I came over to honour the arrangement I made with my young friend on the train. I said, Mr Walker, I would introduce you to the young bagpipe ladies.'

Walker went red and said, 'Oh, I could hardly. . . . '

'But of course, I know them well, you see.'

'You can't miss a chance like that,' said Millingham. 'Go and establish a bridgehead.'

'Oh dear,' said Walker. He got up and Jochum put his arm around his shoulder and led him genially across the room. Walker felt blushes spreading all over his body, and it seemed to him as if his collar had popped open. 'I don't think I know your first name,' said Jochum.

'James,' said Walker shrilly.

The girls looked up and one said, 'Hi, Dr Jochum; what's this?'

'It's a shy young English friend of mine. His name is James Walker. I will let the ladies introduce themselves.'

'Hi, Jamie,' said one of the girls.

Another felt his jacket and said 'Harris tweed, or I'm not Perry Mason.'

Walker said, 'How do you do?'

'Oh, you Yerpeans, so polite,' said another of the girls.

'Now you must make him entertain you,' said Jochum, who was unhooking chairs and bringing them up to the table. Walker sat on one and looked with attentiveness at his knees.

'Hot in here,' he said after a moment.

The girl next to him said, 'You know, I had a teacher in World Lit. talked exactly like you. He couldn't understand why we couldn't understand anything he said. The girls used to say, you know, this hall has bad acoustics, or, I've been deaf since I was three. They didn't like to tell him he talked funny.'

'No, quite,' said Walker.

'What happened to this man?' asked Jochum, sitting down and lighting a small cigar.

'That was Dr Jeffries, you know,' said the girl.

'Ah yes,' said Jochum nodding.

'What did happen?' asked Walker.

'They didn't renew his contract,' said Jochum, blowing cigar smoke blandly.

'He was *fired*,' said the girl.

'Because he talked funny?' asked Walker.

'Oh no,' said the girl, shocked. 'That would be Prejudice. No, he didn't like the course. He kept changing all the books and teaching what he called non-great books in the Great Books Course, because they were better. So they, you know, didn't keep him on.'

'It seems hard,' said Walker.

'Vell, we have another pattern of educational system in the United States, Mr Walker, as you vill see,' said Jochum. 'It is much easier to obtain a post, and much easier to lose one.'

'Oh,' said Walker, feeling uneasy.

'Actually this man was a difficult fellow. He once flunked all

74

the students in his course to show them all standards are arbitrary. That offended the administration. And in an American university you can offend everyone except administration and the football coach.'

Oh, can I last? asked Walker of himself, sweating.

'Of course, he used to date a lot of his students and take them to the racetrack and all,' said the girl.

'I can see that must be a real temptation,' said Walker.

'I guess so,' said the girl. 'Of course a lot of Hillesley girls don't like dating their instructors.'

'Because of their low social prestige,' said another girl.

'Oh,' said Walker.

'He looks sad,' said Jochum.

On Walker's other side, a girl who hadn't so far spoken suddenly tapped him on the lapel. 'I see you're in leaf,' she said.

'Pardon?'

'I see you have this bunch of heather in your buttonhole. Is this some English national holiday?'

Walker looked at her; she was fair-haired, wore a button-down Oxford shirt like a man's, and a corduroy top and skirt. A small button pinned to the shirt said MAKE LOVE NOT WAR. 'Oh no,' said Walker, 'my. . . .' A sudden access of male cunning interrupted what he was about to say; he reformulated. 'A friend of mine sent a bunch of heather to the ship. By telegram. It's amazing what you can do nowadays.'

'Right,' said the girl. 'It is, fantastic.'

Walker cast a quick look around the room. His partner had still not appeared. 'Would you like to dance?' he said to the girl with the button. She put a crisp into her mouth and then, without saying anything, stood up. Walker led her out on to the floor and opened his arms. She placed them carefully where she wanted them, meanwhile looking at him with cool, appraising eyes. Walker set his one dance-step into motion and they moved about the floor. The three Ivy League men danced by with the French girl.

'Well,' said the girl, 'it's kind of you to pick me out. It must have been quite a decision to have to make. Or was it because I was sitting nearest?'

'I suppose it was because you spoke to me.'

'Who didn't?' said the girl.

'I don't think I caught your name,' said Walker.

'No, that's because nobody said it.'

'Is it a secret?'

'No,' said the girl, after some thought, 'it's been bruited around. I'm Julie Snowflake.'

'That's charming.'

'Now why is it charming?'

'Oh, I don't know, it's just a fresh kind of name.'

'Huh,' said the girl.

Walker felt rebuffed and they danced silently for a moment; then the girl said, 'Are you still with me?'

'Yes.'

'Well, look, do try some more conversation.'

'Well,' said Walker, rather uneasily, 'did you have a good vacation?'

'Yes, I had a good vacation. Did you have a good vacation?'

'Am I boring you?'

'No, not exactly. I just don't quite appreciate this Yerpean politeness. Do you all talk to one another this way?'

'I suppose we do.'

'Do you ever get to know one another?'

'Probably not.'

'Ah, well,' said Julie, 'okay, that's Yerp, I guess.'

'That's what?'

'Yerp. Yerp where you come from.'

'You mean Europe?'

'Yes, Yerp.'

'Oh,' said Walker, 'I'm not European, I'm English.'

'Isn't England in Yerp?'

'Yes, in a way.'

'Well, then.'

Walker sneaked another look around the room; his red-headed partner still seemed not to have arrived. He said, 'What are you studying at Hillesley?'

'I'm an English major.'

'I suppose I should salute.'

'Yok, yok,' said Miss Snowflake, looking at him coolly. Walker knew he must try harder. 'Do you find it interesting?' he asked.

'Well,' said Miss Snowflake, 'last year I was popular and nearly flunked, but this year I'm going to shut myself away and really study. This summer I read Dickens and got *him* out of the way. Now I'm starting in on James. I find him a bit *false*, you know what I mean? Actually I can't stand falsity and pretence; it offends me deeply, where I live. Do you read Kierkegaard?'

'Well, I read him a few years back and got him out of the way.'

Miss Snowflake looked at Walker for the first time, raising her head, the top of which came level with his eyes, to do so.

'Now that's some kind of a reply,' she said. 'Well, you know that passage in *Fear and Trembling* about dancing? And he talks about two kinds of people?'

'No, I don't remember it.'

'Well, it's really very fine. Look it up. I wrote it down on a file card and thumbtacked it in the john at home, that's how fine it is. How does it go?' Miss Snowflake screwed up her young grey eyes. 'It's something like this: "Most people live in worldly sorrow and joy, and sit around the walls, and they don't join in the dance. But the knights of infinity" – this is the bit – "are dancers, and possess elevation. They rise up and fall, and this is no mean pastime, nor ungraceful to behold." I think it's marvellous. No mean pastime! Possess elevation!'

'There's a bit like that in Waugh's *Decline and Fall*,' said Walker.

'But isn't it *good*?' said Miss Snowflake impatiently. 'The question is, how do you get to be a knight of infinity?'

'Who knows?' said Walker, 'I don't think I do.'

'Or,' said Miss Snowflake, 'to rephrase the question, why are Yerpeans so stiff?'

'Sitters by the wall?'

'You're getting it.'

'Oh, I see. Well, I don't know. Maybe we've found our

balance. Maybe we think we know what to expect. Maybe we've stopped looking.'

'Could be,' said Miss Snowflake.

'And then,' said Walker lightly, 'we realize we've missed something, so we come to the States.'

'To become knights of infinity? Well, you know, I don't think you're going to make it.'

'Why not?'

'Oh, I don't know, that's not fair. Let's erase it from the record. I'm crazy, I talk too fast.'

The music stopped and they separated. Walker suddenly realized that he was enjoying himself a great deal and didn't want to part from Miss Snowflake. He said, 'They've stopped. Look, why don't we go out on deck? It's a nice night.' Miss Snowflake looked at him speculatively. 'Oh no, thanks,' she said, 'I think I'd prefer to stay right here, if you don't mind, because I've been getting pretty low grades in judo. Why don't we have another dance though? I was just starting to enjoy our conversation.'

'So was I,' said Walker.

Jack Wilks set his group in motion again and they began to dance once more. Walker said, 'Tell me some more about Hillesley.'

'Well, I don't know that I can invest it with much interest. It's a very shoe girl's school in Connecticut where a lot of very expensive girls go.'

'Like you?'

'Yes, well, I guess I'm an expensive girl. Easy, you're kicking me. But the communal IQ is terrific. It's been a kind of proof to me that you can be rich *and* intelligent. A lot of people have questioned that, you know.'

'Have they? I didn't.'

'Yes, socialists and all. Stick around, you can learn a lot. But conspicuous consumption is frowned on at Hillesley. Like a lot of girls have their own planes, but we don't allow them on campus. The freshmen come with wardrobes full of mink-collared sweaters and vicuna coats, all that Miami Beach routine, you know, but we soon put them right. Well, for instance, there's an informal rule among the student body that the only time you can wear a mink coat is going along the corridor to the shower.'

'It sounds very exclusive.'

'Well, maybe, but there are no favours at Hillesley. I can illustrate that. For instance, when there's a prowler on campus, they turn off all the lights so no one knows who gets raped.'

'That seems very fair,' said Walker urbanely, 'does it happen often?'

'Oh, once in a while. But of course there's lots more to Hillesley life than just getting raped. You know, you have to study as well?'

'An all-round education, then.'

'*Exactly*, you've got it *exactly*. An all-round education. A lot of the girls are geniuses – but they're expected to be *all-round* geniuses. One of the problems of genius is the specialization.'

'Well, I suppose there are a lot of problems with genius.'

'Oh, boy, problems. Well, as you know, I guess, a lot of geniuses – I suppose it *is* geniuses not genii – are actually psychos. That's *really* difficult. All our geniuses have this careful psychological testing so that we don't have any really extreme types. For instance, if a girl seems unstable, she has to have a letter from her psychiatrist testifying that she won't commit suicide during semester. In short,' said Miss Snow-flake ironically, 'we allow some leeway during vacation. Actually I hope you won't think because I'm describing this to you I'm approving it without reservation, will you?'

'No, not at all,' said Walker.

'Actually I take a critical attitude towards Hillesley. What about you? What do you think?'

'Well,' said Walker, 'I think my view would be that a college like that ought to take some bigger risks with genius. I have a weakness for genius myself.'

'Well, that's an interesting point of view and I probably agree with it, but just to take the rebuttal position for a minute, you have to protect the name of the school, and then there's another thing. A lot of Hillesley girls marry really shoe Ivy League men, Yalies with balanced portfolios and unique retirement pensions, you know, and marriage for woman is a destiny. Well, for that kind of destiny you really require all-round development.'

'Yes,' said Walker, 'I can see that.'

'Like we have this course on lifting suitcases down from racks without showing our slip,' said Julie.

'I see, so we have to see Hillesley as a kind of marriage bureau as well.'

'A very high-class one. Well, okay, now why not? No, I guess I can see why not, but you see the point. Boys these days are tricky. I mean, they don't care if you've been ravished sixty times by sailors, which I guess is a major cultural break-through, but they do want a girl they can live graciously with, someone they can talk to. A girl with all-round cultural development. And so . . . well, you can be *too* intelligent.'

'Are you too intelligent?'

'Well, I think you've hit it . . . but not the way some girls are. You know, they wear their hair straight, and they're philo-sophically opposed to charm and padded bras, and they don't get any dates and this spurs them on to take their doctorate. I don't think I'm like that, I don't think I'm the doctorate type. No, Hillesley's aim is to produce girls who are mature in *all* directions. This Yerpean . . . this Englishman we were talking about back there at the table, he used to say that Hillesley girls were just normal American girls, but they worried about it more. That seems about right.'

'It sounds,' said Walker, 'more like a way of life than an education.'

'Well, right, and of course the problem is what attitude to take toward it, when they're trying to help you but maybe you can't accept it wholesale. When I was a freshman I tried adolescent cynicism, and wore leotards, and joined SANE and all. But that was a dead end. Now I think I've attained a, well, cooler and more sophisticated irony. I guess it was that you found difficult when we first started conversing.'

'It must have been,' said Walker.

'Cool without being offensive,' said Julie. 'That's the style.'

'And full of elevation.'

'Right.'

Looking over Julie's shoulder, Walker suddenly caught sight of the next couple; it was Dr Millingham, dancing with the red-haired girl. Millingham was facing him, and winked; the girl had her back to Walker. Walker steered Julie round, a complicated manoeuvre, and got behind the cover of two dons twisting with one another. He realized that desperate measures were in order, and said, 'Look, sure you wouldn't like to go on deck? I'm getting awfully hot.'

'I don't know,' said Miss Snowflake, looking at him with a firm gaze. 'You thinking of trying to maul me around a lot?'

'Well, no, certainly not if you don't want me to.'

'No, I don't,' said Miss Snowflake. 'Well, okay, look, I just have to go down to my cabin and get a coat. Why don't you wait for me at the top of the stairway? I'll be right back.'

'Fine,' said Walker, leading her off the floor. They went out beyond the glass doors, and Miss Snowflake left him and went down the stairs. Walker looked at a map of the Atlantic on which a little wooden ship had been moved to a point somewhere off Land's End, and also read a notice about the daily competitions and the Fancy Hat gala. There was also an advice telling him to set his watch back one hour at midnight. 'Having a nice time?' said a voice behind him, and there stood the red-haired girl. She was wearing a long shiny blue dress with a halter neck, and black gloves to the elbow. There were patches of powder on her collar-bones. 'I'm sorry I was late,' she went on. 'That old lady caught me and asked me to help her to unpack. Still, I see you found someone to talk to.'

'Yes,' said Walker.

'Perhaps I'll see you later,' said the girl.

'Yes, buy you a drink later,' said Walker, relieved. She went back through the doors and a moment later Julie Snowflake came back up the stairs.

'Hi, again, all set,' she said; she was wearing an unzipped ski-jacket over her suit. Walker pushed open the outside door. 'Hey, this is some wind blowing,' said Miss Snowflake. A fine wet spray had made the planks of the deck greasy. Deck-lamps picked out the white of the rails and the lifeboats, and the funnel, high above, was floodlit, so that its bluster of smoke was picked out from the darkness.

'Let's go toward the stern,' said Walker. 'Maybe we can get out of the wind.'

'No, I like being out in the wind,' said Miss Snowflake, leaning against the rail and looking out into the darkness; all that could be seen was the bow-wave's faint luminosity. 'We must be way out to sea now. Hey, just look at that illuminated funnel. It's like Coney Island on a lonely night. Nobody around but us. You know something, Mr Walker? You should try zen.'

'Pardon?' said Walker, looking out too.

'Be a buddhist. Take these yellow socks. No, there are a lot of very fine books on zen. All these great stories about masters slapping their pupils in the ear. I think you acquire a sense of reality. You have a good sense of reality?'

Walker said, 'Well, I don't have much to measure it against. I think what I really lack is a sense of unreality.'

'Yes, that figures. Well, that's the thing with zen. You get both. I must tell you about this course at Hillesley called Poise and Co-ordination.'

'Where you lift suitcases off racks?'

'Yes, and how to get out of cars without showing your inner thighs and all. Inner thighs, Miss Snowflake, look to the inner thighs. But the thing is, I use the course a different way. I learned how to relax. It's marvellous. A kind of, well, transmogrification of self. Now you, you don't relax.'

A strand of Julie Snowflake's hair blew against his face, and he felt far from relaxed. 'No,' he said.

'You're trying too hard, you're all screwed up,' said Miss Snowflake. 'So you have problems, we all have problems. Look, let me show you. Try relaxing. Let your arms go all limp. No, go ahead, I'm holding you up. Now, I'm going to lift your arms in the air and let go of them. Let them ooze down. Okay?' She had lifted Walker's arms into the air; she let them go. The knuckles of his wrists smacked him on top of his head.

'Christ,' he said.

'You all right?' asked Miss Snowflake. 'No, Mr Walker, that was way off. You have to ooze down sinuously like a sna-a-ake, you know? You weren't controlling your relaxation. One time at Hillesley a girl broke a ten thousand dollar wrist-watch doing what you just did. She was all tensed up like you.'

'Was she?'

'Now come on, no fooling, try to cultivate detachment from your body. Let each bit of it live for itself. Look, I'm holding you. Now, just sag.'

'Right down?'

'Yes.'

Walker sagged and they both fell heavily to the deck. 'Oh, boy, you're heavy, you brought me down too,' said Miss Snowflake, in whose lap his head had somehow landed. 'I guess you're really far gone. Let me up.'

'I like it down here,' said Walker.

'No, cut that out, come on, get up. Let go my foot, Mr Walker. Give me my shoe back. Thanks. Now, come on, up.'

They got up and went and stood by the rail. 'Just take a look at the back of my skirt,' said Miss Snowflake. 'Is it stained on the, you know, fanny? That deck's greasy.'

Walker, still breathing hard, took out his handkerchief and rubbed for a moment. 'That's fine now,' he said. 'Well, so it looks as though I'll never make it, then?'

'Relaxing? Oh, I don't know. I'm not expert. I was only fooling, I guess. You all right? You're puffing like a blood-hound. You're not going to have a coronary or anything?'

'No, I'm fine,' said Walker.

'Come out from back there and lean on the rail. Sniff this fresh air. Good, no? Of course,' said Julie, reaching in a pocket in her shirt placed square on her left breast, and taking out a pack of American cigarettes, 'there's another great way to relax.'

'What's that?'

'Creative writing. We have this great course. Did you ever try it? It's really therapeutic. That's what I like about writers. They're all such relaxed people, in tune with it all.'

'Well, I have tried that, as a matter of fact.'

'You keep trying, Mr Walker,' said Miss Snowflake, knocking a cigarette out of the pack and hitting it on her thumbnail. 'Cigarette? You ever publish anything?' She cupped her hands round her Zippo lighter and lit both their cigarettes. Their hair touched.

Walker said, 'As a matter of fact, yes.'

'As a matter of fact, are you kidding?'

'No, not at all.'

'What did you publish?'

'Three novels,' said Walker.

'No, come on, tell me the truth. I know a lot of men like to tell girls they're writers because they think girls will go further with writers. But I bless the truth.'

'No, really, it is the truth.'

Miss Snowflake puffed hard on her cigarette and shook her head. 'Well, you're a writer,' she said. 'What was the name again? James Walker? Not the James Walker who wrote *The Last of the Old Lords*?'

'That's right.'

'Well, this is fantastic, and you know why? I'm writing a term paper about the English novel since the war and you're *in* it?'

'Well,' said Walker, 'I can't think why.'

'Now listen, cut that out.'

'I wasn't doing anything.'

'Yes, you were, that modesty bit,' said Miss Snowflake. 'You're an important writer and you just behave like one. Why, you could be anybody. All that "as a matter of fact" and "I can't think why." You should just hear yourself saying it. It sounds like some phoney hack writer for the comics. You mustn't be artificial and embarrassed. You must be what you are. A real human being.'

'Possess elevation, be able to sag?'

'Right.'

'I'd like to,' said Walker, 'but isn't being a real human being acting the way you are?'

'I don't believe so. A writer shouldn't be ordinary. He has to

84

try. He has to feel more, understand more, see more. You have to be able to know the future, to sense moods, to take truth out of the air. Artists are the antennae of the race, Mr Walker.'

'I can't even sag properly,' said Walker. 'I just have to do what I can with what I am. Which is what everyone has to do. A lot of writers finished themselves by trying to do more.'

'No, I don't think so,' said Julie Snowflake. 'You know, you're a disappointment, Mr Walker. You don't believe in yourself, so why should I believe in you? I don't believe you wrote those books you wrote.'

'But I did.'

'No, you didn't.'

'I did, Julie.'

'You're holding my arm,' said Julie. 'You don't know how to feel properly, so how can you have made me feel things?'

'Well, I wrote them,' said Walker petulantly.

'Sure you did,' said Julie. 'Take no notice. I'm crazy. Everyone says so. You mustn't think I don't admire you. I do. But be better, Mr Walker, be better. Christ, I just threw my cigarette over the side. I've probably set the whole goddam ship on fire. Can you see it?'

Walker looked over. 'It's going into the water,' he said.

'Thank goodness. I ought not to be roaming free really. Well, well, well, so I met my term paper. Why are you coming to the States?'

'Well,' said Walker, still looking over. 'I'm going to be a creative writer on a campus somewhere out west.'

'Oh, you should come to Hillesley. I wish you were coming to Hillesley. We have a whole bunch of writers there. A lot of girls like to sleep with them because it's honorific. For the record, though, it's not a view I share.'

'I'm sorry to hear that,' said Walker.

'Hey,' said Julie Snowflake. 'Well, where out west?'

'A place called Benedict Arnold.'

'Oh no, not Benedict Arnold.'

'Why, is there something wrong with it?'

'No, not really. It's just they're a bunch of ski-bums out

there. They won't appreciate you. I know because I have a brother out there.'

'I hope I meet him.'

'Well, maybe, he's training to be a veterinarian. No, it's quite a good school really.'

'Do you ever go there?'

'Once in a while.'

'Maybe we'll meet again.'

'I don't know,' said Julie. 'You want to?'

'I think you're a very fascinating person.'

'Sure you do.'

'I do,' said Walker. 'Are all American girls like you?'

'Yes, but I think about it more. I told you. Well, what about that dancing? We're just sitters by the wall. I suppose that's how you met Dr Jochum.'

'What's how I met Dr Jochum?'

'Well, going to Benedict Arnold. He teaches there.'

'No!' said Walker. 'Really?'

'Moment of truth,' said Julie. 'Isn't that what Aristotle calls a perpety?'

'No, I didn't know that. I met him on the Pullman. I thought just now he taught at Hillesley.'

'He did once,' said Miss Snowflake, resting both elbows on the rail and wriggling her behind till she had gained equilibrium.

'But they fired him because he talked funny?'

'No, he just didn't have tenure. He left at the end of his term. You know . . . I like him. Because he's so sad. Like all the emigrés. All these restless people who drift around from place to place looking for Europe in America. You mustn't get that way.'

'I'll try not to,' said Walker.

'He makes me sad too. He's a bit lost intellectually, too, and because he's sad and drifting and lost no one wants to give him tenure. Well, I'll tell you, if I ran Hillesley I'd give him tenure.'

'That's very kind.'

'Well, I am,' said Julie. 'Now what about that dancing?'

She had turned round to look at him stretching her legs out and putting her backside against the rail. Walker looked at her; he said 'Oh let's wait a minute.'

'You trying to figure out a way to get to kiss me?' she asked, looking at him.

'I suppose I am,' said Walker, feeling a thumping in his heart.

'Well,' said Miss Snowflake, 'be my guest. Politely now.'

Walker's heart seemed now to be thumping so violently that it must, he was sure, be shaking the buttons off his shirt. He came near and put his mouth to Julie Snowflake's. Her hand touched the back of his neck, a touch of sophistication he appreciated. On her lips he could taste lipstick and Manhattans. The kiss continued for a while until she pursed her lips and wriggled her head.

'Well,' she said, withdrawing from the suction.

'Well,' said Walker, breathing hard.

'Cigarette?' said Miss Snowflake, taking out her pack of Chesterfields and her Zippo. 'You know, that's the first time I've ever been kissed by my term paper.'

'What did you write the last one on?' asked Walker, subsiding only a little.

'Tolstoy,' said Julie, 'and I'm no necrophiliac.'

Walker had not taken his arms from around her and he put his lips to her forehead. 'You know?' she said. 'We ought to go back. We're party poopers.'

'We're what?'

'We're pooping the party downstairs. Come on. I'll drag you back. Just let yourself go limp. Okay?'

Walker, being dragged backwards along the deck, was more depressed at leaving Miss Snowflake and at the faults she had discovered in him than he cared to be. There was no doubt about it – Miss Snowflake *was* an all-round education, and that, it seemed, was what he wanted. If he was educable at all.

'You're improving,' said Miss Snowflake. 'Still, that's my limit. You'll have to walk the rest.'

He followed her along the deck and inside, out of the wind.

'Well, it's been nice,' said Miss Snowflake. 'Now I have to

go and tidy up. Come to think of it, it looks as though you'd better go to the john yourself. You have my lipstick smeared around your mouth and on the end of your nose.'

He went into the lavatory and when he came out Miss Snowflake had disappeared and the girl with the red hair was waiting for him.

'You said you'd buy me a drink,' she said.

'And I will,' said Walker.

'I'd like a whisky sour,' said the girl. 'I've never had them before tonight. I do like them.'

At the bar Walker found himself standing beside Jochum. His cummerbund had come undone and hung down behind him like a tail. People kept treading on it and Jochum had a look of profound confusion on his face; he couldn't think what was pulling at him.

'I hear you're at Benedict Arnold too,' said Walker.

'That's true. You mean, you also?'

'Yes, I'm going there for a year.'

'Oh, that is splendid news, splendid. You must come and see me often.'

'In spite of your comments on the dangers of shipboard friendships?'

'Oh, present company is always excepted,' said Jochum, 'except, of course, for our old lady. I shall extend no invitations to her.'

'I wonder,' said Walker, 'if you see the American girl I danced with, Julie Snowflake, would you tell her that I'm rather stuck with someone but I'll see her again.'

'Oh, our other table companion has caught up with you. I thought she had succumbed to your charms. Vell, you must be firm.'

'I find it so hard,' said Walker.

'Vell, it is an old liberal weakness, helping lame dogs over stiles. Be strong.'

When Walker got back to the red-haired girl, she had claimed a bowl of crisps from one of the tables and was eating them with some gusto. 'I thought we'd lost you again,' she said.

'Oh, no,' said Walker.

'I don't know your name,' she said, hitching up her black stole.

'It's Walker,' said Walker.

'Walker the porker,' said the girl. 'My name's Miss Marrow. Like the vegetable. Aren't you going to ask me to dance?'

'Oh yes,' said Walker. 'I thought you wanted to finish your drink.'

'I will, look,' said Miss Marrow, emptying her glass at one gulp. 'There.'

'Be careful,' said Walker, 'you'll fall down.'

'I don't care,' said Miss Marrow. They went on to the floor; Miss Marrow danced in a way that Walker thought of as 'divinely', covering the floor with those great languorous sweeps that he recalled from old films. In this way they dislodged a lot of people and caused several dancing accidents. 'You're not *terribly* good at this, are you?' said Miss Marrow after a while.

'No,' said Walker, 'I did woodwork instead.'

'What do you *mean*, Porker?' cried Miss Marrow.

'At school we had to choose between woodwork and dancing. I may not be much good at the foxtrot, but you should see me make a pipe rack.'

As they swung about, and Walker grew short of breath, he noticed over Miss Marrow's shoulder that Julie Snowflake had come back into the room. If only he could leave Miss Marrow in the middle of the floor, dancing on her own, while he joined Julie; Miss Marrow, since she kept shutting her eyes and was setting the pace entirely, would probably not notice his absence for at least five minutes. But gallantry won out, gallantry to the kind of girl that Walker used to make assignations with on the corner of the street where his parents' home was. She was entirely and provincially familiar; Walker knew a thousand versions of her; but precisely because of that he felt she had a claim. 'Oh, Porker,' she said suddenly, opening her eyes, 'you laddered my stocking, you beast.'

'I *am* sorry,' said Walker. 'They cost a packet, don't they?'

'I think I can stop it running; I've got some nail varnish in my bag. Come outside and wait for me.' She went into the toilet, exactly the sort of girl Walker had always waited outside ladies' toilets for; he waited a moment and then sidled off towards Miss Snowflake. 'Porker!' said a voice; the girl had come back. 'It's no use. Want to dance some more?'

'I don't mind,' said Walker, though he did.

'I'm a bit tired of it, actually,' said Miss Marrow. 'What's it like on deck?'

'Oh, rather windy,' said Walker.

'I *knew* that's where you went!' said Miss Marrow. 'Well, show me around up there.'

A moment later he was on the sports deck again. 'This wind's doing awful things to my hairdo,' said Miss Marrow, 'I suppose I look a fright.'

'Well, no,' said Walker.

'Where's England out there?' asked Miss Marrow.

'Oh, miles away in the darkness.'

'You know, I don't know whether you feel this sort of thing, but I must say I feel a bit mean, leaving it like that. I know fidelity and patriotism and loyalty are rather old-fashioned words these days, but I think when you're doing something like this they suddenly mean something to you again. Don't you?'

'No, not really,' said Walker. 'In any case I'm only going for a year.'

'If you can stick it.'

'Oh, I'll stick it.'

'Well, I suppose you're tougher than I am. I seem to care more about that sort of thing than most people. Damnation! My cig's gone out. Come behind this ventilator, and light it properly.'

They retired behind the ventilator; Walker cupped his hands and struck a match within it, and Miss Marrow penetrated the circle with her cigarette and put it to the match. Once again hair blew against Walker's cheek, and once again Walker's heart thumped a little, though this time not with the cosmopolitan flourish that Julie Snowflake had caused, but with a provincial back-street beat.

'Ta,' said Miss Marrow. 'Well, isn't all this exciting. I suppose we're miles out to sea now.'

'Off Start Point,' said Walker.

'And just think, there are grey-green icebergs glistening in the mist . . . covered with sleeping birds. And sunken hulks on the sea bottom,' said Miss Marrow, sighing, and went on: 'Are you imaginative, Porker?'

'A bit, I suppose.'

'I thought you were. I was always the imaginative one at home. Ever write any poetry?'

'Nothing to speak of.'

'I did. Lots of it. I thought you were sensitive, though. You have a sensitive mouth.'

Walker looked at Miss Marrow and realized that she wanted to be kissed. He looked down at his shoes.

'Oh, my shoulders are getting so cold,' said Miss Marrow.

Her dress didn't fit very well, Walker noticed, and the straps stood inelegantly away from the shoulders. She sat down on a life-raft. 'Have my jacket,' said Walker.

'Oh no, you'll freeze,' said Miss Marrow.

So Walker sat down, put his arm around her, and said, 'Is that better?'

'That's rather nice,' said Miss Marrow. 'I say, do you think this bra I've got is too pointed? My mother thought so.'

'Looks perfectly fine to me,' said Walker.

'That's what I said. Don't you think that old lady's a terror? She'd have me running around for her all the time if she could.'

'Matriarchal England, that's what she is,' said Walker. 'Every man's best reason for emigrating. And then she comes with you.'

'Oh, I think that's a bit hard on her. She's very cultured, you know.'

'Omar Khayyám,' said Walker.

Miss Marrow laughed. 'You're a fool,' she said.

'I know,' said Walker, leaning to kiss Miss Marrow lightly on the cheek. Miss Marrow saw the gesture and turned her face to meet the kiss with her lips. Collision ensued; the kiss

91

went askew and landed in her hair; her nose struck his cheek; and the tip of her cigarette touched the lobe of Walker's ear. 'Bloody hell!' said Walker, leaping up.

'What's wrong?' cried Miss Marrow. 'What is it?'

'It's just that I've burned my flaming ear.'

'How?' asked Miss Marrow.

'Your cigarette.'

'Sit down and let me look at it.'

Walker sat and Miss Marrow twisted his head to face a deck-light. 'You'll live,' she said. 'It's just gone a bit red. You'll have a blister in the morning.'

'On my ear,' said Walker. 'I shall look a fool with a blistered ear.'

'Kissing's dangerous,' said Miss Marrow.

'Yes,' said Walker. 'So I discover.'

'Did you kiss her too?'

'Who?'

'That attractive American girl you were going round with.'

'You shouldn't ask things like that.'

'I think it's a bit awful, kissing two girls in one evening.'

'Why?' said Walker. 'Anyway, I missed you.'

'You know why,' said Miss Marrow.

'You mean I should have picked just one.'

'Well, if that's how you look at it,' said Miss Marrow, 'I'll get off to bed. Still, it was nice, those dances, and talking to you. I hope your ear doesn't blister, Porker. Good night.'

'Good night,' said Walker.

Miss Marrow walked off down the deck, her long blue dress blowing in the wind. Walker sat for a moment and looked at the sea, his hand over his ear. The sea was dark and the birds were sleeping on the grey-green icebergs. He waited a moment, and then hurried downstairs to the bar. He found Jochum sitting at the table with some of the bagpipers, but Julie Snowflake had disappeared.

'What happened to Julie?' asked Walker.

'Oh, she has gone to her cabin, I think,' said Jochum.

'I guess she thought you'd stood her up, you heel,' said one of the bagpipers, 'or else she thought she'd be a heel and stand you up. Either way you lost.'

'Oh dear,' said Walker.

'Sticky wicket,' said one of the girls.

The days at sea passed easily by, and gradually Walker began to feel further and further away from home, more and more en route, going somewhere. The life of the ship grew perfectly customary. Each morning, Walker woke late and in confusion, missing the warm pressure of Elaine's buttocks against his own. But the swaying of the ship, the sound of the washbasin filling and draining, the lanoline smell of shaving-cream, reminded him where he was, in his underwater troglodytic cabin. Looking out from his high perch he could see the quiff of his three cabin-mates as they moved round getting dressed. He got out of bed last and washed himself, humming the Trout quintet, an old bathroom speciality. He shaved with Richard's razor, dipped his fingers in Julian's hair-cream, brushed his shoes quickly with Dr Millingham's discarded undershorts, put on his suit and went to the dining-room. His fellow-passengers had usually almost finished; they sat in holiday trim, beaming at him over the marmalade.

And in this fashion the days went by. The sea lolloped against the side of the ship, his toothpaste went down in the tube, and meal-times came and went, with Lady Hunt-Francis and later, when a slight swell came up, without her. Walker found himself spending his time at the cinema with Miss Marrow, or walking the deck with Dr Jochum, and he became modestly fond of them both. Miss Marrow was shrill, played jokes, and appeared in clothes that drew attention to the droopiness of her behind, the paucity of her bust or the dyed auburn of her hair. Her unfailing lack of art was positively appealing. Dr Jochum maintained a vein of heavy gallantry that brought with it the smell of all the lindens in old Europe. It was like being entertained at some minor palace, and one expected that at any moment the minuet would break forth and life would begin in earnest. Occasionally, across the deck or at a meal, he would glimpse Julie Snowflake, cool, calm and uncollected, unsquired. Aspirations grew in Walker's heart, but Miss Marrow always wanted to see a film or Dr Jochum wanted to swim, and Julie remained in the corner of his eye, an unadopted opportunity. Sometimes he sat on deck and watched her. He had hired a deck-chair, a cushion and a rug, and sitting stretched out in his blue blankets, looking like a patient being carried into a hospital, he lay on his chair and thought about himself.

It was an old subject with him. The wind whistled hard and strong across the ship; his hands turned blue and his body-fat, unused to all this, struggled to keep warm; but every day, in every way, he grew, so he felt, better and better. He started *The Brothers Karamazov*, which was a book he had started often before; he resolved this time to finish it. He accepted, in an absent way, his beef-tea, and often had to be reminded that it was time to go below for a meal. For suspended between the Mansfield Road flat, scented with dishcloths and Elaine's Tweed perfume, and the imagined belfries and balconies of Benedict Arnold, he was looking at himself and wondering at what he found. What he seemed to find was nothing. His parents had always talked about people having good or bad characters; character, in that sense, he seemed to have none of at all. Nothing pushed him very hard. He believed himself to be a decent and rational man who, admittedly, always did indecent and irrational things. He had thought, however, that he was in charge of something. When he looked around, though, every corner of his mind seemed unfledged, and inadequate, and thoughtless, and he couldn't find in himself any immediate machinery for improvement. He was too affable, too reasonable, too ordinary, too willing to drift, for anything like that to happen. His beliefs didn't hold him to anything; they were rarely there when wanted. His body was as flabby as his mind. He was going to seed. His stomach was a great podge of flesh. He ought to get his weight down. He smoked too much. He had lost the power to be excited. Excitement, with him, was like the perfectly boiled egg that we feel we have had once, though when we can't remember, and then spend the rest of our lives pursuing. What should he *do*? He lay on his back and thought of answers. He ought to look again at philosophy, religion, mysticism. He ought to read some energizing work. He ought to ask the world better questions. He ought to change his shirts more often. He ought to be spare. He was in the sere and yellow leaf; he needed insight and vision; he ought to possess elevation. But not, perhaps, yet.

For the voyage didn't, after all, push him very hard. This was equipoise. He accepted the sun, and the wind, and the service. Beef-tea came; the time went imperceptibly by. He had discovered on the first morning that by turning on his side, making a little hole in the deck-chair blankets, and peering with his bright round eye through the wooden slats he could see Julie Snowflake and the other American charmers three rows of people back, talking about Yerp in contralto voices. Charmers they surely were, clad in bermuda shorts of dashing olive twill that threw up the high-toned brownness of their tanned healthy legs, and in handsome sweaters with circle pins on the collar.

On the first morning, while engaged in this exercise, he had been caught and punished. His discoverer was Dr Jochum, now restored from his disorder of the previous night. He tapped Walker on the shoulder and said, 'Oho!' He was wearing white shorts and a sporty foulard shirt that blew away from him in the wind, exposing a round stomach and a deep black navel. He looked down on Walker, snug in his chair: 'Come along, some exercise. Here we are, two fat men. Three times round the promenade deck and then a swim in the pool. That is my prescription.'

'I was reading, actually,' said Walker, holding up like a flag *The Brothers Karamazov*.

'Well,' said Dr Jochum, 'you are like all reformers. You like to reform the world because it is easier than trying to reform yourself. I have met such men.' Walker's expression showed some chagrin and Dr Jochum laughed heartily and at depth. 'Oh,' he said, wiping his eyes, 'you are splendid as you are. But come on, we must take care of our boties. Let's take a constitutional walk.'

Dr Jochum struck out at a brisk pace toward the stern and soon had Walker puffing. 'Not so fast,' he cried, and Jochum allowed his speed to drop slightly but refused to take his eyes off the road. Presently, when his breath was back, Walker said, 'Am I going to like Benedict Arnold?'

'Ah!' said Jochum, 'that depends what you expect of it. No doubt you expect America to set you free?'

'I think I do, yes,' said Walker.

'Well, it is the duty of the young to go out and seek their misfortune. Perhaps you will find it; perhaps you will be set free.'

'Is it a misfortune? Surely it's a good thing for a man to set out and, well, find who he is?'

'So you want to know who you are?' said Jochum, laughing, face forward. 'Well, I am a gypsy. I will tell you the answer. You will go out into the American desert. The air will be pure. There will be no one around. There will be silence, you and the sky. You will open your chest to the air, say, "Okay, shoot, who am I? What am I?" And the sky will say, "Buddy, you're nobody. Now go back to the beginning and start over." '

Walker found this cynical, and protested. 'Surely everything that happens to you changes you.'

'Oh, I don't say America won't change you; I said it won't help very much. The convert takes with him more of his old location than he thinks. Every man thinks he has only to go out of his environment. But there always stays with him *this*.' He tapped, with a gold-ringed forefinger, his dark, intense head. In the desert a Nottingham head, thought Walker. Jochum strode on, his shirt flying out behind him, so that his little drill bermuda shorts were all he could offer against total nudity. A sailor put down his bucket and watched them speed by in some alarm. 'A nice day!' said Jochum paternally.

'That's right, sir,' said the sailor; 'mind you don't walk right off the end.'

'How they look after you!' cried Jochum. 'Such peace, such contemplation, on a ship. You have leisure to do all you want. The mind works. It is like being in a monastery, without the basic disadvantage of those places.'

They turned sharply where the promenade deck encountered the stern, and began the journey back to the bow on the other side. The sea looked just the same. Nothing was in sight. Walker tried secretly to shake his shoe-laces undone. He said, 'It's just the way a university ought to be.' This casual remark caused Jochum's confident step to falter. 'Oh, my dear young friend,' he said, 'I am afraid you are in for a sad disappointment. A fine day!' This last was to the sailor, who had come through, by internal means, from the port side to take another look at them, and who remarked, 'You'll do for yourself, going about like that.'

'I see,' said Jochum, 'that it is necessary to tell you about Benedict Arnold.' He took Walter by the elbow and led him to the rail, and they leaned there together, watching the garbage coming out of the ship's side far below. 'My friend,' began Jochum, 'universities are not better than life. They are just life. It is not you and I who make them what they are. It is the students, and the administration, and the computer, and the alumni, and the football team. Universities are places where people go to get acquainted with one another. Benedict Arnold is very good for that. They can find parking space for their cars. They can date. They can join fraternities and sororities. They can go skiing. And then, oh yes, there is one little thing – they would all like a piece of paper to say they have a degree. In pursuit of this they will come to classes and attack you for higher grades at the end of the semester. If we were just to abolish that piece of paper . . . but no, I am dreaming again.' Jochum looked out at the wide expanse of sea and shook his head at it.

'Actually,' said Walker, 'I don't even know where Benedict Arnold is. Is it in the Middle West?'

'Well,' said Dr Jochum, 'not really. It's on the edge of the middle; it's nearer than the far; it is north of the south. Do you think you can find it now?' Dr Jochum put both hands on the rail and turned his large dark face to Walker to smile at him, screwing up his eyes against the wind.

'Is it pleasant there?' said Walker, trying again. 'Do you like it?'

'Well, beggars can't be choosers, you know the old story. One goes where one is taken in. I am a foreigner, a doubtful case, not a man to keep. Benedict Arnold is not the best of universities, but it took me in and up to now it has kept me. I can think of nothing better to say for it.'

'What do you teach there?'

'Oh, some courses in political science. It is not an easy subject. One has to try so hard to keep politics out of politics. But then I will teach anything. I am something of an all-round man. I have even taught pastry decoration in home economics. And what do *you* teach?'

'I'm going as a sort of resident writer. Actually I've never taught before, not in a university.'

Jochum turned and looked at Walker in evident amazement. He said, 'You are a writer?'

'Yes.'

'Oh, come now, you are much too nice to be a writer. We have had writers at Benedict Arnold before. While they were there they undressed themselves and their students and their colleagues' wives. Then when they went away they undressed them all once more, in books. No, you are not like that.'

'Oh,' said Walker, smiling, 'I have hidden capacities.'

'Well,' said Jochum, taking out a cigarette, 'that is more than the others had – all *they* hid was their incapacities!' He lit his cigarette, inside his shirt, with a book-match.

'Why do they have a writer?' asked Walker.

'That is a good question. Well, for that you must look at the map. Party, that's our town, is in good new country. Near by is cattle country. In another direction there is oil country. All around is mineral country. There is even gold in them thar hills. So . . . there are a lot of rich people there. And they have a writer because they are rich.'

'And a university?' asked Walker.

'Yes,' said Jochum. 'A hundred years ago there were buffalo and Indians. Now . . . a university. Don't ask why; I suppose they think that universities are the proper things to have. They are new people; they want to do things right; they have three fundamental religions – Baptism, Americanism and Philanthropy. With philanthropy comes a university. The problem is it sometimes violates the other two.'

'Then *why* a university?'

'I am not sure. I must try to guess. Let us say that in America it is hard to give money away. You never know when it is going to some organization that may in due course turn out to be subversive. With a university, one assumes, that is the end of it.'

'A dangerous assumption,' said Walker.

'Oh, very dangerous, but very nice. So . . . when Benedict Arnold has an argument about whether to buy a Gutenberg Bible or build a new laboratory for biological research, some man who ten years ago was hanging on the bottom of freight cars appears and tells, Be my guest, please, have both!'

'Are they pleased when they get them?' asked Walker.

'I see, the question really is, will they be pleased with Mr Walker when they have him? Well, they take care of what they have.'

'That's nice, anyway.'

'Don't misunderstand please. Benedict Arnold is not a *bad* place. The Animal Husbandry Department has revolutionized our thinking about the cattle tick . . . do you think about the cattle tick? The Physics Department may reach the moon before the U.S. government. Dr Bourbon, the head of the English Department, is a Shakespeare authority and an eminent man. There is even me. You see, money is a power. It brings leisure and that may even bring wisdom. So . . . we must be optimistic about these things. I expect you to enjoy Benedict Arnold.'

'I shall enjoy leisure,' said Walker.

'Too much. Well, onward, fat men. More exercise!'

Walker heaved himself unwillingly off the rail and they set off along the deck again, their feet clopping on the boards. A puzzled look had appeared about Walker's eyes, as he went over what Jochum had just told him and tried to link it with his destiny. But this was a world of incomprehensibles; the link would have to be forged on the spot.

'I hope I have not depressed you,' said Jochum, noticing his reaction.

'No, I'm just mystified. I wonder how I shall take it. Of course I shall try to take it very well.'

'I thought you were not simply an aimless rogue,' said Jochum. 'You cheer me.'

'Oh, I'm a great believer in behaving right. All I ask is for the world to help me along a little.'

'Ah, *there* is the problem,' said Jochum.

They navigated the bow. The wind caught in Walker's seedy hair and raked out the dandruff. Air poured deep into his lungs. The white paint of the deckworks shone at him. 'I suppose,' he said, 'one has to believe that all that happens is for the best.'

'Not at all, you must acquire some behaviour of your own.'

'In that case,' said Walker, 'I haven't been doing very well lately.'

'Oh, really?'

'I've been trying to leave room for the future, you see. I know what I ought to do. I know what my parents did. But what kind of guide is that, for a man who's going to America?'

'Ah, it is the old problem. Nobody wants to be what he is any more. Everyone hates himself. The priest says, "Ah, if it were not for my silly flock, what wouldn't I be free to believe." The duke says, "Please excuse me, no more duties, it's not so nice to be a lord these days." The writer says, "Culture! Who these days can believe in culture!" The rich man wants to be poor. The Englishman,' he waved at Walker, 'wants to be in America. Everyone wishes he didn't exist! People say "See my nice new picture! This is my style – this week!", or "Look how I behave – these are my morals, until I get some more." You know Karl Marx always talked about people's interest? Well, I will tell you a story about his grandmother. She said, "If our little Karl had made as much capital as he has written about, it would make more sense." That old lady: she knew more about interest than the grandson!'

'But there's no fun in doing what you know you must do. It's freedom that makes the world interesting.'

'Are you so free?' asked Jochum.

'I try to be.'

'Then why do you stay away from Miss Snowflake?'

'Well, I had to talk to that English girl,' said Walker, uncomfortably.

'And why?'

'Because I said I would and because she's rather sad and lonely, I think.'

'You see, Mr Walker, you are a liberal. You are tempted by pathos. I think a really free man would have followed the path of Miss Snowflake.'

Walker, who had lately been following the path of Miss Snowflake to corners behind the lifeboats and had already arranged to meet her for tea in the Winter Garden Lounge, found this very sharp, so sharp as to be disquieting. For the path was not a straight one. How free, really, was he? Walker, to try to suggest the enormity of the problem, said to Jochum, 'How do you like this heather?'

'Fine,' said Jochum, glancing at it. 'You look like a fertility god.'

'It's from my wife,' said Walker.

'Aaah!' cried Jochum. 'What a man! What a man! This is marvellous for a man who is not really interested in love at all! That is my diagnosis of you. You have left your wife?'

'At home.'

'So, you believe in homes too. I think you are in a very interesting position.'

The sailor with the bucket appeared again. Jochum, not noticing that it was the same man, following their progress with fascination, said again to him, 'Beautiful day!'

'Left right, left right,' said the sailor.

'How they look after you on this ship,' said Jochum. 'What a crew!' Walker saw, right by them, the stairway that led to the sports deck, all chairs and comfort and sighed for his deckchair. Dr Jochum said, 'Now, I think, a swim.'

Walker took the occasion to excuse himself: 'I can't redeem my physique in one day,' he said, 'I've got pains from my visick to my gatch, as Miss Snowflake keeps saying.'

'Tomorrow, same time, more weight off,' said Jochum, watching Walker's flabby, lazy body struggle up the stairway. Walker made his way through the chairs, filled with dozers and sleepers, until he found his own. The blankets rapidly warmed his bulk. The virtues of laziness instantly commended themselves to him. He knew he could hold off a while yet the summons of the future. He felt about in his wraps for his book.

'Looking for this?' said a voice above him. A tanned arm handed him the volume; it was attached to Julie Snowflake. 'Jesus, it's great,' she said. 'There's some really fine despair in that book. I read it in Comparative Lit., but I could read it again a hundred times; it's fantastic.'

'It is,' said Walker.

'See you,' said Miss Snowflake.

'Rock-cakes for two at four,' said Walker.

'Thanks for the loan,' said Miss Snowflake. He peered through the cushions until she disappeared into her own blankets. Then he riffled through the volume until he had found his place. The fine Russian despair was soon flooding into his lungs; he took it in in life-giving breaths.

The sea shimmered. A thin sun broke through and beat lightly on his pate. Someone brought him his bouillon and he drank it down and put the bowl on to the floor beside him. The rugs smelled of succour. The pages in front of him began to blur. The next thing he knew was that someone was slapping him savagely above one ear with a newspaper. The blows stung. He looked up to see Miss Marrow, clad in a bright orange life-jacket. 'We're sinking,' she said.

'I like your new bra,' said Walker.

Miss Marrow seized his hand and tried to lift him, all dead weight, from his chair. She could not budge him an inch. 'Come on, it's lifeboat drill,' she said. The ship's siren shrilled a call to duty. The sun shone in his eyes; the day was peaceful; the calls to save himself had no weight at all. 'Come *on*,' said Miss Marrow. 'We're *supposed* to.' But Walker turned on his side and before he knew it was asleep again.

On the fifth night, when they set their watches back an hour for the last time and the dinner-table conversation was entirely about the size of tips to be given to stewards in the morning, tourist class held its Farewell Dance. The mood was like that at the end of some salesmen's conference, when all the fun was ending, friends were parting and everyone had to recollect how they managed to live, day in, day out, with their lives. On deck, fresh-featured, short-haired Fulbright men said to fresh-featured, short-haired Fulbright girls, 'You know, since I met you, I've really found direction.' In her cabin, beside a full bottle of whisky bought that afternoon from the ship's store, Miss Marrow sat on her bunk, talking seriously to James Walker. 'Oh God,' said Miss Marrow. 'Oh God.'

'Don't be silly,' said Walker consolingly, 'you'll really enjoy it.'

'I'm dreading it,' said Miss Marrow.

'It'll do you a world of good,' said Walker, 'make a man of you.'

'I hope not,' said Miss Marrow. She was afraid of America. They sat side by side on the bunk. This was the quiet party she had asked him to. He had his arm round her shoulder in a brotherly way, part of his consolatory role. At the end of the arm his hand held, in the toothmug she had asked him to bring along from his cabin, a half-glass of whisky. He was feeling very uncomfortable. Faintly he could hear through deck above deck the beat of the indefatigable Jack Wilks, calling him to a more attractive duty. Julie Snowflake was in the bar upstairs; he knew it, because he had arranged it. He thought about this and watched with horrid fascination as he saw that his other hand, his free hand, was doing something it had no business doing; it was sliding up under Miss Marrow's skirt, and now it affectionately twanged the elastic of her suspenders, to reassure her and himself that nothing here was ill-meant. Miss Marrow said, 'That's all very well, but I just don't trust you very much.'

Walker affected surprise. 'What's all very well?' Miss Marrow patted his hand through her skirt vaguely, and seemed to go on thinking about the perils of America. Her face was woebegone, her eye-shadow was smudged. Hanging on the back of the cabin door Walker could see her shapeless woollen dressing gown, a nursery dressing gown, and he felt a deep indignation with himself, a deep pitying affection for her. A feeling of the hopelessness of all that was second-rate ran through him, and he knew his pain was because in so many things, he, a man from the provinces, a man without elevation, a man who couldn't sag, belonged with it. He was sorry for Miss Marrow. Miss Marrow was one of his kind, his level. And so he was also here, wasn't he, because Miss Marrow didn't frighten him and Julie Snowflake did. A throbbing mechanism inside him sent his head forward to kiss Miss Marrow on the cheek. She sighed, put her hand on his hair, and said, 'Porker? Do you believe in love?'

'It's a difficult word,' said Walker.

'Yes, it's very difficult,' said Miss Marrow.

'Do *you* believe in it?' asked Walker.

'Yes, I do,' she said.

'Tell me what it means then,' said Walker.

'Well,' she said thoughtfully, 'it means being tied or committed to a person. Feeling fidelity, duty, loyalty. Taking someone seriously. Respecting them.'

'It sounds like the patriotism you talked about on the first night,' said Walker.

'Well, there is a connexion,' said Miss Marrow.

'I don't see it,' said Walker, leaning forward and kissing Miss Marrow on the mouth. This tipped her back on her bunk, so that her upper body lay below him, her head on the pillow, his head above hers.

'Whoops!' said Miss Marrow. Her eyes looked tensely at him. She was afraid. The bunk was narrow and clearly not made for this sort of thing; it was probably made to prevent it. So Walker's rump hung uncomfortably over the edge, sagging toward the floor, and a bar of wood, the edge of the cot at the top, stabbed sharply into his side. The glass of whisky and contents had disappeared somewhere. His trousers had rucked up to his knees. His heart was thumping. The heated machinery inside him stirred against pity, conscience and memory. He bit Miss Marrow's ear. He looked at her face; it had grown flushed and blotchy. She was also breathing hard. Her eyes were closed and she murmured, 'Porker?'

'Yes?' said Walker.

'You are . . . you are just a bit serious, aren't you, Porker?'

'Yes, pretty serious,' he said, kissing her eyelids.

'But honestly?'

'I don't know,' said Walker.

She opened her eyes. 'Just tell me,' she said, 'is it just for fun? Will I ever see you again? When you've finished will you be off just as fast as your little legs can carry you?'

Walker's lips were against hers. 'I suppose I might,' he murmured.

'I thought you were a very decent person, Porker, I've come to think a lot of you.'

'Yes,' said Walker.

'Would that be decent?' murmured Miss Marrow.

'I don't know,' said Walker.

'Well, think about me, look at me,' said Miss Marrow. 'How old do you think I am?'

'Let me guess,' said Walker, stalling, looking at her teeth. 'Twenty-five.'

'Well, you see, I'm thirty-two. And I'm not very marvellous-looking. And I'm not exactly the toast of Rickmansworth. And I'm a virgin, more or less through choice. I admit there hasn't been any really great onslaught, though. So what do I do, Porker? Think about me, study me. What do I do? Are you just making me suffer? I'm good at it, but don't give me more if you needn't. And it's time I got married. . . . ' She breathed hard, turned her face away, and said, 'But I don't suppose you have anything like *that* in mind. Oh, Porker, can I trust you?'

'For what?'

'For anything?'

Walker looked perplexed and sat up. He reached out and poured himself another glass of whisky. Miss Marrow looked at him. 'But I can't be my own conscience, never mind yours,' he said. 'I don't know what I'm doing. How can I think about you, how can I decide what's for you? My own moral motive power's only just enough to keep me from pinching apples from the greengrocer's. I can't give it big jobs like this.'

'But you wanted to sleep with me.'

'Yes, I know. That's because I enjoy fornication and I think highly of it as a way of getting to know people. I have a relationship with you which involves me several ways. You're nervous of going where you're going and so am I. You don't think too much of yourself and I think even less of me. I also feel sorry for you because like everyone going from a little place to a big one you find out all sorts of limitations in yourself; I'm in the same position.'

'I reach you where your kindness meets your lechery,' said Miss Marrow, taking the glass that Walker had poured for her and gulping it like a child. Globes of tears were pinned to her cheeks.

Excuses flooded his mind. I'm sorry for you, and because I'm sorry for you you can't expect so very much. You're a second-class citizen in the world of love, but I'll come down to you and help. He said, 'Look, I ought to go, Miss Marrow.'

As he looked the tears brimmed in her eyes. 'You can't go and leave me like this,' she said. 'You came to cheer me up, and I'm more depressed than ever.'

'I'm not very good at cheer,' said Walker.

Miss Marrow replied, 'Look, please stay. You're right, I'm to blame, I'm asking too much. I'm just a frigid little Rickmansworth spinster who got scared when you started doing what I wanted and tried to throw all the weight of her problems on to you. I'll do it. I'll decide.' Walker watched with growing uneasiness as she leaned forward and took out of a drawer an enormous white male linen handkerchief. She blew her nose on it; the linen buffeted. 'You've been kind. And you were right. I'm a mess. I ought to feel free. I ought to be able to act on my own account. There's nothing much to me and my life is going spare.'

'I wasn't telling you that,' said Walker.

'You were,' said Miss Marrow, 'but it's all right. Please come back and kiss me.' Walker wanted to run away. The heated machinery had stopped beating and all that remained was the pity and the guilt. He leaned on top of Miss Marrow. A storm at sea, a collision with an iceberg; such were the things that seemed to be called for. Miss Marrow squeezed his head to her: 'He's a nice boy,' she said, brushing his hair forward with her hand. 'Now he's Marlon Brando.'

She seemed somehow to have grown enormously bigger. 'Porker, tell me something,' she said. 'Have you had a lot of girls?'

'Well,' said Walker, 'there's had and had.'

'I mean, you know, made love to,' said Miss Marrow.

'A tolerable number,' said Walker embarrassedly.

'More than five?'

'I don't remember exactly,' said Walker.

'What did you do to make them brave?'

'It's not a question of bravery,' said Walker.

The tears came up again. 'Oh, Porker, be kind, be kind.'

'No, but I treated you badly,' said Walker. 'You convinced me of it. I feel ashamed of myself. You mustn't change now.'

'Oh no,' said Miss Marrow, turning her face and looking at the wooden wall. 'You're destroying me. You're telling me every way there is I'm not attractive, I don't rouse you. . . . '

'Oh, I'm roused all right,' said Walker, and he leaned over and kissed Miss Marrow ponderously on the lips, to purge this incredible situation.

'Oh, Porker,' she said, 'you're so kind. And so gentle.' She bit his ear. His hand moved under her sweater, over the shiny nylon, an expedition moving toward Everest to climb it because it was there. A wish for succour made him fire mental flares high into the air. They exploded and were answered. The door, suddenly, was tried; a firm, familiar voice said, 'No talking between meals.'

Beneath him Miss Marrow tensed. The old lady said, 'Open the door, dear, I want you to help me pack.'

'What can I do? What shall I do?' cried Miss Marrow. Walker sat up and scrabbled her sweater back into place. 'She keeps on at me all the time.'

'Tell her to go away.'

'She put masses of her things in my wardrobe. She has the

cabin next door. If I told her to go she'd probably walk along the outside of the ship and come in through the porthole or something.'

'Actually if you open the porthole you sink the ship,' said Walker.

'Don't tempt me,' said Miss Marrow, her tears rolling again. 'I'm coming, Lady Hunt-Francis.' She went toward the door and stepped aside, pulling her bra into shape as she did so. Lady Hunt-Francis came in, her raddled face inquisitive. 'We must all do our good deeds,' she said. 'Fern does hers. You must be kind to Fern.'

'Who's Fern?' said Walker.

'Me,' said Miss Marrow.

'Oh, haven't you been introduced?' said Lady Hunt-Francis. 'How remiss.' She looked at Walker and said, interestedly, 'I see Mr Bigears has whisky splashed all over his clothes. Are you a Christmas pudding, Mr Bigears? Shall we set fire to you?'

'I don't think we should,' said Fern Marrow.

Lady Hunt-Francis took some dresses from the inside of the wardrobe and said, 'Do fasten your skirt, dear. In my day we always used to retire to the conservatory. They are such hot places, they always brought the young men on dreadfully. And those very sexual flowers. I remember once getting a proposal from a young man who turned out to be a private detective guarding the jewels. Quite improper. I always blamed it on the heat in the conservatory. We had tropicals, you see.'

Walker said, 'Actually I must go. Many thanks for the party.'

'Don't forget your glass,' said Miss Marrow.

'Go on deck and cool off,' said Lady Hunt-Francis, 'You can see America. It looks quite the same as anywhere else.'

Walker was breathing hard as he fell into the ship's bar, a disorderly figure, clothes doused in whisky, hair bedraggled. Jack Wilks stood on the podium, looking like the Venerable Bede, and the dancers pounded on the floor in a fug of smoke and streamers. Julie was nowhere in sight. At one of the tables, alone, sat Dr Jochum, his bow-tie undone and his eyes moist.

He looked up at Walker's approach. 'Such a sad evening,' he said.

'Have you seen Julie Snowflake?' asked Walker.

'Ah!' said Jochum sadly, 'leave me, go on with your quest. I am miserable.'

'Come on deck,' said Walker, 'and get some fresh air. They say America is in sight!' This news did nothing for Dr Jochum.

'Oh, this pity of yours!' he said. 'It will stop you getting anywhere. Go after your young lady – leave me to my fate.'

'Come on, it will do you good,' said Walker.

'No,' said Dr Jochum, 'no do-gooding, please.' Walker set off through the dancers and went upstairs.

The sports deck was only thinly lit. The night was cold, clear and dark, and Walker breathed in to clear his head. His breath smelled of Miss Marrow's whisky, his lapels of her perfume, a sour, guilty after-taste hung in his soul. The ship's lights rose and fell on the troughs of the greeny-black waves. The wake flowed luminously outward. A line of people stood by the rail, looking out, and suddenly Walker saw what the fuss was about, for in the windy darkness, far off, a flashing light sparked and faded. 'Nantucket light,' said someone; a scholar disagreed; but the very word struck a note. He waited for celebration, excitement, to strike, leaning on the rail to watch the beacon spell its message. 'Hi!' said the person next to him, and he turned. It was Julie Snowflake. She was wearing a red quilted jacket with the hood up over her head, out of which her face, a cool blur, peered speculatively at him. His heart went into gear; affection swarmed in him like bees.

'How's the elevation?' he said.

'Fine,' she answered.

They leaned together on the rail and looked down at the sea, swaying with its now familiar motion. Further off, in the dark land mass, the beacon of light flashed at them. Behind lay a country one of them knew and the other didn't. Below them the sickly sound of the fiddles rang; the dance still went on. 'Hey, just look at that!' she said suddenly. There were more lights; coming towards them out of the darkness was another liner, a great candelabra of light, every deck illuminated. They could see the figures on deck looking back at them. The ship hung above the sea and was reflected in it, a great confusion of shimmering light to compare with his own mind.

'Oh, Jesus, you know,' said Julie, 'I wish I was on that ship? I wish I was going back to Yerp.'

'I thought you believed in the cool, clear future?' said Walker.

'Well, I do, but maybe your America is my Europe. Those things can work two ways around. A lot of Americans have thought that. And I'll tell you something, going home is hell. There's nothing so terrible as going home. Once out stay out, that's what I say. Of course I don't do it. I'm going right back there to spend the next two weeks before semester starts with my parents. I can describe the whole thing exactly now. I don't even have to go in through the door. Julie, you've grown away from us. Julie, you hate us now you're grown up. Julie, we can't get through to you any more. What's become of you? Are you still a nice girl? Are you still a virgin? Oh boy, am I looking forward to the next few days! Personally I think parents should be assassinated before their kids grow up. I know that's an extreme view, but it's the main plank in *my* platform.'

'Where is your home?' asked Walker.

'New York City, that place right there across the water.'

'I see,' said Walker, waiting for Julie to speak. Nothing seemed forthcoming, but finally she said, 'Are you spending any time in New York?'

'Well,' said Walker, 'I have about five days here before I have to go out to Benedict Arnold.'

'You mean the next five days? The five days from tomorrow?'

'Yes,' said Walker.

'No, you're crazy.'

'Why?'

'Well, don't you know what day it is?'

'No,' said Walker.

'Well, this is Labor Day Weekend. Don't you have that?'

'No.'

'Well, actually you've really goofed. Labor Day Weekend everybody goes out of town. Half of them go to Yerp. You'll be the only man in New York.'

'Will you still be there?'

'I don't actually know. We have a place on Fire Island we go out to. I mean, my parents will have fixed something but I don't know what it is yet. Anyway, there'll be lots of things to do in New York. I suppose you'll be staying at the Biltmore or some place?'

'No, my agent, he fixed my hotel, got me in at a little place somewhere in Brooklyn Heights, somewhere cheap.'

'Wow!' said Julie. 'Still, it could be better than it sounds. Anyway, you can go to some of the places in the Village where they play jazz nights. And hear the folk-singers and the poets. There's a really literary atmosphere in the Village. You'll feel right at home. I'll bet they fête you.'

'I look forward to it,' said Walker.

'Or maybe you won't like it, I'm forgetting you're so normal.'

'I'm sorry,' said Walker. 'I can see it's been disappointing.'

'Well, no, in a way it gives me a kind of hope,' said Miss Snowflake. 'I'd always rejected writing because I didn't think you could be a writer *and* a fulfilled person. Now I see that it's all much easier than I thought.'

'I wouldn't want to say easy,' said Walker. 'And I'm not sure I like being called normal.'

'Well, who would? But you're, well, I guess the most innocent writer I've ever met. I told you, did I, I won this *Mademoiselle* short story contest and thought I'd write?'

'No.'

'Oh, well, I did. But then I looked around at the writers at Hillesley. It's like a meeting of Neurotics Anonymous. You know – "I owe my clear vision to the fact that when I was five I used to watch travelling salesmen laying my mommy" and "I'm a poet because even when I was a kid I carved up cats to see what was inside them." Sometimes they seem convincing and you feel that the only way to live half-way decently in the modern world is to become really corrupt. I know a lot of people think that way. But sometimes I think why don't I just reject my talent and get married and join the PTA and forget about the confrontation with the absurd. So that's why I find you sort of encouraging. You haven't exhausted normality yet.'

'I'm just an old provincial,' said Walker.

'But do you know how to suffer? Do you know how to live? That's the thing, Mr Walker. You know, when I'm with you I feel *I'm* more experienced than you are.'

'Well, so much for Henry James.'

'Oh, him! But do you hear what I'm saying to *you*? Well, one day you'll think of it. Then you could write me, send a message.'

Someone appeared on the other side of her and took her by the arm. 'Hello, ducky,' said Dr Millingham. 'Here I am, back.' Millingham, affable in a brown Italianate raincoat and a small floral paper hat, nodded genially at Walker. 'You know, you did a nice thing, putting us on to these bagpipe lasses,' he said, 'they're great girls. Richard wants to marry one of them.'

'He's crazy,' said Julie. 'Well, look, enjoy yourself in America, won't you, Mr Walker. And I really was glad to meet you.'

'And I was to meet you,' said Walker.

'And look,' she added, shaking off Millingham's hand on her arm, 'why don't you call me on the telephone, if you get some free time, just in case I'm around?'

'I'd like to,' said Walker.

'Fine, write down my number.'

Walker took out his post-office book and biro and looked at Millingham, who said, 'Or I could give it to you later.'

'No, write it down,' said Julie. Walker copied down the number, feeling disappointed and aggrieved and pleased and sad.

' 'Bye now,' said Millingham.

So there was nothing for it but to go to bed; at least this would mean that he could get up early and stand on deck watching the ship come into New York Harbour in the morning.

But, lying in his bunk, he slept scarcely at all. It reminded him that he was nearly there, and all night his head reeled with images and excitement. There were interludes of fear and interludes of pleasure; there were interludes when he lay awake, listening to the soughing of the sea, feeling the ship sway, and wondering whether Dr Millingham was back in his bunk or whether he was still out on deck somewhere with Julie Snowflake. Then he slept fitfully, and saw images of a crazy city, all streets and traffic and high buildings and this made him wake up and wonder about his competence there.

When his watch reached six o'clock, which might well be five or seven, he slid down from the bunk and dressed quietly. Not bothering to shave, he tiptoed from the cabin, its wood-work creaking, where Richard and Julian and, thank goodness, Dr Millingham snored dully into the air. On deck the day was golden, the sea soft and blue, and out of it, close ahead of the white bold bow, rose the high towers of Manhattan, light grey in the sunlight. It was many years since Walker had seen any-thing so close to the dawn, and he realized that he could have chosen no better occasion. It was distinguished, too compli-cated to allow a response. The air was fresh and vital. The ship eased in through the shoals and islands, looking much bigger now there was a world to compare it with. The harbour was crowded with sea traffic. The great bronze shape of the Statue of Liberty stood high on its island, little persons wandering about the crown on its head. Other small figures stood on the ferryboats scudding on the water, Americans who led Ameri-can and mysterious lives. Planks and crates drifted in the dirty river. Red fireboats sailed, and great flat ferries laden with rail-way trucks, painted with Long Island Railroad and Chesa-peake and Ohio and Tidewater Southern, drifted back and forth across the harbour waters. Beyond the Battery, the high wires of Brooklyn Bridge came into view and then, slowly, fell away behind the buildings. On the flat banks of the Hudson on the New Jersey side a vast advertisement for coffee appeared.

It was all totally pleasant, and Walker became a vast recep-tacle of sensation. Here was the country in which he was to remould his own decencies into a new form. Here was the shot in the arm, the new spring. Now they were sailing up the west side, past the piers; on one of them a helicopter buzzed like an angry bee. Behind the dark dirty sheds the expressway ran, with huge, shiny cars chasing back and forth. The high sharp top of the Chrysler building pointed up to a heaven also busy with aircraft. The tugs took them in on the last stretch, round the sharp curve into the dead water of the pier, where they joined the long line of vessels penned to the edge of the island. Inside the vast sheds foreign figures in bright jackets watched the ship touch the wharf-side. Hawsers were hooked, spectators waved, the gangplank went out, uniforms came aboard. America! He could see the taxicabs, yellow and big, swirling along the expressway, read the exhortations on the billboards, see along the cavernous streets that led into the centre of Manhattan. It was all heat and scurry, but there, promising. Sweat ran down inside Walker's tweeds. The steward came along, sounding his chimes, and Walker made his way down below, through excited crowds of English persons jolted out of their national composure, to the dining-room. The service seemed more haphazard even than usual, and at table Lady Hunt-Francis, her face flushed, was crying out, 'We're here, I understand! I'm sure it's all a terrible mistake. Let's stay on board and go back, all of us.' Miss Marrow – Walker could think of his ugly duckling as no one else – took her place in the armchair next to Walker without looking at him; she looked down instead at the cloth, stained by five days of meals.

She said, 'I've used up all the film in my camera, taking shots of it all. It's wonderful, isn't it?'

He said, 'An incredible city. A marvellous day.'

'I didn't sleep a wink,' said Miss Marrow.

'I didn't either, really,' said Walker.

'You're too excited, my dear,' said Lady Hunt-Francis, leaning across the table to his companion. 'We may have to ask you to leave the table.'

'Isn't this luggage business awful?' said Miss Marrow. 'I went to the purser's office and booked my trunks through to Pennsylvania Station by some awful trucking company and they charged me twenty dollars more. That's seven pounds.'

'Too much,' said Lady Hunt-Francis. 'Don't pay it. They're terrible people. Money-mad.'

'You have to pay it,' said Miss Marrow. 'There's no one else.'

'Yes, terrible,' said Dr Jochum, formal and firm as he used to be. 'They are all cannibals in New York. But the rest of America, it is not like that.'

'Thank goodness for that,' said Miss Marrow.

'I hear the immigration people are the worst,' said Walker.

'I know,' said Lady Hunt-Francis, 'they undressed a friend of mine and took away her knickers. She never saw them again.'

'Also,' said Dr Jochum, 'they are very strict about plants and fruit. Did you know that when you drive into the state of California they take your oranges away?'

'No!' cried Miss Marrow.

'Oh, yes,' said Dr Jochum, 'they are afraid of foreign pests, you see.'

'That's us,' said Miss Marrow cheerfully.

'Precisely,' said Dr Jochum, and he leaned over in a jolly way towards Walker. 'I'm afraid, my dear friend, they will even confiscate your wife's heather.'

'The rotten devils,' said Walker, equally cheerfully.

And then, without even looking, he knew that something was happening to Miss Marrow, beside him. She rose up, a terrifying figure in her red box-pleated shorts, and said, quietly, in a hiss, 'You're married?'

Walker turned russet and became afraid. He said nothing.

'You were talking about honesty. Are you then? Are you?'

'I suppose I am, really,' he said, not looking up.

'Honesty, decency,' said Miss Marrow, turning in rage.

'Mind, miss,' said the steward; the bowl of porridge he was carrying left his grasp and came down, upturned, on Walker's head. It sizzled on his pate; milk ran down his face in streams.

'Christ!' he said.

'An accident,' said the steward, wiping ineffectually at Walker's thatch with a very dirty towel. 'We don't get a lot of those.'

'I should go and have a bath, Mr Bigears, before the bath-stewards go ashore.'

'I fear she is right,' said Dr Jochum, looking pained and helpless.

A bath, the last straw, the final indignity with him, turned Walker completely sour. 'That cheeky bitch,' he said, foggy in a world of embarrassment and conspicuousness, knowing he was being unfair; he turned from the table.

'Farewell,' said Dr Jochum, coming forward to shake hands.

'Good-bye, Mr Bigears,' said Lady Hunt-Francis, nodding regally, 'and don't forget to give the m-a-n his pennies. We must all do our bit for those less fortunate. I know. I'm one of them.'

Walker, surly, dipped in his pocket and tipped the steward with the pound he had thoughtfully placed there for the purpose. 'Have a drink with me,' he said.

'Thank you, sir,' said the man, 'been nice to have you here and listen to your conversation. Always interesting, you know. I hope the porridge comes out of the hair. Nasty sticky stuff, porridge is.'

'It had better,' said Walker.

'Never mind,' said the steward. 'If you ask me, it'll bring you and the young lady closer together, if anything.'

The other breakfasters watched him as he went out of the room. Outside, heat buffeted through the public rooms and the ship had been transformed. Sweating in the hot air, Englishmen already stood in long lines, visas and X-ray photographs in their hands, waiting to go through the immigration in the first-class lounge. Luggage now filled the passageways; new doors had opened here, old ones closed there, the crew seemed to have disappeared, all old safety gone. A bevy of longshoremen in lumberjackets, smoking stogies, stood around the corridors, bringing a new and fearful atmosphere. They stopped bundling trunks to look at him with open curiosity, for porridge streamed about him still. 'Take a look a' dis kook,' said one in a plaid shirt. 'Whadya tink? That kind guy dey ouh ta sen hem ride back to Yerrup wit a hart kick up du fanny.' Walker pushed by, to search in the corridors near his cabin for the bath-steward he'd so assiduously avoided all the voyage. Another tip; that was the hardest blow of all. 'You would pick this time,' said the steward, running the salt-water bath. Outside, in New York, cars hooted, traffic roared, civilization buzzed; another life pressed his ears and penetrated his distress. He was no longer at sea; new conduct and new penalties operated now; inquisition and anguish lay ahead. Travel turned from peace to strife, the world from necessity to contingency. Beyond the bathroom the ship's life was dissolving. And they were even going to take the heather, sprouting in his buttonhole, away.

3

America! There it lay, handy and tantalizing, all heat and scurry. All morning they had kept catching glimpses of it beyond the portholes as they stood in long lines, waiting to reach the tables where the immigration men in dacron shirts checked their visas, inspected the X-ray pictures of their lungs that they held in their hands, decided whether to admit them or not. Getting into America was, it seemed, quite as hard as getting into heaven; and the trouble was, thought Walker, standing rancid in the line of sweating aspirants, that as with heaven one couldn't know whether one would like it when one got there. It was unconscionably hot; sweat trickled down their faces and their clothes stuck to their bodies. Outside, signs on buildings reported that the temperature and humidity were mounting steadily. Walker kept wiping his face and fanning himself with the negative of his chest, and from time to time he gave a nod to Miss Marrow, who was in the line some way ahead of him, in a green suit with a mohair collar, and with whom he was uneasily reconciled. She had come back to him for peace.

'I'm sorry,' she said, 'it served you right, but I didn't mean to do it. Upset the porridge, I mean.'

'Oh, never mind,' said Walker, still minding. 'It was rough justice, I suppose.'

'Actually you must admit it was pretty funny.'

'Oh, yes, it was.'

'I was terribly angry with you. But it's hard to stay angry after that, even though you were such a sod. When I think what we nearly did. You might have *said*.'

'It never really came up, somehow, and I didn't think it made much difference.'

'It made every difference, and you ought to know that. Still, you were very kind. I shan't forget that. I hope you'll write to me?'

'If you want me to,' said Walker. As she went back to her place in the queue, a big, chubby girl, the salt of the earth, Walker saw with interest that the hem of her skirt was unattached in at least three places, as if she had been attacked by dachshunds. The sight made him feel guilty; all his kindness and affection had been patronage, easy familiar emotion on the way to bigger game.

The line moved slowly; it was nearly noon when he reached the immigration table. He handed across his X-ray. 'Sorry, this ain't right. You'll have to wait there on that divan till we got this checked by a doctor.' Halted! Walker groaned. A mad craving for America and his destiny, coupled with a profound sense of indignation and fear, swept through him as he stumbled to the divan to wait. My fates! he thought. Was he ill, must he go to hospital? Was he illegal, must he go to Ellis Island? Was he undesirable, must he go back ignominiously to England, perhaps working his passage? What we are denied we want, and Walker wanted America. Unspeakably hot, vilely smoky, the first-class lounge turned into a prison. Tantalizingly, outside, New York boomed and jostled, noise and heat and light. The cushions beneath him told lies about his comfort; he had none, none at all. And when at last the doctor came and released him (the scars were a technician's thumbprint) he blessed the man, wished to call him friend, felt the spirit of victory. Unblemished by tuberculosis or syphilis, found tried and true, proven chaste, he passed ashore, down the gangplank and into the customs shed.

Here all was a bustle of people and trunks and suitcases.

Walker found his own, deposited haphazardly on the dusty concrete floor. 'Bring 'em over here, mac,' said an excise man. 'Okay, open 'em up, spread it out.'

'You mean put the stuff on the floor?' asked Walker.

The customs man put his foot under the nearest suitcase, which Walker had just unlocked, and tipped it over. 'Oh brother, you foreigners!' he said, hoofing into Walker's underwear with a heavy foot. 'You brought anything you know you shouldn'ta?'

'No,' said Walker.

The inspector took a left kick at the packets of tea Walker had brought with him, fearful of not being able to get any in America, and said, 'Okay, go, pack 'em up, get this stuff out of my way.'

A longshoreman led him downstairs to where the taxis, yellow and green, milled about the entrance; amid the jumble of traffic stood Miss Marrow, looking as lonely as he felt. 'Shall we share a cab?' he said.

'Oh good!' said Miss Marrow.

'That worth a buck to you?' said the longshoreman, dropping his cases in the highway.

'Pardon?' said Walker.

'Worth a dollar?' asked the longshoreman.

'I thought it was free,' said Walker. The man was big, bulky and horny-handed, and Walker felt brave in saying so.

'Whyncha stay home, tightwad?' said the man.

'Well, even if I had been going to give you a tip I wouldn't now,' said Walker.

Miss Marrow said, 'What a rude man.'

The longshoreman heard this and stepping forward menacingly he pushed Walker hard over the heart with his big, horny hand. Though, as he hurtled backward, his lips were salty with fear, the one real thought that was in Walker's mind was that of an enormous disappointment, the disappointment one has when one discovers that the reason why children are bad is because they have evil in their make-up. So this was absolute democracy, man speaking to man. The disappointment boomed in his head as he landed upright with his back against something soft; it was Miss Marrow's large receptive chest.

'You sod,' said Miss Marrow to the longshoreman.

'Aw, leave me alone, lady,' said the longshoreman, turning away.

Violence was not a customary constituent of Walker's view of the world, and it surprised him how quickly he could assimilate it. Already, as he regained his balance, it was normal with him. So this, then, was how people coped with the impossible, with death and war; coming into this frantic society, it all made total sense; only the feeling that he was a spectacle of utter stupidity made him feel really hard that it was happening to him, to no one else. Trembling, he went over to a yellow cab whose driver watched impassively, and asked him to take them both. The longshoreman shouted, 'Don't take the tightwad; he won't give you a goddam cent.'

The cabbie was as big and horny-handed as the longshoreman; Walker was afraid they would never get away from all this. But he simply surveyed their two piles of baggage and said sceptically, 'You wanna take all dat wid you?' Walker found that a curious thing was happening; he was nervous of his own speech. Both his wishes and the accent he expressed them in seemed absurd, overly delicate, tea-party stuff; he said, 'Yeah, that's right.'

Not stirring from his driving seat, looking straight ahead, the man said, 'Okay, let's see how it goes.' Walker tried to put on a tough walk as he went round the back and pulled on the lid of the boot. 'Not in the trunk, bud,' said the driver, leaning out and yelling.

'Pardon?' said Walker. 'How's that?'

'What you can't take wid you inside, you gotta take back in the terminal and express. Dat's city law.' Walker glanced over at the longshoreman, who stood bulky and hostile in the terminal entrance, spitting a good deal, and knew that going back inside was one thing that could never be, even if he had to burn his suitcases on the spot. Between them Miss Marrow and Walker strove manfully with the heavy luggage, retaining a tiny intimate spot for themselves. 'You just made it, don't you?'

said the cabbie, turning around at last. 'Where to?' Walker gave the name of Miss Marrow's hotel off Times Square, and his own in Brooklyn Heights. 'You two not staying the same place?' said the cabbie. 'Come on, why not shack up together, and make things easier for all of us. I don't got to drive so far, you got fun. How's that for a suggestion?' He pushed in his gear-lever and they swept under the expressway, over the cobbles and rail-tracks. 'Whadya say, lady?' They turned up one of the cross-town streets, past the unmistakable odour of the abattoir, toward the centre of the island. Dust and paper blew out of lidless garbage cans on the kerbside and iron fire-escapes staggered down the sides of ancient buildings, falling into decay. People sat on stoops, white, coloured. Sun glinted on windows, the city looked dark and hostile, and Walker felt defeated and confused, an animal without a soul, a dead thing. 'No,' said Miss Marrow, winking coyly at Walker. They passed vast skeletons of buildings in the process of construction, crossed the uptown avenues, thick with speeding traffic, joined a long jam of trucks and taxis. Men walked through the traffic with small barrows hung with dresses. Change and rebuilding showed on all sides.

'That porter was very rude,' said Miss Marrow reflectively.

'Yes,' said Walker, 'it's a violent country.'

'I quite hated them all there,' she went on. 'The customs men were terrible, I wonder whether they treat everyone like that.'

'Probably,' said Walker. 'I don't think it was personal.'

'What do you think it was, then?'

'I think they just hate people,' Walker replied. 'And their jobs. And foreigners. But apart from that they're probably very good folk.'

'But why should they? Our customs men aren't like that, are they? They're polite. Why can't these be polite too?'

'Well, the problem is they're afraid it might be mistaken for servility. They think we're so polite to one another because we think other folk are our superiors.'

'And are we?' asked Miss Marrow.

The driver turned right round in his driving seat and looked at them both. 'You know,' he said, 'I finally figured out what it is that's so funny about Europeans. You're limeys, aren't you? Well, I'll tell you. You talk like I ain't here.' They shot through a changing light. 'Actually, back there at the terminal – most folks give those guys sompn.'

'There was a sign up there saying tipping was forbidden,' said Walker.

'There's a sign up there saying you'll feel better in a Maidenform brazeer.'

'They get good wages, don't they?' said Miss Marrow.

'Sure,' said the cabbie, 'they're like most of us. They like loot.' He drove hard at a small old man who was crossing the street at an intersection; then braked hard. Walker and Miss Marrow tipped forward together and went on to the floor. 'Be careful,' said Miss Marrow.

'Lady, you can do it better, you drive and I'll sit in back.'

'You're frightening me,' said Miss Marrow.

'We all need a thrill once in a while,' said the cabbie.

They must be getting near Miss Marrow's hotel, and Walker turned to her and asked about her plans. She was leaving New York the next day. 'Perhaps we could meet and you could see me off,' she said. The city by now had grown so formidable a thing that the prospect of meeting anyone he knew delighted Walker; he arranged the occasion with pleasure, and found that Miss Marrow's prim Anglicanism only faintly extended beyond his own uncertainty in the new world he had entered. Could he bear it? Could he grow to it? He was still trying to rationalize the interlude at the dock, to equate it with his new life, and all he could come up with was the feeling that fear and dislike of violence and aggression was an English middle-class trait that had somehow survived in him, a part of his bad self. He ought, he felt, not to have minded, to have welcomed being abused and thrown on the floor, for the truth it told about the thinness of what he was trying to leave.

'Hey, don't talk, look out the window,' said the cabbie. 'This is Times Square, centre of the universe. You can go to Grand Canyon, Death Valley, them places, believe me, you won't find nothin' like Times Square. Everything happens here. You know there ain't one important person in the world never been in Times Square and looked up at the Camel guy blowing smoke-rings. Right up there, take a look. You got anything like that in Europe?'

'I doubt it,' said Miss Marrow. The taxi now twisted through a few back streets and came to a stop outside a hotel, the one Miss Marrow was staying at.

The cabbie turned round and looked at them. 'What's a matter, lady, ain't you got legs?'

'I'll open it,' said Walker; and he got out and carried Miss Marrow's luggage inside.

'Thank you, Porker,' she said.

'All right now?'

'I hope so.' She leaned forward and pecked him on the cheek, and Walker leaned right back and met her on the lips. 'See you tomorrow,' she said.

The cab was still waiting. 'Thought you'd maybe stay,' said the cabbie. 'She your lady-friend?'

'Not exactly,' said Walker.

'Is it right what they say about English women?'

'What do they say?'

'You know,' the cabbie said, 'they're frigid, don't feel nothing down there.'

'I hardly think so.'

'Tell us what you know.'

'Well, that's not been my experience.'

'That's what I like to hear. A guy whose had experience. Lot of experience?'

'Not terribly.'

'How many?'

'How many what?'

'Different girls.'

'I don't know.'

'That's it, who's counting?' said the cabbie. 'Know that joke? That's a Jewish joke. Well, I'll tell you, you're a guy likes experience, there's plenty of it over here. All you gotta do is look a little. There's no girls like American girls, once you got 'em excited. I can fix you up any time.'

'Oh, I can manage,' said Walker.

'Yeah, an experienced man,' said the cabbie, pulling out into the traffic. 'I thought you English didn't go for that kinda thing much.'

Walker saw that he was being ribbed; at the same time he could feel the city; the most citified of cities around him, with its winos, its shirt-sleeved cops, guns in holster, its clash of races – they were moving through the east side – and knew its violence, its blankness, its hostility. It was all for the viewing. He saw – an experienced man – the temptations of sex, titillation, violence; they came stronger than he had ever felt them. He was isolated, without connexion, without substance; love recommended itself. Shouldn't he at least have *tried* to spend the night with Miss Marrow? She was a half-willing woman; restoration of affections seemed in the air; perhaps she, though tougher, coping better, felt the new world as abrasively as he felt it. Perhaps she was missing *him*. And there was a kind of love that would have helped, warm, cosy, enveloping, comfortable, a welcome of breasts and breathing. An experienced man probably wouldn't even have wished it; but experience was draining from him; he was the provincial in the city.

Finally they reached the hotel, a small, dark tower. Walker got out. 'Now it's all yours,' said the cabbie, as Walker paid him off from his bundle. 'Enjoy yourself.' Walker picked up his cases. 'And hey, muscles – lay 'em and leave 'em, huh?'

Inside, on the desk, a tired old man in his shirt-sleeves looked up Walker's reservation and directed him to a room. There was no porter (bellhop?) and the lift (elevator?) wasn't working; he trudged sadly up the staircase, and in the dark red-carpeted corridors wandered about until he came upon his room. A negro chambermaid listening to the radio on the bedside table got up from the armchair as he went in, and left without speaking. 'Headache?' said the radio. 'Feel like a drill is boring into your brain?' Then followed the noise of a drill. 'Could be that time of the day, that time of the month? Friends, don't suffer. Listen to this.' Fizzing noises. 'That's the sound of an aspirin that won't burn the delicate lining of your stomach, won't hurt those miles of intestine every human body contains. . . .' Walker switched off and went to the window. Below were ceaseless kerbside lines of car-roofs, kids and dogs playing among the traffic; opposite, on a construction site, demolition and construction were going on simultaneously. As he watched, a wall fell down. He pulled down the blind and lay on the bed, exhausted with New York, with himself. Being, after all, a sensitive man, bound up more with self than with the world about, all he demanded of that world was a certain affability, a certain sympathy, a certain tolerance. He knew how to stand up in nature, and even in the small city, so that each got their fair share of what was going, Walker and surrounding universe. But now the circuit seemed broken, the wiring faulty. He lay on top of the green covers and looked up at the pink shade on the light, and felt that all colours and all experiences had turned sour on him, curdled in the heat like cream. In his tweedy suit he lay and bemoaned himself. Had he come to the end of his hopes for the future? Would the power be restored? Could it be that time of the day, that time of the month, or was it going to be this for ever? Friends, don't suffer, said New York; but Walker suffered and didn't in the least know where the blame was to be apportioned.

'Good morning, Mister Wukker,' said the telephone the following morning, speaking his name carefully to reassure him he had one. 'Time's a half after seven, and the weather report promises a new high in heat and humidity. Well, that's the way the cookie crumbles; and speaking of cookies, a word in your ear about the facilities of our Serbian Breakfast Room, now serving, including breakfast specials at attractive prices. Wow!' Walker put down the receiver without hearing the rest of the message. The day lay ahead of him, long, thin and bleak, ready to be worn out and thrown away. Uneasy sensations possessed him; that his mind was slipping, that the emotional content of his life was draining away, that he no longer existed. But down in the lobby the clerk, reading a newspaper amongst his keys, said, 'Good morning, Mr

Wacker!' If America was good at making you lose your identity, it was also good at helping you find it again, even though the one they gave you wasn't exactly the one you'd lost. Walker asked for, and was provided with, the way to get uptown by subway.

'Had breakfast?' said the clerk.

'No,' said Walker.

'Stay away from dis Serbian room,' said the clerk, 'boy oh boy.' Walker wandered outside into the day.

Through the buildings he could see a small park on the heights, overlooking the harbour; he went there and looked down, over the water, to Manhattan, where the buildings stood high. A dog peed on his shoe. The wind, blowing off the water, ruffled him a bit and got inside his jacket, as if searching for the correspondent breeze within. There was nothing there, he had to tell it; that's how it is today. He found his way down into the subway station, which smelled equally of dust, urine, and blood. Along the platform, in the noxious darkness, delinquent youths jimmied the gum-machines. A wild express flashed through on the middle line, packed with souls, glaring with light. Walker read his match-book, which told him how to cure athlete's foot, until the local came, a row of drab, green old cars. Walker poked his head inside and asked if this was his train; no one answered. He got in and sat down, between a midget man, legs dangling off the floor, a straw-hat on his flat-faced head, and a negro in a smart brown Madison Avenue suit. He began to feel hungry, and craved a banana. He sat and looked at the wall while the train dived into the long dark section under the East River; then above the windows, he saw a row of advertisements – SUPPORT MENTAL HEALTH, said one. HELP A JUVENILE DELINQUENT, said another. AID YOUR NEAREST SCHOOL, said a third. Several advertised diseases – BEAT CANCER WITH A CHECK-UP . . . AND A CHECK, and HEART DISEASE STRIKES ALL THE TIME. Beside him, the front page of the tabloid the midget was reading was covered with a photograph of a horrifying car accident, showing in some detail people bleeding to death. His bowels began to churn and there was heart disease moving around inside him, looking for a foothold. The turning fan in the roof of the car flapped his hair and even dislodged his heavy English clothing. The car stopped again and filled up. A fat Jewish woman stepped on his foot. He got up and offered his seat. 'Cut it out,' said the Jewish woman. Walker sat down again, yearning for elsewhere.

When he reached Times Square, he rose and went along the platform, past the booths where you could photograph yourself, an ingrown occupation the direct opposite of what he was looking for. The turnstile that let him out of the system nearly castrated him. He went up the steps, the air stinging his sinuses; then the New York heat hit him like a blow as he reached the street. He was on the town. DON'T WALK said a flashing sign. Walker walked; it was a gesture of the romantic will, the personal imperative. 'Get back on the side-walk,' shouted a cop. He awaited the appearance of someone genteel before asking the way to Pennsylvania Station, where he was to meet Miss Marrow. A man in a white English rain-coat and carrying a small locked briefcase seemed likely; he stopped him and inquired. 'Mind leaving me alone, buddy?' said the man. Finally he went to a newspaper seller and bought a map.

He walked along 42nd Street, where crowds of men and youths jostled under the marquees of the girlie-show movie-houses, and then went down one of the avenues, where traffic ran fast, until he found Pennsylvania Station, a noble classical pile, multi-levelled like all the rest of the city. Miss Marrow, standing by one of the ranks of luggage lockers, was unmistakable; she was big, sure and English, and Walker at once felt about her as colonial officers in India felt about the club. New York had not destroyed her authority. On the ship she had been small; here, amid all the nullity and hostility and foreignness, she took on heroic stature. He felt an over-whelming desire to nuzzle her, to take her clothes off on the spot, to retire with her into the luggage lockers and pull the door shut on them both, in short, to bind her to him. Instead, he said, 'Had a nice time?'

'Smashing,' said Miss Marrow.

'What did you do?'

'Oh, I met a man in the hotel who took me to the theatre, I forget what the play was called. People hating one another in the south, that sort of play. Then we went to a sort of pub and heard some black men playing jazz. Then this morning I've been shopping. I've bought a dress and some marvellous gloves. It's a magnificent place to shop, isn't it? Come in this dinette place and I'll buy you a cup of coffee.'

Blinking at him over the coffee, Miss Marrow said, 'Are you having a nice time?'

'No,' said Walker.

'Oh, *you*! It's marvellous. Let yourself go.'

'I am doing that.'

'Well, drink up,' said Miss Marrow, 'nearly time for my train. It's a Pullman. I've got a cubicle to myself. Now we have to hunt out all my luggage.'

Miss Marrow found a redcap and ordered him round briskly, while Walker marvelled. The redcap explained where the trains were; they had all been hidden underground. They went to the gate, where the attendant refused Walker entrance. 'Well, this is it, farewell,' said Miss Marrow. Miss Marrow and the true humanity of the human race become one and the same; affection for her was a stay against total hostility, obeisance to nobility and inner-direction.

'Let me kiss you good-bye,' said he, delicately, nervously.

'Here?' said Miss Marrow.

'No, come over behind those lockers.'

Behind them, she turned to look sadly at him. 'Not a smudgy one,' she said, 'you can't get on a train like that.'

'Crisp and hard,' said Walker, doing it. 'I wish you weren't going,' he said when it was over. 'Now I shall really miss you. Let me never be left here for long without anyone.'

'I don't think it's me,' said Miss Marrow. 'I think you're afraid and it's made you sentimental. The tables turned, sort of thing. Still, we're two of a kind. We should have given ourselves a chance. But you thought you could do better, didn't you?'

'Yes.'

'Oh, well, maybe you will. Though I just don't understand about your wife.'

'Nor do I,' said Walker.

'Well, must go,' said Miss Marrow. Walker struck again with his lips. 'Now that was smudgy,' said Miss Marrow, taking out her handkerchief and etching the edge of her mouth. 'Well, be a good boy, have a nice time.'

'I'll try,' said Walker. 'You do too. In this strange land.'

'Going our separate ways,' said Miss Marrow. They went back to the gate again. 'Well, take it easy now, as they say here,' said Miss Marrow, as the attendant let her through. 'Cheerio, Porker.'

'Cheerio, Fern,' said Walker. He watched her descending the escalator into subterranea, where her train lay. She waved a hand, a noble Britannia, and went below the earth. The hailstorm of loneliness blew up again.

Alone! Confused, lost, running with sweat, he turned and went back into the concourse and watched the clerks selling tickets from great long racks of machinery, helped by flickering television sets.

While he stared at this mysterious process, a man came up to him; he was a little man, wearing a crinkly transparent shirt, with a pack of Lucky Strike cigarettes showing from the pocket, and a pair of brown pants with wide baggy cuffs. 'How'd you like this necktie? It's wrinkle-proof. Five dollar value for ninety-eight cents.'

'Pardon?' said Walker.

'You from Boston?' said the man.

'No, from England,' said Walker.

'No, really?' said the man. 'What's your name, what do they call you?'

'Walker,' said Walker.

'Walker who?'

'Walker James,' said Walker.

'I'm Harry Dimilo,' said the man. 'Shake.' Walker shook. 'Glad to know you, Walk,' said the man. 'You visiting?'

Walker looked around for escape; there was none. The implications of the confidence trick grew more remote, but confidence trick Walker knew there was. He was really rather terrified, and only grateful that, thanks to the confusion about his name, he was not yet perfectly defined. He said, 'Yes.'

'In New York for long?'

'No,' said Walker, 'I'm leaving almost immediately.'

'You wanna stay around, it's a great little city.'

'Yes, I know,' said Walker, 'but I have to go.'

'What's your line of business?'

'I'm a teacher.'

'I thought you was an educated man, Walk. I'm not, but I'll tell you, I really wish I was. What kinda thing you teach?'

'Literature.'

'Books, poems, that kinda stuff? I know, I love it. I got a whole buncha books in my room, paperbacks. I get 'em down the supermarket. Whole buncha real sexy books there.'

'I must go,' said Walker.

'Goin' far?'

'Fair way,' said Walker.

'Where to, Walk?'

'Madison Avenue.'

'What number's that?'

'Five hundred and something.'

'In the five hundreds, yeah, I think we can find that. I'll walk uptown wid you.'

'Oh, I can find it,' said Walker.

'No, I like talking to you, Walk.'

Walker began to sweat a little. He set off walking; the little man grasped his arm. 'No, let's save ourselves. It's quicker out this way.' They went through the concourse together, the little man slightly behind, tearing the strip of red paper off the top of his Luckies. 'I toit you was from Boston because of your accent. You know you got an accent?'

'Yes,' said Walker.

'That an English accent?'

'Yes.'

'They all talk like that over there?'

'Most of them,' said Walker.

'You still got a queen, don't you?'

'That's right,' said Walker.

'I seen her photograph in the newspaper,' said the man. 'Like it over here?'

'Very nice,' said Walker.

'Better than back home, huh?'

'I don't know,' said Walker, 'I've only just arrived.'

'Yeah, you'll like it here better. It's real crazy country. What d'ya think of American dames?'

'I have yet to find out,' said Walker.

'Stay off 'em, Walk,' said the man. 'I tell ya, I'm through wid these dames. I mean, look at me, I'm not a handsome guy, but I'm better than some. I got it down here what I ain't got in good looks. I tell ya, I spent the best years of my life chasing a nice lay. I screwed dames in every locality in New York. I screwed them in the Bronx. I screwed them in Brooklyn, I screwed them in Flatbush and Queens, I even screwed them in Harlem. I treated them good likewise. One dame I even gave a Motorola air-conditioner to. There wasn't one of them dames didn't run me round in circles. One of them I found in bed with another dame and no less than four guys. That's right.'

'Terrible,' said Walker.

'You hit it, Walk, terrible. You ever fall in love with a man?'

'No,' said Walker.

'Well, you can't live without feelings. Look, you're a foreigner, let me put this to you, another opinion. You think a guy can live without it, like these monks do? You think you can manage without feelings?'

'Yes, I think so,' said Walker.

'Aw,' said the man, 'it's like what they always say about the English. They don't know how to make the scene. All that cricket and roast beef. You wanna try a bit of anguish, Walk. Come on, try. Let's see the steam coming out your ears.'

Walker began to walk a little faster. 'Hold it,' said the man. 'Don't walk. You don't wanna get run down or get a ticket, do ya?' They waited until the sign across the intersection turned to *Walk*, his name. 'All these signs around,' said the man. 'You ever noticed how many signs New York has? You always got sompn to read. That's why you're doing a good job, you know that, Walk, teaching literature to them kids. How else they going to read all the signs? Look up there, what's that say?'

'Niterie,' said Walker.

'There,' said the man, 'that's English. Or don't you call that English?'

'Not really, no,' said Walker.

'Uh,' said the man, 'you know, I like talking to an educated man. I guess we're getting near the five hundreds. What you going to this place to do?'

'I have to see a man in one of the offices.'

'What kind of office is that, Walk?'

'A literary agency,' said Walker.

'Oh, that like a theatrical agency?'

'Sort of,' said Walker.

'Plenty of girls around, model girls?'

'No,' said Walker, growing more and more uncomfortable with his incubus. What did he want? When would he leave him? Would he follow him even right up into his agent's office? Was this a homosexual pick-up, an attempt to sell him something, or a pact at exchanging souls?

'What you want to see this fellow for?'

'He sells articles I write.'

'You a journalist too, Walk?'

'Yes,' said Walker.

'An all-round man, I found myself an all-round educated man. What's the number of the building?'

'I can find it,' said Walker.

'You think I don't know how to help a stranger? What's the number?'

Walker told him. 'It's further on a little ways,' said the man. 'You ought to write something about me.'

'I don't write that kind of thing,' said Walker.

'What kind of thing?'

'I write mostly about books.'

'You're a scholar, Walk. I got a little Jewish guy upstairs from me, a real scholar. He sits on the can all day and reads books. He's got an apartment there with books all round de walls. Furnishings he don't care about, I guess he sits on those goddam books. Look, this is the place.' The man pushed the revolving doors and went inside. 'You gotta check the name on the board, ya see. What's the name?'

'I'd better find my own way,' said Walker.

'No, come on, what's the name again?' Walker told him. 'Right, twenty-sixth floor, I found it for you. Now you wanna take the elevator. Round here.' He led Walker to the elevator. 'Twenty-six, chief,' he said to the elevator man.

'Thanks very much,' said Walker, but the man got into the lift. 'I'll come up wid you.' At the twenty-sixth floor they got out together.

'Look, I'd better go in here alone,' said Walker.

'This the place?' said the man, going inside. 'Guy to see you,' he announced to the secretary, a blonde girl at a Danish desk. 'Nice place you got here. What's all these photographs?' Signed photographs lined the walls of the agency.

'I think Mr Tilly is expecting me,' Walker said, 'my name's James Walker.'

'Take a seat please, Mr Walker.'

'This man's nothing to do with me. He followed me here,' Walker went on.

'I'll tell Mr Tilly you're here,' said the secretary, working the switchboard, 'but I know he's very busy just now.' Walker sat down. The little man joined him and lit a Lucky.

'Take a look at those breasts,' he said. 'I like a girl wid a frontage. Whadya say, Walk?'

'Look,' said Walker, 'I shall have to leave you now.'

'Mr Walker, will you go in briefly?' said the secretary. The little man rose too.

'Mr Tilly is expecting only one,' said the girl.

'Okay, okay,' said the little man, sitting down again.

'Along the corridor to the right, then the door on the left at the termination,' said the girl.

'You got a boy you go out wid?' the little man was saying as Walker went from earshot. He found Tilly's room and knocked on the door, his heart still beating hard from this encounter. Would the man be there when he was finished? Could he ever lose him?

'Entrez!' cried Tilly. Walker went into the office, dark because the venetian blinds were drawn. Tilly, a middle-aged man wearing a bleeding madras jacket, tailored bermuda shorts, a white, button-down shirt with a dark foulard tie, and a grey felt hat with a narrow brim and a madras band, was pouring papers into a briefcase; he looked up with pleasure on his face. 'Jam Walker, as I live and breathe,' he said. 'Come in, Jam, glad to know you at last. A friendship conducted by letters needs this kind of cement. Actually, Jam, I'm just going.'

'Oh, dear,' said Walker, 'I was hoping we could talk about some of my stuff.'

'Nothing I'd like better, Jam, but I have to be at Grand Central in just thirty minutes. But I'm really glad you stopped by, really. You should have come into New York any week-end but this. I wanted you to meet all kinds of people, editors, you know. *Vogue* are dying to take a look at their darling Britisher. Still, I expect you'll be in and out of New York all year, no?'

'I gathered I'd picked a bad week-end,' said Walker.

'Labor Day Weekend. Everybody's out on the Cape. You don't have any friends on the Cape?'

'No,' said Walker.

'The fellows I wanted you to meet at *Esquire*, the lassies at *Vogue*, they're all out of town, or I'd call them up right now. Look, I have to run fast; but Jam, nice to see you. A nice day for me. Just like the photographs, old boy. We'll meet again, of course. Lots of time. Good for me, good for you. Soon, promise me soon. Come back, spend two weeks, we'll really do the thing properly. I'll fix a party.'

'Marvellous,' said Walker.

'Will be,' said Tilly. 'Hotel all right?'

'Not bad,' Walker said.

'I just stuck a pin in the book,' said Tilly. 'You said somewhere away from the centre. Sounded just your dish of tea.'

'Yes,' said Walker, 'it's passable.'

'Not so hot? We'll try something else next time.'

'Yes,' said Walker.

'Walk me down to the elevator,' said Tilly. 'Want to see anyone else here?'

'I don't think so,' said Walker.

They walked out through the entrance hall. 'Leonie,' said Tilly to the secretary, 'meet James Walker. He's going to be a very great man.'

'Hi,' said Leonie indifferently. 'The bum who followed you left. I told him I'd call a cop.'

'Bum followed you up, Jam?' asked Tilly, going out through the glass doors.

'Yes, a very curious experience,' said Walker. 'He latched on to me at Pennsylvania Station and came all the way here with me. I couldn't lose him.'

Tilly, pressing the button for the elevator, said, 'You have to be careful in New York City. People get mugged round here in broad daylight.'

'I don't think he meant any harm,' said Walker. 'Just a . . . democratic encounter.'

'Some kook,' said Tilly, ushering Walker into the elevator. They went down fast, with a whine. In the entrance hall Tilly shook Walker's hand and said, 'Been nice. Come back soon.'

'I will,' said Walker.

Alone again! On the sidewalk he felt curiously stranded. He had come to New York to be great, to make all the contacts Tilly had promised. But instead of grandeur it was expulsion; great you may be, but not on Labor Day Weekend. Now there was little left. He was at the low ebb of his fortunes; the only worse thing would be not to have, in his pocket, that ticket westward that set him free from all this. But it wasn't even the west he yearned for; it was for England, that simple, comfortable hospital of a place. He watched Tilly's head disappear into the crowds of Madison Avenue, largely male, smartly dressed. Then, at a loss, he turned along one of the crosstown streets. This brought him to Fifth Avenue, near the Rockefeller Center. The crowds surged, looking smarter still. There were bright girls in shirtwaisters or plain sheath dresses, simple and smart, crisp and clean as fresh lettuces, carrying themselves with assurance and style. He stared after them; they reminded him that he was in a cosmopolitan city, and they made him only sorry to be alone. He went on up the avenue, beneath the towering buildings, which made him feel like a dwarf.

Then the open space of Central Park, beyond the line of horse-taxis, appeared, a ready relief. His size came back. He took off his jacket, put it over his arm, and crossed the street to go into the park, green, dense, outcropped with bursts of rock. But a patriarchal old man stood in his way: 'Stranger in town?' he said, and warned Walker not to go in there – it was full of hoods and muggers. 'You'll lose your wallet, maybe get a broken nose too.' Beyond him was the green grass; but with a sigh Walker turned and went back down the avenue again. Bargain damask tablecloths and dwarf binoculars tempted him from windows. He compared the prices of shirts and once stopped to watch a gang of men planting a fully grown tree outside a high grey glass building. He looked at the goodies in Tiffany's. Then, again, decked out with flags, was the Rockefeller Center, with tables under sun-umbrellas spread in the open forecourt. He leaned on the balcony and looked down on the drinkers below. When he felt in the pocket of his jacket he found he had lost his fountain pen and sunglasses. Inside, he joined a tour and, with a crowd of midwestern visitors to the metropolis, went up to the top of the building in two wild express elevators, like racing cars. On the observation platform the wind blew and, down far below him, New York looked like a gigantic waffle iron. Down at street-level again, his heart thumping, he peered nostalgically into the offices of the British Railways in the Plaza and then went on down the avenue. There was Greek and Roman statuary at bargain prices in the windows of Brentano's, and an all-glass bank revealed, like a temple now devoid of its mysteries, an open vault in its intestines.

He sat down on one of the benches outside the New York Public Library, behind one of the lions, watching the shop and office girls going by for their lunch hour, carrying paper sacks from Lord and Taylor and the Tall Girl shop. Trim, smart, above all assured, they reminded him of Julie Snowflake. Why didn't he call her? By the side of the library he found a row of glass telephone booths. The dialling system was complicated and the machinery ate several dimes before he managed it. Then a deep low buzzing came out of the American void and sounded in the vibrator against his ear. It was soon replaced by a voice. 'Snowflake household here,' it said. 'Who dat out dere?'

'Is that you, Julie?' said Walker.

'Dis here de Snowflake household. Who dat?'

'Could I speak to Miss Julie Snowflake, please?'

'Ain't nobody here at home 'cept me. Would you care to leave a message? I'll write it down on de pad, always supposin' I kin find it.'

'Don't bother,' said Walker. 'How long will she be away?'

'Dey's on Fah Island. Be five days more before they gets back home.'

'Oh, it's no use then,' said Walker. He put down the phone and felt bereft. The thought of not seeing Julie again – for when she came back he would be gone – depressed him; he peered out of the glass booth at the passers-by, terrorized by loneliness, until he recalled that an acquaintance of his had a copywriting job in an agency on Madison Avenue, and he called him. 'Hallo, old boy,' cried Henry when he had penetrated the switchboard. 'Absolutely topping to hear your voice.' Henry hadn't talked like that when he was in Nottingham, Walker recalled, but then America could probably do this kind of thing to a man. He also had a suspicion that Henry didn't recall him at all, but had simply, with urban bonhomie, responded with pleasure to anyone who actually knew of his existence at all. But then Henry waxed sentimental, recalling the good old days, and it was on a note of intensity that they arranged to have dinner together and show Walker the Village. 'Pip pip, old boy,' said Henry. 'See you.' The booth and something more had made Walker sweat. He went across the road to the Marboro bookshop and looked through the bargains, finally purchasing Sartre's *Being and Nothingness* for one dollar.

Henry Wilkins was an old acquaintance of Walker's with whom he had drunk many a pint in the back bar of Severn's. In those days he had been a quiet, rather sad youth of lower middle-class parentage who worked in a public library, stamping books, fining delinquent borrowers, ushering out hacking old men from the reading-room. The bottoms of his trousers were always frayed and he had a nibble of baldness on each of his temples. He smelled often of bacon fat, and he had a sprayed, blotchy tie which, if boiled, would have made a meaty soup. He was now another man. His clothes were smart and dark; he wore a checked shirt; his tie was English hand-blocked foulard and his temples seemed to have reseeded and grown up again. When he met Walker in the foyer of the vast yellow skyscraper where he worked, he took him surely across Madison Avenue, holding his arm protectively, and into a high building devoted entirely to the parking of cars. When Henry's car came down it was a Triumph Sprite. 'Must keep the old flag flying,' he said, in his more English than English voice, now devoid of its Bulwell twang. He drove the car with American efficiency, holding the right speed so that all the lights changed as he approached them. He took Walker to dine at an Italian restaurant on the edge of the Village where signed photographs of famous writers and actors stared down at them from the walls. The meal was impeccable, and afterwards Henry insisted on paying. He said his apartment was close by, on Second Street, and drove Walker to it along dark shuttered streets littered with wrecked dismantled cars and sleeping winos, seemingly waiting to be filmed by men with cameras in loaves of bread. He stopped off at the liquor store and came out with a bulky package. The apartment, in a faintly sleazy modern block, was furnished inside with Danish settees and low tables and madras hangings. Walker sat in a butterfly chair, his bottom suspended just above floor level in the canvas sling, and drank martinis that were cold and composed almost entirely of gin.

'My rule with martinis,' said Henry, who had never heard of martini when Walker knew him before, 'is just show them the label of the vermouth bottle. No more, you know; I say, I haven't bruised the gin, have I?'

'I don't think so,' said Walker, more and more impressed.

Henry asked Walker whether he had a pipeline – 'People to stay with, millionaires in Mexico, you know?'

'No,' said Walker, 'I don't know anybody.'

'Must give you my addresses. The great thing is to be a free-loader. Americans love it. Sometimes I think that if you're clever enough you need never pay for anything ever again. Until you meet another Englishman.'

'I meant to pay my share for the dinner,' said Walker.

'Nonsense, old boy. And now I suppose you want to stay here. Soon get a day-bed made up. Actually there are four other chaps here too; never met them before. I have to pick them up at Idlewild just after midnight. They've been to Denver to stay with the parents of one of them's mistress. I told Ralph, pick a mistress with a spare car. But he says he prefers to fly.'

'I see there's an art to America,' said Walker. 'I've nearly been missing out.'

'An art indeed,' said Henry.

'Actually,' said Walker, 'I'm booked in at a hotel.'

'Good one?'

'Not really.'

'Well, look, if you want to move out here. . . .'

'Thanks a lot. I'll think about it.'

'How about a wander round the Village? Bookstores, coffee bars, some jazz?'

'Fine,' said Walker.

This time they set off on foot. The winos seemed more threatening and one of them caught Walker by the trouser leg. 'He wants a handout,' said Henry, giving him a dollar bill. The man said nothing, but let go of Walker's trousers. 'I told you,' said Henry. They stopped in Washington Square to watch the emigrés in berets playing chess on the stone tables.

A girl in a denim shirt and tight jeans said to Walker, 'Take a look at these tits,' and opened her shirt.

'Very nice,' said Walker politely.

'Screw you too,' said the girl.

'Nice work,' said Henry, when she'd gone. 'You were real cool. That's what she wanted.'

'It didn't sound like it,' said Walker.

Across the square a man in a leather jacket was talking to a tree. 'You're the goddamest tree,' he said, 'all these other trees are garbage, but you. . . . '

They passed a bookshop where a crowd of old men were reading books on sexual postures. 'Tourists,' said Henry, 'the Village people just steal them.' The whole city was now turning rich blue in the evening light. 'Here's a place I know,' said Henry, 'they serve a good chocolate with an onion in it.' Inside there was a small podium where a couple in powdered make-up were doing a mime. Though the mime was called Leda and the Swan, nothing very much happened. The waitress, a girl who had shaved off all her hair, brought their chocolates, bobbing her shiny bare pate in front of them. Then the proprietor of the place announced the poetry reading. The poet was a young man in jeans and a poncho; he wore dark glasses.

'Night people,' he said; the audience clapped appreciatively.

'Tourists,' said Henry.

'Am I talking to night people?' He looked at the audience and munched for a while on the end of a French roll.

'You're beautiful, boy,' shouted a man at one of the tables.

'Yeah, we all are,' said the poet. He munched for a few moments more, then looked at the ceiling. 'Come, bird, come down, bird, I need you,' he said. 'I'm calling you to help me. Oh, bird, you gonna make it tonight? Make it with me.' The bird must have come, because an expression of ecstasy took his face for a second or so, and then he said, 'A black dog pissed on my lawn. For Gregory Corso.'

'This is the poem,' whispered Henry. The poems were all in the verbal tradition; they mixed wit and intense sentiment in equal parts. Walker enjoyed them, but afterwards, when they left, Henry was disappointed. 'Some nights he takes his clothes off,' he said, 'but I suppose that's just Saturdays.'

'I need a drink,' said Henry when they came out into the street. Two girls in leotards went by and Walker looked after them. 'Cool, man, cool,' said Henry, shaking a finger. A liner hooted, calling the Village Fulbrights to Europe, and a breeze blew off the river. Henry remembered he had some friends in the block and dived into a liquor store to reappear with another package. The friends lived high up in an apartment block; when they went in, the two of them sat typing in their under-shorts on opposite sides of a desk, their little portables singing as the words rolled off. They seemed not to resent the intrusion, and at once, as if they had been waiting all day for it, began a discussion about E. M. Forster and the moral life.

'What I admire about England,' said one of them, a teacher at Hunter College, 'is its moral stability. People even have flowers in their gardens named Honesty. That's the way it should be; moral principles in all things.' Walker felt a warm glow when the words hit his eardrums. 'They still believe in good and bad,' went on the college teacher. 'You know, this sounds quaint, but I wish . . . do I? do I . . . that I did too?'

'But how is it done?' said the other man, an editor with a college publishing house, elbows on his hairy knees.

'Well, we beat it in through the bottom when we're children,' said Walker, 'or at least we used to. It's amazing what you can get in that way if everyone does it too. But I'm afraid you're talking about the past.'

'You should keep at it,' said the editor.

'Why should the English be the ones to spit against the wind?' said Walker.

Much later they dropped Walker off at his hotel, and he went up the stairs to his room. It was hot and fetid and when he had stripped he got between the sheets without putting on his English pyjamas. A mosquito buzzed around his head. After groping for his bed-lamp, which had some kind of patent switch that wouldn't light, he struggled out of bed and went over to his cases for his bottle of anti-mosquito lotion, sprinkling the stuff liberally over himself. Back in bed, he suddenly recalled that his suitcase also contained a bottle of marking ink, but he couldn't care. He felt sweat gathering in his crotch. Through the wall came noises of dispute.

'No, you beat it, she's gonna stay wid me.' 'You wouldn't know how to do it when she got on de bed wid you.' 'Yeah, my good old buddy, pull me down in front of her. This is a friend.' 'You're both crazy, I'm going, I'm wasting my time,' said a girl. 'Walk all over me, good old buddy, break my arm.' There was a hammering in the corridor and a voice louder than any yelled, 'Cut out all that noise, will ya? This is a respectable premises.' 'Now you fetched the desk clerk,' said the girl. 'Shall I bust him one?' 'No, give him a five, he'll go away, won't you, boy?' 'I already had some complaints . . .'

Walker got up and went to the window. Moonlight shone in his navel and a mosquito dived at his buttocks; it must have been marking ink he had sprinkled on himself. Outside, the streets were as busy as day. Shining cars stood at the kerbside, steam surged from a grating, a police siren screamed across the city. Across the street the wreckers, in metal caps and overalls picked out in the arc-lights, went on ceaselessly demolishing the perfectly good building. All New York seemed like a vast confusion; it hummed around him like a steady note of menace. He had asked for a vision; was this the best the created world could do? The vote of appreciation that he felt he ought to give simply would not come; too much that belonged to him, too much of the market-town, too much that had to do with smallness and gentleness and sensitivity and decency, was threatened. He knew that he had made a poor job of the voyage out. His sins – sins of omission rather than commission, for he was always interrupted – stayed the same and felt the same. The future, to which he was trying to give himself, stood ahead of him, hard, insistent, destructive, with very few promises. Further on, in the country beyond the city, where he was soon to go, he envisaged greater follies, greater mess, more incompetence on the part of that crude self that crouched inside him, still believing, as the man had said, in good and bad, still with flowers in its garden named Honesty, still an ugly little dwarf. More was demanded, and more had to come. But would it? A load of rubble smacked into a truck; with a roar of its diesel motor it ripped off down the street. He went back toward the bed. The voices in the next room rose to a scream; somewhere in the building a radio played trauma music for the unsleeping; and the shoot of rubble into trucks went on. Walls fell and the subway shook the hotel. Tomorrow he would take advantage of Henry's hospitality and escape.

Now he opened a new pack of cigarettes and put one in his mouth, tasting the unusual treacly taste on the end of his tongue, and waiting until the telephone rang to tell him his name and invite him to take part in another New York day.

Book Two

A Middle State

Placed on this isthmus of a middle state,
A being darkly wise, and rudely great:
With too much knowledge for the sceptic side,
With too much weakness for the stoic's pride,
He hangs between . . .

Pope : An Essay on Man

4

The visiting lecturer from England came in on the late afternoon of a September day. Bernard Froelich, a lover of meetings, arrived at the railroad depot a little early for the day's one transcontinental train. There was no one around, but he reversed his car with an ornate gesture into the dusty, deserted parking lot, and lay down on the front seat, with his feet sticking out of the window. It was an intensely hot day, without a wind blowing, and Froelich took it as a day of omens, a day for arrivals; he was sure in his heart that the train would stop and Walker descend. His sensations were already disposed to be those of pure awe; it was a day, he felt, he had spent a lifetime preparing for, by spiritual activity and political conniving; it had to go just right, and it would. He looked out across the plain, his head on the hand-rest of the door; it was bare and silent, but after ten minutes had passed he heard suddenly, faintly blown across the hard flat landscape, the cry of the train. The metals began to shudder; a bundle of noise rolled over the platte. The train had to halt; there had to be a Walker on it. And sure enough, the brakes began to groan, the flyer began to slow, the moment took on historic dimensions. He was coming. Froelich watched the train ride by.

The train stopped, and now the ceremonial was beginning. Passengers looked out of the cars to see what was happening, what special event had halted them in the middle of the void. The blue-coated negro porter lowered the steps, wiped the handrail clean with his rag, and handed Walker down from the high car on to western soil. It had to be Walker. It could be no one else. There he stood, dishevelled, panting, his long English hair hanging down; pure poetry. Froelich had one thought as he looked at him; it was: he isn't real, he's a toy. He looked, immediately, so lost, so deculturalized, that Froelich, controlling the urge to rush forward and meet him, stayed in his car and savoured the experience.

'This is it, suh, Bushville,' said the conductor, grinning. 'Sure this where you want to be?'

Walker seemed not to be sure at all. He looked around twice, as if to make sure that what he was seeing was true – he was in the middle of nowhere. The countryside around him was completely, endlessly flat, the only horizon a vague haze that prevented him looking downhill clear to Chicago. In this haze, like big white icebergs, stood indeterminate white shapes, the forms of distant barns and farm buildings. The scene offered only two sensations, of levelness, and dryness. Only the unwavering, shining tracks of the railroad formed a reasonable order, a firm hard line of ingress and egress. Froelich, watching Walker, saw it all anew, in its strange and challenging poverty.

'Oh!' said Walker nervously, evidently wondering whether he could possibly get back on the train; the High Plains always took people that way. What clearly worried him was the fact that there appeared not to be any town, any *place*, here at all; presumably he was thinking that the train had simply stopped at some chance spot on the route, at someone's whimsy, and they had simply decided to put him off. No doubt he was assuming that he would be left to wander about the deserted landscape until, stricken with sunstroke and starving, he stumbled into a drain and died. Froelich could imagine the feeling, the special foreign shiver, the English nervousness (were there Indians, and if so were they friendly?). It was an old experience that the west had always given, felt the sharper now because of the distance this man had come. It was the first lesson, and Froelich lay back and watched while it sank in. This moment, which he had created, was one that he wanted to be a central one in Walker's life.

The porter came down from the coach again and placed beside Walker, to bedeck the barren scene, his two suitcases and his typewriter, all generously covered in flapping labels explaining who he was and where he was supposed to be going, labels that assumed men to read and helpers to direct. The word *Fulbright* stood out, in red letters, appealing to a standard of civilization and urbanity that went without saying in the seaboard states, but said precisely nothing in those western deadlands. Fulbright? Now the porter had taken the ... dime, was it? ... that Walker, confident in his largesse, had given him, and had jumped back into the car and pulled up the steps. The locomotive shrieked, the wheels turned and painfully yet gently the train moved out, the faces of the passengers turning inward again. Left alone, silent, bare, Walker stood for a moment, looking after it. Then he turned and looked at the plain again, waiting for something to happen. Nothing did. Froelich, extending the golden moment, pulled in his feet and imagined the growing doubt in Walker, and within it the profound and English confidence. Froelich knew the English and was a devout Anglophile; he had a psychiatric fascination with the race. People, that English mind would now be thinking, were not left stranded in the middle of what was, after all, a reasonably civilized country. Action was surely being taken. The only question was, what was the action, how was it being taken, what did one do to put oneself in the way of it? There was nothing here except a shuttered house and an apparently empty car. There were no telephones in evidence, no taxis, no people. Froelich, peering with fascination through the spokes of the driving wheel, watched the anxious face turn from side to side. Still the figure made no move, standing there in his baggy country suit, the English genius, the man who was to change Party. The suit was made of thick Harris tweed, and Froelich could see, from this distance, the beads of sweat forming on his brow and dripping on to the jacket, forming pearly droplets on the tips of its shaggy fibres. For this western sun, the getup was farcical, and in a sense noble. Froelich, in spirit, wanted to applaud.

And now Walker suddenly seemed to resolve his dilemma. He buttoned up his tweed jacket, picked up his suitcases, tucking the typewriter under his arm, and began to stride confidently along the tracks as if he had made up his mind to walk back to New York, two thousand miles to the east. Froelich, in whom there was endless fascination but no cruelty, felt he had let the matter go on long enough. Now he wanted to know and love this man. He opened the car door and hurried after Walker, who was stepping off into the skyline like the end of a supremely hopeful movie. He wanted to succour him, to save him, to win him in friendship. He was a genius and a soulmate, and it was he, Froelich, who had won him for the west. Froelich prided himself on his cosmopolitanism; he had, so to speak, graduated from England, and had a special love of its men and its minds. He had done the voyage in reverse; he had had a Fulbright to London University. There he had been almost odiously American, as Walker now was being English; in the British Museum, in the professional academic hush, he would lean over some English scholar, smelling as musty as the books he was reading, and say, 'Say, *those* books look interesting. More interesting than mine.' But now, back home, he usually wore imported British shoes and spoke with an imported British accent; they were part of his academic style. Harris Bourbon, his department head, one day had stopped him in the doorway of the faculty lounge and complimented him on his looks – skilful use of tweed sports-jacket, briar pipe, hair cut slightly long. 'I like your style, Dr Froelich; all you need now are a few publications,' he had said, puffing on *his* briar and knocking the ash off *his* tweeds (he was a local man who had been a Rhodes Scholar in the twenties). Froelich was so touched by England as to be, in a sentimental way, something of a monarchist. 'I think he's a communist; he says the United States ought to have a *king*,' one intense girl student of his had complained when she went to Bourbon to ask to have Froelich fired. Froelich could hardly wait to introduce Walker to all these congenial sympathies, to show him that here he could be at home. 'Hi! hi!' he shouted. Walker turned, saw Froelich, and increased speed perceptibly. Froelich caught up and tugged at the tail of his jacket, jerking him to a standstill and tumbling his suitcases round him. 'Hey there, old fruit,' he said. 'It's good to see you.' He held out his hand in hospitality.

'How do you do?' said Walker, not taking it. 'I wonder whether you could give me some directions?'

'You are James Walker, aren't you?' asked Froelich. The evidence was plentiful; there could scarcely be two such Englishmen wandering the plains in this way: but there was just faint room for doubt. Walker had been classically vague about his arrival; his cablegram had said, with simple purity, '*Arrive station 5 p.m. Walker.*' Isn't that cute? everyone had said; one of the graduate assistants had taken it home to frame it. Meanwhile Harris Bourbon had assigned various members of the faculty to cover the three train stations and, as an after-thought, the three bus depots in a thirty-mile radius, at one of which, he hoped, Walker would arrive. This was the west; there was no station in Party. It had been suggested in the Department that the heavens would open up at five and Walker would descend in a golden car, like Juno in *The Tempest*, but though this had been dismissed as improbable everyone felt that one didn't know with the English. Subdued excitement had grown; and thus, even now, faculty members up to the rank of distinguished service professor were bound-ing up to strangers in places of public concourse throughout the state, asking the question Froelich was now putting. But of course Froelich had struck lucky; Walker's face shone, as if a new bulb had been put in, and said, 'Yes, I'm Walker. Are you someone from the university?'

'That's right,' said Froelich, 'my name's Bernard Froelich, and I'm an associate professor in the English Department here. Look, you weren't leaving, were you?'

'Oh, no, not at all!' said Walker.

They shook hands, and then Froelich reached out and took the two suitcases as Walker bent to retrieve them.

'Not going anywhere special?' asked Froelich.

'No,' said Walker.

'Good, that's fine. We'd hate to lose you now you've got this far. We've all been looking forward to having you here very much.'

'No, I was just looking.'

'Looking?' said Froelich, stepping out toward the car. 'Where is it?'

'It?'

'The university.'

'Oh, that. Well, we're about fifteen miles out of town here.'

'Rather a funny place to put a railway station, isn't it?'

Froelich began to laugh; it took a finished social world, twenty generations of teapots and civilization, to produce a remark, indeed a cultural artifact, like that. 'You see, there's no railway station' – it was a pleasure for Froelich to use the English phrase – 'in Party itself. The western habit is just to drop you off in nowhere. Of course there's a good historical reason. The railroad was built before most of these towns were settled. People went further west before they came to Party. What you have here is the Great Plains – the high plain west of the platte that Cooper said was like the steppes of Tartary. It's all treeless, shortgrass prairie, buffalo country; people thought it was unfit for cultivation. In fact, a lot of people around still think the same.'

'I can imagine,' said Walker, 'it's very unvaried. It doesn't look like a landscape. Just a concatenation of circumstances.'

'That's right,' said Froelich, reaching the Pontiac and opening up the trunk, 'when you come out here you have to develop a new brand of aesthetics. I'm still groping for mine; I'm a stranger here myself.'

'Is this your car?'

'That's right,' said Froelich. In fact the car wasn't his but Harris Bourbon's; Harris, knowing the broken-down state of Froelich's own automobile, had lent him his expressly for the purpose of hunting down Walker and bringing him to the English Department faculty lounge, wherein the faculty were even now assembled and currently passing bowls of pretzels over one another's heads and developing a tension over the new arrival. 'You look after it very well,' said Walker. Froelich realized they were in the midst of one of those Anglo-American confusions that gave life such relish; he had simply meant that it was the car he was driving. But Walker had meant, of course, as he ought to have known, do you possess this car? Is it your property? Ergo, do you exist? The English, Froelich recalled, didn't think they'd described anything until they'd said to whom it belonged. 'Like it?' asked Froelich.

'It's very big, isn't it?'

Froelich got in behind the wheel and noticed that Walker was waiting politely outside until, presumably, Froelich unlocked the passenger door, which was not of course locked – this was the west. 'Come on in,' said Froelich, reaching over and pushing it open. 'If there's anything you want you don't see, just ask.'

Walker got in and sat close to the door, his hands on his knees.

'Do you drive?' asked Froelich.

'No,' said Walker, looking ahead through the windshield.

'Well, I'm afraid you won't get by in this section of the country without a car of your own. As you've seen, the public sector of life isn't very well supplied out here. We're all individualists. You'll have to learn.'

'I'm quite prepared to,' said Walker.

'Here,' said Froelich, 'why don't you try? There's nothing round here you could hit.'

Walker looked nervously at him and said, 'No, I'd better not.'

Froelich pressed a button and the windows went up and down; he pressed another and the seat whirled upward and backward. Walker looked even more frightened. 'We have all the gadgets,' said Froelich. 'Do they make cars like this in England?'

'I wouldn't know, I ride a bike.'

'Well, let's go,' said Froelich. 'I hope you don't mind meeting a lot of people. Out here you're a real celebrity, because we get so few visitors.'

'I'm a bit nervous of big gatherings,' said Walker.

Froelich, looking for signs of stature and genius, felt a faint wave of disappointment, sensing that here was a man not quite cut out for his destiny. This did not lessen his genial regard for him; if anything, it increased it. But it did mean that more depended upon him, Froelich, the man who had claimed stature for Walker and was determined that he should have it. 'You'll like the people here; they're simpler than they would be in the east, but they have a lot of style and interest. The west's a special place, another state of mind,' he said, switching on the ignition and letting out the clutch. The car reversed and smacked into the paling fence behind them. 'Jesus,' said Froelich, 'what was that?' He looked at Walker, who appeared to have noticed nothing; he gazed steadily ahead into his future. Froelich fiddled with the gearstick and let out the clutch again. The fence swayed in his driving mirror but the car failed to move. 'We'll have to wait a second,' said Froelich. 'We're in some trouble.' He got out and went round the back to survey the tangle. The fender was neatly fixed over a metal spike.

'Oh dear,' said Walker, coming round the other side of the car.

'Well, that's how it is,' said Froelich, 'no matter how careful you are, there's always the other fellow.'

'Bit of a mess, isn't it?'

'Isn't it?' said Froelich.

'You must have been in reverse,' said Walker, his longish roundish English face peering seriously into the damage, as if a word or two from him might rectify the situation.

'Well,' said Froelich, 'don't just do something, stand there. Now look, will you give me a little help? Why don't you bounce up and down on the fender, and I'll try to drive her out.'

'All right,' said Walker.

As Froelich got into the car again, he was worried. Though luckily I have tenure, he thought. Still, the idea of damaging Bourbon's new car wasn't very freshening. However, the sight he now had in his mirror, of Walker pumping himself up and down on the fender, his eyes round with surprise, his expression serious and slightly dispirited, as if to imply that this was not quite what he was used to – this reminded Froelich that he was living out a classic day. He could have wished for a photograph; it would have been a superb illustration for his book. He released the clutch again and let the car go gently forward. The fender on Bourbon's new car stood up as it might have been expected to do on a highly finished piece of modern engineering, the flower of American experiment – it ripped away from the bodywork and fell with a loud clang to the ground. Walker toppled precipitously from his perch. 'Come on, Mr Walker, jump in before someone sees us,' shouted Froelich through the window, noticing that the fence was also down. Walker got in dejectedly and put his hands on his knees again, saying nothing; Froelich drove off at some speed. 'What happened back there, Mr Walker?' he asked when they were on the open road.

'The bumper came off and the fence broke when I fell on it.'

'You fell on the fence? I hope you're not hurt.'

'As it happens, I don't think I am,' said Walker. He looked displeased and Froelich grew worried for the friendship he felt was growing between them.

'So, here you have it, the shortgrass plain,' Froelich gestured out of the car, 'your spiritual home for the year.' The land was flat and lightly cultivated. Corn stood, seemingly withered, in the fields, in gross misshapen clumps. A sign on a barn end said: *Chew Mail Pouch Tobacco. Treat Yourself to the Best.* Strange prehistoric mating calls, ferocious cries, sounded out of the haze. It was the whistle of the train Walker had come on, heading out towards the Rockies. Dust flitted into the car. 'It's hot here,' said Walker.

'This is about the average for the season. Actually you're fine if you dress for the climate. You'll feel it as long as you stick to those clothes.'

'I'm certainly sticking to them now,' said Walker. This touch of whimsicality didn't soften his face, which still seemed to detest all that was happening to it. Froelich grew embarrassed, as if it was he who had brought this man here to make him unhappy.

He said, 'Why don't you loosen your necktie?'

'I'm all right, thank you. In a new place you have to be careful not to catch cold.'

'I suppose so,' said Froelich, driving close to the centre line, not quite sure how wide the car was. A farm truck coming the other way made him swerve over, and he ran up on the shoulder, tilting the car and scattering gravel. Walker winced and put his hands on the instrument panel. Froelich began to hope piously that he would get Walker to Party alive. There might be faint credit in being found dead in a roadside smash with a distinguished British novelist, but Froelich had more complicated plans for Walker than that. He hoped he was going the right way to achieve them, but with one thing and another the relationship didn't seem to be taking the turn he would have wished. He tried anew. 'Tell me, Mr Walker,' he said, 'are you an Oggsford marn?'

Walker looked at him and said, 'Pardon?'

'Did you go to Oxford?'

'No,' said Walker. 'To tell the truth, I went to one of the provincial universities.' Froelich knew this – he had researched his subject thoroughly, and knew all the essential factual details, even down to Walker's poor degree – but he wanted to prompt some of that intense social observation that had made Walker's name hit the quarterlies.

'Which one?' he asked.

'You won't have heard of it.'

'Why won't I?' asked Froelich, rather stung at this.

'It's not particularly well known.'

'I've been in England.'

'Oh, very nice. Which part?'

'All of it, it's not so goddam big.'

'Well, it's big enough,' said Walker.

Froelich was a sure, confident man, not used to rebuffs, and it came hard to him to discover that he was doing very badly in this relationship, one he had come to prize intensely. He had been thinking about Walker for weeks, worrying about him, planning this good day, planning this good year. But as he looked at Walker, his side pressed against the side of the car, he felt his failure. Was he pushing too hard? That, of course, the English didn't like; there was something craggy and hard about their personalities that discouraged access. Americans knew this problem of old. Froelich could remember saying to his wife, in the Earl's Court days, as they sat lonely and huddled for warmth over the one-bar gas fire, beneath that iron there's solid gold. You've simply got to keep chipping away, and forget the notion that if you haven't established a relationship in the first five minutes these people don't want to know you. They don't spend themselves in relationships until they know what the odds are; long hours spent as babies lying in the rain outside greengrocers' shops have made them tough.

So they drove on in silence for a bit, the big car humming on the concrete. Now wide low automobiles, their visages set in bright metal grins, began to flip by them; here and there, a large hog, lowslung and menacing, rooted on wire-fenced land. Occasionally they saw a steer, carrying with it the whole ethic of the west. These were lands that Froelich had come slowly to love, and he wanted to share them, but Walker seemed only to gaze on them in mystery, as if vainly trying to discover their imaginative principle. He tried again and said: 'What do you think of America, old boy?'

'I don't know yet,' said Walker. 'I think it's confusing. I can never make up my mind whether people are being friendly or hostile. Most of the time they seem to be both simultaneously. And in New York . . . well, in New York I never knew whether I was going to be welcomed or murdered. You don't know who to trust.'

Trust me, Froelich wanted to say, except that he wasn't trustworthy. He said, 'I suppose we make relationships differently.'

'If that's what they are. I was beginning to think that in America relationships had nothing to do with people at all.'

'I can see that. We make up our minds first and then spray the attitudes we have on to the people we meet. Not like jolly old England.'

'No, quite.'

'Talking of relationships, are you married?'

'I'm not a homosexual, if that's what you mean.'

'I didn't mean that.'

'Oh, sorry, so many Americans seem to think that Englishmen are.'

'No, I tell you, I've been to England, you can go easy with me.'

'Well, yes, I am married,' said Walker, as if he was loath to make the confession.

'Good, that's nice. Any kids?'

Again there was a silence, until Walker forced himself to say, 'One.'

'A girl or a boy?'

'A girl.'

'Great.'

'It's all right, I suppose,' said Walker.

'Why didn't you bring them along with you?'

'The money wasn't good enough,' said Walker, as if pleased to be slightly discourteous again.

'You should have written and told us. We might have been able to rustle up a grant from somewhere.'

'Well, no,' said Walker. 'Actually, I think I shall work better on my own.'

'Are you planning to do some work out here? I mean, besides your teaching?'

'I want to start another book, if I get the time and the ideas.'

'Well, this really is the place. You couldn't come to a better one. It's a really creative atmosphere. All the men write books and all the women get pregnant. One long fertility rite. I suppose the point really is that we're so cut off there's nothing else to do.'

'I see,' said Walker. 'Do you write?'

'I'm writing a scholarly book, but I don't write novels, if that was your question. I have this block: I can't bear to put my friends down on paper.'

'I suppose someone has to stand by and watch.'

'Oh, I do that,' said Froelich. He was pleased to see that Walker was growing more genial; the day brightened again for him, like the sun coming out on the dark plain.

'By the way,' said Walker, growing forthcoming. 'I met someone you probably know coming over from England on the boat.'

'Did you? Who was that?'

'Someone who teaches here at Benedict Arnold, a man called Jochum.'

'You met Jochum?' cried Froelich. It was a name that brought Froelich no pleasure at all, and he was worried to think that someone else not of his spirit might have reached this man first, have taught him about a different west and a different Benedict Arnold.

'Yes,' said Walker patiently. 'He was on the *same ship*.'

'There's a person you need to watch,' said Froelich.

Walker bristled and grew distant again. 'He seemed a very pleasant man indeed,' he said.

'Oh, he's pleasant. We have a whole crowd of those people. They're our *emigré* colony. They all play chess and eat apfelstrudel together. And shake their fingers at you. "Ach, mein friendt, you Americans, you are zo innocent, zo liberal." '

'That's it,' said Walker. 'Nice man.'

'Yes, good with the finger.'

Walker went silent once more. They drove past more hogs, more gullies, more cars. 'Tell me something, Mr Walker,' said Froelich, after some minutes. 'What's all this you've been getting so mad about over there in England?'

'Mad?'

The point of Froelich's question was that Walker had been described in the press as 'an angry young man'. He had been pictured in *Time* magazine, leaning against a tree, in the rain, a long scarf down to his crotch, over the caption: 'Phoneys make me puke.' Froelich had the clipping in his wallet, along with several others about Walker. But far from seeming, now, angry, Walker looked excessively phlegmatic. As for being an angry *young* man, he didn't look all that young either – though the English were notoriously deceptive, since none of them took enough exercise, except those who took too much. He was going bald; his stomach was potted; he wore a dotard's knitted cardigan, and his suit made him look as if he had been rolled over by a sheep. The general impression suggested middle age. Nor, clearly, was he a scintillating conversationalist, if this car ride represented his talents in that direction; in fact, you couldn't get a tweet out of him. Froelich was still prepared and ready to respect him, but truth to tell he had been expecting, when he drove out to the depot, someone a bit more like Tom Wolfe or D. H. Lawrence, someone burning with tension, articulate about his plan for saving the world. Walker looked like that kind of Englishman who seems to have been rained on too much. Froelich said: 'Aren't you an angry young man?'

Walker said, angrily, 'No.'

'This angry young man business just doesn't make sense to me,' said Froelich. 'The way I understand it, and I may be wrong on this, but the way I see it is that a lot of fellows who have been sent free to university by the government are complaining that the government is lowering standards by letting fellows like them in. I suppose this is English liberalism.'

'I'm not one,' said Walker. 'Admittedly there are a lot of things I dislike about England just now. I've written about some of them.'

'What kind of things?'

'Well, I think we're being over-Americanized, for a start.'

'How tough,' said Froelich.

'I didn't mean to be rude.'

'No, I agree with you.'

'I mean that we take the wrong things and we use them badly. It means American hamburgers that don't taste like hamburgers and American television programmes of the worst rather than the best kind. . . . I'd like us to take other things, some of the excitement and freedom that Americans seem to have. But I'm not an angry young man. It's a silly label and I hope it won't be pinned on me. It makes me so furious.'

'Oh, don't worry,' said Froelich, trying to forget the posters for Walker's public lecture in the Fogle Auditorium (which he still didn't know about) which, draped all over Humanities Hall and the English Building, used the phrase with what Froelich now recollected as ceaseless repetition. 'So you came to the States for the excitement of it?' asked Froelich.

'Yes, if it really exists. Does it?'

'Well, you'll see. I think you'll find a certain amount of excitement in Party. It's mainly a university town.'

'Where is it?' asked Walker.

'Don't worry, *that* really exists. It's over this next rise. You'll see it in a couple of minutes.'

'So there's plenty going on, is there?'

'Intellectually? Yes, I suppose there is. Scrabble, red-baiting, wife-swapping. The auditorium series brings visiting plays and orchestras. There's an art theatre just off campus, mainly showing Sellers and Bergman. There's a university bookstore with the best selection of ring-binders in the state. It's a mixed campus. We teach things like driver education and animal husbandry, but the English Department, well, they're not entirely committed men, but they have character. I don't know how you'd measure it against the civilization you come from. My guess is that you'll find what you take for granted in England is only veneer out here in Party. But that's the thrill, I think. Oh, there's one thing. It's a dry campus. There are no liquor stores in Party. If you go into the bars they serve 2.5 beer. To buy real liquor you have to go a couple of miles away from campus.'

'Why is that?' asked Walker.

'It's a state law. Benedict Arnold is slightly paradoxical in that it's both a private and a state university. We draw on some state funds. This means that the state has some power over us, and that means they can keep us dry and also apply the loyalty oath. In fact, because of our constitution, their rights are a little hazy, and we keep challenging them. You'll see some activity in that direction while you're here, I would guess. Are you a liberal?'

'Yes,' said Walker, 'I think I am.'

'Good.'

At that moment the car topped a rise and they could see the town, quite suddenly, laid out on the slope in front of them. It was set in trees. They drove downward to meet it. As they did so, they could see, on the long dark line of the horizon, something new. Where the grey grasslands seemed to end, a row of wigwam-like formations, some straight, some tilted, some grey-brown in colour, others streaked with green, some touched at the top with white, were scribbled upwards into the sky. Froelich heard Walker gasp at his side. 'What's that?' he asked.

'Those are the Rockies.'

Walker said, 'Aren't they marvellous?'

Froelich looked at him and loved the man. The eye, embedded in that cold flesh, saw, then; passion could take root, enthusiasm grow, in that fleshy rind. Froelich warmed, as he had intended to do, to his genius, and felt the man grow in stature.

Walker too knew an occasion when he saw one. 'Actually,' he said, 'I think I will take off my tie.'

'Do that,' said Froelich. He watched Walker spread the great wings of his collar wide, English-style, as in old movies, across the lapels of his jacket. The gesture was important: it was assertion of comradeship and commitment; it was an abandonment of a whole culture; it was a promise that here was a man who would yield and give something to America and to Party. Froelich knew that there was more than a collar to be undone over these next few months. 'There,' he said, feeling a strange warm glow of triumph and promise, 'now you're a beatnik.'

Walker looked at the mountains and knew that they had come just at the right time. For the Walker who descended from the transcontinental flyer into the middle of the American void, and now sat beside his terrifying companion in the car, washed over by landscape and incomprehensible discourse, was not the man, was less than the man, who had sailed in, a few days before, past the Statue of Liberty with a note of hope in his spirit. So much had happened since then; and all of it was bad. What was sought, on his part, was sense and design; what was offered, on the world's part, was the other – violence and meaninglessness and anarchy. Was this then the promise, the liberty? If it was, why grumble at chains? The days had gone by, immersing him in disjunction. What New York had begun, the train journey westward had finished. For nearly two days now he had sat in lowered spirits as the train perambulated the country, while cities faded and were replaced by untiring plain. The tree became a forgotten European elegance. Onward they drifted, coursing, bells ringing, through the backs of middle-western towns and cities, where grey cupolas had peered through the window glass at him over liquor stores, and where networks of iron fire-escapes had competed with high-tension wires to give a sense of temporariness and disorder and clutter. The towns were as he expected Russian towns to be, half-staked settlements clinging to the steppe. Dogs in dustbowls celebrated a somnolent deadness; small boys exposed their genitals on ashpits; birds with heavy feet plodded about the landscape. America grew vaster and vaster, then the train had stopped, to deposit him and him alone, to put him between naked sky and naked ground, to leave him stranded where his style and his thoughts bounced against shimmering mirages and unwatered desert.

And from out of the desert, like a djinn in the Arabian Nights, had come Froelich, big and bouncy, threatening and cajoling, all bonhomous destruction, demanding an accounting. In the car, watching the concrete road stretch ahead of him into the unpromising future, Walker thought again of home. A faint name stated itself: it said, Elaine, Elaine. Walker wanted to let it go, wanted to be here, but it sang and sang. Froelich picked it up, as if by intuition, and twisted it with a question. It needed the mountains, and they came. He had seen the Rockies, wigwams of stone, and the seed that had grown enough to bring him here began to sprout again. They dominated the sky and designed it. Below them, as if in response, the world began to change. Signs began to flick past. They said WATCH FOR SNOWPLOWS and YIELD and REACH FOR A CIGARETTE AND DIE. A few houses appeared on each side of the highway; a sign said THICKLY SETTLED. Then a vast spread of roadside services appeared, small restaurants and diners and service stations, recognizing human existence and human need. They addressed the traveller with monosyllabic communications, clearly knowing he must be exhausted: EAT, they said, and GAS and SLEEP and (rather more mysteriously) WORMS. Then came the boundary of the citadel, the social note: a sign said *Party : Pop. 15,000 Happy People and a Few Soreheads*. The Lions, declared a sign adjacent, met lunchtime Thursdays in the Van Der Pelt Sunshine Hotel. The Hallelujah Baptist Church on Main Street was 'the Church where Jesus is REAL.' The K.K.K. Motel was recommended by the A.A.A. Here was life and God and love; all these things could still go on, even out here; man in his

163

inexhaustible inventiveness could be social anywhere. That in itself gave a sort of hope.

'Here we go!' cried Froelich, waving his hand around him, 'Party!' The car wobbled and he grabbed the wheel again. 'There's your neighbourhood shopping centre, out here we buy our groceries.' Walker looked out at a large expanse of parking lot, around which a few stores had congregated; the Grabiteria, advertising a free bear's paw with a five-dollar food order, a laundromat called the Doozy Duds, and an establishment called the Big 'n' Beefy dominated by a sign showing a gross, meatladen hamburger. A few girls clad in clothes that suggested they had just come off the line of chorus girls at the theatre walked among cars carrying small trays. Then came society of greater complication yet. The fire station, a palace of crystal with an incongruous Swiss chalet roof, looked like a romp of Eero Saarinen; the court house, one block later, was a domed institution in high gothic style, capped with a lead roof and defended on two sides by a Civil War cannon, muzzle packed with paper, and a small naval aircraft missing its propeller. Loungers sat on the low walls around, chewing Mail Pouch tobacco and reflecting with all the sagacity of the local yokel on the passing parade.

'Can we stop at the post office?' said Walker, feeling vastly better, able to plan and to prognosticate. 'I'd like to send a telegram. It's to abroad.'

'You can't send a telegram from the post office,' said Froelich. 'You send it through Western Union.'

'Where's that?' asked Walker.

'Oh, you can call them from my place.'

'We're going to your place?' asked Walker.

'I guess you want to wash up.'

'Wash up?'

'You know, clean yourself up a bit.'

'I see,' said Walker, relieved. 'Well, if it won't inconvenience the university. . . . ' And indeed he did want to go to the lavatory; he had not liked to go on the train, because he was afraid of missing his destination, and that little walk up the line into the desert, which had perplexed Froelich so, was no more than a search for a public convenience. Now to be clean and new was Walker's first ambition. He looked out at the town. A prairie schooner stood out on Main Street, and a number of the inhabitants, walking through the stretch of active life that extended from Penneys, where farm overalls hung in the windows, to the First National Bank, which was giving away free balloons, wore prospectors' beards and string ties. Two rodeo riders horsed showily down the street, blocking traffic and delighting the tourists heading west, canvas sacks of water hanging off their fenders. The motif of ancient and modern was repeated right through the town centre: here was a store in glass and aluminium, where ski clothes and western boots shrivelled in the sun-glare, and there was a Victorian structure in gargoyle style, called the Van Der Pelt Sunshine Hotel ('Party's Coolest Finest Driest Martini'). Of the university there was no sign, no hint, almost no possibility.

'Where's the college?' asked Walker.

'Doesn't look like the place where you could have one, huh?' said Froelich. 'Well, that's about right. Still, Party does have its provincial virtues. Actually you have to drive eighty miles to the state capital – Dimity – to find out the right time, but time is, after all, a relative concept. No, the university's just out on the edge of town.'

'How do you mean? *Why* don't you know the time?'

'All the townships round here can vote their own time. There's sometimes a two-hour difference between two settlements five miles apart. That's what we call out here *real* democracy.'

'It sounds like anarchy, to me,' said Walker.

'Well, that's right, that's another word that fits the case. That's what people forget about the States. They think it's a land of conservatism and conformity. Okay, there is that, there's plenty of it out here, and you'll meet it. But the important thing is that at bottom America is free-floating and anarchic. You'll find it in the students. The real Americans are the free-floating, do-anything students who don't believe in a goddam thing except life. Riding on the back of history, flux and flow.'

'Well, I have some sympathy with that,' said Walker, 'but I think I take a stand on time.'

'Yeah, that figures. The English think of time as being made in England . . . all that Greenwich Mean Time bit. Greenwich Mean . . . that's *real* time, the fundamental absolute time, and you can live by it because no one's challenged it yet. They may do but they haven't yet. But in the States we have five time-zones, *and* variations locally. So we know time is relative . . . you can manipulate it, cheat it.' Froelich took the car around three bermuda-shorted girls who were crossing the street, and said 'Hi, luscious,' through the window at the one nearest to him. 'Hello, fella,' said the girl.

'Am I the man I was ten years ago?' asked Froelich. 'I believe, as an American, no. I'm not the man I was last week. Now you . . . you *know* what you are. You stay the same, through every situation. You put out the flags, old school tie, Englishman's suit, all the fitments that keep you right there in line. But what's the line? Who made the line? Our clothes change with our personalities. We change our whole psychological and physiological systems when we go from one room to another. Call me Proteus.'

'Everyone sees foreigners as more static than they are,' said Walker. 'That's because the first thing you identify us by is by our nationality. I don't lead the moral life of my father. . . .'

'Sure,' said Froelich. 'That's right. But *we* don't even *remember* our fathers.'

Now they had reached the residential part of town. Great boat-like American cars oozed past on the streets, and slid silently up driveways sprigged with exotic greenery. The houses behind were white and shiny in the sun. Housewives sipped cool drinks on patios; sprinklers revolved on green lawns; there was an aroma of peace, and no one seemed put out about time at all. Walker looked at the life and liked it. 'This is where the fathers live,' said Froelich. 'Republicans and proto-fascists. You can bet there's a bomb shelter under every patio. Rigged out with machine guns to keep the hicks from downtown getting in.'

Presently Froelich turned the car off the street and parked in the driveway of a small, noticeably unpainted property with a long decaying porch. 'Well, this is it,' he said, opening up the car door. 'It takes a heap o' heapin' to make a heap a heap, as the Hoosier poet once said.'

'I suppose so,' said Walker, getting out too.

'It does. Sometimes I have the urge to set fire to the goddam thing and collect on the insurance. But it's all right. Anticonspicuous consumption. It has real style.'

They walked up the path. Suddenly some trigger mechanism in the lawn sprinkler turned it through ninety degrees and it sprayed fine water brightly over Walker's tweeds. Froelich had stepped up on to the porch and opened the screen door.

'Hi! hi!' he shouted.

'Hi!' said a female voice.

'Come on in,' said Froelich.

Walker stepped into the entrance, which gave directly on to a living-room furnished in modern, or primitive, style, the general aim of which seemed to be to suggest that one wasn't buying real furniture since one might be moving to a better place soon. There was an old divan, and four chairs made of tangerine canvas stretched over a metal frame, and shaped for people with two heads. The bookcases along the walls were of unvarnished planks and unpainted bricks. Over them hung a medley of decorational devices: Aztec masks, bongo drums, spears, and a Speed map of Leicestershire. Hi-fi wires trailed around the walls and there were unpainted speakers in at least two corners; the record player itself stood on a shelf, all its technology exposed. An opening gave directly into a bedroom, where an unmade bed was evident, on it a nightdress, a girdle, and two empty Coke bottles.

'Hi!' said Patrice Froelich, coming out of the kitchen. She was wearing a shift dress which made her look as if she might be pregnant; she had dark hair and a delicate thin face. 'This is Mr Walker,' said Froelich.

'Hello,' said Patrice, holding out her hand, 'you're all wet.'

'She is good, isn't she?' Froelich said.

'Oh, very,' said Walker.

'Well, don't be so goddam polite,' said Froelich. 'Say what you mean around here.'

'I did mean it. Your wife's a very attractive woman.'

'Damn right she is,' said Froelich.

'Would you care to use the bathroom?' asked Patrice.

'Oh yes,' said Walker, relieved. 'I've been wanting to go to the lavatory for ages.'

'Show him the john, Bernie.'

'Right here,' said Froelich. He led Walker to the bathroom, on the door of which hung a little card which Froelich turned to reveal a message saying *Seat occupied. United Airlines.*

Walker sat in the toilet and heard the Froelichs laughing outside. It made him uncomfortable. Once he heard Bernard Froelich say: 'What a character.' At one point something seemed to be being shouted at him. A moment later the door was pushed open. Walker, sitting there contemplatively, crossed his hands in front of his face and said, 'Go away.'

'I just wanted to know, martini or Manhattan?' said Froelich, adding, 'what have you got to hide?'

'Martini,' said Walker. When he came out, Froelich stood outside the door, stirring martinis with a glass stick. 'Pardon me,' he said, 'you know how it is. This is the free-and-easy west.'

'Quite,' said Walker.

'Don't mind Bernie,' said Patrice. 'He's a psycho case from way back. Well, you're here. That's good. I hope you like Party.'

'Let's go outside on to the porch,' said Froelich, 'and really get to know one another.'

'Well, take it easy,' said Patrice. 'I expect Mr Walker's had a really tiring journey. How was it?'

'Yes, tiring,' said Walker.

'He'd be disappointed if we didn't keep up that fast pace of living they talk about all the time in England,' said Froelich. 'Okay, now let's ask him some really searching questions. Look, sit over there out of the sun. Where we can't see you.'

'I love that suit,' said Patrice, 'is that Harris?'

'Yes,' said Walker, 'it's all wet.'

'You want to change into something of Bernie's?'

'No, he doesn't,' said Froelich. 'What are you trying to do, destroy his character? That suit is his nature. Don't worry, the sun's hot, it'll dry right away.'

'Speaking of Harris,' said Patrice. 'Is that right you're staying with the Bourbons?'

'Harris is Bourbon's first name,' said Froelich.

'That's right,' said Walker. 'He invited me to stay there until I found somewhere suitable to live.'

'Very good,' said Patrice, 'though we could have taken you in here. You'd have liked that better.'

'Yes, why not?' asked Froelich. 'We intended to ask you, but Harris got in first.'

'Oh, I can't do that,' said Walker.

'Well, okay, if you can't, you can't.'

'No, he's right, Bernie, he already made an arrangement.'

'I guess not, it's just that Bourbon has these crazy kids. They'll give you a terrible time.'

'Yeah, we should have warned him ahead of time. Then he could have come here.'

'What's the matter with these kids?' asked Walker suspiciously.

'Well,' said Patrice, 'the oldest boy, that's Crispin, is a j.d., a juvenile delinquent. He graduates from high school next year.'

'Then he'll be an adult delinquent,' said Froelich. 'That's progress; if you're going to be a delinquent, why be juvenile about it?'

'What does he actually *do*?' asked Walker.

'Oh, he runs around with a funny crowd, steals cars and drives them off cliffs for kicks, takes drugs, that kind of thing. I'd guess you'd say he was a normal child of intellectual parents. If intellectual is the word for Harris Bourbon.'

'He's shook up,' said Patrice. 'They all are, but he's extrovert and has become a delinquent, whereas all the best kids

169

round here are introvert and become psychotics. I much prefer that kind.'

'That's right,' said Froelich. 'What we need in this country is a government that will come out on the desirability of suicide over murder.'

'Then there are the twins. The Bourbons abstained for about twelve years after they had Crispin, cut out intercourse entirely. I guess they felt it had failed, once they saw Crispin. It worries *me* sometimes. But then they went to it again and came up with these twins.'

'I guess, if there are any real measurements on these things, they're worse.'

'How?' asked Walker.

'Well, they figured they were too permissive with Crispin, so they tried to repress the twins, made them hate their father and venerate him and all. Dr Bourbon worked on his super-ego and developed a bunch of authoritarian traits. My guess is they'll ask you to try some of that English discipline on them. Dr Bourbon had a cane shipped over from England. Brandy, that's the girl twin, hit him across the face with it. He was two days in the hospital.'

'I told Bourbon he should have stayed continent or tried adultery, but this monstrous sexuality bowed him down.'

'What's he like?' asked Walker.

'Harris? Oh, well, what *is* he like, Patty? I find it so goddam hard to remember him once he's out of the room.'

'Well, he's a sort of cross between Dr Johnson and a Texas cowpoke. He's sort of impressively unimpressive.'

'No, he's not. I'd say he's even unimpressively unimpressive. When I went out there this morning to borrow his ca . . . his electric mixer, he was out shooting bottles in his yard in a Brooks Brothers suit. That seems to me a kind of basic image of him. And he said to me, waving this revolver at my gut, "Ho, there, boy, you know, son, this her-ed-it-ary business gits mo' and mo' mysterious to me ivery day. Alphonse, that's one of mah little fellars, he come into the bunkhouse this mo'nin' at sunup and his maw said sumpn or other to hum and, you know, he started to laugh. Ah bin scratchin' mah brains all day but it still don't figger. Cause his maw and me – we don't *niver* laugh." '

'Oh come on, Bernie, you're giving Mr Walker the wrong impression.'

'I don't believe so.'

'Why does he have a revolver?' asked Walker.

'Well, this is the west, you know, Jamie,' said Froelich. 'It's really tough country. Out here, well, a fella gotta be able to defend himself. Keep your mouth buttoned and shoot from the hip.'

'Don't believe him,' said Patrice.

'You shoot a-tall, Mis' Walker?'

'No.'

'Well, walk in the middle of the street and keep looking around.'

'It's not that way any more,' said Patrice. 'Dr Bourbon happens to be a morsel of the old west, to a point.'

'Yeah, well,' said Froelich, gulping his drink, 'time we was hittin' the trail, stranger. Whole bunch of fellas lookin' out for you ahead a-ways.'

'Are people waiting?' asked Walker, 'I was wondering about that.'

'Yes, they've been waiting a while,' said Froelich. 'Better not tell them we stopped in here.'

'Well, I really enjoyed meeting you, James,' said Patrice. 'Do come round and have dinner with us soon. And if you have any problems or difficulties, you know, just call us. We've all been waiting for you here. You're just what this town wants.'

Outside the house, the sprinkler, awaiting his reappearance, turned again through its angle and once more filled Walker's trouser cuffs with water. He got into the car and they drove towards the campus, past the fraternity houses and by the lake, Bernard Froelich and the man who was just what the town wanted, the stranger from the east.

Meanwhile on campus, in the faculty lounge of the English

Department, the assembled guests were waiting. They had convened some two and a half hours earlier, in the heat of the afternoon, when they had had to drink iced water and blow on one another to keep cool. Five times their emissaries had returned with tales of barren buses and Walker-less trains; five times they had poised themselves for a welcome. Now President Coolidge had gone to keep another appointment and Dr Bourbon had, in a wild issue of departmental funds, bought Cokes all round, which had revived some and finished others. Old ladies in flappy dresses who taught children's literature sat on the floor with their shoes off, penned in by forests of legs, thinking vaguely of little Hans in the forest and the gingerbread house. Young instructors in Ivy League suits, bright Jewish fellows who had been Ph.D'ed at Columbia at the age of eighteen, argued fiercely about the incest theme in the *Ancrene Riwle*. The faculty's one beatnik, who taught a course in The Novel and Fascism, leaned against the wall and said dreamily, 'Man, listen to that silence.' The pretzels had run out, the peanuts had gone, and there were some who had forgotten what the occasion was convened for. Nonetheless all obscurely recognized their duty to stand firm until something happened – until someone had a coronary or Dr Bourbon left. Wallowing in corporate unhappiness, they handed glasses about over their heads and swallowed in cigarette smoke, secretly swearing that they never wanted to see their fellows again until this time next year.

Dr Bourbon, his six feet six inches leaned against the wooden wall of the English building, was worried. He thought back to the Visiting Writer he had most detested – a poet from the east coast who always wore sneakers and shirts open to the waist, who managed to get through 400 reams of departmental quarto paper, an all-time record of consumption, and who had since been picked up by the California State police for broadcasting obscene messages on short wave to patrol cars. He had an uneasy feeling that the experience was to be repeated. He did not know what he would do with the man if and when he arrived. Some of the younger staff members, the group Dr Bourbon thought of as the *Partisan Review* clique, bright young fellows who believed in at the most one God and had petitions to sign whenever you went to see them, had argued at a departmental meeting that the resident writer should not be asked to do anything at all; he should not mean but be. Dr Bourbon had been compelled to protest; he could think of only one word for the suggestion, and he said it. 'Socialism,' he cried.

But what was happening? The wooden floor outside resounded with footfalls, and the door swung open. Bourbon craned over the mob; at the same time a voice cried, 'Froelich's found him!'; and the throng galvanized into action, pressing forward, snickering, pinching one another. Before them stood a muddled, tired, dispirited figure. They noted the corpulent shape, the Harris tweed suit, so signally inappropriate as to be a considered eccentricity. Walker, who in his slim social past had got by on an argument about abortion, a habit of reading while talking and a few desultory spurts of lechery, tried to take command of resources he had not got. He stood silent. It was, as it happened, enough. 'Pip pip, old top, what ho!' cried jovially a large man at the front of the assembly, a Phi Beta Kappa key dangling ostentatiously at his side. 'I'm afraid we didn't wait tea.'

'Take no notice of Hamish,' said a large woman, coming and gripping his elbow, 'I'm Evadne Heilman. I'm a Chaucer man.' She seized one of her bosoms in an intimate gesture, which Walker only understood a moment later; for, suddenly, she reached forward, grabbed him by the lapel, dragging him sideways and downwards.

'Awk!' cried Walker.

'Just a little ceremonial,' said Miss Heilman through clenched teeth. 'Now you're ready to face them.'

She let him go and he discovered on his lapel a little cellophane-covered ticket that said, like a gravestone, JAMES WALKER, A.B. (NOTTINGHAM, ENGLAND), GUEST OF HONOR. He saw that all the company wore the same. A tall and lanky man, pipe clenched between his teeth, showing whiteness of dentistry against the hard brown tan of his skin, broke through the crowd. 'Howdy there, son,' he said.

'Mighty honoured to have you with us. Have a pleasant journey to find us?'

'Terrible,' said Walker, feelingly, 'I thought I was lost in the middle of the desert.'

'Waal, we lost five faculty members jus' last year in accidents while travellin'. You do well to be scared. I'm Bourbon, chief of this little outfit. I have apologies for you from President Coolidge. He was due at the state penitentiary at six. But you'll meet him again.'

'Oh, I see, splendid. On parole, no doubt,' said Walker.

Bourbon chuckled, and then said confidentially, 'There's something I ought to tell you right now. And that is I hain't gotten round to readin' yore fine books. I usually stick around in Elizabethan territory, that's a big range to ride, so I leave most of them moderns to . . . well, you met Dr Froelich. Ride much, Mr Walker?'

'A bicycle.'

'Never on a horse?'

'No.'

'Not even a high one?' said Bourbon with an amiable chuckle. 'Forgive me. You ought to try it some time. We're an athletic set of hands round here.' He tapped his pipe on the heel of his hand and stuck it in his top pocket, drawing himself up to release another half foot or so of physique, and said, 'Let's mosey over to the other side of the room and meet Mrs Bourbon; she really wants to meet you.'

'Tip-top trip, eh?' asked the large man with the Phi Beta Kappa key as they passed him, 'and how's the Queen? Well, I trust.'

'I suppose so,' said Walker.

'This is Dr Wagner, Dr Walker. Dr Wagner is medieval.'

'How do you do?' said Walker.

'Nicely, thank you,' said Wagner. 'See you around, pip pip.'

'A droll, Dr Wagner,' said Bourbon, dragging him onward.

'I was wondering,' said Walker, 'whether there was anything to drink?'

'I'm afraid you're right out of luck, Dr Walker; we're dry

here. Tell you what, though, we're drinking Cokes. Miss Handlin.' He called over a younger girl, around twenty, who looked Walker over with bright eyes. 'Miss Handlin, this here is Dr Walker, the English novelist and our guest of honour, and I was wonderin' if you'd do us the privilege of takin' this dime and walkin' down the hall to the Coke machine and bringin' one back for Dr Walker, seeing as how he's come all the way from England to be with us today.'

'I surely will,' said Miss Handlin, smiling richly at Walker.

'I didn't know you could run a university without sherry,' said Walker, trying a bit of patter.

'We git along, we git along,' said Bourbon slowly. 'I was a Rhodes Scholar in Oxford myself, but there's some things the same and there's some things different, and that's one of the things that's different and I guess that's the way life is. This here is Mrs Bourbon. She's an English lady.'

So this was the mother of the twins, previously without intercourse for twelve years, thin and sharp-nosed; she said, 'Yeah, we met up in Oxford all those years ago. I still remember and love that city. Know it at all?' Her accent was hybrid, so was she. 'Amazing how quickly one forgets, though. Stay here in the States and I give you two years. For two years you can stay an Englishman and do all those quaint things that Englishmen do and everyone thinks it's fine and dandy. Then . . . you become an American, or you go home. Either way the privileges are withdrawn. So you must enjoy them now, Mr Walker, while you can. You're in a favoured position.'

Walker looked in her sharp eyes and knew she was saying something interesting. He said, 'That can be tiring too.'

'And false,' said Mrs Bourbon, 'I know that. Still it's a nice lie while it lasts. So long as it doesn't become everything you have.'

'Well,' said Walker lightly, 'perhaps I'll try and enjoy it, then. It'll be the first time.'

'Oh, come now, you're a famous man. . . . '

Walker was spared answering this; 'Coke?' said Miss Handlin. 'Dr Walker, I just want to tell you that I'm going to be in your creative writing class next year and I'm looking forward to it very much. I just finished your last novel. It's a fine noble book.'

'Thank you,' said Walker.

'A fascinating book.'

'Thank you,' said Walker.

Walker let Miss Handlin lead him away. 'Oh, that Mrs Bourbon, she's a lovely person,' she said. 'Now, what I wanted to ask was, you know, how do you write? I mean, you know, do you write straight on to a typewriter or in longhand first or how, how do you write?'

Miss Handlin had a bosom which rose and fell rapidly as she spoke, quite the best thing it could do.

'Does it matter how I write?'

'Oh, sure it matters because you have to find the way that's right for you, you have to have everything exactly right. I mean, I write a little, you know, and I've tried all kinds of ways of writing, you know like sitting in chairs and lying down and in the bath and all, and I find sometimes I'm fluent and sometimes I just block. Do you block at all?'

'Not often. Well, I write in longhand and copy on to a type-writer.'

'And that's all?'

'Yes.'

'The guy who was here last year could only write when he could smell horses near by.'

'I'm sorry,' said Walker, 'I wish I could say that I wrote suspended on pulleys from the ceiling, but it's just not true.'

'Well, that's a pity, because I think if you can find a new position it makes it more interesting.'

'You still mean writing?' asked Walker surprised.

'Well . . . oh, you mean *sex*.'

Walker found Miss Handlin's bright young eyes fixed on him inquisitively. 'I'm glad you said that. That means you've found the analogy, too. It *is* like sex. Did Freud say that somewhere? He should have.'

'I don't know. I can see we're going to have a great class,' said Miss Handlin.

'I hope so.'

Suddenly Walker found that Miss Evadne Heilman, whose sturdy shoulder had for some time been rubbing familiarly against his own, whose buttock met his, as they stood back to back in the press, had been gyrated round to face him. 'Can I wrest you for a moment?' she said. 'Let's sit on the floor and talk. Can I have a sip of your Coke?'

'With pleasure,' said Walker, when they had found a space on the wall.

'Like it here?'

'I don't know.'

'Miss your afternoon tea?'

'No.'

She handed back the Coke bottle.

'No, do finish it,' said Walker.

'You know, you're so *polite*? Well, it turns out you're a very splendid writer. I've just been reading an article about your books, and if you're doing all that, then, brother, I congratulate you.'

'Oh, what am I doing?'

'Disentangling the fibres of existence was one thing I particularly remember. Placing in an immediate and urgent social context the sempereternal problems of man; presenting and yet challenging the anarchy of modern life and morals; evolving a metaphysic out of your uncertainty and your despair. And more,' said Miss Heilman.

'Who wrote this article?'

'Why, our own Dr Froelich.'

'Froelich?'

'Yes, the man who met you at the depot. It was in *Studies in Modern Fiction*, I'll let you have my offprint. You could have it tattooed behind your ear.'

'I didn't know Dr Froelich had written about me.'

'Yes, that's why you're here, he's an expert on you. Knows about your bowel movements at the age of three. You didn't know?'

'I didn't know anyone was an expert on me,' said Walker, 'even me.'

Suddenly Dr Bourbon raised his hand high, so that it touched the ceiling, and said in a deep booming voice, 'Well, folks, we're hittin' the trail; good evenin' to you all.' The group fell silent and as Dr Bourbon nodded to him Walker realized that he, too, was expected to say a word. 'Good night,' he said, 'and thank you very much.' Then, realizing that this sounded a little pallid, he added what he believed to be a standard American rubric. 'Take it easy now,' he said. Looking round the assembled faces he saw Bernard Froelich hooting with laughter. The Bourbons led him to a car that looked oddly like the car Froelich had met him in. Bourbon, with cowboy gallantry, held open the front passenger door for his two riders. As Walker made a motion toward getting in the rear, Mrs Bourbon pulled his arm. 'We can all get in front,' she said. Then Dr Bourbon went around the back to get into the driver's seat, and they heard a cry go up from him. 'Goddern it!' he yelped, and his face appeared in the window. 'Pardon my french, folks, but some skunk ripped off my rear fender. We'll have to figger that one out in the morning.' He got in and started the engine.

'Isn't this Dr Froelich's car?' asked Walker in his innocence.

'Dr Froelich's car is a '37 Chevvy he ain't managed to git started for a few weeks now. Did he tell you this was his car?'

'I must have misunderstood,' said Walker.

'Did he do that damage?'

'We had an accident at the station.'

'Really now,' said Dr Bourbon. 'You hit a lot of traffic out there?'

'No, there was no one around.'

'I think we'd better talk this out with Dr Froelich,' said Mrs Bourbon grimly, and they set off through the campus paths.

'He didn't say nothin' to me,' said Bourbon reflectively. 'There's a mighty strange fella, Dr Froelich. A clever enough man, but with no ethical basis.'

'He's an out and out liar,' said Mrs Bourbon.

'But a mighty clever fella.' There was something staid and

comforting about the Bourbon family, and Walker sat back to enjoy his ride while he was still in their good books.

'I feel sorry for his wife,' said Mrs Bourbon. 'She's a very nice girl. You'll meet her.'

'I already have,' said Walker, 'she is very nice.'

'Can't figger out whether she's carryin' or not,' said Dr Bourbon.

'She could do more with that house,' said Mrs Bourbon.

'I rather liked it,' said Walker.

'I thought,' said Mrs Bourbon, 'you told him to bring Mr Walker straight to the reception?'

Dr Bourbon looked wearily at his wife. 'I did,' he said.

They were moving out of the campus. 'Isn't it big!' said Walker.

'It'll be bigger,' said Dr Bourbon. 'I suppose really I ought just to say a word of warning. I say this to all my new men. A lot of folks come out from the east expecting to find a progressive atmosphere here. In some ways there is. The west is really moving. This is new country, we are working out our own life here. But you won't find here the fancy-dan educational experiment you find in City College, Hunter, Bennington, them places. Our biggest benefactor, he's a Texas oil-man, only the other day gave a speech where he said the mistake America made was not to desegregate slavery and open it up to whites as well. Now I call that backward-looking thinking. But you have to take account of that kind of thing out here.'

'I see,' said Walker, crouched between the two Bourbons, and feeling the winey air driving him toward sleep.

'We live out of town a ways,' said Dr Bourbon. 'These are the town limits. See the package store? You can buy liquor out here.'

'Can we stop?' said Walker.

Bourbon looked surprised, but said, 'Well, sure,' and pulled into the parking lot.

'I shan't be a minute,' said Walker.

Inside the store the owner, wearing a stetson and smoking a panatella, appeared from the back and said, 'Howdy there!'

'Hello,' said Walker. It seemed to be the wrong remark.

The man said, 'You over twenty-one?'

'I'm over thirty,' said Walker. 'I've got a child of seven.'

'Got an ID card?'

'What's that?'

The man grew more suspicious. 'Identification. A driver's licence.'

'I don't drive,' said Walker.

'Then how the hell you get here?'

'I was brought.'

'Well,' said the man, 'I can't serve you unless you swear an oath.'

Walker looked at the little pad the man pushed forward. *In giving the oath*, it said, *both you and the purchaser should raise your right hand. You should ask : 'Do you swear you are 21 years of age or older?' Purchaser should reply 'yes' or be refused the purchase.*

'You unnerstand the penalties for perjury?' said the man. 'Okay, raise your right hand. Do you swear all that bullshit there?'

'I do,' said Walker.

'Sign the form. Now, what can I do for you?'

'A box of matches' was what Walker wanted to answer, but the owner seemed too menacing, and he asked for the bottle of scotch he had come for. When he got back to the car, the Bourbons had turned face to face and were discussing him. Mrs Bourbon was saying, ' . . . you can always tell with that puffy complexion, I knew the minute I saw him he was a lush.'

. 'Didn't even drink all his Coke,' Dr Bourbon said. Walker got in and presented the scotch to his hosts, for whom he had intended it. 'Waal, that's mighty kind of you,' said Dr Bourbon, letting out the clutch. 'Mrs Bourbon and me almost never touch the stuff, but when we have guests around . . . mighty kind.'

'I had to swear an oath,' said Walker.

Bourbon turned off the main highway, which disappeared back into barren land, and on to a dirt road, saying, 'It don't mean nothing, lots of the college kids come out there and perjure themselves black and blue.'

The Bourbon house, along a dirt track off the dirt road, was long, low, and modern, of a kind that Walker had learned from the billboards to call 'ranch-style'. It was a house of paradoxes; for instance, Walker gathered, as Mrs Bourbon showed him round with the pride of an Englishwoman who has raised her station in life, that the bedrooms were on the ground floor, while social living took place either above or outside. Walker's bedroom was as commodious and central as an English drawing-room, and was decorated with remarkable attention to detail – the towels, as Mrs Bourbon indicated, matched the bindings on the backs of the books. Beyond the screened window in the luminous light was a view, uninterrupted by a single human object, of the wigwams of the Rockies. Walker stared for a moment until suddenly, all interruption, there came into it a youth in jeans; he was firing a large gun into the undergrowth in a desultory, inhuman sort of way. 'That's my son,' said Mrs Bourbon in tones that mingled pride and disgust.

A moment later Dr Bourbon came into the room, unpuffed, carrying Walker's suitcases suspended round him. 'These all, boy? You travel mighty light for a stranger.'

'Well, you never know when you might have to run, do you,' said Walker.

'Guess not,' said Bourbon, taking the remark rather coolly.

'Well, Mr Walker will want to take a shower,' said Mrs Bourbon. There was, in fact, nothing further from Walker's thoughts, but he knew a hint when one was given.

'Oh yes,' he said.

'Well, come and join us in the conversation pit when you're all washed up.'

Walker didn't understand this but said, 'Yes.'

'The bathroom's right here,' said Mrs Bourbon, opening the first door in the passageway and switching on the light. Immediately a frantic whirring and buzzing and whirring began in the room; Walker jumped back. 'It's just the extractor fan,' said Mrs Bourbon. 'It's activated by the light. You'll find us through here.'

When they had gone Walker locked the door and took off his clothes, which smelled of Pullman. He piled them in a corner of the bathroom and got under the shower, turning the handles. A blow of hot water made him jump out again and he found that the shower water had soaked the bathroom and all his clothes. For decency's sake, he clad himself in his dirty wet underwear and his trousers and ran back along the corridor to his bedroom, clutching the rest of his outer gear. Here he stripped again and began to unpack his cases, looking for his underwear and thinking that he must really write to Elaine. This thought stirred up a complex of emotions that he did not know what to do with, so he sat on the coverlet and peered out through the window, only to discover a small round female face looking curiously at him from outside. 'Hello,' said Walker. The child pointed coldly at Walker's private parts and said nothing. 'Go away,' said Walker. The child puffed out a large round globule of bubble gum, shrank and enlarged this for some moments, and then walked off. Walker drew the drapes, completed his toilet in some unease, and tried to restore his hair, which adhered in a thick wet cake on his pate, before entering into company. He found Mrs Bourbon in a large room quite big enough for a dance hall, sitting surrounded by space and time, time and space. She sat on a bergère settee, stroking a Siamese cat and reading the supermarket advertisements in the *Party Bugle*; before her, tea was laid.

'Here comes Mr Walker,' said Mrs Bourbon to the cat, which went away. 'Hullo, feeling fresh?'

'Very fresh,' said Walker.

'Good. Do take a seat, please. Harris is just frying us up some steaks. How do you feel about outdoor cuisine?'

'Oh, I like it,' said Walker, who could not remember having eaten anything outdoors other than fish and chips.

'It's adventurous, we all do it out here.' While she spoke, there appeared, through an aperture which in England would have been blocked by a door, a small child, wearing a Confederate general's hat and pedalling a tricycle. 'Charge, man, charge, wipe out the enemy,' he cried, speeding dramatically across the room until he slapped hard against the opposite wall, which dismounted him and cracked open his tricycle wheel.

'Don't show off, Alphonse,' said Mrs Bourbon from the conversation pit.

'I wanted to see the crazy Englishman,' said Alphonse. Walker felt a shiver of foreboding. 'What's your name?' said Alphonse, looking hard at him. 'And talk fast – or I'll let you have it.'

'His name's James Walker,' said Mrs Bourbon.

'Huh,' said Alphonse, 'well your teeth are all crooked. Whydya got such crooked teeth? Whycha go get 'em straightened? Whycha wearing a brace like me?'

'Cut that out, Alphonse,' said Mrs Bourbon. 'Look, isn't it time you were hitting that old sack?'

'England's a nutty crummy country,' said Alphonse.

'How do you know?' said Walker.

'That's the word,' said Alphonse.

'It's time you were in your bunk,' said Mrs Bourbon.

'Okay, okay, I'm just going. But I'm hungry. Can I take a piece pie out the icebox?'

'Yes, just one piece, and then get right undressed.'

When Alphonse had gone, Walker stroked his eyebrow with one finger and said, 'And do you have a small daughter also?'

'That's right,' said Mrs Bourbon. 'My twins. Do you have children too, Mr Walker?'

'Yes, one daughter.'

'I'm afraid we haven't made too good a job of ours.'

Alphonse passed by the entrance space, carrying a whole pie and shouting, 'Nutty crummy Englishman.'

'I always felt that if I'd brought them up in England . . . they wouldn't, you know . . . have been such bastards.'

'Oh, you can't say that,' said Walker, much excited to discover in nuance that same mythical England to which several people had already referred, fulcrum of moral sanity, fine and formal society.

Outside the house a gong boomed sonorously. 'Come and GIT it,' cried Dr Bourbon's booming voice.

'He loves the kids,' said Mrs Bourbon. She got up and led the way out on to the patio where Dr Bourbon stood in an attitude of warm anticipation, like a big amiable dog, wearing a chef's tall hat and an apron with *Danger : Not Recommended by Duncan Hines* inscribed upon it. Smoke was rising in some quantity from a barbecue grill of modern design. Beyond the eating pit Walker noticed a small kidney-shaped swimming pool, in the blue water of which a small kidney-shaped girl without clothing lay on an inflated air mattress. 'I thought you were in bed, Brandy,' said Mrs Bourbon.

'Aw, go jump in the lake,' said the girl, whom Walker recognized as the Face at the Window.

'Time you was bedded down, Brandy baby,' said Dr Bourbon. 'Come 'long now for yer paw.' The child tipped off the float, swam to the steps and padded in past Walker. 'Huh,' she said. Mrs Bourbon followed her in.

'Don't lit your steak git cold, sweetie,' cried Dr Bourbon after her.

Then Walker and Bourbon ate their steaks together silently in the half-light, while monstrous flies pierced holes in Walker's leg and tapped the vein. The steaks were on paper plates and were intensely flavoured; Dr Bourbon had apparently been overly generous with a bottle labelled *SMOKE : Gives That Real Smoke Flavour to Your Bar-B-Q*. Finally Mrs Bourbon came back and began to eat. The night was clear and cool and the mountains were still visible. They seemed to speak of a world away from families, a world away from mankind altogether, a world of pure action and pure being. The threads and frenzies of family life that he had met in the Bourbon household reminded him of home; but the mountains suggested something better, the thing that had summoned him away. And thinking in the darkness, Walker brought his mind round to a thought that had been hunting through his mind since the day he left home, and which the mountains had brought to fullness. He looked up and said, 'I wonder if I might send a telegram, Dr Bourbon.'

Dr Bourbon swallowed and said, 'Sure, boy, go right ahead.'

He reached down, lifted a large stone, and produced an extension telephone in a pleasant shade of light blue. 'What do I do?' asked Walker.

'Call Western Union and give them the message,' said Bourbon.

'What's the number?'

'Hold on,' said Bourbon, putting a last morsel down his throat. 'I'll git 'em for you.' He hooked his long fingers into the dialling mechanism and presently said, 'Hi there, Western Union. Hold the line, I got you a customer.' Then he nodded to Walker and passed the mouthpiece over to him, saying, 'Just talk into this bit right here, and the girl who's on the other end will take your message. It's pretty simple.'

'I wonder . . . it's rather personal, this,' said Walker.

'He wants us to go inside, Harris,' said Mrs Bourbon.

When they had disappeared inside and shut the door behind them, Walker, speaking quietly but firmly, dictated his message to the girl who was treacling on the other end of the line. The message said ARRIVED SAFELY STOP WILL YOU GIVE ME DIVORCE QUERY MESSAGE UNSUCCESS STOP LOVE JAMES. The operator, without concern, repeated the message to a Walker now shaking all over with it. 'That's it,' said Walker.

'I guess from the nature of the message you'll want it reply paid?'

'Oh yes, please,' said Walker.

'Address for reply?'

Walker thought for a moment and then offered the address of the English Department at Benedict Arnold; a wise caution told him that Dr Bourbon might not like to receive this kind of message at his home. After he had replaced the receiver and put the apparatus back beneath its stone, Walker sat back and found that he was feeling very upset indeed. And he realized something else also. The tall lanky youth in jeans, the one who had interrupted the mountains a little earlier, was sitting in a patio chair behind him. He was smiling and directing at Walker a pair of hostile sunglasses with mirror-faced lenses in which Walker could see only two shrunken images of himself. It was Crispin, the Bourbons' third child; Walker looked blankly at him. 'Boy, oh boy, oh boy,' said Crispin, grinning. 'What a story . . . boy, oh boy.'

5

The fall semester at Benedict Arnold had not begun; there were four more days of peace before it did. Party and the campus rested on in the summer sunlight, and the mountains sat quietly behind them all. In the university buildings, classrooms stood empty and cavernous, their desks with little curved writing arms waiting to be filled. The soda fountain in the union contained only faculty members in nylon shirts and the campus maintenance men and policemen. In the university bookstore, behind a display of university pennants and sweatshirts with cartoon characters on the bosoms, a single, bored clerk read, for curiosity's sake, *Up from Liberalism*, a required text in the sophomore course on International Affairs in the Modern World (Dr Jochum). At the Bourbon household Dr Bourbon was up with . . . if not the lark, then the vulture. Clad in a handsome Japanese kimono, carrying about a peanut-butter sandwich, he did half an hour of push-ups on the patio and turned on the sprinklers before going into his study to write, before breakfast, a thousand words of *Marston : the Man, the Moment and the Milieu*. The keys of the typewriter flicked; the pages of reference books flipped; and new horizons of Marston thinking opened while the sprinklers bubbled outside. The carillon on campus began a morning rendition of 'Rudolph the Red-Nosed Reindeer'. In bed James Walker slept further on into the day.

The heat thickened. The mountains grew hazy. Late night adulterers walked quietly home. Crispin, the Bourbons' maladjusted son, rose, showered, pulled on his levis and a sweatshirt, fixed himself some fruit juice, got into his hot-rod car and roared away in a scurry of dust, heading for town to exercise his devil. The carillon played 'These Foolish Things'. Walker stirred but slept on. The sun rose higher and the areas of shade disappeared. Mrs Bourbon, in a Japanese kimono that matched Harris's, got up and went into the kitchen to ladle out breakfast, a feast habitually used by Alphonse and Brandy as missiles in substitute for other forms of communication between them. The carillon rendered 'Bless You for Being an Angel'. And Walker stirred and began to heave himself into consciousness. The day shone bright into the room, penetrating the vestigial drapes. The light had a colour and vigour that he was not used to and he found himself meeting it – was it the light that did it, or something else? – with expectation. His dreams seemed curiously energetic; his body, this last few days, seemed to be taking on new power. He no longer needed sleep so much; he no longer felt away from where he belonged, and he no longer awoke missing Elaine's big bulk beside him. In the mountains the train whistles echoed and America seemed to him a landscape of excitement. He got out of bed with some pleasure, ready for the day. Having already adopted the American custom of sleeping in his undershorts, and now viewing his own body with a good deal more interest as a result, he padded through the bathroom and took a shower. It no longer annoyed him; now it cleansed and neatened him. Because it wet his hair, he had resolved to have it all cut short; perhaps that would thicken it up, too, like turf. The extractor fan, whirring mercilessly over his head, no longer irritated him either. When he had showered he stood naked on the bathroom scales and looked at the measure; he was going to watch his weight. He opened the medicine cabinet and took, from among the rows of deodorants and dandruff remover, anti-congestants and purgatives, eyewash and shower talc, Dr Bourbon's dental floss, now his favourite method of cleaning his teeth. Then he sat on the lavatory pot and lit one of Dr Bourbon's cigarettes, which lay on the flushing mechanism, and read a few pages of Bourbon's lavatory book, A. C. Bradley's *Shakespearean Tragedy*. In the distance the carillon played 'I'm Sitting on Top of the World'. 'In the circumstances where we see his hero placed,' he read, 'his tragic trait, which is also his greatness, is fatal to him. To meet these circumstances something is required which a smaller man might have given, but which the hero cannot give.' He put a match in the place to mark it and went back into the bedroom. His clothes lay in piles about the room. He put on trousers and a shirt, gazing out as he did so at the high furry peaks in the distance, the sprays of water rising from the sprinklers on the lawn, and the Japanese wind-chimes that tinkled in the breeze where they hung under the house eaves. When he was dressed, he opened the door and paused for a moment in the corridor, taking a deep breath to ready himself for the generous syrup of American hospitality that he knew was to be poured over his head.

The Bourbons, from the first, had been poised to be kind to him. As soon as he reached the kitchen, Dr Bourbon, Japanese robe open to a furry navel, appeared at the door of his study. 'Guess that puts me 'bout two thousand wuds ahead this morning, boy,' he said cheerfully, cracking two eggs into the skillet with a practised and professional motion that came from doing, apparently, all the household cooking. 'How'd you like 'em? Done both sides?'

'Right,' said Walker.

'Right right,' said Dr Bourbon, pouring out juice into a breaker. 'You got to be mighty sharp to git ahead of me. Read plays at all, Mis' Walker?'

'Some.'

'Marston?'

'No, I'm afraid not.'

'That's a mighty underestimated man, that Marston,' said Bourbon, slapping fat around the eggs with a fish-slice. 'You read him, boy, you take a look. Immoral, though. That egg look right to your taste?'

'It looks fine to me.'

Bourbon sprinkled some Tabasco sauce over his concoction and put it in front of Walker, still in the skillet. 'There now, git some of this good grub down you and meet the day right.'

'Give him a glass of milk, Harris,' said Mrs Bourbon, who

had been operating the dishwasher in another corner of the big kitchen.

'You want some toast with that?' asked Bourbon, pouring the milk into a glass.

'No, thanks,' said Walker.

'Yes, give him some french toast,' said Mrs Bourbon.

As Walker ate they stood around him, high and lanky the one, round and maternal the other, working out his plans for the day. Did he want a freewheelin' day, just moseyin' around, or a programmed day, with a picnic and a trip somewhere? Would he care for something on the hi-fi while he breakfasted (Dr Bourbon rushed into the community room to put on Copeland's 'Billy the Kid', which boomed out western euphoria through the seven speakers scattered about the house)? Or would he care to listen to KNOW, the campus radio station (Mrs Bourbon flipped the switch, and Dr Lee Fichu came bubbling through with a sunshine course on astral physics, carefully directed to the taste of fact-oriented morons)? The campus carillon changed to 'Pale Hands I Loved Beside the Shalimar'; the coffee bubbled in the percolator; the kids made a rumpus in the rumpus room. 'I'll do what you think,' Walker said. The Bourbons strove to commit him to decisions, pointing out, in effect, that America was a democratic country, and it was every man's task to create his own fate – even if he had no background on which to decide it. 'It's your choice, Mis' Walker,' said Bourbon, looking distressed. Bourbon suggested trips here, Mrs Bourbon suggested trips there. There was Party to see, and the campus, and the county, and the mountains, and the mines, and the ranches, and the state as a whole, and the next state, and the state after that. 'I leave it entirely to you,' said Walker.

'So polite, the English,' said Mrs Bourbon, adding as an afterthought, to restore community, 'Aren't we?'

On the first day they had gone up to the mountains, and had a picnic in the pine forest. 'We got a course in picnicking at the university,' said Dr Bourbon. 'It's called Geology, but it's really picnicking.' Coming back, they stopped on the ridge of the foothill range and looked down upon Party, a green tract in the distance identifiable by the phallic campanile of the university. On the second day they drove the other way, into the shortgrass plains, until the mountains dipped out of sight and the endless flatness that Walker had seen on his arrival became the only landscape. Today, on the third day, Dr Bourbon, forced to make Walker's decisions for him, revealed that he really had a meeting at the university and ought to go there. 'Well, I'd love to look around the campus,' said Walker.

'Well, right, good,' said Bourbon. 'Actually I was goin' to suggest it, if you'd wanted to do anything else. . . .'

On campus great cranes lifted new buildings into place. They drove down fraternity row, past the houses, some castellated and defensible, some modern and indefensible; they looked to be interesting mixtures of formal luxury and informal squalor. Rows of red MGs and white Corvettes were parked outside. 'All those cars,' said Walker.

'You ain't seen nothin',' said Bourbon. 'Why, most of the brothers ain't even back yet.'

Further on were the sororities, where brown baked girls in two straps played basketball or sat outdoors reading in aluminium garden furniture. 'Hang on to him here,' said Dr Bourbon. 'Don't let him leap out the car.' Then along the campus roads, of which there were several miles, past the lake ('You might want to do a bit of swimmin' there, but there are plenty of garden pools among the faculty. Trouble is you got to talk to them'), past the tower of KNOW ('a truly stimulatin' project; I reckon that's made us into a real educated little town'), and the football stadium, where grotesquely shaped monolithic men struggled with padded machines against the fence ('team's down a bit this year; they lost their coach, he was bribing high school kids with cars to come to BAU.' 'What happened to him?' 'He was demoted to full professor').

'What's that building?' said Walker, spotting a small version of Caernarvon Castle, dwarfed by the football stadium.

'I guess that's the library people keep talkin' about,' said Bourbon.

'He knows it is,' said Mrs Bourbon. 'Why, Harris spends a whole lot of time in the library.'

Bourbon stopped the car with a screech. 'Want to take a look? We got some good stuff here. First Folios, that kind of thing. But you ain't a Shakespearean, are you?'

'I'd like to see it,' said Walker.

'Harris teaches a one-semester course in library use for entering freshmen,' said Mrs Bourbon, as they got out. 'Isn't that right?'

'Tellin' 'em how to find it, mostly,' said Bourbon. An inscription over the portcullis, one letter obliterated by trailing ivy, declared: A GOOD OOK IS THE PRECIOUS LIFE BLOOD OF A MASTER SPIRIT. At the head of the steps, whereon several students sat smoking, was a large statue, representing innocence, female, naked and immense, taking a draught of learning from a stone jar. On its backside, which faced the visitor, the Greek letters of a fraternity had been inscribed in blue. They went through into the catalogue hall, freshened by air conditioning, and then, past an elderly attendant female with blue hair, into the stacks. Suction equipment cleansed the air of dust and the only hazard was the perpetual twang of static electricity as they touched the shelves. Finding around him so much scholarship, Walker tasted for a moment the thought of writing one of these big books, solid and reliable, as a symbol of his election into a new community. But his mind, as he thought on, seemed not to be tuned to it. There was a time when novelists could decently write, in six weeks, a small tome on *Novels I Love* or *Sport and the Novel*, but those days had passed; now the new academic creator wrote *Mimesis* or *The Road to Xanadu* and took it quite comfortably along with his fiction. But he really hadn't come that far; he didn't know that much; and a sort of guilt about his lack of competence began to affect him as he stood in the bowels of this new world. 'Lots of people wukkin' in here today,' said Dr Bourbon to him. 'That's because the library's the coolest spot on campus. We made it that way by design. I'm always tellin' my students, "Use the library; it's the coolest spot on campus." We infect a lot of very good kids that way.' Bourbon's bumbling scholarship, the foreignness of the students moving about in the stacks, even the fearsome American static electricity, conspired with Walker's self-consciousness about his own academic qualifications to make him feel a stranger. How could he teach here? What would he do?

Dr Bourbon continued the tour, pointing out to Walker the shelves devoted to the English literature classification and the special reserve section, into which Walker would put reserved copies of the course books he was going to use. Even this was something about which he had not thought. Did his academic innocence show? Was even the self-centred Bourbon beginning to worry about the man he had brought here? But why fret? Bourbon seemed to accept everything; he took Walker into the undergraduate reading room, where, even now, a few early students on study dates read books with their arms around one another, and was unfazed by that sensuous spectacle; he paid no attention, as he led them back out of the door, to the fact that someone had pasted, on the pudenda of the statue, a notice declaring 'Made in the Virgin Islands by Virgins'. The world was all one to him. They came back to the car and got in. 'Lots of folks,' said Bourbon, letting out the clutch, 'call Benedict Arnold a play school, figurin' that our kids just come here for a good time. 'Course we do have a lot of good sports at this U, but that's only a part of the students' life around here. I get annoyed when people say our kids don't learn nothin'. They learn a lot. They teach us and we teach them. We expect 'em to learn a lil and live a lil and play a lil. That's what a U is for.'

'I suppose it is,' said Walker, watching a boy student walking by with a girl student on his shoulders.

'And over here, right there where those panties are hanging out the window, that's Thrump Hall, the girls' dorm. And this here in front of it is student parkin'. President Coolidge was one of the first Prexies in the States to realize that one thing students require of a U is good parkin'.'

They drew up outside the English Department, in its wooden hut. 'I guess I'll take the car and go down to the supermarket,' said Mrs Bourbon.

'Okay, sweetie, you take a bite downtown somewhere and we'll git ourselves a snack in the Faculty Club. That way I can introduce Mis' Walker to a few of the guys. Then maybe you'll stop by around the middle afternoon and pick us up.'

The car drove off, and Bourbon watched it go, his face dropping as he noticed the damaged rear end. 'Wonder if Froelich's in the buildin' today,' he said. 'Come on in and we'll do a tour around.' Bourbon pointed out all the salient features of the premises. He showed Walker where the Coke machine was, and where to find the janitor. He took him into the English Office and introduced him to the four secretaries, neat young girls who sat behind typewriters painting their nails and beaming goodwill when people came in. 'I want you to shake hands with these girls. Kiss 'em if you like. You're going to depend on them a lot. If they moved out the building would fall down.'

'Hello,' said the girls. After Walker had told them how he was liking it over here and the girls had told him how much fun it was to have him here, Bourbon took Walker's arm and led him to a wall which had been neatly boxed out with a mass of pigeon-holes.

'Here's where you find your mail,' he said.

'Are these all staff pigeon-holes?' asked Walker, for there seemed to be hundreds of them.

'Oh, er,' said Bourbon, pleased at his surprise, ' 'course most of them is graduate assistants, part-timers. We do a lot with part-timers over here, boy, you know. Comp. and all that.'

'What's Comp.?'

'Well, it's a course in basic essentials of English we teach to all enterin' freshmen. Readin', Writin', Speakin' and Listenin'. How to underline. Speakin' from the diaphragm. It's a service course to enable them to communicate with one another without sex, that's how I always see it.'

Walker found a pigeon-hole with his name on it and was surprised to see that it was already filled with letters. 'I put a telegram in there for you,' said one of the secretaries, Miss Zukofsky. Walker found the telegram on top and put it in his pocket. Underneath it was a letter, cyclostyled, from President Coolidge, welcoming him to this U and looking forward to many years of happy association and contact. Then there was a cyclostyled invitation to take a season ticket to the auditorium series, which opened in early October with an evening of Chamber Music by the campus string quartet, the Gold Nugget String Four. There was a map to show him how to find his way about campus. There was a free desk copy of a large dictionary. There was an invitation from the Foreign Students Group, asking him to join and also to put on for them a special supper composed of the endemic foods of his country. There was a letter telling him the number of his office and enclosing a key to it; there was a letter containing parking permission for his car; there was a temporary Identification Card, with a notice asking him to keep this until he had a permanent identity. There were several social invitations. There was a package of forms which constituted his contract with the university. 'All the bumf,' said Bourbon. 'We got plenty of that. Have to give those I B M machines something to do. I was a number for the I B M. Well, boy, what say we go take a look at your office? We got nice rooms here, but I'm afraid we got to ask faculty members to share. Let's see, who d I put you in with?'

They stopped at a door which had Walker's name at the bottom of a list of four. The other three names were Luther Stewart, William Van Hart, Jr, and Dr Bernard Froelich; Bourbon read them to him, rather laboriously. 'Sounds like there's someone here now,' he said, and opened the door. Inside there were three persons who were playing a game. Having placed a waste-basket on top of a large bookcase, filled with fat, pretentious texts, they were playing a kind of basket-ball which involved landing squeezed-up balls of paper in the bucket. 'Hell, I hope this isn't a student,' said Bernard Froelich as they came in: he was standing on a desk reaching into the basket. 'Oh, hi, Harris! And Jamie, well, good to see you.'

'So this is what you boys do,' said Bourbon, standing at the door and looking a little sour.

'We try to keep in trim,' said Froelich. 'Too many consti-pated teachers around these days.' He got down off the table and clasped Walker's arm. 'Men, I want you to meet our new writer. You all know his name, now this is the face that goes with it. Luther Stewart.'

Stewart was a large, thin young man with a small moustache, wearing a kerchief in the neck of his tattersall shirt. 'I'm very glad to know you. I've got a whole pile of questions I want to ask you sometime.'

'Fine,' said Walker.

'William Van Hart, here,' said Froelich.

'How do you do, Mr Walker?' said William Van Hart, who was tall, elegant and rather sophisticated. 'Thank God we've got someone intelligent out here at last.'

Bourbon, who was still standing in the door, as if he feared to be assassinated if he advanced any further, interrupted: 'I think we ought to be getting over there to the Faculty Club. You boys will have plenty of time to talk to Mis' Walker.'

'We look forward to that,' said Luther Stewart.

'See you soon, Jamie,' said Bernard Froelich. As they walked out of the English Building, and into the heat of the campus at noon, Dr Bourbon said, 'You know, boy, these young kids come out here from the east, read Cassirer and Buber and all that stuff, they're pretty darn sure of themselves. They think they're mighty good. 'Tain't always so. I always make it my rule, beware of intellectual arrogance. Now take me, I'm a scholar. That's what I'll be hung for. But those boys, know what they are?'

'No,' said Walker.

'Critics!' said Bourbon in some disgust. 'That means they can go around spoutin' their own opinions all the time as much as they want, without ever havin' to check a fact. Needn't use the library ever.'

The campus path they had been following now brought them out at the Faculty Club, a small and elegant stone building with a hotel-like marquee over the entrance door. Donnish men, lit by green table-lamps, could be seen discoursing wisely within, and Walker felt, with some nervousness, that he was entering hallowed academic ground. Bourbon held the door open with his foot while Walker passed through, and then led him into the urinal. Here, with one hand against the wall, he sang 'Git Along Little Dogie'; his good spirits had evidently returned after the short spell of personal doubt. 'Oh, shoot,' he suddenly said, 'fergot to ask Froelich about that rear fender.' The thought occupied him for a moment. 'Of course,' he went on, 'bein' a scholar in this country, and this part of the country, it's a burden, Mis' Walker, and part of the pain is the problem of not bein' understood.' As he spoke he took two ties out of his pocket and handed one of them to Walker. 'We're formal here,' he said. When the ties were on they went through into the lounge. 'What can I git you to drink?' asked Bourbon. 'All we're allowed to sell here is 2.5 beer. That to your palate at all?'

'Fine,' said Walker. Bourbon went over to the bar, where an elegant student in a white shirt and a string tie was pouring beer from cans into glasses. Walker sat in his armchair and straightened the creases in his trousers. Then he picked up the student newspaper from the table in front of him; 'BAU students arraigned on drug charges,' said the banner. Suddenly he looked up and there in front of him was Dr Jochum, looking smaller, more American, less sure of himself. Jochum brought back Julie Snowflake and Miss Marrow and a lot of old sensations.

'Vell, this is a good surprise,' said Jochum.

'It certainly is,' said Walker.

'And tell me how is Party?' asked Jochum, sitting down. 'Is it not all I said it was?'

'It is.'

'And is America up to your expectation? Is the freedom all you wanted?'

'Oh, it's much too early to say. I haven't even started being free yet.'

'And what happened to our little American innocent?' Jochum asked.

'Miss Snowflake? Now that I don't know. I called her in New York but she was away.'

'Well, the thing about America is that there is plenty of everything for everyone. That is why we all come here. Is America being a good host to you?'

'Ah, he can't answer that,' said Bourbon, returning with the drinks. 'He's house-guestin' with me.'

'Oh, then he is being very well received,' said Dr Jochum, smiling. 'Of course it was not this vay, you understand, when I first came. I spoke almost no English. I was another refugee. Who was to pick out Jochum? My books were not translated. I had written no distinguished novels. But America gave me what I did not have; that was a country. So that is why I am grateful.'

'America's grateful to you for comin',' said Bourbon, very sincerely, as he sat down.

'Well, here England's loss is America's gain,' said Jochum, gesturing at Walker.

'Well, thank you,' Walker said, 'but I'm only staying for a year.'

'No, you will stay longer,' said Jochum positively. 'Where will you find people so nice? And chairs so comfortable to sit in? Does this happen so often?'

'One can outstay a welcome,' said Walker.

'I hope you do not mean me.'

'No, not at all,' Walker replied. 'I'm thinking of myself. I expect I shall end up a perpetual commuter. That's what happens so often.'

'Ah, yes, mid-atlantic man, happy in neither place. Yes, I see that fate for you.'

'Hi, hi,' said the voice of Bernard Froelich, beaming as he sat down and joined them. 'Are they treating you well?'

'Why, Dr Froelich,' said Jochum, 'I don't believe we've encountered one another since I returned from my European trip. Are you vell?'

'My diseases are under control,' said Froelich. 'And how was the European land-mass?'

'Ah, with Europe, who knows? A little tired, perhaps.'

'Not what it was when you were there.'

'No, not what it was at all.'

'Dr Jochum,' said Froelich, 'is an *emigré* from Poland.'

'Ah no, there is no such place,' said Jochum. 'I am from America only.'

'That's right, Jock,' said Bourbon, looking around the room. 'Hey, kind of quiet in here today. Wait until the semester starts.'

'Yes,' said Jochum, 'I am waiting. I love these students.'

'Especially the ladies,' said Froelich.

'That's right,' said Jochum, 'I vant to marry every damn one of them.'

'You should, Jock,' said Bourbon.

'Oh no, von at vonce, please, I am not a young man,' said Jochum. 'Actually I often am vondering why I stay single. Perhaps I should find a nice little American vidow off the cover of the *Saturday Evening Post* to sew all these buttons on. And to mend the socks. Still, as Johannes Brahms, you will remember, said, "It is impossible to live with a woman together." '

'Nonsense, Jock,' said Bourbon. 'Every man ought to be married. Gives him a stake in sumpn. My lady's been with me twenty years now. Ain't nothin' like marriage, is there, Mis' Walker?'

Walker tried not to notice the glint in Jochum's eye as he said, non-committally, 'I suppose not.'

'What about the merits of unwed fornication?' asked Froelich. 'That has a lot of rewards and a few less of the penalties.'

'Dr Froelich, I don't like to hear a married man and a member of the faculty talkin' that way,' said Bourbon, 'and that reminds me 'bout sumpn else I wanted to ask you. . . . '

'Yes, fine,' said Froelich, 'but do you mind if I take a rain check? My meal ticket's standing over there by the dining-room waiting for me.'

'These young radicals,' said Bourbon when Froelich had gone.

'Yes, vell, I must go too,' said Jochum, standing. 'Vell, my good friend, it has been good to see you. Now we must arrange to meet. I have a nice little apartment, I do my own cooking, and it is a temptation to extend the range of dishes if I have a visitor. That is why you must come.'

'I'd be glad to,' said Walker.

'You are vitness, Harris,' said Jochum leaving.

'There goes a great scholar. And a great American,' said Bourbon. 'Well, now, boy, there are a whole bunch more people I ought to have you meet. Now. . . . '

At this moment there was an interruption in the doorway; a flotilla of men in dark suits, all walking at the same speed and very close to one another, as for protection, came in. At their centre was a craggy-faced, healthy fellow who clearly functioned as their leader. 'Well, Mis' Walker, you're very fortunate,' said Bourbon, getting up. 'I want to try to have you meet a very important person indeed. That's the President himself.'

'Which president?' asked Walker.

'President Coolidge, President of this U,' said Bourbon, leading Walker across the room and breaking into the flotilla.

President Coolidge's face beamed automatically as Bourbon introduced his guest. 'Ah yes, Walker, our literary man,' he said, putting out a hand to crease one of Walker's affectionately.

'Pleased to meet you,' said Walker, on his best behaviour.

'Look,' said the President, making a decision of evident political import, 'let's have lunch together.'

'That's a real honour,' said Bourbon in Walker's ear. 'He don't even *take* lunch very often.'

The cavalcade moved into the dining-room, where a waitress rapidly cleared a table. The President seized her arm. 'I'm going to take a peanut-butter sandwich,' he said, 'but I want to see these important men tie into something really good. Steak, fellars? Steak all round.'

The President sat down and the group sat about him, allotting places according to their relative importance. 'Here, Walk,' said the President, patting the seat next to him. 'You know? As soon as I met you, I thought, here's a man who has a real resemblance to my favourite Englishman. Know who I'm talking about, Walk?'

'No,' said Walker, 'I don't.'

'The Duke of Windsor. Ever met him?'

'No,' said Walker.

'I've had the honour a couple of times. See the resemblance, Har?'

'No, cain't say I do,' said Bourbon, seated on Walker's other side.

'I see it,' said one of the other men.

'Let me introduce you to all these good fellows,' said the President. There was the Dean of Men; the Fund Raising Secretary and an assistant described as 'a computer man'; and there was a reporter from the *Party Bugle*. 'We're very proud,' said President Coolidge, 'to have Mr Walker here from England as our Creative Writing Fellow. He's a fictionalist and is responsible for many very fine books.'

This said, the President suddenly stood up. The rest of the group rose and Walker made it too, just before the President said '*Benedictus Benedice*' and sat down again. The steaks had arrived, and a rather regal-looking peanut-butter sandwich, crowned with cress. 'I guess we have this written down some place, Walk,' said the President, 'but tell me – are you from Oxford?'

'No, I'm not, exactly,' said Walker, exploring a strange fruit compote frozen in gelatine, which had been placed on top of his steak.

'My favourite university,' said the President, 'I often wish Benedict Arnold resembled it more.'

'Why?' said Walker.

'I often think, if we only had a river here. . . . '

'You have a lake, haven't you?'

'Oh yes, a lake. But what's a lake, compared to a river? If you had to choose, which would you pick?'

'I suppose I might pick a river,' Walker admitted.

'Spender, Stephen Spender,' said the President, 'isn't he an English writer?'

'Yes.'

'Friend of yours?'

'Never met him.'

'Nice man. Know Durrell?'

'No.'

'Oh. Snow?'

'No, I don't know any of that lot,' said Walker.

'Sir Charles gave a lecture here last year. Very good. Remember that, Har?'

'Yes,' said Bourbon, 'very good, but the freshmen didn't understand it.'

'And where do you come from in England, Walk?' asked the President. Walker thought a moment and remembered. 'Nottingham,' he said.

'Well, that's a real coincidence. My seven-year-old daughter has a bicycle that was made right there in your city.'

'So have I,' said Walker.

'A bicycle?' cried President Coolidge. 'Well, isn't that something?'

'Yes, I go chugging all over the place on it.'

'You artists,' said President Coolidge.

'I didn't think there was anything strange about a bicycle.'

'Well, only kids and college students ride bicycles in America. We have a car civilization over here. Drive-in movies, drive-in banks, drive-in drive-ins, you don't really need to get out for anything.'

'I was only saying to Dr Bourbon how many cars the students seem to have. Particularly sports cars.'

'Well,' said President Coolidge, flashing his bright smile, 'you see, Walk, we have one substantial advantage out here. That's our climate. It happens to be very healthy, like Switzerland. In fact I'm in the habit of calling Party the Geneva of the States; to people who have travelled a lot. We get a good many faculty and students just for that reason. They love our air here. Someone once said it was like – wine.' The analogy came so freshly from Coolidge's lips it seemed to have been minted anew.

The man from the *Party Bugle* leaned across the table. 'I'd like to ask you, how'd you like Party? Nice place.'

'It seems to be,' said Walker.

'You bet it is,' said the reporter. 'Find the people warmhearted and kind, the best of American folks.'

'Yes, they seem that way to me.'

'They are, the greatest people on God's earth. Well, let

me ask you this, what brought you over here to Party?'

'I was asked.'

President Coolidge leaned over and intervened smilingly: 'Mr Walker is an English angry young man. We had a very interesting lecture on the Angry Young Men. By a Professor L. S. Caton, just passing through, didn't we, Har?'

'Mostly 'bout Amis, though,' said Bourbon.

'Well, let me ask you this,' said the man from the *Bugle*. 'You've just been described to us, right, as an angry young man. Now, are you still angry now you're over here?'

'I never was angry,' said Walker.

'But there's nothing makes you angry in Party?'

'No.'

'So you find things better here in Party than they are at home; is that right?'

'No, I don't feel so concerned about the problems of this country because I haven't been here long enough to know what they are.'

'But there are a lot of things you don't like about England, right?'

'Yes, some.'

'So there's no place like home but I like it here better? Well, thank you. You just gave us a real good story.'

'You're not going to print all that?' cried Walker. But the President, who had finished his sandwich, got up. 'Been nice to know you, Walk, see you again. Don't hurry boys, finish up that good steak. . . . '

'Oh, I'm through,' said the Dean of Men; 'Me too,' said the Salaries Accountant. The reporter snapped his notebook shut. A moment later Walker and Bourbon sat alone at the table, surrounded by unfinished beef.

'There goes a great administrator,' said Dr Bourbon, 'and a great American.' Walker, sculpting large pieces out of his steak, said nothing. He was worrying about America, and him in it. He was not used to a public manner, in others or in himself. He had never consciously had a public thought, and when he met men like President Coolidge he thought of them as actors, role-players. But such men seemed naturally at home here; indeed, all around him were people who were inviting him to be an actor himself. The invitation said, Be an Englishman, Be a Writer, Tell Us Your Beliefs, Reveal to Us Your Thoughts. He had a kind of intrinsic scepticism about such things, and it occurred to him to wonder whether this was a personal or a national trait. Was he being inadequate, or was he being English? It was obviously better for him if people believed the latter, and though he wasn't prepared to make this into a moral excuse he was certainly not prepared to become an American. These doubts about his competence in this new world brought into relief the basic problem, the question of his duties here, and whether he could fulfill them. He decided to ask Bourbon about this. 'Actually,' he said, 'I wonder whether you could tell me about my teaching and so on here?'

Dr Bourbon screwed up his paper napkin, wiped his moustache with it, then put it into his empty coffee cup. 'Surely, Mis' Walker,' he said, 'I been thinkin' about that. Let's go back to my office. Talk about these formal things better in my office.' They walked back across the campus to the temporary structure of the English Building. Outside it, a co-ed on a bicycle nearly ran Walker down; she fell off and smiled brightly at him from the floor. Her skirt was above her knees and Walker looked down into it and said, 'Hi.' This made him feel that he was getting closer to American life and he followed Bourbon into his office with less unease. 'Sid down, Mis' Walker,' said Bourbon, lifting a pile of *P.M.L.A.s* from a chair. Walker sat down and looked around. The room was lined with bookcases, holding large American academic volumes and long runs of scholarly periodicals. They were dusty and some were tumbling from the shelves; in two or three cases the runs were supported in position by old boots. Dr Bourbon sat down in his chair and, opening a bottom desk drawer, put his feet into it. 'Waal,' he said, 'first of all I'd like to welcome you formally to this Department. We hope you'll be happy with us. Lot of people are. Some aren't. We want you to be one of the happy ones. Waal now' – he picked up a yellow note pad from amid the desk papers – 'I'd like you to tell me a few things 'bout yourself. You know about us. You'll find in all that paper we gave you all there is to know 'bout our courses here and such-like. Now we have to get to know you. Ph.D.?'

'Pardon?' said Walker.

'Do you have your Ph.D.?'

'No.'

'Oh look, I got a file on you here some place.' Bourbon's head disappeared below the desk. 'Done any university teaching before?' said his voice.

'No, none.'

'Well, let's see,' said Bourbon, bringing up a file and opening it. 'We usually ask our creative writing fellow to do six hours a week. That don't seem too much to you, does it?'

To Walker, who had nothing to compare it with, it seemed unbelievably pleasant, and he said, 'No.'

'We usually expect him to take one graduate course and one undergraduate course in creative writing, they meet twice a week, and one other course. We ought to talk about the other course. . . . '

'What are the creative writing courses like here?' asked Walker.

'The usual kind of thing.'

'What's the usual kind of thing?'

'You ain't done this kind of thing before?'

'No, we don't have creative writing, as such, in English universities.'

'Oh, that's right,' said Bourbon. ' 'Course I was in England, I told you. Well, the graduate course is writing pomes and novels. Plays are Drama and Theatre Arts; you don't touch plays. Pomes, well, tell 'em how to write pomes. Novels, well, construction and plottin' and characterization and thematic unity or design and keepin' the reader interested. Tell them what James said. Tell them what Wolfe said. Show the kids how you do things. We give an M.A. in creative writin' here. That means they can write a novel or book of pomes in partial fulfillment. Tell them about that. You'll find we got some good kids here. Make 'em great, Mis' Walker, make 'em great.'

'Just in the graduate course?'

'Well, undergraduates, you have to go more careful there,'

said Bourbon, taking out his pipe and lighting it. Blossoms of smoke grew around his head. In the next office the typewriters of the secretaries clacked. 'That's more manuscript mechanics and typin' and the blessin' of creativity. Then a bit later in the year get them writin' short stories and pomes. That's the way it's been done in the past. But those are your courses, Mis' Walker. We want you to give what you want to give. Now there's one other thing, we usually ask our creative writer to give a public lecture to folks, folks from the university and outside it, durin' the first semester. You'll see some posters up about it if you look around. We didn't trouble you for a subject, so we took the liberty of calling it "The Writer's Dilemma". So you can talk on anythin'.'

'Will there be a lot of people?'

'Well, Mis' Walker, you're a good writer, you've got a lot of press publicity locally since we appointed you, you should get maybe a thousand people. It's an occasion we all look forward to. So you might be thinking about that. And now that leaves us with the other course for the year. Lot of writers in the past have taken a course on a specialty, but we talked this over in the Department, Mis' Walker, and we wondered whether you'd care to do a Comp. course. We like to give everyone in the faculty an experience of Comp.'

'That's Reading, Writing, Speaking and Listening?'

'Yeah, it's one of the most valuable services we do here. Lot of these kids come here, Mis' Walker, from all kinds of little red schoolhouses all over the state. We're financed in part from state funds, that's people's money, and we don't impose strict entrance requirements on in-state students. Fact is, almost any student who has the gumption to actually find out where the U *is* is admitted. Well, I'll tell you, some of these kids, I mean they're all good kids, but they've not had the schoolin'. Some of 'em can hardly write their names in the dust with a stick. That means if they're going to get any benefit out of a U at all, and by that I mean intellectual benefit, they've got to be taught to communicate. So here in the English Dep. we run these courses for entering freshmen, tellin' the kids how to talk and write and pass messages on and avoid parkin' where it says

"No Parkin'". It's a very valuable function for English in the technological world of today, and I don't mind tellin' you, Mis' Walker, it's sometimes the only way we have of presentin' English as a university subject at all to the other departments like Science and Business. A lot of folks who come here from Europe think that literature has a kind of status in its own right, but I don't mind admittin' to you I think they got a case, but it ain't an easy case to present always. But tell the U that you're teachin' scientists to talk to one another and teachin' business majors to write memos and reports and they listen to you, because they know that's important. So I figured I'd put you down for two hours a week of Comp., because you ought to see that course and because anyway a couple of graduate students from out east we hired got theirselves fixed up elsewhere and I got to assign eight sections to regular faculty. I think you're goin' to find that a fascinatin' course, Mis' Walker. Teachin' the comma and all.'

The door opened and Mrs Bourbon came in. 'Waal, we're all set, sweetie,' said Dr Bourbon, taking his feet out of the drawer and getting up. Walker followed them both to the car, and on the way Bourbon tapped a printed placard on the noticeboard. It said, 'James Walker, British novelist and angry young man, will speak Wednesday, December 1, Fogle Auditorium, on The Writer's Dilemma.' A small passport photo, which Walker had submitted earlier in the year, had been blown up and set at the side of the legend, revealing traces of acne and wrinkle that he never before knew he possessed. The lecture worried Walker, because of its size and the fact that he had no notion what to say. His absence of literary ideas and beliefs had never been an issue to him before, but now, faced with the need to testify, he felt a blankness where his standards ought to be. More and more it occurred to him that in the public sense he wasn't a writer at all. He was just a half-writer, a man who simply wrote, and it wasn't going to do out here. The challenge to be himself excited him a bit, but depressed him rather more. He sat between the two Bourbons, the sun-visor shielding him from the afternoon glare, and tried to urge himself into self-awareness and new insight.

There was an impulse there, he found, an impulse that came from the uneasiness he had felt when, looking around this university, gazing at its students, listening to Bourbon talk, he had recognized that literature and literacy didn't have the same permanence in this new world he had come to that he had always believed it to have in his old one. The winds of change, the winds of democracy and technology and an inhuman future, were blowing hard in these western plains, with its few bare sticks of civilization. There was testimony to be given. But the desire to give it didn't entirely quench another feeling – the feeling that the lecture itself was something of a breach of hospitality. It had been foisted on him. He didn't, he couldn't, he shouldn't be expected to do things like that. He sat still and said nothing until the car reached the ranch house and they all got out.

After they had taken the supermarket sacks into the kitchen, Walker went straight to his bedroom. He wanted to read the letters, open Elaine's telegram, know the future. The bundle of papers in his pocket had much to tell him. But when he opened the bedroom door, something had happened. The contents of his suitcases had been up-ended on the bed, and the two Bourbon twins, evident executors of the deed, were in the room. Brandy stood in front of the mirror wearing one of his sweaters, which came down to her feet. Alphonse had knotted all his ties together and was using them to pull one of the cases after him round the room. The experiences of the day suddenly crystallized into irritation.

'Get out of here, you little fiends!' he shouted.

'Nerh,' said Alphonse. Walker took Alphonse by the ear and led him out into the passageway. 'Lemme go,' said Alphonse, but Walker didn't, so he said, 'Do you want me to grow up repressed?'

'I don't think I want you to grow up at all,' said Walker grimly.

Alphonse looked frightened and kicked Walker on the shin. 'It's my house,' he said, 'I can do what I like here.'

'I know it's your house,' said Walker, 'but let me tell you something. You're a child, and a child is a pretty stupid thing to be. Don't come back to me until you're socially responsible. And that goes for Brandy too.' Alphonse began to cry; since he had never actually seen him do this before, Walker felt a certain satisfaction, until a shoe thrown by Brandy hit him in the small of the back. He went back into the bedroom and got hold of Brandy's ear. 'Now stay out of here and leave me alone,' he said, 'I've got some work to do.'

He sat down at the desk and felt almost gay. It was the first time he had asserted himself for a while, and it gave him great pleasure. He was in a very positive mood as he took out the morning's post and laid it out in front of him. The telegram seemed to promise another step in freedom; it was impossible to imagine, as he looked at it, that the world wasn't even more his oyster, that Elaine hadn't cut the cords that bound. But she hadn't; the message said: DON'T BE SO DAFT LOVE STOP ELAINE. The trouble with Elaine, thought Walker savagely, crumpling the telegram, is that she can't take anything seriously. She treats me like a small boy, she doesn't want *me* to grow up. But his were rightful claims, good claims. Grow he would, and free was what he intended to be. He could see a real prospect of that now, an infinity of futures. He lived now in an expanding universe, an America. It was not the country's democracy, or its permissive child-rearing, or its wild technology, that gave the hope, but something grander and vaguer. It was that unformed, free-style landscape and the hints of mountain beyond. Vague, yes; but not daft.

Walker dropped the telegram into the waste-basket, and turned to look at the documents of his new aspiration, the introductory papers to the university, which said *Welcome* and *Hi there* and *Good to know you*. Here were identification cards and keys to unknown doors and passports to park and eat. He thumbed through wads of American-size quarto paper, packed with mimeographed promises and instructions. Here were his teaching materials. The Creative Writing classes were documented with a list of last year's assignments, mainly reading assignments in texts with titles like *Write That Novel* and *The Path to Poesy*. The real bulk was the documentation on Course 101, Composition, T-Th 10-11

A.M., on which a mass of intellectual energy had clearly been expended. 'There is no course more important than this in the university,' said an opening brief by Bourbon. 'We like to think all who teach it are good 101 citizens, thinking and working as a team, believing with such men as Sapir, Hayakawa, Wittgenstein and Margaret Mead that to learn one's language is to GROW, not just in thought and organization, but in emotions and response to LIFE. People with linguistic skills live better. They also know how to write a good business letter.' The course's first aim, Walker read, was to reduce the students' most serious errors of grammar and mechanics to a reasonable minimum; there were seven basic grammatical errors (GROSS ILLITERACIES), so abhorrent as to win an automatic F for Fail on any student theme. The Gross Illiteracies consisted of such syntactical follies as The Unjustifiable Sentence Fragment ('I came to college. Having graduated from High School') and the Dangling Modifier ('If thoroughly stewed, the patients will enjoy our prunes').

Walker dug further into the pile, turning over the sheets, signing various contractual forms (LAST NAME: GIVEN NAME: ETHNIC GROUP). One paper was of a kind that worried him. It was headed 'Oath', and had to be signed before a public notary. Walker read it through again and went and knocked on the door of Dr Bourbon's study.

Bourbon had put on his oriental robe and was bent over his typewriter, making the keys rattle with two infinitely busy fingers. 'Howdy,' he said, stopping work.

'It's about this,' said Walker, handing him the form.

'Oh, the loyalty oath,' said Bourbon, looking at it.

'Do I have to sign it?'

'Well, yes, sure, we get state funds here and that means that the state legislature can ask us to give a signature to our loyalty.'

'Even if one isn't an American citizen?'

'Well, it don't mean nothin', it's just a formality.'

'Like the liquor store oath?'

'That's right, everyone signs it. The commies all sign it. Only people who don't sign it are New York liberals and they don't teach so good anyway.'

'What happens to them?'

'Well, we can't appoint 'em. Have to ask them to go home. Most of 'em don't like it here anyway. Miss the bagel shops, I guess.'

'So I have to sign it.'

'Well, you don't want to overthrow the government by force, do you, Mis' Walker?'

'Not at all.'

'Waal, I don't think I quite see your problem,' said Bourbon, putting a sheet of carbon between two clean sheets of typing bond.

'It's just that I'm a British citizen. I shouldn't be signing an oath of loyalty to another government.'

'Don't think they'll let you back?' asked Bourbon. 'Thought we was in alliance.'

'Oh, we are, as far as I know. No, I'm trying to define a scruple.'

'Well, I'm not sayin' I agree with this here oath,' said Bourbon, 'but it just don't make no difference. No, take my advice, you just sign it and fergit about it, Mis' Walker. Don't mean nothin'.'

At this moment the telephone on Bourbon's desk rang; he picked up the receiver and listened to it. Then he reached out and passed it over to Walker. 'For me?' said Walker, surprised, 'I don't know anyone.'

'Someone askin' fer you.'

'Hello,' said Walker into the phone.

'Hi, Jamie, how are things?' said a voice.

'Who is that, please?'

'Bernie,' said the voice.

'Who?'

'Bern Froelich,' said the voice.

'Oh, hello, Bernard.'

'Hi!' said Froelich. 'I want you to come over to dinner tonight. I have some people I want you to meet.'

'Oh, I can hardly do that, the Bourbons are expecting me here.'

'Ditch them.'

'I couldn't do that.'

'You don't want to come?'

'Yes, I'd be happy to, at longer notice.'

'Well, tell Harris you've been invited to my place and you want a pass-out.'

'But Mrs Bourbon's in the kitchen cooking a meal now.'

'You're willing to come if I can fix it?'

Walker looked at Bourbon, who was putting paper in his typewriter and affecting not to be listening. 'I don't have transport,' said Walker.

'I'll fix that,' said Froelich. 'Just say you'll come.'

'Well . . . ' said Walker.

'Is Harris there?'

'Yes.'

'Okay, just put him on.'

'It's Dr Froelich,' said Walker to Bourbon, 'he wondered whether you'd have a word with him.'

Bourbon reached out for the phone. 'Bernard,' he said. He listened for a while and said 'I guess so' a couple of times. 'You want me to drive him over there?' he asked at one point. 'Okay, I'll have him there right on seven,' he finally said. 'Oh, Bern, before you hang up, I want to ask you a question about the fender. . . . Hung up,' he said, turning to Walker. 'Well, he wants you to meet someone. Says it's important, it's a dinner date. I'm going to drop you by at seven.'

'I'm sorry if it's any inconvenience to you,' said Walker. 'Actually I tried to put him off. . . . '

'Well, that's Bern,' said Bourbon. 'Meant to ask him about the fender on my car. Hung up.'

'I'd better go and get ready,' said Walker, getting up.

'Waal, boy, you don't worry your head 'bout that oath,' said Bourbon. 'Could look into it for you, if you like.'

'Yes, I'd be very grateful,' said Walker.

' 'Kay, boy,' said Bourbon, flapping his oriental robe, and then he added, putting his big head down, and looking shy, 'Mind if I ask you a question, a friendly question?'

'Do,' said Walker.

'You ain't a communist, are you, Mis' Walker?'

'No, not at all, I'd call myself a liberal.'

That word seemed to depress Bourbon a little, and his moustache dropped as his mouth went down. 'It's just that you realize it could look a little funny if you refused to sign this thing.'

'Funny for a British citizen? Because that's the point. Though I must say I don't much like the assumptions behind it. I thought the McCarthy days were past.'

'Oh, this ain't nothin' to do with that nut McCarthy.'

'But that's nothing to do with me, that's your problem. Mine is simply that, well, the word loyal never did have a lot of place in my vocabulary, but if I'm loyal to anything I'm loyal to, well Britain, I suppose.'

'Well, fine, and I want you to know I respect your scruples. You gave me your word that you wasn't a commie, and I'll believe that until something convinces me different. But you got to watch the impression you make around here, Mis' Walker. Like with kids for instance, you mustn't go around beating up kids. Alphonse told me you just grabbed him by the ear.'

'Oh, he told you that, did he? Well, I didn't like to complain about him and Brandy, but they were both interfering with my things.'

'Waal, you know how it is, Mis' Walker, they're just kids, healthy normal kids. We think a lot of our kids round here. It's their life, Mis' Walker, it's their life. Mustn't go around attacking folk's kids, whatever you do at home. And, since we're speaking frankly, Crispin just came by and told me somethin' mighty disturbin'.' Bourbon stopped, looked grave, and ponderously lighted his pipe. ' 'Course,' he went on, smacking his lips round the stem, 'I know writers are mighty unusual people, and if I may say so, you look to me like one of the nicest we've had here. That's why I'd be sorry to lose you on the oath issue. But Crispin says he heard you were divorcin' your wife. Is that true, Mis' Walker?'

Hearing a public statement of his private deed, Walker felt deeply uneasy; he had never thought of this as a matter for others: but 'I suppose it is,' he said.

'Well, that's your own problem, Mis' Walker. I always say marriage is like fishin'. Some folk are always content with what they caught, and some always figure there's a better one that got away. But I'd say this. I know there's a lot of divorcin' and humpin' goes on here, and Party looks like a kinda progressive sort of town. But there's a lot of folk, responsible decent folks, who still look on marriage as a sacrament. My lady and me been together for twenty years. So don't let this atmosphere go to your head. If you take my advice you'll think it over, Mis' Walker, for the sake of yore little lady and for yore own. Mrs Bourbon and I, we was just sayin' last night, you're a mighty nice fellar and we don't want to see you make a bad start. I'm saying this all in friendship, Mis' Walker.' Dr Bourbon was now so embarrassed that he had nearly slid down from view behind his desk, and so Walker said nothing except 'Well, thank you' and went back to his room, the unsigned loyalty oath in his hand. He sat at the desk and looked at the place on the form where his signature ought to be; then he took out a piece of paper and wrote, *Dearest Elaine, I know what I said was a surprise, but you must believe that I meant it all. I am asking you for my freedom, because.* . . . But no more words came, and he stopped and looked out of the window. The sun was tipping down below the mountains, and there were great creases of shadow in the foothills. In Bourbon's study the typewriter was rattling again, but Walker looked inward and couldn't find a word to say.

'They chose a mighty funny place to live,' said Dr Bourbon, stopping his car at the end of the Froelich's drive. On campus, the campanile was chiming; Bourbon's sense of time was impeccable. Walker got out and stumbled up the steps on to the porch.

'Hi, come on in,' said Patrice, coming to the door. She saw Bourbon, shadowy in the car, and shouted, 'Come in for a while Harris?'

'No, I gotta get back to a steak,' boomed Bourbon. 'Give me a call when you're ready for me to pick him up.'

They stood for a moment on the porch to watch Bourbon

roar away. 'I see someone hit his rear fender,' said Patrice. 'Well, now, want me to take your jacket?'

'Oh, no, that's all right,' said Walker.

'I'm all alone,' said Patrice. 'Bernard had the Naughtys, that's Robert and Eudora Naughty, drive him out to the package store. We were right down on liquor, and our car's at the repair shop. Actually, that's nice, because I can get to talk to you. Sit down.'

Walker sat in one of the tangerine canvas chairs and looked around the room. 'There's a little gin and some vermouth,' said Patrice, rattling bottles. 'How about a martini with the proportions reversed? That sound exciting? Still, I guess it's just an English gin and It.'

'Oh, that'll be fine,' said Walker.

'We were in England, you know. How is it?'

'Oh, fair to middling.'

'Fair to middling. Funny how you all talk the same. You know, I ought to tell you about the Naughtys. We wanted you to meet them because we figured you'd be getting the wrong impression of Party from Dr Bourbon and his set. They're the old guard, you know. Been here for ever and are still living in the old America. Mrs Bourbon once asked me where I bought my antimacassars.'

'Yes, they are a bit that way,' said Walker. 'Dr Bourbon is worried that I'll get off to a bad start. Because I tweaked Alphonse's ear.'

'Yes, well, the Naughtys aren't that way a bit. Bob's from Chicago, a real union background. They're both liberals. You know, the type who make their own shoes. They have a baby called Buber, after Martin Buber, and they don't put diapers on it because they don't want to repress it.'

'I think I know,' said Walker.

'Bob teaches political science. He's trying to organize the faculty, get them unionized. So they can have strikes and go picketing and have mob-violence like everybody else does.'

'It sounds like fun,' said Walker.

Patrice brought the drinks over and sat down on the divan.

She was dressed in the same shift dress that she had worn the previous time he had come to the house and met her. But her dark hair was done differently, pulled up into a French pleat at the back. She had dark, intense eyes. She sat and put her head on her hands and looked at him. Like many American women, she sat closer and looked longer than he expected. He found this both pleasant and uncomfortable, for it brought to his attention things he wasn't quite ready to notice – that she had freckles on her arms, that the loose dress fell into a good shape because of the lines of the body inside it, that she had a very full and attractive mouth and an active and mobile face. She said, 'You know, this is interesting, because I've just been reading through all your novels. Bernie made me read them when we knew you were coming because he said I ought to know what you were like.'

'And did they tell you?'

'Not too much, no, they didn't. Well, now, do you want me to tell you what I thought of them or not?'

'Yes, I'd be interested.'

'I'll tell you sincerely.'

'Do.'

'Well then, sincerely. I thought they were great . . . '

'But you have another candidate for the fellowship.'

Patrice laughed. 'Well, I thought they were sort of confused, disoriented, a bit too obviously uncommitted. I don't know. They didn't seem to say enough or know enough about life; you know, not enough authority.'

'Oh, well, you did find out a lot about me.'

'And there's something else. They didn't have very much affection, feeling. Maybe it's just very American of me to say this, but I think people are less rational, and communicate more, have more intuitions about one another, than your characters do. Your books give me the feeling that you felt a bit exhausted, just living; as if you didn't want to do anything or know anyone, and had just given up and decided to drink yourself to death in a corner.'

'Well,' said Walker, 'I suppose I do think something like that.'

'Don't you like people?'

'Oh yes, but they are a terrible expense of spirit. Sometimes I wonder whether they're worth the effort.'

'Well, we won't let you believe that here,' said Patrice, looking at him intensely. Walker looked back. Her clean modern style of being, her very American willingness to talk and debate about the inner life, which Walker wasn't used to putting into words, made him feel much more at ease than he had all day.

'That's what I came here for,' he said.

'We're going to redeem you? Oh, that's nice. And how will you know when you're redeemed?'

'Ah, now that I can't tell. I've had truths come to me before. And a lot of old garbage most of them turned out to be.'

'A wary man. Well, fine, you've come to the right place. I know Bernie's been working on a big plan for redeeming you. Are you pleased?'

'I don't know.'

'You know it was Bernie who got you out here?' asked Patrice. She put her feet up on the divan.

'Yes, I heard that,' said Walker. 'They say he's writing a book about me. Which makes me not want to do anything at all.'

'Oh, it's not a book, it's a chapter. You overrate yourself. Anyway, it should give you some leeway for action.'

'Yes, just a bit.'

'He likes you,' said Patrice, 'so you don't really have much of a chance. When Bernie likes someone they're through. He likes me, too. Being liked by Bernie is a full-time job in itself. He's so hostile to the people he likes.'

Walker sipped his drink and looked at Patrice. Then a car stopped outside and he felt indignant. There were footsteps on the porch and people came into the hall. 'Hi, hi,' said Froelich, coming in carrying two large clinking paper sacks. 'Stand up and be introduced to these people we've dragged out here to meet you.' Robert and Eudora Naughty came in; they were both tall, and blond, and very healthy, and they were both wearing jeans and white sneakers. Both of them put out long arms to be shaken.

'Glad to know you,' said Bob. 'We got enough bottles to make this an all-night session.'

'I'm sorry we're late,' said Eudora.

'Yeah, it was our fault. We were supposed to be picketing this barber shop till five, but the guy stayed open longer than usual,' said Bob Naughty.

'Well, it shows we're cutting into his custom,' said Eudora.

Froelich, unpacking bottles, said, 'Don't apologize. He'd much rather have had another hour with Patrice.'

'Yeah, that's right. Well, I apologize for being so early.'

'Can we bring this conversation down to chair level?' said Froelich.

'Won't you take off your jacket, Bob?' said Patrice.

'Sure. If you ask me,' said Bob, 'I'll take anything off.'

'How about you, Mr Walker?' asked Patrice.

'Yes, I will now,' said Walker.

'That's a necktie *and* a jacket,' said Froelich. 'We're getting there.'

Then they all sat down and Froelich went into the kitchen to mix martinis. Walker, politeness itself, said, 'Why are you picketing?'

'Oh,' said Bob, 'this guy doesn't like cutting spade hair.'

'We sent in three different negro boys and he refused them,' said Mrs Naughty.

Patrice went into the kitchen and came out with a bowl of tomatoes and a cheese dip, into which they started popping the tomatoes. 'You have this problem in England?' asked Eudora Naughty.

'Well, we do, yes, a little.'

'I read your books,' said Eudora Naughty.

'Don't talk about his books,' said Froelich, handing round martinis. 'He has a very big ego but he'll be tired of his books at the end of a week. Talk about yourself.'

'Okay,' said Eudora. 'What about?'

'You ought to know. Tell him about your childhood. Tell him about your prolapsed uterus. He knows all about *him*. He knows how good he is.'

'Know anything about American politics?' asked Bob Naughty.

'No, I don't,' said Walker.

'What about your politics back home?' said Bob. 'Which ticket do you vote?'

'Guess,' said Froelich.

'Socialist?' said Bob.

'Yes,' said Walker, 'rather unwillingly.'

'Why unwillingly?' said Bob.

'Oh, because I don't like any of the futures they have waiting for us. Any of them.'

'Are you a member of the British Labour Party?'

'No, I'm not.'

'Why not?'

'Well, I don't think I could approve of a party that took in people like me,' said Walker.

Froelich laughed and said, 'There you have a definition of English liberalism.'

'A divided man,' said Bob Naughty.

'The point about England is that everyone is a liberal,' said Froelich, 'they all listen to one another and everyone who thinks knows everyone else who thinks. That's why there's no radical right in England.'

'What is the radical right?' asked Walker.

'Oh,' said Bob, 'the people who believe that God is a communist because he made other countries besides America. You'll meet up with a lot of politics here. I don't know whether you know this, but in this country university administration is considered a public matter. Not just the right but the left, the unions, get involved. And then there's a whole bunch of contenders inside the university as well. Who was it defined American society as a variety of contending views raised permanently to a shout?'

'Me,' said Froelich.

'What kind of views?' asked Walker.

'Well,' said Froelich, 'one of the things about American politics is the wide spectrum of opinion.'

'A spectrum with every colour except red in it,' said Bob Naughty.

'So the Yipsuls – that's the Young Socialists – won't talk to the young Democrats, and spend all their time attacking Castro. The people you dislike most are the people nearest to you, and you form alliances with the extremists at the other end. The Young Conservatives on campus just published a manifesto which said they were against governmental interference, and not just against fluoridation and medicare, they were against government interference with premarital intercourse, and government interference with drug taking, and homosexuality . . . '

To Walker this was all intensely confusing. He disliked politics because he disliked the political imagination, which divided and hated and judged. He resented the loyalty oath, but that was an individual and not a political resentment; in fact, to hate it was to attack politics, where they tried to impinge on the kind of personal life he wanted to lead himself and wanted others to lead with him. Politicians would say that that, too, was a political belief; but then, they said everything was. He believed in democracy and liberalism because they diminished political belief and stressed individualism and debate. People over politics; that was Walker's cry. Present company, the pacts and alliances of those he knew, the prods of friendship and the probings of sexuality and the pursuit of inner vision, these things seemed the only possible reality. None of the organizations and schemes that politics proposed for the future had any charm whatsoever; wherever he looked, he saw a promised attenuation of the kindness and personal space and individual freedom that seemed to him the real and worthy core of living. What if his gestures in that area were poor and confused, and the wake behind him was scattered with blunders; only open space and private people made sense. Froelich and Naughty went on talking; Walker, following a more natural and ready line of interest, looked at Patrice, curled on the end of the divan, her shoes off, her hair coming out of the French pleat, and thought about the politics of sexuality and personal relationships.

'The point is,' said Froelich to Walker, 'that American politics isn't a dichotomy or *zweischplitten*. It's a *fünf* or *siebenschplitten*.'

'We forgot to mention the *emigrés*,' said Bob Naughty.

'Like your friend Jochum,' said Froelich. This brought things home a bit and Walker said, 'Who are they?'

'Oh, they're a bunch of refugees from Hitler and Stalin who are so anti-communist they want to pass an ordinance against wearing red underwear,' said Bob Naughty. 'They're running a campaign to have Russia put back the way it was before the 1917 Revolution.'

'Is Dr Jochum one?' asked Walker.

'Well, for instance,' said Froelich, 'he gives lectures to the women's clubs around attacking the communists for cutting down the plane trees in Prague.'

'How about dinner?' said Patrice.

Outside, on campus, the carillon was ringing out nine, and Walker realized he was very hungry indeed. The steak with the President had been more of an ordeal than a meal, and Walker hadn't eaten much of it anyway; he was a slow eater, and if he talked, he lost pace. 'Oh, let's have another drink,' said Froelich.

'I'll get them,' said Patrice. 'Then we ought to eat.'

'Well, you'll have to make another pitcher of martinis,' said Froelich, 'unless anyone wants another thing. How about it, James?'

'Oh, I don't mind,' said Walker, 'anything.'

'Got any varnish?' said Bob Naughty.

Patrice went into the kitchen, and Walker watched her, looking at the delicate back of her neck. He felt rather exposed when she was absent, and he took out his cigarettes and passed them around. 'Oh, are these English cigarettes?' said Eudora Naughty. 'I don't smoke for survival reasons, but may I take one to keep?'

'Do,' said Walker.

'The handing around of cigarettes in England is an interesting ritual,' said Bob Naughty. 'Anyone know why?'

'Of course,' said Froelich. 'It's because you're offering something valuable. In America cigarettes are so cheap it's like offering people one peanut. In another way it's a form of niggardliness. The English are niggardly.'

'Okay, Bernie,' said Patrice.

'No, goddam it, this is important,' said Froelich. 'Here you have a spectacular English niggard. Sociology demands we seek out his values.'

'Goddam it, Bernie, you're just a goddam walking megaphone.'

'Yeah, well, we all know that. Now put your knees together and let's listen to Mr Walker, the well-known niggard, goddam it. All we want to do is to get at some truth around here. Okay?'

'You know, Bernie, I've finally found out what it is with you. You talk to people as if they were a group.'

'Well, they are a group. Mr Walker here is an English group of one. Now I'm going to ask him some questions because I ask the right questions and everyone else asks the wrong questions because they aren't going any place. Okay, now all I want to know is, why do the English like their fathers?'

'I didn't know they did,' said Walker.

'Sure they do,' said Froelich. 'English history is all about men liking their fathers, and American history is all about men hating their fathers and trying to burn down everything they ever did. I hate my father. Patrice spits on her father. Bob throws rocks at his. That's the way we change the society every generation. It's called the Pursuit of Happiness or the American Dream. Why isn't there an English Dream?'

'I don't know,' said Walker, 'perhaps there was once.'

'Right,' said Froelich. 'You see what we all need to know is that this man doesn't believe in anything. And that's because he's an Englishman. Ask him where he stands and he's polite and non-committal. You see, James, what I'm telling you about is the difference between English liberalism, of which you're an example, and American liberalism, of which I'm an example. I'm explaining to you why you're here.'

'Well, now he's here, let's give him some dinner,' said Patrice. 'We've cooked him a dinner and he's goddam got to eat it.' They moved to table. It was a card table with Japanese plate mats on it. Patrice had served roast beef, red with gore, and a salad; that was all. There was Californian red wine to drink. It was very good indeed. While they ate, the Naughtys talked for a bit about the parking problems they were having at the nudist camp they both frequented. After a while, Froelich said, 'Well, how are the Bourbons looking after you, James?'

'Oh, quite well,' said Walker, 'very luxuriously.'

'Are you staying at the Bourbons?' asked Naughty.

'Oh, no,' said Eudora Naughty. 'That Harris is such a dimwit.'

'No, he's not,' said Froelich.

'He's a dimwit,' said Eudora.

'No, he's a dullard.'

'He's a dullard who, if he worked hard, could be a dimwit,' said Eudora.

'He's a nice old guy who doesn't know what's happening,' said Froelich. 'He's fought a good deal for English here. It's never been a popular department and that means you need an advertising man like Bourbon. It's like the ads for aspirin. "Now here are three apparently similar products. Watch this simple laboratory test. French has sediment. Business Administration has sediment. But English – no sediment." '

'Why don't you elect a different head now?' asked Naughty.

'Oh, that will come. He knows that. That's why he's frightened of me. The people he's frightened of he calls New York liberals. He calls me that. Even though I'm from Medford, Oregon.'

'I like him too,' said Eudora, 'he's so anal. I mean that as a compliment – he's so orderly and all.'

'He's your daddy,' said Froelich. 'No, he's doing fine.'

'What I can't understand, Bernie, is why he hired you,' said Bob.

'He hired me because he's on the right side. You've heard him. "We got a very liberal department here. We got a Quaker and a New Critic and a Catholic Aristotelian and a New York liberal and a Buddhist Leavisite. Course we can't hire this man 'cause we've already got one Buddhist Leavisite and now here comes another guy, he's a Buddhist Leavisite too. Throw the whole department out of kilter. Still, I'll recommend him to a friend of mine, head of a department in the middle west, don't believe they got a Buddhist Leavisite." '

'Oh, Harris is all right,' said Patrice. 'Mr Walker said he'd had a bit of trouble with him, though.'

Walker blushed and looked down at the beef, so much redder than he was. 'What kind of trouble?' asked Froelich.

'Well,' said Walker, 'he thought I was getting off to a bad start. It was a mixture of things really. I twisted the ear of one of the twins, and then I'm, well, getting divorced. . . . '

'Wow,' said Bob Naughty, 'you really are hitting at all his verities.'

'You didn't tell me that,' said Froelich reproachfully. 'Why are you doing that?'

'Oh, we don't get on,' said Walker. 'We just don't seem very happy. . . . '

'You're English, aren't you?' asked Froelich. 'The English don't believe in happiness. I thought England was a family-oriented society. Marriages stayed together and people went to prostitutes.'

'Well,' said Walker, 'I must be getting Americanized. And then I think I offended him over the loyalty oath. . . . '

'Boy,' said Bob Naughty, 'is that thing still around?'

'Of course it's around, goddam it,' said Froelich. 'Don't pretend you didn't sign it.'

'I don't remember,' said Bob.

'Everybody signs it. The only people who don't sign it don't come. The commies sign it. The rightists sign it. The only people who don't sign it are people who don't think the question should be asked anyway, and we never see them.'

'*I* don't think it should be asked,' said Bob.

'Well, okay, so you're a hypocrite,' said Froelich. 'I'm a hypocrite.'

'I thought that it was wrong of me, as a British citizen, to sign an oath of loyalty to another government,' said Walker. 'My motives weren't any more complicated than that.'

'You know, Bernie,' said Bob, 'that's quite an argument.'

'Sure it is, just keep it as simple as that.'

'Of course,' said Walker, 'Bourbon said the oath was only nominal, a safeguard.'

'That's right,' said Froelich. 'If you overthrow the American government by force, they've got a comeback: they can take your job away.' He cut some more meat and said, 'How about seconds?'

'Thank you,' said Walker, putting out his plate.

'Well, what are you going to do?' Bob Naughty asked, looking excited about all this.

'Well,' said Froelich, 'think it through. He doesn't sign it. He's not a citizen; his loyalty is required elsewhere; he's got an absolutely sound reason for standing out.'

'Okay, then people get hold of it and it becomes a big story. Won't they ask him to leave?'

'We could come in on that,' said Froelich.

'I thought I might sign,' said Walker.

'Well, the only reason I could think of for signing is that you're a communist and you want to teach some subversive materials,' said Froelich.

'No, I'm not, my subversion is all in favour of literature.'

'Why not do this? Just put in a protest to the President of the University? Get him to give you an answer, a ruling. It's going to trouble him, that's all we want.'

'You shouldn't ask him that,' said Patrice.

'Sure, he's a decent man, he likes performing moral actions,' said Froelich.

'The only problem,' said Walker, 'is that like everyone else I don't know what a moral action is any more. I'm away from my household gods; I'm living in a world of someone else's ethics; I don't know what I'm saying or doing when I say or do. How am I qualified?'

'You're a man, that's all,' said Froelich.

'Well, who isn't? What do I have? If I had a moral life I

224

wouldn't be here. I'm here for the confusion. So why me? Why here?'

'You didn't stand,' said Patrice to her husband. 'Why should he?'

'I did stand. I crossed my fingers when I signed it,' said Froelich. 'No, look, this is the point, friends. *Because* you're from outside, *because* there's no cause or flag you've got to wave except a simple matter of principle that has to do with the one thing you are, which is that you're English – that's the only existence you've got, pal – you're the man. The finger points, James.'

'I don't know,' said Walker.

'It points, buddy,' said Froelich. 'A time to choose.'

Patrice came out of the kitchen with a cheese cake. 'I only have a spatula to carve it with, is that okay?' she asked.

'Oh, fine by me,' said Walker.

'See, you can make decisions,' said Froelich.

All the things that were being said to him disturbed Walker very much, though he tried not to show it. He had always tried to preserve in himself that little slender growth of concern, a dangerous taste for good humane doing. It was his most precious possession and he didn't care, therefore, to bring it out too often. It seemed to him that he lived in a primitive world, in which this thing he stood for had little place. People believed in the broad sweeps of history, not in moments of individual decision. Walker could take history, and he could leave it alone. He was nervous now because here was a political matter, a public matter; and he felt he was being invited to do something rather improper, to perform an indecent exposure of his moral core on the platform and the stage. And expose it, too, in a world of political nuances he didn't understand and couldn't control.

All his values were private values, he was just James Walker, naked as they come; all else was pretence and rôle-playing. But now the invitations were flowing. Tell us your beliefs, your truths, your commitments. Noticeably, in the last days, he had begun to feel the robe of Englishness. Little shivers of nationality, almost of patriotism, came to him now.

'Of course you know the background to all this,' said Froelich. 'They used these oaths to press charges of perjury against faculty members with a past, in the McCarthy days. Some universities used to have microphones hidden in the classrooms during classes in those days. I wasn't here then, but it was fought hard here, and the oath was amended. There was a Democrat president then, and he came out on the good side. Then when we got a Republican administration in the State he was eased out, you know? But the atmosphere's more liberal now. They even have intellectuals in government. Pouring into the White House waving *Dombey and Son*.'

These evocations suddenly sounded a chord on Walker's liberal heart-strings; he said, 'All right, I'll fight it.'

Patrice said, 'You think about it, Mr Walker. Don't et these hustlers talk you into anything you don't want to do. Let's move back to the chairs and I'll serve coffee and cookies.'

They moved, and Froelich put on the gramophone a record of Cynthia Gooding. The wires around the room twanged; the two speakers boomed; the singer sang Scottish folk ballads about lords poisoning one another; and Patrice brought in the coffee, which was served in pots that had once held Keiller's Dundee Marmalade. 'We brought these back home with us, we thought they were so beautiful,' she said.

'They're great,' said Eudora Naughty.

'Marvellous,' said Walker politely.

'That means he hates them,' said Froelich, 'because he knows what they're used for.'

'He said they were marvellous, goddam it,' said Patrice.

'Sure he said they were marvellous,' said Froelich, 'but how do you know he means what he says?'

'Why did he say it, then?'

'Because he's polite. The English are polite by telling lies. The Americans are polite by telling the truth.'

'Oh, fix some drinks,' said Patrice.

Froelich went off into the kitchen, and Patrice said, 'He's manic tonight.'

'He's a great guy,' said Eudora.

'He's a hundred per cent ego,' said Patrice. 'Look, Mr

226

Walker, don't you let him pressure you like that. He just likes to run the whole show. You do what you want. I think it's crazy to get mixed up in these schemes of his. He's probably working to destroy the whole goddam university.'

'Somebody ought to fight this one again,' said Bob Naughty. 'Bernie's right.'

'You admire that man too much,' said Patrice.

'He's a squirrel,' said Eudora. 'He collects nuts.'

'Well, okay,' said Bob, 'but he knows what he's doing.'

'Well, I don't know what he's doing.'

'I'm pissing in the drinks,' said Froelich from the kitchen. 'You know what I think? I think Mr Walker there wants to go to bed with my wife.'

'Well, who doesn't?' said Bob Naughty.

'What do you think, spicejar?'

'I think you're going crazy,' said Patrice.

Froelich came in with the drinks. 'Did I ever tell you about all my wife's lovers?' he said, handing the drinks round with overtly meticulous care.

'You're drunk, Bernie,' said Patrice. 'You're so high it just isn't true.'

'Hi hi,' said Froelich, 'and these lovers work in relays and come up the drainpipes the minute I go out that door. They're even wearing out the brickwork.'

'This is a total lie,' said Patrice.

'Oh, don't believe her, believe me.'

'Why?'

'Because I'm more interesting,' said Froelich. 'You didn't answer Mr Walker's question, spicejar.'

'I didn't hear any question,' said Patrice.

'He's too shy to ask it. He's an Englishman and that means he's polite.'

'You should take some lessons,' said Patrice.

'Well, answer the question, please, baby, and quit stalling. Mr Walker is a normal healthy human animal with the usual male appendages and the impulse to go to bed with you has possessed him. Actually he's crazy. But we can't help that, can we, Eudora? Eudora and I are going to kiss one another for the next couple of minutes, so just get a good conversation going and don't pry.'

'Well, honey,' said Eudora.

'It's your left ear that's always attracted me, baby,' said Froelich. 'Take a look at that lobe. It's the sexiest lobe in town.'

'I'm glad you appreciate it,' said Bob.

'Bob, I've been taking a statistical survey around here, and figures prove that you're kind of the odd man out in this ménage. So why don't you go boil up some more coffee?'

'I'd love some coffee, Bob,' said Eudora.

'Now will you two kids in the back seat pay attention to each other and leave us to our business?' said Froelich.

Walker said, 'Well, this is quite a party,' to Patrice.

'It's Bernie's favourite kind of party,' said Patrice.

'And what about you?'

'Well, I don't know, that's how it goes.'

'Why don't we take a walk outside?'

'I'll get some real shoes,' said Patrice.

Outside, on the block, it was dark. Sprinkler hoses hissed in the silence. 'Why are you divorcing?' asked Patrice.

'Oh, we've grown away,' said Walker.

'What's your wife like?'

'A nice girl. Very nice. Big and good-looking.'

'She work?'

'She's a nurse.'

'Does she nurse you?'

'Well, that's exactly it,' said Walker. 'What about you? Do you work?'

'I have a job in admissions on campus,' said Patrice.

'Like it?'

'Oh, it's kind of fun. I run around a lot.'

'It's nice out here with you,' said Walker.

'It's nice out here with you too,' said Patrice.

Walker turned so that he stood in front of Patrice, and lifted up her face to kiss her. She put her arms round him and said, 'Well, hi hi.'

'Hi hi,' said Walker.

'You should have got your jacket,' she said. 'You'll catch cold.'

'No, I'm fine.'

Patrice ran her hand through his hair and said, 'I like doing that. I love English hair, it's so long. They'll cut it off when you go to the barber shop. For me, don't let them. Take a stand.'

'I will,' said Walker, kissing her again. He grew so engrossed that he failed to hear the car that drew up beside them. 'Hey,' said a voice. It was a police cruiser with a big red pimple light on the roof.

'Did you want us?' said Walker.

'What's going on here?' said the cop.

'We were just taking a walk,' said Walker.

'Where's your car?'

'I haven't got a car.'

'Come here and talk where I can hear you,' said the cop. 'What are you playing at, walking around this time of night?'

'It's a nice night.'

'Yeah, beautiful, stars, moon, all the usual crap. I don't like to see people walking around at night. I get the idea they're up to somethin'. Got any identification? What about you, girlie?'

'I live right up the block,' said Patrice.

'Oh yeah?'

'Right back there where that light is.'

'Well, let's see some identification.'

'I don't see why,' said Walker. 'We weren't doing anything.'

'Look, bud, I already seen you doin' sumpn. Now come on, no lip, or I'll take you in for drunken driving.'

'I don't even have a car.'

'Look bud bud, if I take you in for drunken drivin' you were drunken drivin', car or no car. Where's your identification?'

'I don't have any.'

'A funny guy,' said the cop.

'I'm just a visitor here.'

'Yeah, where are you visitin' from?'

'England.'

'Oh, you're from England? Hoity toity. And what about you, girlie? Are you a limey too?'

'No, I told you, I live right up the block.'

'You're a resident.'

'Yes.'

'Well, I'll tell ya sumpn, girlie, I don't like to see a resident screwin' with these foreign kids. Why don't you stick with a good American boy? What's wrong with American boys?'

'Nothing,' said Patrice. 'This man's just a friend.'

'Yeah, I saw what kind of friend. Well, let me see you go right back in there where you live. And, girlie. . . . '

'Yes?' said Patrice.

'Keep your screwing instate, okay?'

'I don't think you should talk like that,' said Walker.

'Come on,' said Patrice. 'Don't talk back. This isn't an English bobby.'

'That girlie's talking sense, Limey,' said the cop. 'Now beat it. And you, Limey.'

'But he's no right. . . . ' said Walker.

'Whyncha take the potatoes out your mouth when you're talkin'?'

'Now just a minute. . . . ' said Walker.

'Come on, for Christsake, Mr Walker,' said Patrice.

'I ought to write down that name,' said the cop, ' 'cause I don't remember too good. But maybe I'll remember. Okay, walk. And don't forget I'm cruising right behind you and I want to see you go into that premises. You'd better really live there, lady.'

'It's like a fascist state,' said Walker, as they turned round and went back.

'Oh, he thought we were students.'

'Is that the way they treat the students?'

'Well, the cops don't like the university kids. They give them a lot of work. Then there's this drugs thing. It's made them a bit too smart.'

'I've a good mind to complain.'

'The police chief's worse than that guy.'

'Sitting there, holding on to that gun, just playing around with us. What was it all *for*?'

'Oh, people don't walk in America. And you talk funny. And he's just plain exercising power.'

'He looked like an executioner.'

'Well, we have executioners,' said Patrice. 'It's a violent country. That's why you have to be careful with this oath thing. What do you know about America?'

'I know, but that's a simple matter of principle.'

'Only it's not so simple.'

They were on the porch; Patrice waved to the cruiser, which had turned round and was moving along very slowly at the kerb edge. She opened the door and the cop suddenly gunned his engine and roared away. Inside, Froelich and Eudora had disappeared and Bob Naughty was lying full length on the divan, with his shoes off and a martini in his hand.

Walker found his drink and picked it up. 'Let's have some music,' said Patrice. 'Why don't you go and pick a record you like and play it for us, Mr Walker? They're through there in the bedroom.'

When he got into the bedroom Walker heard heavy breathing. 'I was looking for a record,' he said into the darkness.

'Hi hi,' said Froelich, 'grab the pile from down there by the door.'

'Got them,' said Walker.

'Bysie, bysie,' said Froelich. Walker went back into the living-room to discover the lights were off and there was heavy breathing here too.

'I got the records,' he said.

'Great,' said Bob. 'Strike a match and put something on. Music to screw by.'

'How about the 1812 Overture?' said Walker.

'God, no,' said Bob. 'What are you, a militarist?'

'There's the Appassionata,' said Walker.

'We ought to talk to Mr Walker,' said Patrice.

'Oh, come on, you've got a whole year to talk to Mr Walker.'

'Well, look, here's a stranger in a foreign land. I guess if I'm going to neck, I'd rather neck with a stranger in a foreign land. It's more pathetic.'

'Oh, God,' said Bob.

'Where are you, Mr Walker?' asked Patrice.

'I'm by the record player. I can't work it.'

'Come over here.'

Walker moved forward and stumbled over some shoes. His hand went into a potted plant and prickles stuck in his palm. He crawled the last bit to the divan. 'Hi hi,' said Patrice, 'give me a kiss.'

Suddenly there were three faces together, breathing heavily over each other. 'Hey, easy,' said Bob, 'keep it heterosexual.' Walker found Patrice's face and kissed it.

'You have parties like this in England?' asked Bob Naughty.

'I can't remember any,' said Walker.

'Whose hand is that?' said Patrice.

'Why these speculations about identity?' said Bob Naughty.

'I like to know whose hands are in my dress,' said Patrice.

'Not mine,' said Bob.

'Well, it's not mine,' said Walker.

'It must be your own,' said Bob, 'unless there's another guy here we haven't identified yet.'

'It's you, Bob, cut it out,' said Patrice. 'Why don't you make some drinks?'

'James hasn't made any drinks yet.'

'Well, I want him here.'

'See,' said Walker.

'Maybe I should hit him,' said Bob.

'No, make some more drinks,' said Patrice.

'I don't even want a goddam drink.'

'Well, I do and James does,' said Patrice. 'A beer and a scotch. A neat, tidy scotch.'

'Let the guy on top of the pile do it,' said Bob. 'I'm parked where I can't get out.'

'So we'll all get up,' said Patrice.

'Oh Jesus,' said Bob. He got up and stumbled into the darkness. They heard him open a door and Froelich's voice said, 'Bysie, bysie.'

'Hell, wrong door,' said Bob. Patrice put her head against Walker's and said, 'Hi hi.'

'Hi hi,' said Walker. 'Patrice, I was wondering. . . . '

'What?' said Patrice.

'Is dandruff infectious?'

'You got dandruff?'

'Yes. And America seems to make it worse.'

'Well, treat it,' said Patrice. 'I'll give you something you put on it in the shower.'

'That's very kind of you.'

'Oh, you got friends here.'

'I see I have,' said Walker, putting his hand where Bob's had been. 'Mine,' he said. Patrice pressed the hand and said, 'It doesn't have a wedding ring.'

'Men don't wear them in England.'

'Oh no, I know that,' said Patrice. 'Is that because they don't need them, they're so good, or because they refuse to be tied down?'

'The second.'

'Oh, those poor English women,' said Patrice. 'Why don't they stand up for themselves?'

'Who wants them standing up?' said Walker.

'I wonder if you're a very nice man.'

'I wonder myself.'

'Maybe you do have a mind of your own.'

'You have very smooth skin,' said Walker. 'Is it brown in there?'

'I'll show you sometime,' said Patrice. The carillon on campus rang out two, and Patrice said, 'Those Bourbons will wonder where you got to.'

'I'd better call them and explain.'

'Great, let's call them up and say Nerh,' said Patrice. 'Nerh, Harris, and another big Nerh for the rest of the family.'

'Oh, don't get up,' said Walker.

'Sure, don't you want to do it?'

'No, not really, on reflection,' said Walker. 'I'm staying with them, you know.'

'I know, it's crazy,' said Patrice.

The door of the bedroom opened and Bernard Froelich stumbled out. 'Hi hi,' he said. 'How goes it?'

'Fine, Bernie, fine,' said Patrice.

'Eudora wants to hear the bongos,' said Bernard, 'so I said we'd beat out something. Ever play the bongos, Jamie?'

'No,' said Walker.

'There seems to be a lot of goddam things that you ain't never done,' said Bernard.

'I know, but I'm learning.'

'Here, give him the drums,' said Froelich. 'Now beat them out, boy.'

Walker put the drums on the floor in front of him and hit them. 'No, not like that, goddam it,' said Froelich. 'Put them between your knees. Sit on the floor. That's it, now, beat 'em.' Walker began drumming. The noise pleased him and he tried some syncopations. 'Beat 'em, boy,' cried Froelich. Walker opened up the front of his shirt and then set to again. 'Come on, come on,' cried Eudora. Walker maddened to the rhythm. Sweat poured down his body. 'Take off his shirt,' said Eudora.

'It's like King Lear, over again,' said Froelich. 'Oh, boy, now you're a negro.'

When they left, the light was coming up. A bird was singing in a tree. The fresh pink light was rising over the shortgrass plain and picking out the undulations over toward the mountain. The peaks showed faintly. Walker got in the back with Patrice and held her hand as they drove through the empty streets of Party. 'I feel like we were driving west,' said Bob Naughty. 'What time do we hit Amarillo, Texas?' They found a diner on the edge of town and ordered eggs. The bright sunlight slanted in now through the windows, and outside the town's garbage trucks were meeting together. There was the dust of sleeplessness in Walker's eyes and he began to nod over his eggs.

'You were really turned on with those drums,' said Patrice.

'I'm tired now,' said Walker.

'Okay, come on, I'll drive you back to this Bourbon place. Where is it?'

'I don't know,' said Walker. 'Out in the country some-where.' They drove back through the fresh morning light. The Bourbon house was shuttered and silent. 'Thanks,' said Walker, getting out. He walked toward the house.

'We'll wait until you get inside,' said Froelich. Walker tried the front door; it was locked. He was about to turn and go back home with Froelich when it opened silently and Dr Bourbon, in his Japanese kimono, stood sadly on the step. 'I was sittin' up in a chair waitin' for you,' he said. 'Thought you didn't have transportation. Was waitin' for you to call.'

'Sorry I'm late,' said Walker.

'Then I heard the car. Figgered for a moment it was prowl-ers. Nearly shot you all up.'

'I'm glad you didn't.'

'Is that Bernard Froelich out there?' asked Bourbon. 'Wanted to ask him 'bout my fender.' But as he spoke, the car gunned and drove off. Walker, watching it, saw Patrice's hand waving at him through the rear window. Then they were gone and solemn Dr Bourbon ushered the guilty Walker indoors.

6

On the first day of the new semester, Walker woke in his bed at the Bourbon house to hear a strange hum and buzz in the air. The bright American day shone in through the thin gauzy drapes, and balmy winds blew in from the direction of Party the sound of yells, and screams, and shouts. Closer at hand, on the gravel outside, someone was walking; the steps ceased and suddenly a clear 'Goddarn it' was superimposed on the distant noise. It was Dr Bourbon, taking another look at the place where Froelich, in his wildness, had torn the fender off his car. Walker got out of bed and dressed quickly. When he got into the kitchen Dr Bourbon was already there, slipping his apron from the hook.

'Hear that? All that noise?' he said, nodding his head in the direction of town. 'The kids are all back.'

'Is that what the racket is?' asked Walker, feeling suddenly like an old resident.

'Yup,' said Bourbon, tying the apron, 'they're all registerin' for their courses.'

Walker sat down and Bourbon cracked two eggs into a copper pan. 'So it's all starting,' said Walker. 'Yup,' said Bourbon. 'Oh, take a look in the *Bugle*. I put it there. Nice little story about you, son.'

Walker picked up the newspaper, folded to reveal an item headed 'Angry Young Man Loses Anger in Party'. It began: 'Angry young man author James Walker, visiting Party from England to head Benedict Arnold's creative writing programme, announced Wednesday that he had stopped feeling angry since he arrived in town. "In Party there's nothing to feel angry about," chunky, tweed-clad Walker told a *Bugle* reporter . . . '

Walker put the paper down, positively red with anger. 'I didn't say that,' he said.

'Nice piece,' said Bourbon.

'I think it's terrible. I shall have to go down to the newspaper office and ask them to retract it.'

'Oh, I wouldn't do that, Mis' Walker,' said Bourbon, surprised. 'You know how it is, they write these things up a mite.'

'It's nothing like what I said,' said Walker.

'Seems close to the gist of it to me,' said Bourbon. 'Seems to me you're just regrettin' you said it.'

'I didn't say that, did I?' asked Walker.

'Well, sumpn like it. Any case, I wouldn't go down there, don't want to get off on the wrong foot with the press.'

'I seem to be very good at getting off on the wrong foot,' said Walker.

Dr Bourbon, who had been subdued ever since he had sat up all night waiting for Walker to return from his visit to the Froelichs', didn't seem disposed to refute this. The Bourbons had been nice to him, the matter had never been mentioned. The day before, Mrs Bourbon had taken him downtown and shown him the stores he might want to know about – the best men's store; the Doozy Duds, a coin-operated laundry; the

Rexall Druggist; and the First National Bank, where an amiable western character in a string tie and stuck-on mutton-chop whiskers had opened his account and given him a cheque-book with his name on it, a wallet for his statements, and a piggy-bank inscribed JAMES'S BANK. At the super-market, for supermarket orientation, she had taken him in through the self-opening doors and he had been introduced to a black-and-white check elephant and been given a free balloon and a genuine china cup and saucer. Even so, Walker felt that the fine glow of relationship was dimming out, that the pleasures of hosting were losing their savour, that the best thing a guest could do was, after all, go. So the previous afternoon he had visited, at the Froelichs' suggestion, the International House on campus and been shown a room with a small desk with a snaky-coiled lamp, a closet full of wire hangers, and two bunk beds. 'By the way,' he now said to Bourbon, 'I've fixed my living arrangements. I'm moving into a room in Inter-national House.'

'Waal, I'm told it's a mighty comfortable little place. 'Course they're mostly foreigners there, but you won't mind that. Indians and Japs and all. Did you take a look at the room?'

'Yes. It's a double, but they're letting me have it as a single. I shall have plenty of space and a place to work, you know.'

'Yeah, well, I guess that's the best. Waal, it's been mighty nice havin' you here, Mis' Walker. When do you plan to move?'

'Is today all right?'

'Oh, when you like, boy. We ain't wantin' to use the guest room for a few more days yet.'

'Well, thank you,' said Walker, 'and for all your kindness and hospitality.'

'Fun for us, Mis' Walker,' said Bourbon. 'Sweetie, Mis' Walker's leavin' today, movin' into International House,' he shouted through to the conversation pit. Mrs Bourbon came through, her cat on her shoulder.

'Oh, that's nice,' she said. 'They have English tea on Sunday afternoon once a month. I always go. They make it with those, what do you call them? – leaves. Not the bags.' Walker said his thanks and shook hands. Then he went into his bedroom and packed up the cases; Dr Bourbon was taking him down on his way to the university. The last thing he heard was a shout of 'Good-bye, turd' from Alphonse in the pool; the last thing he saw was the hostile face of Crispin, lowering from some bushes close to the drive. And then he left.

Bourbon dropped him at International House, a big, white-painted house with colonial pillars, on the edge of the campus, where town met gown and hated one another. An Arab student led him up to his room. 'Remember, please, this is a democratic place,' he said.

The phone on the wall rang. 'Su,' said a high little voice.

'Pardon?' said Walker.

'This is Mr Su. Welcome to International House. I am head of Foreign Students Committee. Good to know you.'

'And you,' said Walker.

'Remember, call Su when you're in trouble here. Any information or aid. I will invite you to all meetings. They are very democratic.'

'Thank you, Mr Su,' said Walker. After he had put down the phone, Walker picked it up again on a whimsy, for it was the first time he had had free access to this means of communication, and called Patrice Froelich in the admissions office.

'Hi hi,' he said, 'it's James Walker.'

'Hi, how are you?'

'Just to tell you I've moved into International House.'

'Fine, how is it?'

'Very democratic,' said Walker.

'Let me write down your number,' said Patrice.

Walker gave it and Patrice said, 'Now you can do what you like.'

'Fine, well, I'll call you again, then. I like that.'

'Well, do that,' said Patrice. 'Good to hear you, James.'

Walker put down the phone and heard the carillon, nearer now, playing 'It Ain't What You Do It's The Way That You Do It'. It was now his ambition to find his way to the English Department and sit in his office and prepare for his first class, tomorrow. He picked up his map and the pile of papers marked

Faculty Orientation and set out. On the way out of the House, he looked in on the bathrooms. There were no doors on the lavatories; a row of olive skinned Asiatics sat contemplatively, their trousers down, on the pots in each stall. Very democratic, thought Walker.

Outside, the students had taken over Party. College boys drove by in cars with their feet out of the windows. On the sloping roofs of the student apartments and the sororities, co-eds in simple bikinis sunned their brown skins and threw peanuts at people passing by. It made Walker want to wait there to catch one when she fell off. On campus, the girls walked along the campus paths, their notebooks in their arms, wearing neat bermuda shorts or tight skirts, with darts under the rump to make their bottoms stick out. Despite his map, it took Walker some time to find the English Department's wooden hut; at one point he crossed a stream and found himself plodding through bushes, up to his ankles in mud. Finally the hut appeared before him, vibrating with activity. Inside, students in large numbers walked up and down the corridors, making the floors bounce, and worked the Coke machine. In his office his colleagues were already sitting at their desks, giving student conferences; boys and girls sat beside them, spreading their knees, chewing gum, arguing about their destinies. A co-ed, a sorority pin at the tip of her left nipple, was saying to Froelich, over in his corner: 'Hi there, Mr Froelich. Are you going to want me to *think*, like my last teacher did?'

'Hi hi, James,' said Froelich. 'The peons are here.'

'Good morning,' said Walker.

'Want to use your desk?' asked Froelich. 'I left some teaching notes in the drawers.' He pulled out the drawers and tipped them upside down on the desk top; papers, old cigarette packs, books of matches and a Coca-Cola bottle tumbled about. 'The guy who had this desk last year drove off the top of a mountain halfway through the second semester,' said Froelich. 'You've got to be tough to survive.'

Walker sat down and opened up the instructions for his first class, trying not to think about his predecessor. The instructions said: 'Meeting One. Introduce yourself and spell your name; also write it on blackboard. Check the names of the students. Make sure no students are in your section who have been assigned to other sections. . . . ' It went on, but the print blurred in Walker's eyes and he found that he was feeling very frightened indeed. Across the room he heard Froelich's voice rise: 'Of course what I tell you is right, because if it was wrong I wouldn't tell you it. Okay, my colleagues might disagree with me, but *they're* wrong. Have confidence.'

But confidence was what Walker had not. America was a society where the words right and wrong were, from his point of view, inapplicable. Anybody could do anything. And amid this chaos stood up a few pedantries of grammar. The truth, tablets of revelation! 'It should always be made clear who is addressing whom, and on the subject of whom.' Walker made some notes for the class, despairing, and a moment later Froelich came over and proposed that they go to the faculty lounge for coffee. The lounge was full of teachers, none of them lounging, all of them tense. They were mostly young men who had just come in, pulling Hertz trailers from New York and Wisconsin and Santa Barbara. They had supposed they were individuals, intellectually unique, and now here were hundreds more like themselves. They stood in the lounge and looked at one another in desperate inquiry, seeing their intellects, their critical responsiveness, their high literary awareness, their special quality of mind, multiplied by scores. In the corner of the lounge an old man tended a coffee machine; they paid five cents each and filled their cups. 'See that man behind the machine?' said Froelich. 'He's an emeritus professor. He watches the coffee and then he goes downtown to get the latest word on the used car prices. Can't bear to give the old place up.' They sat down, and Froelich said, 'You look unhappy.'

'Well,' said Walker, 'I am. Here we are in America. A pluralistic society where nothing is not allowed. Everybody goes his own way. But we have to teach them grammar. What do you say on its behalf? "Grammar is what you feel good after. And our sermon today is on the rewards of the good grammatical life. Live grammatically, and all shall be open to

240

you. Your employer will appreciate the clarity of your memoranda, or other kinds of report required in business." '

'Oh, don't worry about it,' said Froelich, 'wait until later in the year. You'll feel a really fulfilled person when you call up one of your students on the telephone, to ask her for a date or something, and she answers: "This is she speaking." That's the day when it all comes right.'

'Is that all teaching is? Remember there used once to be a thing called morals? Does that come into it at all?'

'Now morals,' said Froelich, 'well, there, you must wait and see.'

'I know I shouldn't pine like this,' said Walker. 'After all, this is such a challenge. A wide-open country. Responsibility or non-responsibility – you can choose. It's a moral supermarket. The trouble is I get so confused, I decide to buy nothing at all.'

'You need consumer advice,' said Froelich. 'And that's what I'm here for.'

'I'll remember,' said Walker.

Standing in front of the letter pigeonhole later, Walker found his name at last. There were four letters. One, from Elaine, had been posted before the telegram. It reminded him about his underpants, and said it had rained in Nottingham, and told how the librarian downstairs had come up twice to unstop the sink in the kitchen. 'I do wish these nine months would hurry up and go away, because I miss you,' the letter ended. The second, from New York, contained a file card. On it, in rather unformed handwriting, was inscribed a quotation: 'Fools and young men prate about everything being possible for a man. That, however, is a great error. Spiritually speaking, everything is possible, but in the world of the finite there is much which is not possible. This impossible, however, the knight makes possible by expressing it spiritually, but he expresses it spiritually by waiving his claim to it. The wish which would carry him out into reality, but was wrecked upon the impossibility, is now bent inward, but it is not therefore lost, neither is it forgotten. Kierkegaard, *Fear and Trembling*.' Underneath was written: 'I was sorry we missed in N.Y. So –

come again. On the wall of the women's john at a bar in the Village: If you love life, despicable is thy name. How's the co-ordination? Julie.' The third letter, from St Louis, said, '*Isn't* it a funny country? I'm loving it though. And one has so much money. Are you going to travel? I am, and don't be at all surprised to see me descend on you. I can offer, if you come to St Louis, a bed-settee in the living-room, all quite respectable. You're a nice boy, and I remember you well. Remember me. Love, Fern Marrow.' The fourth letter said, 'Dear Friend: I am giving on the evening of next Thursday, at 7 p.m. (19:00), a small dinner party, and at this party you are the guest of honour. Since you will be the only guest, you will not, I think, be able to plead excuses of "previous engagements". The proceeding for arrival here is so: take westwards the crosstown bus on Main and request to descend at Mountview. Here is a fire hydrant. From here walk north on Mountview one block. You cannot fail to observe this house. It is really the house in which the elves make those toys for Santa Claus. There is a bell on the doorpost and against it my name. F. Jochum.' Walker read all the letters blandly, and felt free of all their claims. He put them in his pocket and went to finish the preparation of his class.

On the day after, the teaching programme began. The wooden hut occupied by the English Department was next to one of the main paths that led across the campus, so that from their offices the members of the faculty could see the co-eds flouncing past the windows, notebooks in their arms, on their way from class to class. On fine days they wore neat blouses and skirts, tight at the rump, or else cut-off jeans with the Greek letters of their sororities painted in white across their behinds; on wet ones they wore slickers in red and blue and yellow or, if it was cold, quilted or fur-lined jackets with hoods. The men wore denims and shirts, or sweaters with the university crest across the bosom. They were a bright sight, and Walker spent a good deal of time peering through the fly screens on his windows at this campus display. It took place every hour, when the bell rang, the floors boomed, and classes emptied out.

The faculty dashed in and out of their offices, taking off and putting on their jackets, servicing the many needs of the students. You could see them as you walked down the corridors, teaching affably, the door open, their voices genial from the podium. The teaching associates, who taught only the composition classes and were usually working for graduate degrees as well, were packed six or eight to an office and could be seen there, with the doors again open, marking themes, preparing classes, writing novels, smoking and occasionally eating lunch. All these people were mentors for Walker in the conduct of his academic life, these men of abstract ideas who read Shakespeare in the morning and played with a football on the grass in the afternoon. It seemed hard to know where they got their inspiration from, why they went on being wise men at all, and it was only from a kind of intellectual optimism that Walker sensed in the American air, a fondness for discovery and growth, that he could relate all the varied parts of them together. They were neither convincingly intellectual nor convincingly philistine; they mixed the materialist and the aesthetic approaches; they were coarse where they might be sensitive and sensitive where they might be coarse.

From his own classes, Walker began to learn. He suspected that he ran them rather differently from the other teachers; for instance, he was always careful to shut the door. He taught, too, in an atmosphere of amiable mystery, unsure about his standards, unsure about his function, unsure even whether his words were being understood or not. The composition class was his most difficult one. It met twice a week in the Chemistry Building, opulent new premises which lay about a half a mile away from the English Department, and involved him in a long walk on which he occasionally got lost completely. The classes were held in a large amphitheatre with a sink and some gas taps on the teacher's desk. When he leaned forward excitedly he fell forward into the sink, and on occasions when he grew abstract he was apt to play with the gas taps and turn them on. The class consisted largely of beautiful girls, all about eighteen, splendidly made up; they sat in the front rows, close to him, exposing beautiful legs, and distracting him with intense perfumes. The men sat separately, on the other side of the aisle, occasionally throwing pieces of paper at the girls. One of them, a big bulky youth with fair hair in a crew cut, put his feet up on Walker's desk. All of them appeared to write down everything he said. On the first day he had told them his name – they wrote that down – and had written on the blackboard the number of his office in the English Department. 'Where is the English Department?' asked one of the girls, all of whom had started to knit. It was impossible for Walker to answer this and he had to turn for help to others in the class. Presently another girl asked him where he was from, and a boy had asked about the supposed stodginess of English women, and Walker found himself talking about his wife and his sexual habits before marriage and the way in which his parents had brought him up. It had gone on this way ever since. The class seemed to like him, and he liked them. Often he suspected that they only understood a few words of what he was saying, because of his accent, but they were extremely jolly with him and told him a great deal about the dating system. One of the girls offered to knit him a sweater; he felt that, there, he was well on the way to acceptance.

The creative writing classes were simpler but not less challenging. They met in the seminar rooms in the English Building in an atmosphere of pleasant informality. The class members sat round the oblong table, smoking, and reading things they had written, or asking questions about submitting manuscripts and whether they should send self-addressed envelopes or not. The graduate class was the more demanding, because it lasted for two hours and because many of the students were his fellow teachers in the composition course. They were also intense and bright. There were extravagant Emersonians in white socks who wished to recreate in fiction all of human history and human knowledge; there were strange Southern girls who said little but occasionally sketched out plots for stories about extravagant rapes on poor white smallholdings; there was Miss Handlin, the girl whom Walker had met on his first day in Party, who was keeping a visionary spiritual diary about the way she was trying to attain progression through hallucination. The practical, finite pitch of Walker's thoughts embarrassed him as he discovered that his students were all romantics; they tapped their cigarettes on the old tins used as ashtrays in the seminar room and asked, 'Well, Mr Walker, what is truth?' or 'What does it feel like to die?' or 'Where are we going, in this world of ours?'

'You're a writer, Mr Walker, so you have to tell us the truth that nobody else tells us,' Miss Handlin said in the first class. Walker wriggled and went red. 'You must have a vision of the world; tell us what it is,' she went on. Walker groped to find it and got nowhere. The classes went on and he began to doubt. Was he a writer at all? Wasn't he a half-writer, a man who had chanced into this as he might have gone into any profession, a man without dedication or intensity? Had he ever given anything to the imagination? Did he take chances, believe in it as a force? Where and how did literature flow into him, and in what way did it seed or grow? The class pushed him and pressed him and groped with him, and watched to see his spirit stir. He was on the way, though, and he knew it. The provinces, and domesticity, and the home he had left behind, had all lost their grip on him. At night he sat in his room and watched the mountains, while oriental students played ritual basketball in their shorts below his window, and tried to grasp at infinities, at the unethical and irrational immensities that would give him the vastness of spirit he craved. America seemed, through these students, the world of freedom and aspiration he had hoped for it to be. Miss Handlin's diary, headed with a phrase of Santayana, 'The imagination, therefore, must furnish to religion and to metaphysics those large ideas tinctured with passion, those supersensible forms shrouded in awe, in which alone a mind of great sweep and vitality can find its congenial objects', set the pace of the class. She read from it her visions, achieved through the stimulus of drugs, occasional fornication, and contemplation of nature, keeping the class active in interpretation and Walker alive in his hope that romanticism was not, then, exhausted.

Amid the finite and the diurnal, Walker and his kindred souls wrestled onward, for two hours a week. There was a gay antinomianism about the graduate students, too, and he spent long evenings with them in their rooms in the Graduate Halls, listening to records of Lotte Lenya, eating pretzels, then driving up to parties in the canyon, where the air was sulphurated with sexuality and everyone drank Californian wine. Walker developed a taste for and a loyalty to it all. The graduate students and younger faculty members, who had all spent long years in college, also had an intellectual style Walker envied. They had vast terminologies for talking about literature, and freely used words Walker had never before heard in anyone's speech vocabulary – *mimesis*, *epistemology*, *mythopoeic*. They had strong specialisms which they talked about in detail – a strong Shelley group banded together in the faculty lounge to talk about *Epipsychidion* over cups of Maxwell House – and Walker was struck by their real concern with ideas. Walker got on with all these well, and his only difficult encounters were with Hamish Wagner, who always prefaced any conversation with him with the phrase 'Pip pip, old boy,' and saw him as a stage Englishman, and some of the older faculty members who had spent time in Europe and for whom he had a glow; they were vastly disappointed when he set aside his tweeds on purchasing a seersucker suit in blue and white stripe that made him look like a sunshade.

One evening, at the end of the second week of the semester, Dr Bourbon invited out all the faculty and graduate students to his house, in order to introduce them to one another. In the doorway Bourbon and Hamish Wagner, Head of Composition, stood, pinning tags on lapels, giving the wearer's name, degrees, and a short list of his publications. Inside, the house where Walker had stayed was transformed. People swayed back and forth in eddies. A Spenser specialist stood outside on the patio to prevent people falling into the swimming pool, and a Swinburne man was stationed by the barbecue pit to stop people from skewering themselves on the spit. The realization that their colleagues were so many in number brought a return of the depression that everyone had felt on the first day; people went about, one eye low down, reading the tags on lapels. Some of the women looked rather red. Walker got himself a drink and hid in one corner of the room, talking to Cindy Handlin. 'I've just been reading *The Magic Mountain*,' said Miss Handlin.

'Ah, yes,' said Walker, 'a splendid book.'

'*Is*n't it good? *Is*n't it?' said Miss Handlin. 'Didn't it just give you an orgasm?'

'Well, it didn't actually,' said Walker, 'but I'll look at it again.'

'Oh, do,' said Miss Handlin.

Across the room, Hamish Wagner asked for silence and said that Dr Bourbon was going to speak. The crowd all sat down tailor-fashion on the floor, and Bourbon appeared in the serving hatch, a curiously effective podium. His head and shoulders stuck through, his moustache catching the light. He smiled and said, 'First of all I just want to say "Howdy" to everybody, ole friends and new ones.' A few people said 'Howdy' back at him. 'Folks,' he went on, 'in these times a lot of people don't realize how important English is. Now we know that, that's why we're all here, teachin' and all, but we've got to convince these kids of the importance of English. I want you to think that after a year these kids will go away and say, "Boy, that was a great teacher I had there in Comp., or World Lit. Maybe I'll take some courses in Lit. next year." Teach 'em right, and these kids will come back for more.' Bourbon then went on to define some of the fundamental axioms of teaching as he saw it: avoid intellectual arrogance, never criticize another teacher to a student, don't smoke in the corridors of wooden buildings. Gifts of money should not be accepted in exchange for favours. If teachers were attacked by a member, or members, of their class, they should report it to the Dean of Studies, even if they were not wounded. 'Now,' he went on, 'I want you all to introduce yourselves to one another. I'd like us to get up in alphabetical order and announce our names, our degrees, and our list of publications.' People began to stand up and testify, as Bourbon read out their names. When he got round to Walker he rose sheepishly and mentioned his degree. 'A special welcome to Mis' Walker from England,' said Mr Bourbon. 'He's our creative writin' fellow and he's published some fine novels. Tell them the names of your novels, Mis' Walker, so they can go right out and order them.' Walker gave the titles of his novels and was rewarded with a small round of applause.

Afterwards Walker took his drink out on to the patio and stood in the darkness looking out over the lights of Party, shining through the trees. It was neat and small and comforting, and after the ceremonial of acceptance Walker felt himself a citizen, an approved man of mind, a spoke in the cycle of learning. He was of this élite, and it had accepted him. An accredited teacher, he felt his loyalties growing to include these visionary souls. They were of one body; materialists of grammar, but on the path to higher things. Then he heard someone in the darkness behind him, blundering through a bush, and Dr Bourbon appeared by his side.

'Shoot,' he said, wiping his brow. 'Have to git a bigger house, if the department keeps on expandin'.'

'It's an enormous party,' said Walker.

'Yip,' said Bourbon, 'they've drunk all my supplies. Had to send Crispin out for some more ice. Well, must git back in there, but I just wanted to tell you somethin'. I wrote a memorandum to the President 'bout the loyalty oath business. Got a reply today. Said all members of staff had to sign it, accordin' to state law. But he says if the British government did require you to overthrow the American government you'd be covered under international law. He looked it up.'

'Well, thank you very much,' said Walker. 'I'll have to think about it again. It seems an equivocal position.'

'Waal,' said Bourbon, 'I guess Britain and the States are goin' to see pretty much eye to eye for the rest of the academic year. Might as well sign.'

'I'll see,' said Walker.

They walked back inside. Elderly faculty wives were making gracious rounds among the graduate students, and a fairly rigid class system was operating. The graduates all seemed rather subdued by the formalities of the occasion, but there was considerable delight when Hamish Wagner, pouring a bagful of ice into the punchbowl, got into difficulties – the ice exploded upward in a high pillar of smoke, scattering a fine spray over the people near-by.

'Mighty violent ice, that,' said Bourbon, waving ineffectually at the smoke cloud.

'I got dry ice,' said Crispin, leaning against the wall and cackling with laughter, 'the kind they use for starting rainstorms.' Harris Bourbon shook his head sadly and the graduate students poked one another and hid suppressed mirth. Miss Handlin took it rather differently however.

'Oh, wasn't that ecstatic?' she said to Walker. 'Did you ever see anything so beautiful? I guess that's one of the most beautiful things I ever saw. Doesn't it make you want to take your clothes off?'

'It certainly does,' said Walker politely.

On the next evening Walker took the crosstown bus, found out where to deposit his fare, and sat on the bench, watching Party unroll through the windows, until the driver said, 'Here's where you want out.' Dr Jochum lived in a part of town that Walker had never visited and never really knew about; it was composed of extravagant gothic houses in wood, and was a relic of the rich mining days when Party felt confident about itself. The house where Jochum roomed was distinguished by onion domes on the roof, so that it looked like a smaller version of the Kremlin, and by doors at all levels, with steps up to them and steps down to them. Walker found the right door, then the right bell. Jochum appeared instantaneously, beaming, wearing shorts, a gay shirt, and moccasin shoes. 'A big welcome here,' he said. 'Now we must go carefully up these stairs.' He led the way up a tortured, big-banistered staircase to a tiny room in the roof; it had wooden walls, a high bed in the centre, and at one end, in a gable window, two chairs and a maple table. 'Please take off your jacket, I will hang it carefully in the closet, and then sit down,' said Jochum. 'Then I will serve you first some tea. It was with tea that we first met each other, do you recall?'

'Yes, I do,' said Walker.

'One moment,' said Jochum, 'I vill be back. In the meantime here is a newspaper to read.'

But before Walker had even unfolded the *Bugle* Jochum was back with a tray. 'Vell,' he said, 'has the desert worked? Have you found the lost character?'

'I think I'm finding it.'

'How does it look?'

'Oh, pretty bad.'

'Vell, that at least is interesting. Most people find they haven't got any at all. Please eat while we are talking.'

'Thank you.'

'See, I am eating too. Of course, character is not a fashionable concept. Now we think that we act because our family situation was so, because our historical location is so, because we are sailing with the tide of history, or because it has abandoned us as reactionary deviants. Today all our actions are really performed by our grandfathers; we take no responsibility, like the owners of umbrella stands in hotels. So, you see, nobody believes really in people any more. People, well, they are a nineteenth-century concept. Now man is a focus of forces.'

'Well, I feel that's true,' said Walker. 'I haven't succeeded in finding much self yet . . . as you warned me I wouldn't.'

'Ah vell, what do you expect? The good ship you sail in is called *Eclectica*; you are blown about by the winds as they come. You have no idea how to conduct yourself, so you make a virtue of whim. That is quite natural.'

'Yes,' said Walker, eating a large sandwich filled with tuna fish. 'But that can be a nice mode of being.'

'Oh yes, but such an atomized one. The Marxists always tell that the nineteenth century was the age of atomized behaviour. Individualism. As I am telling my classes always, it was not so. Those were the great days of being, the grand carnival of existence. And why? Because everyone had a large piece of society in his head when he was six months old, and a vast ethical system when he was adult. That is why there was Freud; everyone thinks that Freud knew about insides and Marx about society, but it was the good Sigmund that knew about society. It starts here, in the head.' Jochum rapped hard with his fist on his skull.

'But we all live under the pressure of the facts,' said Walker. 'I mean, look how the world is going. Look at this vast urbanized and technologized mass-society that we are going to have to live with if we don't evade the issue – as I do. What a foul empty life that promises to be to people who have some idea of what the good life was like. But that's the future America is looking so brightly towards. I can't help thinking that England's wise in politely pretending that it can't really exist.'

'You are telling me that our time is one when we are learning how to live worse. Well, I am telling that to you.'

'But how does one be a man among men now?'

'Ah, there is the question. You want me to give you ethics. But you must find them for yourself.'

'But as you were saying, there seem very few around. The moral space in our lives seems to be shrinking fast.'

'That's so. And so we invite in politics. The ethics of politics tells: eliminate these, kill those, declare war, start revolutions. It drives out the ethics of personal living, of being a person, which tells: be kind, respect others, do good things. So I like your search. You are foolish, my friend, and you will always do silly things. But I am admiring you a good deal. More tea for you?'

'Thank you,' said Walker, holding out his cup. 'Actually it all grows more difficult. I feel very burdened just at the moment.'

'Of course, ever since I have known you on that ship you have been so. Vell, let me guess. You are in love with fifteen vomen at one time, and now they are all pregnant and vish to marry you.'

'Close,' said Walker. 'But not quite. I'm trying to divorce my wife.'

'Vell, no doubt this is a more stupid thing than all the rest, but I vill assume there is some special Walker sense to it.'

'I want to be sure I'm doing right, you see.'

'Oh, you are not, but no matter.'

'I don't want to hurt her, you know.' He felt in his pocket for

251

a letter which had come that morning, a reply to the letter he had finished and sent, asking for his freedom. Elaine said, 'You ask me to give you your freedom. But I haven't *got* your freedom, Jim. I don't remember ever seeing it. I think you must have taken it with you – do look through all your things. If it's not there, I don't think you ever had it. You can do what you want; you always could. You owe some things to me, but they're not claimed very often. No, it's not your freedom that's missing, really, but your love. I think you ought to have a look for that too, because I think you'll find it. And if it's not over there, shouldn't you come back home and look before you decide on this? I think that would be much better than coming back to me in a couple of years and saying it was a terrible mistake. And you know you're quite capable of doing *that*.' Walker handed the letter to Jochum; Jochum took out some old, wire-framed spectacles to read it. 'Vell, are you capable?' asked Jochum, when he had finished.

'I suppose so. It depends on whether I go on finding what I think I'm looking for.'

Jochum looked at the letter again and said, 'I'm afraid it is difficult. I think she loves you.'

'Oh, she does.'

'And you do not love her.'

'Well, I don't know. I'm not sure what it feels like, not sure what the word means.'

'Ah, I understand,' said Jochum. 'Love is an emotion that other people feel towards you.'

'No, not that. It's just that my loyalties have changed. My mind has gone another way. I'm committed to things she doesn't share. She holds me back from them. And in a way I've gone beyond that kind of affection.'

'Oh yes, the cruelty of the writer. He must sacrifice his loved ones to write the better about love. It is a very old story.'

'Well, it is like that, yes. I've grown a lot here. I'm moving towards things I've long missed. I think I'm moving towards being a real writer, a real artist. That means cutting some ropes, untying oneself from the shore.'

'You want to marry someone else?'

'No, it's divorce, not marriage, I'm on with. I want to marry the universe.'

'Ah, those old romantic weddings. The trouble with the universe is that it is so unfaithful. It runs around with so many people.'

'But you see what I mean?'

'No,' said Jochum, 'I don't see. I think you are mad as a hatter.'

'I am?' asked Walker, looking pleased.

'We all are, but it is always a good lesson to look hard at the victims who suffer by your ideology.'

'There are always victims.'

'Oh, I know, I am a victim from way back, that is why I am an exile. However, I must retire to the kitchen. Now I become a hausfrau. Read please the newspaper.'

Walker picked up the *Party Bugle*, and found in it, again, his own name. 'Angry young man author James Walker, presently visiting BAU from England, lectures Wednesday, December 1, on *The Writer's Dilemma*. Walker, one of Britain's leading authors, earlier picked out Party as a town of "real nice people", and said he preferred it to England. Maybe that's Mr Walker's dilemma.'

'Did you see this?' said Walker, angrily marching into the kitchen with the paragraph.

'Ah, yes, I see you know how to please the press.'

'Those aren't my views.'

'Of course not.'

'And I didn't say that.'

'It is simply what you are expected to say. No one believes it, but it is nice to think that one day someone might really say such a thing. Now I would say it and mean it, but I am never asked.'

'Say it and mean it?'

'Of course,' said Jochum, throwing some lentils into a pan, 'I am a loyalist. This is the only country, the only town, I have. I love it much more than the citizens. I only see its virtues.'

'I meant to ask you,' said Walker, 'did you have to sign a loyalty oath when you came? As a foreigner?'

'I signed such an oath, but I am not a foreigner.'

'You didn't complain?'

'I was pleased to sign it. This is what I am telling. I feel very loyal here.'

'It offends me,' said Walker.

'Well, of course, you are a liberal.'

'And a foreigner.'

'But I thought that you told me you had discounted those old loyalties. You had cut the ropes.'

'I have.'

'Ah, you want to be a loyalist of nowhere. I want to be a loyalist of somewhere.'

'A loyalist of the imagination,' said Walker.

'Well, I hope you will not make a cause of this. There are many people on campus who would be only too happy to use you to further their ends.'

'Mightn't they be good ends?'

'Some of them.'

'I have a taste for preserving freedom, because I enjoy it so much myself.'

'Since I came here for freedom,' said Jochum, 'I have the same taste. On this we agree.'

'But isn't prescribing what we teach – and doesn't the loyalty oath mean that? – a limitation of freedom?'

'How does it prescribe what you teach?'

'Well, how does one define what contributes to the overthrow of the American government? Supposing I praise the British National Health Service in class? Isn't that menacing to the government, in a sense? I'm told there are people who think it is.'

'I have never understood that the misuse of a device means that we should eliminate the device, only the misuse.'

'But the device is a symptom of the prevalence of the misuse.'

'Ah, now I agree. But you will find that American universities are very vulnerable. Someone once defined liberals as people who embrace their destroyers. I think protected democracy is proper in a world where there are many destroyers. But please, why do we talk of these things on a pleasant evening?'

'I have to decide what to do about the oath,' said Walker.

'Well, I can offer a solution. I believe in personal solutions and here is one. Do not sign it – that will ease your conscience – and hope that the filing system in the Administration Building is so terrible that nobody will know.'

'I've already raised the matter with Dr Bourbon.'

'Even so.'

'It's a thought, a nice thought.'

'Just a friendly suggestion,' said Jochum, looking like a kind father as he beamed at Walker. Walker beamed back and sucked in the thick vegetable smell that rose from the pot Jochum was stirring. He was looking forward to a real, European meal.

Walker spent most of the next week writing his lecture on *The Writer's Dilemma*. His writer's dilemma was that he couldn't think of anything to say. One day, when he was sitting in his office, late in the evening, when the rest of his colleagues who shared it with him had gone home, he was interrupted; Dr Bourbon had heard him typing and put his head in. 'Hi, boy,' he said, stuffing threads of tobacco into his pipe, and looking round to see whether Walker was alone. 'Just come in to tell you President Coolidge is givin' a little reception before yore lecture next Wednesday. 'Bout six. Drinks and a buffet. It's a real honour, boy.'

'I hope I finish writing it in time,' said Walker.

'That it? Well, I won't look. Let it surprise me.'

'It may,' said Walker, smiling.

'Be a lot of very important people there. The President and his wife; in fact the President may introduce you. Real honour. Then some of the state officials may come down, there's an athletic meeting that afternoon. Be a good turnout from the faculty, I guess. Thought I'd better warn you case you was thinkin' of makin' it informal. Better make it formal. Press'll be there. Guess they'll send a man down from the *Dimity Gazette*. That's the biggest paper in the state. Dimity's the state capital. I'd stick in some extra carbons so they can have copies of the text. These pressmen, they're nice fellows, but they don't all write shorthand very good.'

'I know,' said Walker, thinking of his recent press experiences.

'I look forward to it, Mis' Walker,' said Bourbon, nodding and going out.

Walker didn't. On the evening of the lecture it rained, the mountains went from view; and the trees were wet and fragrant as Walker set out in his mackintosh to the President's House, or rather mansion, a large white property in the colonial manner hidden behind trees on a corner of the campus. Here President Coolidge and his wife, a handsome woman in a flame-red dress, stood formally just inside the door, shaking hands with the entrants.

'Nice to see you, Walk,' said the President, crinkling his smile, 'you're our guest of honour tonight.' He put his hand on his wife's arm – she was talking to Harris Bourbon, who looked ill at ease in a vast black area of dinner jacket – and said, 'You must meet our guest of honour, Hetty.'

'Oh, the great man himself,' said the President's wife, turning, 'I've heard so much. . . . '

'The students really love this man,' said Bourbon. 'Why, I was talkin' to Miss Handlin, she's wild about you, Mis' Walker.' Bourbon ushered Walker forward into the big, elegantly furnished room, a concord of decoration, done by a designer with a taste for big hangings and Aztec masks. 'I got some new people you ought to know,' said Bourbon, introducing him to Selena May Sugar ('she's one of the committee brung you here'), a local novelist, a moustachioed man clearly modelled on Mark Twain ('writes about the west – begins with the creakin' of the covered wagons and ends with the discovery of oil'), two reporters from Dimity ('bastions of the press'), and the Mayor of Party, a dapper little man in a string tie and a lightweight suit with gold threads shining in it. 'Howdy, sir,' said the Mayor. 'We're real glad to know you like it here. We do.'

Walker had been feeling nervous all week; now he felt

virtually hysterical. His speech, under his arm in a blue folder he had bought for ten cents from the college bookstore, seemed utter nonsense to him. He drank three martinis in quick succession, and talked to the Mayor about the history of Party. 'My granddaddy and grandmaw came out here in a covered wagon, to settle. Grandmaw still talks about it. Recollects coming out here in a covered dish. Her mind's going a little. Lot of people in town who came out that way. You can still smell the frontier here. There were people coming through here still looking for gold when I was a boy.' The President interrupted to ask Walker to partake of a buffet supper. At the long cloth-covered table where the morsels were laid out, Walker found himself in line with Hamish Wagner. 'Pip pip, old boy,' said Hamish.

'Hello,' said Walker.

'Come for a dish of tea?'

'Yes.'

'How's the Queen?'

'Very well, thank you.'

'You know,' said Hamish, 'the last big lecture we had of this kind was when Auden, that's W. H. Auden, came through. Lectured in a tweed hat. It was brilliant.'

'I'm afraid you'll be disappointed tonight, then.'

'Not at all, old boy. Keep your pecker up, what?'

'All right,' said Walker.

Walker filled his tray and sat down. He sat next to Bernard Froelich, hoping for comfort. 'Hi hi,' said Froelich.

'This is turning into quite an occasion, isn't it?' said Walker, trying to keep the tray steady on his knee. 'The only disappointment will be the actual lecture.'

'Oh, you're safe, you're an authority. You became an authority by leaving home. In England there are fifty of you; in Party you're the only one of the kind. So we give you martinis and potato salad and we'll all come to look and see what you wear and what shape your head is.'

'I see, they won't listen to me.'

'Oh, they'll drink in your nonsense as words of wisdom,' said Froelich, encouragingly. 'That's why you have so much moral power around here. That's why you can take a special stand on the loyalty oath issue.'

Walker looked around to see whether anyone was listening, but though they were at the heart of a crowd no one visibly was. 'I think I've solved that,' said Walker, 'I shall simply not sign and hope that no one notices.'

'A secret protest,' said Froelich. 'A sneaky way round the existential dilemma. The only trouble is that it's no good.'

'Why not?' asked Walker.

'Well, do you want a political answer or a moral answer or a religious answer? Look, I'll tell you. It's no good because you're an authority, as we've said. That means you're a charismatic figure. You're a psychopomp, a public conscience. You've been appointed. So now you have to grow up beyond morality in secret. You have to stand up and be counted. You have to state your beliefs, because people want to hear them and you want people to hear them.'

'But I don't, I happen to believe in privacy of choice.'

'A writer who believes in privacy of choice. You know, privacy, I thought we'd vanquished *that* concept. We're members one of another; we're social beings; we're political animals.'

'I'm not, I never liked Joan of Arc; I've always thought sainthood was too public. I want to do what I think right, but I do it to please *me*. I don't want that exploited, I don't want to change the world.'

'You want to act without consequences. Well, I don't think that opportunity has ever been vouchsafed.'

'Oh, I've managed pretty well so far, and I shall keep on trying until I'm stopped. All I want on my headstone are just three fine words: "He eschewed definition." '

'I suppose that's what's called liberalism in England.'

'In a way, yes.'

'It sounds like self-hatred to me,' said Froelich. 'It's a logical inconsistency, and it will beat you yet, James.'

'It may, but it hasn't.'

'You don't believe in yourself, you don't accept what you do, is that it?'

'I believe in it personally, but I'm not a causes man. I don't believe that what is right for one is right for all.'

'You want your own salvation but everybody else ought to go to the devil,' said Froelich. 'I get it.'

At this moment the President came over to the couch where they were sitting. 'Well, now, look, fine,' he said to Walker. 'I think we ought to be getting on over to Fogle. I've got your biog. right here, Walk, and I'm going to give a welcome and a biog. and then it's yours. Got your script?' Walker picked up the script and put down his unfinished meal. He felt cold in the stomach. 'I'm going to take you over in my car and then we'll rest a moment when we get there and let the others take their places.' Coolidge led the way outside and they got together into his car. 'I'd reckon about an hour's spiel, then a pause of about five minutes to let people who want to get up and move around, and then, if you're amenable, we'll take a question or two. I put out a glass of water on the podium, and don't forget to speak into the mike because we're taping it.' Coolidge drove through the darkening campus and stopped at the rear entrance to Fogle. He led Walker through a backstage and property-room section and showed him a lavatory. Then it was time to begin.

The Fogle Auditorium, which could accommodate about three thousand people, was a vast series of tiered crescents with plushy green seats. The audience for his lecture comprised about eight hundred people, clustered together just below the stage. As they went on to the platform, an organ was intoning, sombrely, 'Abide with Me'. The organ stopped and the platform party sat down, three chairs behind a large speaker's desk from which innumerable microphones bristled. To one side of it was a limp American flag. Below the platform a student crouched with a tape-recorder. Then came the audience, in which Walker, though nervous with fear, could vaguely discern the features of Bourbon, Froelich, Dr Jochum and Cindy Handlin. In the front row was the Mayor of Party, who had somehow acquired an Alsatian dog, and the men of the press, including the reporter from the *Party Bugle* whom Walker now detested. After a long silent pause, while audience and Walker looked at one another, President Coolidge rose and went to the desk. 'Ladies and gentlemen,' he said. 'In the eighteenth century, I guess it was, it was the custom of important men, men in power, to employ the services of a professional hermit. This guy sat in rags in a grotto and he offered, well, a practical demonstration of the virtues of solitude. The rich men employed him as a kind of cure for their consciences. These worldly fellows led practical lives, you see, but they could imagine another kind of life that was dedicated to more, well, spiritual things. Today, ladies and gentlemen, we, the universities of America, are the new patrons of these hermits. Now sitting with me on the platform tonight is B A U's own hermit for the year. His name's James Walker and he's an important, a very important, English writer. We have a writer here at B A U so that he can live with us and we can examine him and look at a less practical kind of life than the one we live in the modern world of today. It is in this belief that the creative is no less important than the practical that we welcome James Walker, author of three novels, a writer of no mean repute, to this campus and this country. Mr Walker is not only a great writer but a great Am.. great Englishman. I'll ask him to speak to us now on, ah, on *The Writer's Dilemma.*' The audience applauded and so did the President. Then, standing at the desk, he summoned Walker over with an outstretched arm and put something – a laurel bay? No, it was a microphone – round his neck. The applause died and Walker was alone.

He looked down at his speech in the blue folder. The first page of the typescript said neatly *The Writer's Dilemma.* After that followed reams of windy persiflage, hammered out in the security of isolation. He looked at it, then out at the audience, and then decided to stay away from the text.

'Well,' said Walker, 'I've been asked to speak tonight on the writer's dilemma, and the way the topic was put to me made it evident that it was taken for granted that dilemmas were things no decent modern writer could afford to be seen without. I don't deny that writers do have dilemmas, and that there are more dilemmas than ever for writers to have. As I look at you all out there, sitting in those nice green seats, all come out from your warm houses and apartments, I can't help but feel grateful that you should turn out, when you needn't, to listen to me talking about my dilemma. I ask myself, would I come out and listen to yours? Would I ever hold still on a bar stool long enough to hear about the dentist's dilemma? Or the doctor's dilemma? I have a nasty feeling that I wouldn't. What makes the writer's dilemma so interesting or important I don't care to think. But I'm touched and grateful for the goodwill and generosity with which the matter is treated. Here am I. For the first time in several years I have a new suit, this is it, bought me by this college. I have a new pen, a madras watch-strap, a new pair of socks. My thinking has been stretched. My attitudes have changed and expanded. I can't grumble. What dilemma?'

A flashlight bulb exploded and the Mayor's dog growled.

Walker found himself more confused than ever. He tried to grasp for something. 'The writer's dilemma today is, it seems to me, every man's dilemma, sharpened for certain evident reasons, due to the writer's social location and the commitments that literature as a profession puts on him. The writer today is talked of as an outsider. He is called disoriented and disgruntled. But was he ever the inside man, the loyalist, the patriot? Was he ever oriented? Was he ever, well, gruntled? Literature, it seems to me, has always, or for a long time, demanded that writers be concerned with matters of conduct and good living. I suppose if I have a dilemma it's not meeting up to the ethical demands of the profession, because of course we are more confused about good living than ever. We know too much; we know the falsity that lies behind our professions of honesty, the vanity that lies behind our moral stance.'

Walker thought he had talked enough now, and looked at his watch; there were forty-five minutes more to go. He took a glass of water and caught the face of Dr Jochum, looking wryly at him. He smiled. He found a few more things to say about his moral confusion; that it did not distinguish him from other men, that only because he thought of himself as a writer did he feel justified in talking about it at all. He located a clock on the side wall and watched its fingers turn slowly. He observed, as he talked, the spinning wheels of the tape-recorder on the ground just below his podium. He was talking, he found, about the complexities of commitment and of attitude in the modern world, which was now no longer national but international. 'I have to come to America,' he said, 'to be called a writer, to feel like a writer at all. And that raises the question of what it is that today we owe to the imagination. Should we let it bring us away like this, from our wives and our children and our hearths? Should we all have stopped at home? I don't know. Perhaps there are things we should put first – other loyalties. But I do think this. If we are going to show our piety to the liberal ideal of the writer, the disinterested man, and have him in our universities and have him lecture to us about his dilemma, then we have to do it freely. I came here for the chance to be uncommitted; it was a marvellous chance, and I'm proud to be here, I suppose. Yes, I think I am. It was very disloyal of me to come, really. But I came to be loyal to being a writer. That means not being limited. As I say, I'm not sure whether this is a good commitment. But if you think enough of it to ask me here, then don't limit it at all by anything like, well, the loyalty oath that I have on my desk in my apartment. That's a mistake.'

Walker hadn't really intended to say this, and he was surprised that his own mouth should have come round to this position before his heart did. He paused a moment, and then noticed that there was some confusion in the audience. The Mayor of Party was sweeping out, tugging at his dog. There were several rapid flashlight shots, one of the audience and not of him at all. One or two people were talking, and the press was writing furiously. An old lady seemed to be hitting someone with her purse. More people followed the Mayor down the aisle. On-stage, the President appeared to be pushing back his chair away from Walker. All Walker could think of was that he had to keep going for thirty more minutes; he used the pause to think of more things to say. It occurred to him that the argument against what he had just said might be the argument that Jochum used: that the speciality of liberalism is the betrayal of the society in which liberalism is permitted to exist. He went on to argue with this one, pointing out that he himself wasn't dangerous to anyone. He could quite see that there were others who might be: that the danger of freedom of ideas, the possibility of literary commitment and disinterestedness, was that it gave equal freedom to non-ideas, to the free play of the stupid cause or the stupid assertion. There were never any guarantees that bad ideas wouldn't drive out good. But the bad ideas came equally from both sides, and had their own variants on repression. He talked about this a bit more and then it was time to close. So he said: 'Well, that's my dilemma. I think I want freedom and I shall take it if you give it me. That's what I came to America for. You might like my dilemma or you might not. All I'm saying is that it is, in a way, yours too. I just hope it's been worth talking about.' He walked backwards from the podium and sat down. The audience seemed to be slightly relieved. They applauded politely, save for one or two who sat silent. Only in the second row was there slight uproar. It was Cindy Handlin, who had risen to give him a standing ovation.

Book Three

They came largely to get *away* – that most simple
of motives. To get away. Away from what? In the long
run, away from themselves. Away from everything. That's
why most people have come to America, and still do come.
To get away from everything they are and have been.
'Henceforth be masterless.'
Which is all very well, but it isn't freedom.

D. H. Lawrence

7

When people asked Bernard Froelich why he had gone into the academic life, he usually answered, 'Oh, for the prestige, the power.' It was a joke, but a half-true one. He had always been an ambitious man. When he went to the east coast college where he had done his undergraduate and graduate work, a college with many intellectual but few social attainments and a student body composed of enterprising socially mobile Jewish boys like himself, he had seen himself ending up in one of the more prestigious professions; he should have been a doctor or a rabbi. Something – probably success – had diverted him into university teaching; something – probably ignorance – had brought him out west to do it. Once in Party, he had found himself happy in the west; at the same time, his glances went eastward frequently, and it was for this reason, in part, that he had grown into Anglophilia. He had a generic liking for the English; he liked them because they came not out of the woods but out of a culture. However, there was only so much room in the spirit for Anglophilia to take up; and Froelich had larger causes. He had, therefore, a wealth of ends in view when, that spring day, sitting next to Selena May Sugar at the meeting to appoint the next creative writing fellow, he had proposed the name of James Walker. There had been the thought of the service he could do for the book he was writing. There was the desire to bring into the English Department a concealed bomb or catalyst. There was, too, the desire to bring into Party's frontier plainness a soul-mate, a portion of the loveliness he had left behind back east, a man who could also recall to him the good days in London.

And then, also, there was a reverse impulse – an impulse to do something *to* that same England. For, sitting there on their island, the English had seemed to him a settled race, a race that had taken the things of the mind for granted and lived easily with them, a race that had acquired forms for living and had assumed that concert halls and bookshops and libraries and writers were permanent and eternal – a race, in short, that hadn't faced the future. And Froelich had wanted to put that kind of view to the test, to see what would happen to it in a place where things of the mind could only be appendages. The faculty of the English Department at Benedict Arnold looked impressive in their classrooms as they discoursed on Dickens and Dostoevski and Blake, clad in their tweed suits, smoking their pipes, thinking up their articles for *P.M.L.A.* For part of the time, at least, they might have been at Harvard or Oxford. But what a veneer it all was! On week-ends they put on levis and went up to their cabins in the canyon to clear snow, fish in creeks, and saw logs for their stoves. They became deeply ambiguous men, who looked at the world with two faces, the man and the mask. Froelich's image for the type was Dr Bourbon, who could be seen, still in his Rhodes Scholar's tweeds, shooting at bottles in his back-yard with a six-gun after a day of classes. It was the thought that the English wore their disguises all the time, had no sense of independent self, so to speak, that helped to motivate Froelich. He wanted to confront an Englishman with confusion, and see what part of the equation would change.

The disappointment he had felt on Walker's arrival had waned a little in the following weeks. It seemed to him that it would be Walker, and not Party, who would change. It was a despairing notion, because he had hoped for the other thing, hoped to see Bourbon's head drop in shame and the department realize that it had to turn its face toward the east from which he himself came. He had watched Walker carefully, over those weeks, as he threshed and flailed, watched his every assurance and his every embarrassment. He felt that he had offered this man a whole new world and he wondered what he would make of it. He, Froelich, had brought him to Party, given him joys and tortures and problems. He had given him work, dinner, and was prepared to do more; Walker was, he decided, of the same spirit as Froelich, and whatever he wanted – Froelich's home, his work, his wife – he could have. He felt the kinship between them grow daily. When Walker had grasped at the loyalty oath question, he had felt that the intellectual world of liberalism was awake in Party at last. And when Walker, perplexed, had come to him before his lecture, Froelich had glowed, counting the threads he had tied. He had tried to follow and to lead; to show the way and let the way be found. Walker's very English brand of liberalism, a faith of unbelief, struck Froelich as a cultural artifact. Its most committed assumption seemed to be that you shouldn't do anything to anybody because people, and the world, like to be the way they are. Froelich's own liberalism was more militant, as, in America, it had to be; the English had not had to fight for it for a very long time, and they didn't recognize, even now, that the odds were against them, that every freedom, every cultural moment, had to be won by political energy. Walker, left without a sense of society or of historical change, could speak only out of himself. He was striving for no future; he held only on to a past that was familiar enough in his own land but sounded like the voice of a ghost out here on the plains. Froelich had a function to play in relation to Walker's sublime subjectivism; he was objectivity, history, leading him on.

Now, he sat in the third row of the audience in the Fogle Auditorium, and watched Walker, a little figure behind the microphones, wriggling with embarrassment, beside the American flag, at the English perspectives he had to put. His English socks poked out beneath the too-short trouser cuffs of his American seersucker suit. The ghost spoke, and sounded more like Hamlet. It was not the kind of statement that Froelich would have wished for, had he been a totally political man. But he was not. What he felt, as Walker's halting words at last turned to the loyalty oath, was a sense of personal triumph. What had happened was that he had given Walker what he had come here for, a moment of truth and test, an historic moment of growth. Visibly the man had changed and grown, won himself and destroyed himself. Walker's statement was almost incidental, really: he had taken up a cause that he knew little about, one he had not much right to, one that others could have handled better. But the real point, for Froelich, was his own personal achievement in doing all this; he had linked Walker so inexorably to himself that their spirits now had to sing in tune. The words spoken had Froelich in them. They cut Walker off from Bourbon (who was contorting himself excruciatingly in the row ahead); they cut him off from President Coolidge (who was looking down urgently at the pressmen as if to stun them into deafness). They might well cut him off from his Fellowship because the state legislature was not going to like this one little bit. But there was another fellowship that they didn't cut him off from, the right-minded fellowship, the warmth and the goodness, of Froelich himself. Here was the lesson given.

As the audience, or what was left of them after the walkout, applauded politely, Froelich got up from his seat and caught up with the man from the *Dimity Gazette*, who was making for the exit door to reach the telephone.

'Quite a story,' said Froelich.

'It was?' said the journalist suspiciously.

'The most remarkable speech I ever heard on this campus,' said Froelich confidently.

'You think it's big?' asked the pressman.

'Well, I don't know, but it's coast-to-coast stuff if you ask me,' said Froelich. This work done, he followed the man out of the exit doors and found his way back through Fogle into the wings. Walker and President Coolidge stood nodding at each other in the semi-darkness of the wings; ropes hung around them, and Walker was clutching his blue file under his arm.

'Yes, well, now, Walk, that was very interesting,' President Coolidge was saying, 'but I think it was probably a betrayal of hospitality. That's dangerous ground you were treading through, there, Walk. I was sweating inside my shorts, I don't mind telling you.'

'I don't think I said anything very extreme, did I?' said Walker.

'Yes, well, I'm not blaming you, Walk, because I don't think you saw what was coming, but I think we're going to have to do some real talking to the regents to make them like this if it slaps the front pages tomorrow. Maybe we can get you on television to disclaim it; there's ways round, we're not beaten yet. But I don't know, I'll tell you. I've seen men put back in the breadline for this kind of thing.'

'I don't see why.'

'Well, that loyalty oath's a real bone of contention in this section of the country. I'll tell you, Walk, in the days when it was a really live issue we ran this one up the flagpole and shot at it from all directions, and I mean it, it was a real bomb from start to finish. The previous president got the golden hand-shake over it.'

'I didn't realize so much had happened,' said Walker.

'Oh, it was a bomb, Walk. This is why I came to this campus. I came here determined to reconcile all the factions. The faculty were all resigning because the loyalty oath existed or else because it wasn't tough enough. I did a real Potsdam agreement with it. I got all the reds on campus, and I got all the rightists on campus, and I put them round a table, and I said "Boys, we can blow ourselves to pieces over this one, or we can stay quiet and play it by ear and wait until the shouting's all through." I prognosticated what would happen. I told those men, I said, "Look, friends, this is the poop. Two years ago everyone was worrying about fluoridating the water. Two years from now they'll be worrying about cancer-causing deodorants or civil rights. This is a phase and we're going to weather this phase and I'm going to tell you here and now how to weather this phase." And by God, Walk, we weathered it.'

In the darkness Froelich trod on something, perhaps a discarded pretzel, and Coolidge said, 'Hey, there's somebody back there. Who's that?'

'It's me,' said Froelich, coming forward.

'Oh, hello,' said Coolidge, the look of despair on his face wiped off as rapidly as a smear in a television commercial, 'I remember the face but the name's slipped. I'm Coolidge.'

'I'm Froelich, President.'

'English?' said Coolidge.

'Yes,' said Froelich.

'You know, Walk,' said Coolidge, thoroughly his old discon-
certed self, 'I hate to forget a name. We've got a big faculty
here, but I try to remember all my men. You were out there,
Dr Froelich? How do you think they all took it?'

'I thought very well,' said Froelich, 'except for the people
who walked out. They didn't like it, but we don't worry about
them, do we?'

'Well, you know, Dr Froelich, I think we do,' said Coolidge.
'We mind what everybody thinks. We have civic responsi-
bilities in this U, and we got to be responsible to those re-
sponsibilities.'

There was then the sound of someone bumbling through
ropes and over the scattered props in the semi-darkness, and
the big bulk of Harris Bourbon appeared. Worry was designed
across his features. 'How'd it all go, Har?' asked Coolidge.

'Well,' said Bourbon, taking out his pipe and playing with
the threads of tobacco that overhung its bowl, 'it was a nice
talk, but the citizens didn't understand it.'

'Talk to the press at all, Har?' asked Coolidge.

'No, they all rushed out in a hurry.'

'Goddam that, I ought to have acted,' said Coolidge, 'but
I'll act now. I'll call up some editors I know. We'll have our
rebuttal out before they have their story. Don't worry, Walk,
we'll get this straight if I can.'

Walker stood and looked confused; his moral growth was
evidently not yet complete. Froelich felt for a moment that he
ought to trip Coolidge or grab his coat, anything to delay the
man on his mission of concealment, but he was gone. 'I felt I
could have done so much better,' said Walker to them both.

'Waal, Mis' Walker, all I kin say is thank goodness you
didn't,' said Bourbon.

'I don't quite see the need for all the fuss,' said Walker.

'Waal, maybe you don't, Mis' Walker, but this isn't just a
university matter, you know. You're moving in the realms of
state and national policy when you touch this loyalty oath
business on a public occasion. It's one thing to raise it in the
department meetin's or in the U, and another to raise it
here.'

'I didn't think I said anything very much.'

'You didn't,' said Froelich, 'but maybe the world will make it into something.'

'Waal, I guess there's nothin' we kin do 'cept go home,' said Bourbon. 'Can I give you a ride back, Mis' Walker?'

'Thank you,' said Walker.

'It was very good,' said Bourbon. 'Nice talk. Just that the folks didn't really get the level you was talkin' at.'

The following morning, Froelich was out on the porch, in his Black Watch tartan dressing gown, almost as soon as the delivery boy had hurled the packed-up copy of the *Dimity Gazette* from his motor scooter in the general direction of the house. On the front page was a photograph of an old lady who was hitting a middle-aged man, with some energy, with her purse; inset was a photograph of Walker speaking on the podium, his hair ruffled, his paunch looking particularly vast. *British Author Lashes Loyalty Oath*, said the headline; Froelich began cracking open his breakfast eggs with some glee.

'It looks like your friend James Walker's in a mite of trouble,' he shouted to Patrice, who still lay in bed clad in the lower half of a pair of pyjamas and reading *Moby Dick*.

'I guess we all know who got him into it,' said Patrice.

When he reached the door of his office in the department building later that morning, Froelich found waiting outside it a very large student with a crew cut, his long arms holding his notebook neatly lodged in front of his crotch. His name was Jabolonski and he was present at BAU largely because the football coach had been drawing heavily on the college patriotism of his tutors.

'Oh, duh,' said Jabolonski.

'Looking for someone?' asked Froelich, unlocking the door.

'Duh,' said Jabolonski, 'I was lookin' for my teacher, this man Walker. The president of the fraternity I'm pledging said I gotta withdraw from his course.'

'Why?'

'Oh, duh, I dunno, he says we all got to withdraw 'cause of

sumpn he said. I dunno, I'm all confused, shoot, what's it all about, why are we here, what have I gotta take these courses for anyways?'

'The mystery of life, Mr Jabolonski,' said Froelich.

'Is that what it is?' said Jabolonski doubtfully.

'That's right,' said Froelich.

'Well, duh, okay, I'll come back when he's in and see if he is,' said Jabolonski.

Froelich went inside and sat down at his desk, awaiting the moment of Walker's arrival. A few minutes later the door opened, but it was Luther Stewart and William Van Hart; they had a cabin in the canyon and rode in on motorcycles, together.

'Seen friend Walker?' asked Froelich.

'No,' said Stewart. 'Maybe he's been kidnapped by the Party Friendly Mortuary.'

'I thought he gave a cute lecture,' said William Van Hart.

'What did he say?' asked Froelich.

'Okay, the sharp-edged mind of Froelich says what did he say, but I'm a Chicago Aristotelian and I say how did he say it?' said William Van Hart.

'A lecture should not mean but be,' said Luther Stewart.

There was a knock on the door. 'Come in,' said Froelich. The door opened and one of Froelich's freshman students, a tall, confident, handsome girl with ringlets falling down to her shoulders, and named Willa Anne Papp, came in. 'Can I see you for a moment, Dr Froelich?' she said.

'Okay, come on in and sit down.'

Miss Papp sat down and said, 'You've got a big problem here, Mr Froelich. It's me.'

'Oh, yes,' said Froelich, 'and what's your trouble? Pains in the abdomen? Titillation of the middle ear?'

'No, it's about these grades I been getting. You keep giving me Fs and I know I'm more capable.'

'Well, let's take a look. Is this your last theme?'

'Yes,' said Miss Papp, handing over a theme paper on Shakespeare and the Sonnet, which began: 'Petrarch had one foot in the Middle Ages while with the other he became the father of the Renaissance,' and which had been heavily marked by him in red pencil. Miss Papp leaned her ringlets close to him and said, 'I don't understand why you marked this bit here.'

'Well, let's take a look and see,' said Froelich. 'You say, "This poem is almost, but not quite, unique," and I recommended you to turn up a page in the *Handbook for Writers*. That's what HW means. Did you turn up the page?'

'I didn't know what HW meant,' said Miss Papp. 'I think you ought to tell us those things.'

'I did, in the second meeting,' said Froelich.

'Well, I missed that.'

'Well, if you turn up the page in *Handbook* you'll find it says you can't have comparatives of "unique".'

'I don't see why not, in the modern world of today.'

'Oh, hell, Miss Papp, you just can't. A thing either is or it isn't.'

'I think that's ridiculous,' said Miss Papp.

'Well, it's like saying "almost but not quite a virgin".'

'What's wrong with that?'

'Or "almost but not quite pregnant".'

'What's wrong with that?'

'Well, how are these situations possible, Miss Papp? Tell me, baby.'

'You haven't been around very much, have you?' asked Miss Papp.

'Maybe I'm the one who needs teaching,' said Froelich.

'I'd gladly do what I can,' said Miss Papp.

'How about if I call you sometime, Miss Papp, and we talk about those grades some more.'

'Okay, fine,' said Miss Papp.

Miss Papp rose, and Froelich noticed that Walker had come in. 'Oh, hello, James,' he said, 'how's things?'

'Hellish,' said Walker, sitting down, 'I've been getting phone calls.'

'Good. What kind of phone calls? Obscene ones?'

'Yes. There's a woman who keeps calling me and thinking of new four-letter words.'

'She'll soon run out of permutations,' said Froelich. 'Take it easy. Any favourable calls?'

'One or two college kids called to say it was the best speech they'd ever heard.'

'Fine, it's going nicely.'

'Well, I didn't think it was such a sensational speech.'

'No, it was kind of wishy-washy, but you picked a good occasion for it.'

'I liked it,' said Miss Papp. 'I thought it was almost but not quite sensational.'

'Well, that's Mr Walker,' said Froelich. 'He has one head cocked in the general direction of the nineteenth century while with the other becoming the father of the modern world of today.'

'Well, I just want you to know that a lot of the kids liked it,' said Miss Papp. ' 'Bye now.'

When Miss Papp had gone, Walker looked at his shoes and said, 'I wonder whether I ought to issue some kind of modification, saying that it was a general point and not a specific attack on the university.'

'No,' said Froelich. 'You've done your bit, as they say. Oh, I forgot to tell you. Mr Jabolonski was looking for you. It turns out that his fraternity president has put him up to withdrawing from your class in protest.'

'I didn't realize I'd caused so much trouble.'

'Oh, it doesn't mean anything.'

Just before Walker set off across campus to meet his composition group, Bourbon came in. He stood haltingly in the doorway and warned Walker to beware of trouble; two of the students in the course had come to him to ask for Walker to be fired, on two grounds: because he was a fellow-traveller, and because nobody could understand his accent anyway. 'He doesn't even talk the English language properly,' one of the students had said.

'They don't even attend class anyway,' said Walker.

'They want to be absent from the classes of a different instructor in future,' said Luther Stewart.

'Waal, Mis' Walker,' said Bourbon, looking at his booted feet, 'I felt I had to accede to their wishes, particularly as one or two sections is running a bit lightweight. But it don't mean anything.'

Walker said nothing, but put on his belted raincoat and set off for his trek across campus. Froelich, whose composition class was in a closer building, was back in his room to see Walker's reappearance. He was evidently in a mood of increased dejection. It emerged that one of the students had asked him if England was a communist country, and when he turned round to write on the blackboard, halfway through the class, he had found that someone had chalked on it, 'If you don't like it here, why don't you go back to where you came from?' Walker had marked the grammar of this, finally giving it an F for the repeated preposition, but his heart had not been in it.

'One of the great mottoes of American democracy, and you give it an F,' said Luther Stewart.

'It doesn't mean anything,' said Froelich.

Walker, swirling his chair round on its centre stalk, said, 'How will I know when something means something? When I get hit on the head with a stick?'

'Easy, buddy, you're getting all tensed up,' said Froelich. 'Look, I think the best thing for your comfort and protection would be if you came over and stayed at my place a few days. No one need know where you are. You can just hole up until this thing works itself out. It's just starting, now. Soon it's really going to move.'

There was yet another knock on the door, and Froelich went to open it. In the corridor stood two male campus nonconformists, both wearing sun-glasses, beards, and sweaters and levis. 'We're looking for Mr Walker,' they said, 'is he around?'

'Why do you want him?' asked Froelich.

'We just want to shake him by the hand and tell him he's real turned on.'

'Also to invite him to a party,' said the other beat.

'Come on in, then,' said Froelich, 'there he is.' Walker, whose head was drooping further, gave each of them a limp hand to shake.

'Hi, James, real glad to know you,' said one of them. 'We just wanted to apologize for this sick society we have here, and thank you, for, you know, being a saint.'

'That's right,' said the other. 'There's a party tonight we'd like you to come to. A real scene. There'll be a like turned on crowd there, and they're all wanting to meet you. A whole lot of girls, real sweet chicks. It'll be a pot party too.'

'Thank you very much,' said Walker, 'but I don't feel up to a party at the moment.'

'Sure, you go,' said Froelich, 'I'll drive you round there.'

'No,' said Walker, 'another time.'

'Okay, that's a date,' said the beat, 'see you somewhere.'

Froelich felt a sincere desire to jolly Walker back into emotional health. 'You should have gone there, man,' he said. 'I tell you, all the real people round this place are looking for victims like you. You don't come so easy; you fill a real need. You stand for truth suffering against ignorance for a whole bunch of folk on this campus.'

'Do I?' said Walker.

'Yes, you're a hero, I mean it. Why, there are whole crowds of nice girls, like my sexy Miss Papp, you know, who are really breathing hard to lay someone who's been wronged. They've been going around for years looking for a sufferer like you, a man misused by society. All you have to do now is to take it while it's going. What a feeling, hey, Jay? What a feeling!'

Even the pleasures of being a victim seemed to be lost on Walker, however; his face made no move, no spark came to his eye.

'Well, look, why don't we go by International House and pick up your things and take you back home? You could rest up this afternoon.'

'Well, thank you,' said Walker. 'That's probably a very good idea.' He got up and they went out to the car.

As they drove, Walker sat in silence, and Froelich thought back to the day when he had picked him up at the railroad depot and had brought him into town for the first time. Then, too, Walker had been surly, as if afraid of what he might expect; it was a characteristic thing with him, evidently. The future disturbed him. He was never a man for impassioned fire, it was clear; and he didn't know how to hold or hunt a cause when there was one going. In a sense, Froelich was disappointed; he hoped he could count on Walker more to work his way through the next few busy weeks. On the other hand, though, the ball was now in his hands, and he was a man, he knew, capable of carrying it. He knew all the next moves; and perhaps it was even better if Walker was, as he seemed to be, anaesthetized. All was going brightly.

Walker glumly packed his luggage as Froelich watched. Once the phone on the wall rang. Froelich picked it up and listened. 'Could you say those words again, madam?' he said finally. 'I'm doing a survey of vernacular obscenity and there's some material there that I don't think I have on file.' He listened a moment. 'She hung up,' he said. 'I'm going to put this phone off the hook. No use waking all the foreign students in the building. I see what you mean, though, Jay; that was real fierce.'

'What do they do it for?' asked Walker.

'Oh, people live naked in this country. If you get steamed up you let everyone know. She seems to think that you've got at her family, and her womanhood, and her Americanness; they're all bound up. It's fear of the future.'

'I think I suffer from that myself.'

They drove through Party to Froelich's house. 'Watch the sprinklers, Jay,' said Froelich, as they got out of the car. Indoors, Patrice stood in the living-room. 'Hello, James,' she said, looking pleased, and coming forward and kissing him. 'I'm sorry I missed last night. I hear all over you were great.'

'He wasn't great,' said Froelich. 'He doesn't even know what he said.'

'Well, that isn't what I heard.'

'Well, we don't have to worry too much about him just for a while, because now we're concerned with something bigger, which is called politics.'

'Oh, Jesus, Bernie,' said Patrice, 'be careful you don't take this thing too far.'

'You think I don't know how to handle it? Look, let's have a drink. You two sit over there and I'll fix something. I like to hear you necking whiles I'm in the kitchen.'

Walker's face seemed to clear a little at the prospect, and Froelich's glow of joy began to return. 'Watch him, he's a bum,' he heard Patrice say to Walker as he reached in the ice-box for the cubes. 'You're both being very kind,' Walker replied. He slid the serving hatch open slightly, and saw that Walker and Patrice were kissing. Mutual self-congratulation! Froelich spied through the crack and felt an intense kind of pleasure. Here was a duet in which two spirits, one English, one American, sang in tune at last. They were Walker's, and Froelich's. They were united souls, of an ambience, sharing a single cause and having a taste for one woman. The comradely glow spread outwards into a sense of hope for the future. Never had Froelich felt so close to literature, to his book and the world of letters to which it contributed. And all we do now is wait, he thought, wait for the world to take up Walker and define him, wait for the sides to pick themselves, wait for causes and affections to work their way onward, wait for Walker's role of positive genius to become historical. Who would have thought, on that day of the creative writing fellowship meeting, that those calculated words about a man Froelich didn't even know would bring him here, sit him on this divan to kiss his wife, while around him history was being made and all America was defining attitudes towards him? He felt an achieved man. Singing quietly, in his fieldhand's voice, 'There a man goin' roun' takin' names,' he poured a little martini, a lot of gin, into the shaker and mixed the contents slowly and deliberately, seeing no need whatever to hurry.

On the morning after his lecture Walker, waking in his room in International House, had felt as if the world had come clear to him; a gay, good glow spread through his body and told him he had done well. He recognized the feeling; it was a return to the ethical jubilation of his earlier days as student and liberal bohemian, when causes were just and righteousness was assured. The intervening years seemed to have slipped away—those years of moral flabbiness, when marriage and a sense of the sheer complexities of living had brought him into ethical confusion. Why then, now, had truth taken him by the scruff of the neck, shaken him hard, made him do the great good thing? He didn't know, but the glow of honest innocence was a prized possession, the more prized because it was a renewal of something he had known before. He got out of bed in joy. Outside his window a strange foreign bird sang and his spirit went gaily along with it all, in tune. He felt healthy; his pallid skin seemed to him to have browned, his uncoordinated body to have tightened, the loose muscles in his stomach to have grown hard. The sense of personal renewal was just what he had come here for, and all these intimations were goodness.

He ought to have known that it couldn't last, that it never lasted. A moment later the phone rang, and he was in a world of recriminations. Ethical joy was never pure; he had not pleased everyone by pleasing himself. The moral fog came down again; the rocket went up; Froelich hove alongside. Into Froelich's car his luggage went, and, sulky and shocked again, with the world whirling by out of control, he let himself be led forward. From that point onward, the confusion worsened. The strange marriage of causes that linked him with Bernard Froelich was just like the marriage with Elaine; here, too, were ties that he didn't remember knitting, but were evidently felt from the other end; here too was the sense he was committed to something of which he wasn't the single master. He slept uneasily on the Froelich divan, wondering why he had been chosen. And if Froelich beckoned onward, intellectually and morally, then Patrice beckoned in other ways. Walker, wanting to understand and to be understood, knew of only one real place to go for that; it was a female place, and he felt that that, too, was waiting, was almost part of the bargain. Why? Froelich's bland tolerance, and his very insistence that Walker and Patrice be affectionate, Walker thought he understood. After all, he had been a bohemian himself; he still was confused in that general area, and Froelich, he knew, was a man beyond outmoded ethicalities, a bohemian and a playboy himself. Everyone knew, including presumably Patrice, that he dated his students and took them for meals at Lucky's Place; after that his car could be seen phutt-phutting painfully out of town, bearing its burden of two, leaving behind a student moral debate about whether it was right to hope, by advances in the world of affection, to gain elevation in the world of grades also.

And so Walker, who was only a provincial bohemian, and knew it, found himself amiable but floundering in the world of the cosmopolitan variant. In an odd way, he yearned for the old simplicities, yearned to be back in marriage with Elaine. Those feelings, simple bourgeois matrimonial affections, returned to his mind and senses and were newly focused. He felt that it was this fear of going too far that had taken him away from Julie Snowflake, back to Miss Marrow, on the boat coming over. Sitting at the Froelich breakfast table in the morning, while the Froelichs needled each other across the pop-up toaster and the eggs Hawaiian, Walker realized that Patrice mediated the relationship between him and Froelich. That was tacit all round. And Walker knew too that he was fascinated with Froelich. Froelich's assurance, his pure sense of direction, his sheer energetic manipulation of his acquaintance, impressed Walker as he had not expected to be impressed in the States. It was a sheerly intellectual admiration, an admiration of finesse of mind and of a positive intellectual will. At first Froelich had been to him simply a bore; his moral importunities had been too pressing, too intense, too violent . . . the obsession of a biographer for his victim. Now he saw that Froelich's role was more creative; he was a reforming spirit; intellectually dissatisfied with his subject, he was taking him onward to something better. Perhaps it was that he had already written his chapter and now had to make Walker live up to it; better to change the man than to retype fifty pages. Even if that was so, well, Walker had come all this way to be open to change. Change was his one commitment, his one demand of the world. He believed in search; he always had; if someone could lead and guide, then let him.

So the days went by and Walker waited for things to fall into shape again. And one thing you *could* say . . . the world now seemed interested in him. Froelich, bringing Walker's mail home from the department, came with challenge and praise and blame from all quarters. One letter Walker particularly cherished; it said: 'I read about what you did in the *N.Y Times* and I think it was just really great. Forget those things I said, yes? You're a knight of infinity; you made it. Here's a kiss I had around someplace. Julie.' On the third day of his stay at the Froelichs', the *Party Bugle* appeared, bearing a hostile account of Walker's lecture (*Walker Offends Laws of Hospitality*) and a versified advertisement which read:

> We gave foreign aid
> See how it's repaid
> So why do we listen?
> Walker . . . go back to Britain.

> But loyal Americans will want the aid of Party's
> Friendly Mortuary, for a friendly all-in interment
> at a difficult time.

On the following Tuesday, Walker drove into the university with Froelich to meet his classes. On campus, many of the trees were now bare, the campanile stood out stark, and the convertibles now had their roofs up. 'Only two weeks now to the Christmas vacation,' said Froelich. 'If anything's going to happen, it'll have to happen soon.'

When Walker went into the English office to get his mail, the secretary looked up and said: 'Dr Bourbon wants to see you, James. Will you go in?'

Walker knocked on Bourbon's door. 'Come right on in,' cried Bourbon. He was sitting behind his desk, smoking his pipe, and when he saw Walker he let his body slide down in his chair behind his papers. 'Ah, Mis' Walker, mind if we have a little talk?' he cried.

'Not at all,' said Walker.

'Waal now, I just wanted to keep you pooped on the situation caused by your furore. There's a few things bin happenin'.

One of them is that the state legislature has sent President Coolidge a memo saying that he should either require you to sign the oath or fire you.'

'I see,' said Walker.

'So President Coolidge sent back a memo saying that if you don't sign he'll refuse to renew your contract at the end of this year, that's this academic year.'

'But the contract was only for one academic year, wasn't it?'

'Well, that's President Coolidge; he out-thinks people every time. So, we don't know what's goin' to happen about that, but I'll let you know what happens when it happens. Okay, well, the other thing is that the local chapter of the American Association of University Professors, that's a kind of, you know, union, is discussin' the matter noontime Friday in the Faculty Club. Figured you might want to be there. Are you a member? No? Waal, you have any friend you could send along?'

'I'll think of someone.'

'Waal, it's a sticky wicket, Mis' Walker, and you know I wish it hadn't never happened. But looks like the U's tryin' to look after you, and I hope you're feelin' mighty grateful. But this could get worse. We're under fire from without and within. Without means the press, the townspeople, the state legislature. Within, waal, that's all these here students who have protested to me, and some of the faculty. Number of the faculty have protested to the President 'bout your indiscretion.'

'They have?' asked Walker. 'Who?'

'Well, seems a pee-tition was started by a man you know.'

'A man I know?'

'Yes, by Dr Jochum.'

'By Jochum? The man I came on the ship with?'

'Yes, that's right, Mis' Walker.'

'I can't believe it.'

'Well, frankly, that didn't surprise *me* none. Jochum is an old campaigner for loyalty. But I'll tell you what did surprise me, and I guess you ought to know this. Pee-tition came round this department yesterday and I did hear, didn't come to me a-tall but I did hear, that it was taken round by Mr Van Hart.'

'Mr Van Hart in my office?'

'That's right. Waal, Mis' Walker, I'm independent in all this, and I'm in a mighty difficult position, appointin' you and lettin' you not sign and all. But what all this means is that you're in a mighty difficult position too. Pressure comes on too hard I may have to fire you, and that's the truth, Mis' Walker. We don't fire easy here, but you don't have tenure with us. I think we're goin' to be able to keep you for the rest of the year, and I don't mind sayin' I'll support that. Spite of the trouble we've always had with writers. The U hasn't forgotten Elvis Flea.'

'Who's that?'

'That was the creative writin' fellow two years back. Said he was a poet. His trouble was seducin'. Story is he humped the faculty wives in alphabetical order. They got him in jail somewhere west of here, didn't surprise no one. There's a lot of people on this campus don't ever want to see a writer here again So . . . go careful, Mis' Walker.'

Walker was so confused about these things as he went back to his office that he bumped hard into the water cooler and sent the paper cups flying. 'Go careful!' The only person in the room was Froelich, making up a list of grades.

'Bernard, you didn't tell me about any petition,' said Walker.

'It's not good for you to know everything,' said Froelich. 'You might get scared.'

'Or the meeting on Friday.'

'Which you can't go to anyway. And even if you could I wouldn't want you there, boy.'

'Harris said it was Bill Van Hart who brought the petition round the department.'

'That's right, Bill did that.'

'But why did he? I'm surprised at Bill. . . . '

'Maybe because I told him to.'

Walker felt an enormous confusion. 'But why did *you* do that?'

'I can't answer,' said Froelich, scrawling F on a theme. 'I plead the Fifth Amendment.'

Walker sat down in his chair and made it spin round to match his wonderment.

'It's time for your class,' said Froelich.

Walker picked up his teaching plan and the Freshman Reader and set out across campus, into the cold air. An aroma of treachery seemed to fill the world in which he had been moving so unsuspectingly. Even the trees and the paths seemed no longer reliable, and the faces of the students he passed seemed very foreign indeed. Though he was unsure of his alliances and his connexions, and hadn't thought about them very much, missing all that sensitivity to the political which those trained in institutions possess, Walker had felt that there were certain stabilities – human ones: that Jochum was his friend, that Froelich was, that the teaching staff of the department was on the whole behind him. He knew now that his appointment had been disputed; but he assumed that the human appeal of his existence had put an end to that. And he also assumed that the human took precedence over the political; this he took to be an essential rule of life. But now the wind seemed overnight to have overturned all these connexions and assumptions. The sensation of being a foreigner and of having done things a foreigner shouldn't do affected him deeply, because the easiness of American life had brought him to feel that foreignness wasn't an issue. So he stood at his desk and looked at his students, wondering what he should teach them, perplexed by the cast of their minds. For some reason Jabolonski was back. 'I thought you transferred to another instructor,' he said.

'Yeah, well, I did, but it all seemed kind of crazy to me, so, well, shoot, I come back to you.'

One of the girls, with long fair hair and white bobby-socks, a Scandinavian type, said, 'Are you really a red, Mr Walker?'

'No,' said Walker. 'Did you read the assignment?' The assignment was Swift's *Modest Proposal*, one of the few works of any pretension in the Freshman Reader. 'What did you think of it?'

'I disagreed with it,' said the Scandinavian girl. 'I don't think even under any circumstances people should eat children. I mean, I guess there's another point of view, but I don't think I'd agree with it.'

'That's a very humane view, Miss Lindstrom,' said Walker, 'but why don't you think people should eat children?'

Miss Lindstrom looked at Walker with bright blue eyes. 'Are you really in favour of eating children, Mr Walker? Are you *really*?'

'Not really,' said Walker. 'Was Swift?'

'Was who?' said Miss Lindstrom.

'Was Swift? Jonathan Swift who wrote the essay I asked you to read.'

'Well, I guess he must have been,' said Miss Lindstrom. 'He wouldn't have said he was if he wasn't, would he?'

'What about that?' Walker looked round the class. He began to feel a little uneasy, for a number of the class looked distinctly hostile; he was now bearing not only his burden, but Swift's as well. His gaze went round the room and he noticed, huddled in the back row, holding a large cleaner's bag, a large man wearing a raincoat and a trilby hat. The hat didn't entirely conceal the red hair of Hamish Wagner. Walker knew that one of Wagner's tasks was to sit in on the composition classes and check on the competence of the teachers. The graduate students were the usually selected victims, and they had interesting stories of the considerable lengths to which Wagner went in concealment, donning janitor's coveralls, appearing in bermuda shorts and a freshman's beanie, and the like. What disturbed Walker was that it should be this class, and this particular time, that Wagner should have picked on him; in any case, he had the impression that it was only the graduate students who were supposed to be checked on in this way. Walker dropped his gaze and noticed that, at the front of the classroom, Jabolonski was sitting straining, with outstretched hand. At Walker's glance he said, 'I think the guy was kidding.'

Miss Lindstrom looked at Mr Jabolonski. 'Why would he be kidding?' she asked. 'What would he kid about a thing like that for?'

'Well, duh, I dunno, but maybe he was tryin' to get sumpn done about all dat famine and all.'

'What's the name for that kind of literary procedure?' Walker asked.

Mr Jabolonski ducked his head and scratched it with a large hand; after a moment he said, 'Duh, I dunno, lyin'?'

'It's irony,' said Miss Hackle, an independent and bright girl in a dirndl. 'It's an oblique procedure which suggests the opposite of what's said.'

'In this case, yes,' said Walker, feeling more at ease now. 'And why would he want to use it, do you think, Miss Hackle?'

'Well, to shock people into what Mr Jabolonski over there said just now,' said Miss Hackle.

Miss Lindstrom shook her head in confusion. 'You mean he didn't want people to eat children at all?' Students all around her began saying 'Yes' and 'That's right' and her face grew flushed. 'Well, I don't understand it,' she said. 'Supposing someone had taken him seriously and they had. He'd be responsible, then, wouldn't he? Anyway, I don't understand why these writers have to be so smart. Why can't they say what they think right out, 'stead of going around confusing people?'

Miss Hackle said, 'I guess he thought nobody would do it. I guess he thought people couldn't do anything so terrible.'

'I don't know about that,' said Walker. 'He didn't think so very much of human nature.'

'You see,' said Miss Lindstrom, 'I guess he did mean it. And I think it's terrible, Mr Walker, I really do.' At this a gallant, anarchistic student who wore a Mohican haircut, his head scraped bare except for a thin band of hair across his skull, and who had in previous classes expressed a high regard for Walker, was roused to sudden protest.

'I think,' he said, 'we ought to look at this one again. Maybe there is a real case for cannibalism, but we haven't thought it through properly yet. I mean, a lot of races have practised this thing; are we right to condemn it unheard?'

'That's crazy,' said Miss Lindstrom.

'That's because you're prejudiced against it from the start,' said the student with the Mohican haircut.

'Is nothing sacred in this class, Mr Walker?' asked Miss Lindstrom.

Walker flushed red and looked uneasily at Hamish Wagner, but he had gone right out of sight behind his dry-cleaner's bag. 'Swift wasn't in favour of cannibalism,' he said. 'He took up a complex intellectual position which I'm now going to explain to you.' He talked for a while and when he had finished he saw Mr Jabolonski's hand waving in the air. Mr Jabolonski's question was why literary guys had to be so confusing. 'Why do they have to make everything so difficult? Why don't they just accept things the way they are?'

'What was it John Stuart Mill said?' asked Walker: ' "It is better to be a human being dissatisfied than a pig satisfied; better to be a Socrates dissatisfied than a fool satisfied." '

'Well, I can't stand these guys who question everything,' said Mr Jabolonski.

'You like yourself as you are?'

'That's right,' said Jabolonski. 'I'd be crazy if I didn't. I didn't come to university to improve my *mind*, Mr Walker. I come here to, duh, train me for a job. That's what you guys don't realize. You're always wantin' to change my values. You want us to think like you do, irony and all that crap. And what happens? You just get yourselves into trouble is what happens.'

'Yes,' said Miss Lindstrom. 'And I don't think it's right for you to call people who don't agree with you pigs.'

'I didn't mean . . .' said Walker. But Miss Hackle and the student with the Mohican haircut were deeply roused.

'He's right,' said Miss Hackle. 'People who refuse to think about themselves are just animals.' The class dissolved into bedlam. When the bell trilled on the hour, students went out of the classroom raging at one another, and Walker tucked his books under his arm in exhaustion and embarrassment. Hamish Wagner had contrived to leave the room in the middle of a press of disputants, and he foresaw his report: subversive teaching, abuse of the students, expression of an untenable opinion. He hurried out of the building and noticed Wagner striding along the path ahead of him, his cleaner's bag over his shoulder, on his way back to the English Building. Worry made him chase after him. 'Hello, Hamish,' he called.

'Oh, what ho, old chap,' said Hamish.

'I saw you in class,' said Walker, 'I'm afraid it was a bit confused. I think probably they're a little upset because of the fuss about my lecture.'

'Yeah, well, I thought it was a nice class,' said Hamish. 'I have a few criticisms. Maybe you don't want to hear them, but I have been teaching a good few years now, and with increasing experience and study has come wisdom. . . .'

'I'd like to hear them,' said Walker.

'Well, good, that's how it should be,' said Hamish. 'No, I thought there were some weaknesses in presentation. I'd mark you high for teaching content, but I'd put you low on a few other things. Like standing and sitting. I like to see a teacher who moves around a lot, keeps the class interested. You sat on the corner of the desk without moving except to go to the blackboard once and write down *sustenance*. And that's another thing, blackboard use. I like to see a full use of visual aids in a class: blackboard, mimeographed materials, use of opaque projector. You know, those secretaries in the office will mimeograph any teaching aids you want any time you want them. You just have to give reasonable notice.'

'Yes, quite,' said Walker.

'Hope that don't sound critical. Look at it as my job.'

'I will, Hamish,' said Walker.

'Of course you were right,' said Hamish. 'They are pigs. In the sense defined in that passage.'

'Oh, not all of them,' said Walker. 'Some of them understand what it's all about – Miss Hackle and the boy with the funny haircut.'

'Yeah, that's true,' said Wagner. 'They're not pigs; they're nuts. Well . . . all very interesting.'

Watching Hamish Wagner retire into his office, Walker realized that the encounter had strengthened him rather; he was capable of fighting back. And so instead of returning to the office where he belonged he went into the English Department telephone booth and made a call. 'Is that Dr Jochum?' he asked.

'Who is this here, please?' said Jochum's voice, shouting into the telephone.

'It's James Walker.'

'Ah, my friend, I have been vondering about you. But first I have a rebuke to make. I am disappointed in your lecture.'

'I gathered that you'd led a protest about it to the President.'

'Ah, I thought you were not calling just to get acquainted, as we say in America.'

'Did you?' asked Walker.

'Did I inspire that protest? Yes, but it was not a protest about your lecture. It was a protest that the President had not publicly affirmed that academic freedom and the loyalty oath are compatible.'

'How are they?'

'Oh, vell, it is quite simple, surely. I know you will not agree, because you are a liberal and you do not understand conspiracy. Do you not think there is more academic freedom here than there is in Russia or Hungary or Estonia?'

'Yes, clearly.'

'Then what happens when, within the context of academic freedom, men use that freedom to advance the view that it is intellectually necessary to create a society in which that freedom is taken away?'

'That's just saying that in the open market bad ideas drive out good.'

'And is there no evidence in the world that that is true?'

'I suppose in the short term there is.'

'But in the long term truth will prevail. Is it doing? It didn't prevail where I came from. There are no guarantees. You see, you are an optimist and live on hope. I am a pessimist and live on experience. I told you all this before. You are my friend; I am not attacking you. But I have had a harder life than yours; I learned my lesson. Now it is necessary to say what I have learned. Of course I hope it will cause no trouble for you. . . . '

'I don't see how it can't.'

'Vell, it is a silly business, it will soon be forgotten. Then we shall meet again, I hope.'

'Yes, I hope so.'

'One day you will believe these things too.'

'I don't think so,' said Walker. 'But we'll meet. After all, that's what academic freedom is about.'

'Ah, vell, good fortune and a good Noel,' said Jochum. 'Soon the snow will fall and you will see another Party. It is so lovely here.'

'I hope they keep me here to see it.'

'They vill,' said Jochum. 'Of course they vill.'

'I guess it's going to snow,' said Patrice Froelich. 'That means a white Christmas, great. Funny how it always snows around the beginning of the Christmas vacation.'

'Yeah, we arrange it so the students going west can get trapped in the passes,' said Froelich. 'It leaves us with some places vacant for next semester.' Walker sat on the divan reading the first chapter of Cindy Handlin's novel, *The Eye of My I*, which she had submitted to the graduate creative writing class: it began 'Who is any of us?', and Walker didn't understand it. It was the last day of classes before the vacation began, and Walker was to return to his room in International House the following day. For over a week there had been no news of the Trouble, no reports in the press, no letters in his mail. The A A U P meeting had taken place a week ago, but about it no one, not Froelich, not Bourbon, had spoken a word. Froelich, when pressed, just said 'It went fine,' and since there had been no demand that he leave, not even an insistence that he sign that cursed blank form on his desk, he had not thought about the matter again. He thought that, if asked, he was prepared to sign it; all the benefits of his stand had been reaped, none of them by him. Unless, perhaps, there was a tiny glow of pride and principle? If so, the zest of that had gone; he felt himself back where he was before, cold winter Walker, with nothing achieved to speak of except a new veneration in the creative writing class, where he was freely spoken of as a 'genius'. It struck him as odd, yet not inconsistent, that this praise came, not because he wrote like a writer, but because he had spoken like one. And that, at least, was something achieved, if he could hold on to it. Perhaps he had grown, then, but how did he know?

'There's a call for you, Jamie,' shouted Patrice from the kitchen.

Walker said 'For me?' and picked up the phone. 'Hello,' he said.

'Hi,' said a voice.

'Who is that?' said Walker.

'Who is this? You don't know?'

'No,' said Walker.

'Guess,' said the voice.

'It would be easier to be told.'

'But not so much fun. I'll give you a clue. It's an old friend from way back.'

'I didn't know I had any old friends,' said Walker.

'Only new ones?'

'Yes,' said Walker.

'Well, tell me something. Are you a knight of infinity yet?'

'Is it Miss Snowflake?'

'Sure it is,' said Julie Snowflake.

'How nice,' said Walker and then, since he was in America, 'how marvellous.'

'Isn't it great? I'm here. I've come. How are you, duckie?'

'Oh, pretty well. How are you?'

'Just fine, really fine. And can't wait to see you. Who is this Froelich you're staying with?'

'He's one of the English faculty.'

'Nice?'

'Well, yes.'

'Married?'

'Yes.'

'Nice wife?'

'Yes,' said Walker. 'Look, how long are you here?'

'I don't know. I'm heading out west for Christmas.'

'How did you come?'

'I have a car. I just rattle around all over now. I'm staying at my brother's apartment. Boy, what a creep that kid is. Still, it lets me see this town. I think I like it. It looks like fun. Is it fun?'

'Yes, it is really,' said Walker. 'Well, we must meet.'

'Okay, fix it. I'm free all the time.'

'Tonight?'

'I hope so,' said Julie.

'I'll just check,' said Walker. He put his hand over the telephone and said to the Froelichs, 'Am I doing anything tonight?'

'We're all going over to Dean French's for a buffet supper. Who is this?'

'A friend of mine from the ship coming over.'

'A girl?'

'Yes,' said Walker.

'Well, bring her along. Does she have a car?'

'Yes,' said Walker.

'Have her stop by here for you.'

'What time?'

'Oh, any time,' said Froelich, 'around seven.'

'Julie?' said Walker into the telephone, 'write down this address.' He gave it. 'Have you got that?' he went on. 'Well, can you stop by at seven and I'll take you to a party?'

'Fine,' said Julie, 'a faculty party?'

'Yes,' said Walker.

'Great,' said Julie, 'I always love gate-crashing faculty parties. On seven. I'll bring you a bouquet.'

'This is nice,' said Walker.

'Well, we'll see,' said Miss Snowflake, hanging up.

Froelich said: 'Is she a student?'

'Yes, she's at Hillesley.'

'How old?' asked Patrice.

'Oh, I don't know, about nineteen.'

'And you slept with her on the boat coming over,' said Froelich.

'No, I just talked to her.'

'Ah-ha,' said Froelich. 'And she came out here to see you.'

'No, not at all, she has a brother at Benedict Arnold, a veterinarian.'

'Well, it's a good story,' said Froelich.

There was something in Walker that made him want to believe that Froelich's hints were right, that Julie Snowflake had come out here just to see him; and at seven o'clock he stood in excitement at the window, looking up and down the street. 'Oh, just look at him,' said Patrice. As the campanile chimed out seven, a black Volkswagen turned the corner and pulled up in front of the house. Julie got out, wearing a cashmere coat and a blue straw hat. Walker grabbed his coat and went out on the porch. 'Hi there, Mr Walker,' Julie called from beside the car. 'Just walk slowly down the path. I want to check your co-ordination.' Walker went slowly down the path, reached her and kissed her on the forehead. 'Hi,' she said. 'Yes, I guess you've improved slightly. Boy, it's cold here, let's get in.' They did. Julie turned the ignition. 'You know the way to this place?' she asked.

'No, we have to follow the Froelichs. They're coming right now. That's their car.'

'That's a car? I thought it was an ancient monument. Well, okay, let's hope they make it. Well, hey, Mr Walker, together again!'

'Yes,' said Walker, 'it's splendid.'

'We'll celebrate. Reach in the glove compartment. There's a box of panatella cigars. Have one. Light one for me too.'

'You smoke these?'

'I smoke anything,' said Julie. 'Hey, you were all written up in the press. It really changed my image of you. I thought it was virtually heroic, what you did. And out here too. I suppose they almost lynched you.'

'No, not really,' said Walker.

'Oh well, never mind,' said Julie. 'You can't have everything.'

'I can't?' said Walker.

'No, but you can aspire,' said Julie. 'Hey, we're here. Just look at that.'

Dean French's house was a modern A frame, composed

almost entirely of glass. There was, apparently, only one room in the house, right in the centre, into which you couldn't directly see from outside, and this one you could watch people going into. 'I guess that's the can there in the middle,' said Julie, 'if people who live this way use anything like that.' The downstairs rooms were full of folk, and Julie said: 'This is quite a party. I'm going to feel a real ringer. At Hillesley the faculty parties are quite different. I went to a couple. They serve tea and then somebody plays, you know, the lute?'

'I don't think Dean French's parties are like that,' said Walker.

'Come on in, you two,' said Patrice Froelich, putting her head into the car. 'We're abolishing small groups.'

'Hello,' said Julie. 'I'm Julie Snowflake, from the east coast.'

'I always thought Jamie liked the young ones best,' said Patrice. Walker looked down in embarrassment and scratched his nose. Inside, Dean French, a very big man who wore a monocle and a velvet smoking jacket, welcomed them. Dean French, a bachelor, had the reputation of setting the social pace in Party; his main role in life was introducing everyone to everyone else, and when people couldn't recall where they had met someone before, they always said: 'We were introduced at one of Dean French's parties.' He had an expensive and very public house, and even during the day, if you drove past, you could see people sitting around in the living-rooms, drinking martinis, people perhaps left over from last night's party or arrived early for that night's.

'I hope you don't mind,' said Walker. 'I've brought along an old friend of mine.'

'No, I love that kind of thing,' said Dean French, taking Julie's hand and squeezing it. 'And how did you get mixed up with this ivy-covered ruin from limey-land?'

'I met him last summer coming back home from Yerp,' said Julie.

'Let me show you around the house,' said Dean French, 'and then we'll go out back and I'll show you the pool. Did Dr Froelich tell you we were going to swim?'

'Oh no, that's a pity, because I don't have a bathing suit.'

'You don't need a bathing suit,' said Bernard Froelich.

'I think we'll get by,' said Dean French. 'I'll take you on the tour, honey.'

'Let's get some drinks,' said Froelich, leading Walker over to the bar, which was being kept by Hamish Wagner.

'Pip pip, old top, keep your pecker up,' he said to Walker.

'Hello, sir,' said a graduate student in the department, coming up to Walker, 'I've been meaning to ask you – but first I ought to say how much I enjoy your novels – are you writing about us?'

Froelich said to the graduate student: 'Who are you?'

'I'm Ewart Hummingbee, sir, I'm in your department.'

'Well, don't ask Mr Walker silly questions like that. He doesn't have to answer that kind of thing.'

'Maybe he wants to,' said Hummingbee.

'I'm looking after him, and he doesn't. So blow. I love this man and I want to talk to him.'

'I'm sorry,' said Hummingbee.

'Blow,' said Froelich, and turning to Walker he said: 'Hi hi.'

'Hi hi,' said Walker.

'Tell me something,' said Froelich. 'Right, now, what have you learned since you came here?'

'I'll tell you at the end of the year,' said Walker.

'Tell me now, goddam it,' said Froelich. 'Have you learned anything?'

'Yes.'

'What?'

'Well, I've learned how to hold my trousers up without braces, and how to work a coin-operated washing machine, and . . .'

'What have you *learned*?' demanded Froelich.

'Well, all right, I've learned that, well, the things I believed in aren't as secure as I thought. I've learned that literature is a bit more precarious in the future than I expected, that the new world of technology is one I don't understand at all, that democracy is not what I thought it was, and that there's more than one way of being a writer.'

'Yes,' said Froelich, 'that's a good answer you gave me. You're a clever man, Jamie. So – what are you going to do?'

'Do?' asked Walker.

'Yes, you'll have to decide, won't you?'

'Decide what?'

'Whether you're going to stay here or to go, whether you're going to go back to your large domestic wife or marry that kid you brought here tonight.'

'Oh, I don't think there's much chance of *that*.'

'Is your divorce arranged?'

'No,' said Walker. 'My wife doesn't like the idea.'

Froelich shouted over the crowd: 'Julie Snowflake, come here.'

'Don't,' said Walker.

'Hi there,' said Julie Snowflake, squeezing through the crowd, 'I got a kind of a hint you wanted to speak to me, Dr Froelich.'

'Right,' said Froelich. 'You see this man I'm talking to, this excellent man? Well, his name's Walker and I'm his friend.'

'So am I,' said Julie. 'He's a very well-endowed guy, don't you think?'

'Well, I want to ask you a question about him. I want you to tell me briefly just what your sentiments are towards him.'

'You don't need to answer,' said Walker. 'Please don't.'

'She does need to answer,' said Froelich, 'because I asked her a polite question and polite questions have to be answered.'

'Well,' said Julie, 'if you really want to go through with this, I think he's, like you say, an excellent man.'

'How excellent?'

'Very excellent.'

'Do you find him sexually attractive?'

'Yes, I think I do,' said Julie. 'But then I find a whole lot of people sexually attractive. It's amazing. You expect there'll be just one and then there are these dozens and dozens, just walking about.'

'Would you marry a man like that?'

'Hey, I don't have to answer that kind of question, Dr Froelich. I make up my mind when it's put direct to me by the man who's proposing. I think that's a reasonable enough approach to the problem.'

'Would you marry a man like that?'

'I could do, I guess, if all the things were right, which they aren't. Mr Walker knows what I mean.'

'You mean he's a married man.'

'Yes,' said Julie. 'I didn't know whether he'd told you. He doesn't tell everybody.'

'Okay, fine, that's all we want to know. Go back to Dean French. He's leering at you.'

'I don't want her to go,' said Walker. 'I've hardly talked to her yet.'

'Oh, don't worry, Mr Walker, I'll come back,' said Julie.

'She'll come back,' said Froelich. 'So – what do you want to do, Jamie?'

'God knows,' said Walker, confused.

Julie had gone back to Dean French, who put his arm round her. This reminded Walker of Dr Millingham, and the talk on the ship, and the heather Elaine had sent him, and of Elaine's last letter in his breast pocket, telling him to remember to change his underpants.

'No, He doesn't,' said Froelich. 'I do, but He doesn't.'

Walker had become oriented towards Froelich's advice, he didn't know quite how, and he found it natural to say: 'What am I going to do, then?'

'Well, you're going to go home, aren't you?'

'Am I?' asked Walker.

'Yes, because you're afraid? And because if you stayed you'd turn into Mrs Bourbon or that madman Jochum? And because Julie is young and deluded about Englishmen and writers? And because everybody looks better when they're away from home, and it embarrasses them?'

Walker felt uneasy about these words, for he began to suspect that Froelich was telling him he had been fired. But that seemed too simple, and he had long understood the complexity of Froelich's motives. The truth might be that he was telling him the truth. The complicated feelings that Walker had long felt toward Froelich, the man who had drawn so much from him, suddenly turned into a sense of affection and gratitude and kinship. Froelich had, out of some remotely conceived sense of affinity, chosen him and, as Patrice had promised, he had changed him by making him see. Walker looked out through the great windows at the mountains, and felt at once depressed by what Froelich said and convinced of its kindness and its wisdom.

Evadne Heilman came by and handed Walker a plate of rare roast beef and salad. 'You look ready for some food,' she said. 'I'm sure you're losing weight around the middle.'

'It's this healthy life I lead,' said Walker. 'Marking fifty themes a night is real exercise.'

'You know you have to swim later?' said Evadne Heilman, big and booming.

'Oh, not me,' said Walker. 'I'm not athletic.'

'Yes, you,' said Evadne.

'Out there?' cried Walker. 'It's much too cold. The temperature's probably below freezing. I'd drop dead.'

'The pool heating's been on all day,' said Evadne. 'Oh, we're counting on you, buddy. For the honour of the English.'

Walker took his plate and went with it into the study. The house was packed with people, all in a state of high euphoria, and Walker had an image of Party as a vast nudist colony. In it people had no privacy and no defects were concealed. Sex and friendship hung in the cold air like summer pollen, and exposure, of self and of others, was the essential ethic of the place. The rooms were full of asserting, sensual souls. Near him a girl in a grey swimsuit was having her left buttock caressed by a man in a red blazer, a professor of French literature. 'What an ass, baby, what an ass,' he was saying.

Walker watched and listened and ate his beef, and presently Patrice Froelich came and sat down beside him. 'Hi, honey,' she said. 'What happened to your friend?'

'I don't know,' said Walker. 'She's here somewhere.'

'She's with that fat-assed Dean French,' said Patrice. 'He's really taken a shine to her. Still, she's having a great time. She's a marvellous kid.'

'Yes, isn't she?'

'Are you in love with her?'

'I don't know,' said Walker, embarrassed. 'I like her a great deal.'

'Ah, it's that old yearning for innocence. Which we never find, remember?'

'Well, she's hardly innocent,' said Walker. 'I think it was Dr Jochum who was telling me the roles are reversed now. European innocence chases American experience.'

'And is that what you've been doing over here?'

Walker saw this was dangerous ground, and said, 'Well, something like that.'

'Now what does *that* mean?' said Patrice, 'remembering I'm just a little involved here.'

'I mean intellectually; and in spirit. As Bernie was just telling me, I've learned a great deal over here.'

'Bernie means from Bernie,' said Patrice. 'Still, we're always glad to help.' She put down her plate and said: 'Come and take a look at the pool.' They went through some glass doors and out on to the patio, in the middle of which was set Dean French's enormous pool. It was a dark evening, and the only illumination came from four flambeaux, stuck into the turf, their flames burning brightly, and some pool lights which lit the green water from below; clouds of steam blew off from the pool's surface into the darkness. 'Feel how hot it is,' said Patrice.

'Wow,' said Walker, dipping his hand into the water; it was as hot as a good bath.

'Were you expecting her?' asked Patrice.

'Julie, you mean? No, that was a great surprise.'

'Yes, Julie I mean; does Bernie want you to have her now?'

'I don't know what he wants. I don't think so. I think he probably wants me to go back home.'

'To your wife?'

'Yes.'

'When?'

'Oh, I don't know. I suppose at the end of the year. *If* they let me stay here.'

'Yes,' said Patrice. 'I can see how going home would be the best thing, after you've pleased him so much. I mean, you'll have done all you can for him then.'

'What pleased him so much?'

'I expect he'll tell you all about it, when he's ready. I'm surprised he hasn't told you now. I wonder why?'

'Yes, I do.'

'Perhaps he's afraid you'll be upset,' said Patrice.

'Why, what at?'

'Oh, I don't know. Will you go home?'

'I don't know, it depends whether I can choose. In any case it's my decision, not Bernie's.'

'I hope it is, I hope everything has been.'

'I think it has. You know, it will be very hard to leave this place. I love it here. Just look how beautiful it is. See the mountains?'

'Yes, it's fine,' said Patrice. 'And we'd miss you, Jamie. I would. Even Bernie would. He really cares for you a lot.'

The glass door opened again; it was Julie Snowflake. 'I'll go inside,' said Patrice, 'you want to talk to her.' Walker did.

'Come on, Mr Walker,' said Julie, 'we're going swimming.'

'Oh, I'm not the swimming type,' said Walker. 'In any case, I've just eaten.'

'Look, Mr Walker, I thought I was teaching you poise and co-ordination. I want to see you right there in that pool, I mean that. No fooling.'

'All right,' said Walker. The cold had already kept him shivering. Now he had to undress, get his hair wet, no doubt catch a cold. He was not as healthy as these citizens of an outdoor society. But he went into the men's cabin and took off his jacket and shirt. The cold was hideous. He unbuttoned the ancient British flies on his trousers and dropped them round his feet, standing there in his underpants.

'How are you doing?' shouted Julie from the other side of the partition. 'I've got my suit on.' Walker took off his underpants and looked down at his shivering body, at his puny arms and graceless paunch, and hastily picked up and put on a pair of undershorts with green porpoises etched on them. 'Come on,' said Julie, banging on the door. Walker went outside. The winter night wind hit him hard and raised up goose pimples. Julie, already standing by the pool in a rather slack red one-piece swimsuit, shouted, 'Get in quick, Mr Walker, it's cold.' He watched as she poised her arms in the air, and then tossed her long lithe body into the water. 'Oh, it's great,' she said, surfacing. 'It's the most splendid sensation, really.' Walker, who couldn't dive, hurried over to the pool and slid into it, scratching the backs of his legs on the concrete edge. The pool was painfully hot, but the bits of him sticking out of it, his head and neck and his hands, were, equally, painfully cold. His meal felt heavy in his stomach and his scratched buttocks hurt. 'Isn't it great?' said Julie.

'Yes,' said Walker.

'You don't swim too well, do you, Mr Walker? Don't you like getting your hair wet?'

'Oh, I don't mind,' said Walker, in cavalier fashion, though he did. Miss Snowflake's expectation of him, always strong, seemed to have risen. His success in the American press had got him into an exciting position with her, but one that, with his pain in his legs and stomach, he doubted he could live up to. But her sweet young face, and her cool inquisitive concern, made him want to do nothing more than to try.

They swam to the deep end of the pool, Julie fast and gracefully, Walker slow and gracelessly. When they reached the end they held on to the edge and looked at each other. 'Oh, Mr Walker, I'm very pleased to see you,' said Julie.

'You look very pretty,' said Walker.

'Oh yes,' said Julie. 'This swimsuit's practically falling off me and I've lost my tan. I'll say I look pretty.'

'Let it fall off,' said Walker, breathing hard, and he pushed himself forward in the water and kissed her. This made him lose his grip on the side and he disappeared beneath the surface. When he spluttered up, Julie said, 'I like you doing that, but I'm afraid you'll drown. I was wondering. Have you ever made love in a swimming pool?'

'I can't say I have.'

'We'd probably both drown,' Julie went on. 'At the height of our relationship. Might be fun.'

'I'm sure I would,' said Walker.

'You know why? You don't trust the water.'

'I don't sag,' said Walker.

'That's right. You remember,' said Julie. 'Take a look at that stomach of yours. That's not healthy fat. You should see mine.'

'I'd like to.'

'Well, just feel it.' Walker felt the stomach; it was splendidly firm.

'You should train,' said Julie. Walker ran his hand up and inside the top of Julie's swimsuit. 'They're too tiny,' said Julie, 'I wish they'd fill out more. Big but neat, that's how I like them.'

'I like them like this,' said Walker.

'Hi hi,' said a voice from the pool-side darkness.

'Oh, that friend of yours,' said Julie, wriggling away. 'You know something? He may be a nice guy and all, but he's a bully.'

'Bernard? Yes. I suppose he is. He's a kind man really, though. I wouldn't be here if it weren't for him.'

'Okay, but he's still a bully. He's the kind of guy who'll splash water on us.'

'Look out,' said Froelich, and he squirted a hose of cold water on them both from the other side of the pool.

'Hey, Dr Froelich, Jesus,' said Julie.

'I thought you needed cooling off,' said Froelich.

The spray of cold water had added to Walker's feelings of ill-health. His head was beginning to reel. 'Hey, get us a drink,' said Julie. 'Bring us some martinis.'

'Righty righty,' said Froelich.

'He shouldn't have asked me those questions,' said Julie, when Froelich had gone inside.

'No,' said Walker.

'What did you think of the answers, though?'

'I liked them.'

'Well, it's real hard to answer when you're put on the spot

like that, but I guess I was pretty frank. Didn't you think I played it cool?'

'Did you mean them?'

'Oh, Mr Walker, you know how I tell the truth. I'm committed to truth, I told you that on the ship. It's beautiful, you know? And I'll tell you more truth still, Mr Walker. I came out here to see you. My brother, well, I can see him any time at home.'

'To see me?' cried Walker. 'Why?'

'It was seeing your picture in the paper. I was mad at you when you got off the ship. Because you didn't tell me you were married. So I told the girl to tell you I was out when you called. I was right there by the phone.'

'The truth,' said Walker. 'What about the truth?'

'Well, that was imaginatively true, I was out as far as you were concerned. And then I started thinking a lot. I read your books again. I thought, this man is a conniver and he doesn't know how to live even, but there's real aspiration there. You can help him. And then you did that, came out against the oath. I admired it; I thought it was really fine. You know me, writers don't snow me as a general rule, I've seen so many of them. But I did think well of that. Not just because of what you said; it's said all the time. But because you said it, in spite of your difficulties. I knew it was hard for you. I thought it showed you'd really come on.'

'I thought that too, but it wasn't quite so simple.'

'But you did it. I once asked one of my teachers at Hillesley, this funny old lady who looked so wise, I asked: "Can you improve your character by trying?" She thought a bit and said: "No." I didn't want to believe her but I thought she might be right. But I understood that you don't believe that. You gave me hope.'

'No, I don't believe *that*.'

Julie stretched her legs out in front of her and floated on the water. 'Just checking I still had my suit on,' she said. 'You know, I was wondering. What do you plan to do over the Christmas vacation?'

'Stay here.'

'Any special reason?'

'No, unambitiousness. Except I have an invitation to Christmas dinner.'

'Can you break it?'

'It's with the Froelichs.'

'Ditch them, 'said Julie.

'But why?'

'Well, I thought I might put an invitation to you. You don't have to accept, but it's one of those brainstorm things that occurred to me. Why don't you come out west with me?'

'With you?' cried Walker.

'Yes, with me. I'm not going anywhere special, not meeting anybody. I'm just travelling around on my own really, taking in my country. And I could use a little company, especially if it's yours, Mr Walker. To share the writer's eye. I'm sure you could teach me what all these mountains and deserts mean, if you wanted to.'

'I certainly do want to,' said Walker.

'Then shake,' said Julie, 'you've struck a bargain.' Walker took one hand off the edge, slipping a little into the water, and they shook. 'How long is your vacation?' asked Julie.

'A fortnight.'

'And what may that mean?'

'Two weeks. I felt so pleased I forgot I was in the States.'

'You thought you were back home with your wife, didn't you, Mr Walker?'

'Don't say that.'

'Well, okay, two weeks. Good, so's mine, only I have to get right back to the east coast. So I'll drop you by here a couple of days before, if that sounds all right.'

'It sounds fine.'

'You're not just being polite about this? Because I didn't know whether to make this invitation or not.'

Walker, trying hard not to think of Elaine, said: 'I'm not being polite at all. When do you start?'

'Oh, any time,' said Julie. 'Right now, if you like.'

'Here are your drinkies,' said Froelich behind them; they

took the glasses and began to drink. 'Oh, what a sensation,' said Julie. 'It's everything. What more do we want?' At the other end a few people had come into the pool. Dean French swam toward them.

'Let's see you swim,' he said to Miss Snowflake.

'Okay, here goes,' said Julie, letting go of the side and breast-stroking for the other end.

'That's a very fine girl,' said Dean French, holding to the edge next to Walker. 'Why is it that foreigners always manage to find out the best we've got?'

There was a shout from Julie at the far end: 'Hey, it's snowing,' she cried. And it was; large soft flakes dropped silently out of the dark sky above them and melted into the water of the pool.

'Yes, when it snows like this, it makes me wish I could spend my life here,' Walker said.

'I'm very glad to hear you say that,' said Dean French. 'Makes me glad we're not going to fire you.'

'Oh, you're not?' said Walker, deeply relieved. 'That's what I've been waiting to know.'

'Maybe I shouldn't tell you that, maybe everyone was planning to keep you on the hook a little, but I'm too drunk to care.'

'The meeting went in my favour, then,' said Walker.

'Very much,' said Dean French. 'Want to hear about it?'

'Very much,' said Walker.

'Well, I don't know why I'm building you up so much, when you're running around with the nicest girl I've seen in years, but okay. I'll have to treat you to some history first.'

'Go ahead,' said Walker. 'I can even manage that.'

'Well, it all goes back to the McCarthy period, when there were a lot of firings round here. A character called Leonov, who's still at the U, but on leave this year, was behind that. So anyway, the local chapter of the A A U P rallied round, a bit late in the day, I have to admit, and they resolved democratically to support the principle that college teachers shouldn't be forced to declare their political allegiance, by oath or any other means, and they shouldn't be fired on solely political grounds. The AAUP here has taken that line ever since, and we've put a hell of a lot of pressure in the college admin. at different times to withdraw the state oath. The last president, who was a lazy but very well-meaning guy, finally agreed to do that, but he was caught up between the faculty and the regents and the regents finally got at him and he resigned, quit.'

'I see.'

'Then we got Coolidge. Of course he tried to play it all ways, but the point is he never fired anyone for disloyalty. You know that careful line he walks.'

'Yes,' said Walker, 'I know it very well now.'

'So you see you came in at the end of quite a battle. Now what happened after your crazy speech, which incidentally was pretty innocuous stuff, was that the Leonov faction got moving again. Another of the émigré wing, a man called Jochum, presented a petition asking the college to affirm in favour of the oath.'

'How did Jochum get tied up with these people?' asked Walker.

'Oh, he's a friend of Leonov's, they have sad Russian pasts in common. Jochum wouldn't hurt a fly, he's carrying the can for Leonov. So our friend Bernie got up at the meeting and accused the petitioners of prejudicing the AAUP stand. Jochum tried to fight him, but the point is that the meeting supported Bernie. So then Bernie moved that the meeting counter-petition the university to come out in opposition to the oath. Now obviously it can't do this, because of the state backing, but Bernie proposed it as a gesture, to repudiate the Jochum petition. So we approved it. Then there was a big scene. Coolidge saw Jochum and Bernie on Monday and condemned the first petition, so Bernie withdrew his. Then Jochum resigned and that's it.'

'Jochum resigned?'

'Yes, he resigned, quit his job.'

'But he loved it here.'

'He had no choice, he was really out on a limb,' said Dean French. 'He'll find a post somewhere else.'

'But that's terrible. I stay and he goes.'

'But more terrible for him than you,' said Dean French, diving into the water and swimming toward Julie.

Walker hung in the water, clinging to the edge, his head sticking out of the water, decked out with snow. The storm of flakes blew down into the pool. The story he had just been told possessed him with horror. Jochum, who had been expelled from his country, Jochum who had drifted without a nationality, Jochum who had been taken in here and there for a while and then dropped again, Jochum who had so often said to Walker 'Beggars cannot be choosers', had lost the grip on his security and happiness that he had only just recently found. His own part in this was obscure, but he had a part; through lack of insight, through political ignorance, through his blundering approach to life, he had deprived him of his hard-gained possessions. And what was most distressing was that his own part was so vague, so that he could not know where to start taking measurements. And then something darker occurred to him, as he looked up at the snow; it was, this is why I was brought here, this is what I was appointed to do, this is what I am all about. This was Froelich's end in view; this was why his name had been proposed, why the letter had come to him in Nottingham, why he had given his speech, why he had been tempted with Patrice, why he had heard from Froelich nothing about the meeting.

In fury he dived away from the side and toward the other end. He pulled as hard as he could through the water, and felt something unfortunate happening; his over-large shorts had slid down his legs and were pinioning his feet together. He began to sink. People stood round the side of the pool; his face looked up at them in horror. He heard Froelich, on the side, say: 'The day he arrived in Party he didn't even want to take his goddam necktie off.'

The next thing was that someone was pulling him up to the surface; it was Bernard Froelich, who had walked into the pool fully dressed. Walker looked down and saw his exposed privates and reached down to pull up his shorts. 'Thanks,' he said to Froelich.

'Bring him inside,' said Dean French. 'We'll give him some brandy.' Walker let himself be led, shivering, through the cold air into the house. His stomach now pained him a great deal, and the cold made him feel faint, but the biggest pain was the profound embarrassment of his indecent exposure. Froelich sat him down in a canvas chair and knocked the pat of snow from his head. Beyond the windows, the pool lights, the snow whirled. Froelich stood over him, urgent, concerned, but beneath the honest emotion was something else, Walker knew. He could think of nothing more to say to him.

'You'll have to be careful, Jamie,' said Froelich. 'You're a precious possession. We don't want you to die while you're here.'

'I won't,' said Walker.

'Good oh,' said Froelich.

Walker took his clothes when Julie brought them and went into the bathroom. When he came out, Julie was dressed, and had her car keys in her hand.

When they got into the car, Walker said: 'Let's leave this town now.'

'Go west?' asked Julie.

'Yes,' said Walker.

'I'll have to get my luggage,' said Julie.

'I have to get mine too. Drop me at the Froelichs' and I'll be ready when you get back.'

'Okay,' said Julie. When he got back to the Froelichs' empty house, Walker hurried round and packed his bags. It was about three-thirty, and it was just getting light. A bird was singing somewhere. Afraid that the Froelichs might come home, he climbed out of the window like an adulterer and hid himself and his bags in the bushes, which flipped snow over him. The bottom of the sky was pink and there was pinkness on the white of the mountains. The long plain was also touched with white, but the snowfall had stopped. One speeding car passed down the street. Then, presently, the black Volkswagen crept round the corner and stopped.

Walker put in the two cases and the typewriter and climbed in front. 'We're off,' said Julie, 'Westward ho. Pike's Peak or bust.' Walker watched as the car began to move and then, exhausted, he immediately fell asleep.

8

When Walker awoke, the sun was up, slanting in through the car's rear window, and they were high in the foothills. The big peaks, which from the plain around Party had looked so close, retreated before them, spreading out their white caps in all directions. There was a fresh snowfall here too, on the road and among the rocks and pines. 'Hi,' said Julie, holding tightly on to the driving wheel as the car slid about the road in old ruts. 'You're awake. It's a beautiful day.'

'What time is it?' asked Walker.

'Oh, around eight. We have to stop and get some breakfast soon. And we need some groceries, because I've got a pump-up camping stove back there and we can make our own meals. You a good cook, Mr Walker?'

'I don't think so.'

'It's real cold out there,' said Julie, 'I wouldn't like to be a brass monkey.'

'There seems to be a lot of snow around.'

'I know. I didn't think of that. With this new snowfall the ploughs won't have got to it yet and we could be blocked in. That happens in the mountains. Like the Donner party. I guess that was west of here, in the Sierras, but they got overtaken by winter and they had to eat one another to survive, or for some of them to survive. The question is, if we get snowbound, who eats who?'

'You eat me,' said Walker.

'Now you're just being polite and English again; why? Let's be rational. Who's the most useful of us?'

'You're younger than me; and you're beautiful.'

'Well, you've published more and you'll publish more yet if you survive. No, you eat me.'

'You eat me.'

'Look, I'd better try the radio and see what the weather report is for this region, don't you think?'

'I should,' said Walker. Julie switched on and a disc jockey on a local station came through announcing early carols for people who would be killed on the roads before Christmas.

'Oh lord,' said Julie, pressing the button again, and getting country and western music, where lethargic cowpokes sing about their dogies. On a third station was a commercial for horsefeed. 'Horsefeed to you,' said Julie, switching off. 'You eat me, don't forget. You snored in your sleep.'

'I must have been tired,' said Walker.

'You nearly drowned, remember? I sang you lullabies when you were sleeping.'

'Let's hear one now when I'm awake,' said Walker.

'Okay,' said Julie, and sang:

> Hush, little baby, don't you cry
> Cause you know your mammy was born to die
> All my trials, Lord, soon be over.

'You know that one?' she asked.

'Yes,' said Walker, and sang:

> If livin' were a thing that money could buy
> The rich would live and the poor would die
> All my trials, Lord, soon be over.

'Okay, all together now,' said Julie, 'and let's have it loud and clear:

> I've got a little book with pages three
> And every page spells liberty
> All my trials, Lord, soon be over.

'Good,' said Julie. 'What do you do in cars in England? Apart from laying one another? We have this whole car culture here.'

'We sit and look out of the window.'

'Sitters by the wall,' said Julie. 'We always sing. Know any English songs? Isn't that where our folk songs came from originally?'

'Do you know "Ilkley Moor Baht 'At"?'

'No,' said Julie, giggling.

'All right, I'll give you that.' He gave that, and then sang 'Oh, Sir Jasper' and 'Three Old Ladies Locked in a Lavatory'. He felt absolutely fine.

At a roadside diner they stopped for breakfast. The man sweeping the entrance wore a Stetson and said, 'Howdy strangers, welcome,' looking at them suspiciously.

'Hi,' said Julie. 'You have to say "hi",' she said, 'this is the west, man.' They sat down at the counter and looked across at display cards of No-Doze and nail clippers. Julie picked up the menu and said: 'You going to have the breakfast special? How'd you like your eggs fried?'

'I don't remember.'

'Oh, you have to be smart with these short-order cooks. They're real tough. Ask for two fried looking at you.'

'Two fried looking at you,' said Walker.

'This the breakfast special? You don't want the short stack?' asked the waitress.

'Two fried looking at you,' said Walker.

'There, you sounded tough, now she respects you,' said Julie, putting on her sun-glasses.' I can't bear to look at naked fried eggs.'

'I really know I'm abroad in these places,' said Walker.

'Cream with?' asked the waitress.

'Sure, set it down,' said Walker.

'Oh boy, oh boy,' said Julie, 'you'll be running for President next.' When they went back to the car, 'Oh, that cold's good,' said Julie, huddling her arms across her breasts, 'we're coming up to the high peaks now. We'll soon be hitting the Continental Divide. Once you're over that you're really in the west.'

They saw the Continental Divide signs about an hour later; Julie stopped the car and Walker got out and urinated on the ridge, hoping to fill Atlantic and Pacific at the same time.

The summits all around them perpetually reorganized themselves as they went on. They went through miners' towns, with abandoned workings by the roadside, and high cattle country. 'We'll stop in the next good place and I'll fix us some food,' said Julie about noon, when the sun was filling the canyons. They found a picnic area, deep in snow. In her cashmere coat and straw hat, Julie opened cans and unwrapped packages. 'I'm going to fix soup and frankfurters and beans, is that all right?'

'That's good,' said Walker. They sat on the running board of the car to eat these things, watching the new snow drop from the pines.

'See any bears around?' asked Julie.

'Are there bears here?' said Walker.

'Of course,' said Julie, 'they come out of the National Parks and live wild for a spell.'

'We seem to be living very dangerously,' said Walker.

'Yes,' said Julie, 'especially with my cooking. There's just some Hostess cup-cakes now. I'll fix some coffee. It'll have to be in the same saucepan as the beans.'

'Good,' said Walker.

'How was it?' asked Julie afterwards. 'Am I a good cook?'

'Excellent,' said Walker.

'I like cooking for you,' said Julie.

'The coffee tasted of beans, though,' said Walker.

'It's called boffee,' said Julie, 'it's a specialty of the house. Okay, let's get packed and we'll start again. I want to hit Salt Lake City tomorrow some time.'

The Rockies were still with them as they drove on into the afternoon. The sun began to slant down again, coming full into the front of the car. Then, in front of them, there was suddenly the plain again. 'This was the pioneer's dream,' said Julie. 'Think of those Mormons coming out from the passes and finding this. You know what they said? "This must be the place." It was the Happy Valley, the land God had saved for them. Actually it just looks like anywhere, but it's those mountains that make it, I think.'

'The trouble's before,' said Walker. 'It is beautiful, though. But what impresses me about America is the way everyone saw it as a God-designed landscape. Every journey was a myth.'

'I think we still have something of that feeling,' said Julie. 'That's one reason why it's so big to come to Yerp. Keep your eyes skinned for some roadside cabins, Mr Walker, cheap ones. I think this is about my capacity for driving in one day. We have to decide. Are we going to share a cabin?'

Walker said, 'I would like us to.'

'Well, then, we have to register as a married couple. Do you know about the Mann Act? It's a federal offence to transport a girl across a state line for immoral purposes. That's why lots of guys do it just for extra kicks.'

After a while, they found some weather-beaten, white-painted wooden cabins at the roadside, in the pines. There were only two cars there already, and a sign hopefully said, *Vacancy*. 'I'll turn in here,' said Julie, skidding the car up the snowy slope. 'Look, you don't happen to carry around a wedding ring with you, do you, Mr Walker?'

'No, I don't.'

'Never thought you'd get lucky, huh?' said Julie. 'How come you don't wear one?'

'We don't use them in England.'

'Not even women?'

'Oh yes, women do.'

'You have one law for women and another for men. Okay, well, I'll just have to put my gloves on. Maybe I should tie a bit of cord around my finger to make a hump. At least we have luggage.'

'What about the labels?' said Walker, as they stopped outside the first cabin, which said *Office*.

'We'll have to unload when he's not looking. Now, you go in there and find out the rate. Then come and tell me what it is.'

'Shouldn't you?' asked Walker. 'You know what's what.'

'Goddam it, no,' said Julie. 'I drive, I cook, you ask the rates, Mr Walker.'

Walker went into the office and rang a bell on the counter. A small old man in grey denims came out from a back room and said, 'Howdy, stranger.'

'Howdy,' said Walker, and asked if they had a double room for one night. 'Reckon we do,' said the man. 'Number six.'

'How much is it?'

315

'Four bucks the pair,' said the man.

'Thank you,' said Walker. He went outside to Julie and told her.

'Okay, now ask to look at it,' said Julie. Walker went inside again and asked to be shown the cabin. The man took down a key and led him through the snow. 'Ain't no dinin' room here but we got cookers in the cabins. There's a store 'bout a mile down the highway. Coke machine back there in th' office. Guests out by ten in the mornin' for cleanin'.' The man unlocked the cabin door; it had a double bed with a maple headboard and footboard, an old cooker in the corner, and a small bathroom and toilet in the back.

'Yes, that's fine,' said Walker, and he went back to the office and signed the register, writing 'Mr and Mrs Caliban, Tempest, N.Y.' in the book.

' 'Kay, Mr Caliban,' said the man, 'you can drive right up there.' Walker got back in the car. 'Sleep good, Mrs Caliban,' said the old man, on the step. Julie backed the car and drove up to the cabin.

'What's this Caliban bit?' asked Julie.

'That's our name,' said Walker. They unlocked the luggage and took it inside.

Walker went over to Julie, lifted her face, and kissed her. 'Hi,' said Julie.

'Hi,' said Walker.

'Well, it's not the honeymoon suite at the Waldorf-Astoria, but at least the bed bounces,' said Julie. 'I don't think it will do discredit to the occasion.'

'Good,' said Walker, kissing her again.

'It's kind of cold, though,' said Julie.

'We'll warm each other,' said Walker.

'I know we will, duckie,' said Julie.

Walker sat on the bed and said, 'Come and sit down.'

'Not so fast, Superman, I'm going to cook us a meal first. Then I'll test the bounce.' She got out some cans and opened them. 'Oh, and there's a little question I have to put to you,' she said. 'This little question of your marital status. I guess you wondered why I put you down that last evening on the ship.

Well, your friend Millingham told me you were a married man. Now, what about it? Let's have the whole story, Mr Walker, duckie.'

'Well, it's true, of course.'

'Yes, I got that. So, what do you have to offer me?'

'I'm trying to divorce her.'

'What does the word "trying" mean here?'

'She doesn't want me to.'

'Why not? You're so attractive, I should have thought any girl would want to divorce you.'

'I suppose she likes me, and thinks I'm being foolish. And she's a traditional sort of English girl. She thinks marriage is for ever.'

'It's beans again,' said Julie. 'Oh, and you don't?'

'Well, I don't honestly know. On the whole the English have always believed in making the best of a bad job. The English have always really clung to their marriages, because they don't see them as places and the achievement of happiness. If it doesn't provide positive pleasure at least it offers safety and security.'

'You mean that English wives are no good in bed?'

'I'd say they don't put so much effort into that area of life. Americans live so much more through the sexual relationship, they demand more of it.'

'And you don't?'

'Ah, me,' said Walker. 'Well, that's a different matter. Come here and I'll show you.'

'Eat your beans,' said Julie.

When they had eaten, Julie went into the bathroom and took a shower. Walker, listening to the water cascading, lay on the bed. The sleep he had missed the night before fought with his excitement about Julie. You mustn't sleep, he said, you mustn't sleep; this is the best thing that has ever happened to you. And the more he thought of it, the more it seemed it was. His affection and fondness for her ran deeper than any he could recall. Her coolness and style and her physical neatness, the very composition of her body and her heart, pleased him more than any woman he had known. Even in the shower he missed her. He went and knocked on the plywood door and said: 'Can I come in?'

'Okay, duckie,' said Julie. He looked at all the neatness of her naked body under the flow of water, every aspect of it neat, rightly shaped, proudly there, and his heart beat wildly. Julie turned the shower head and soaked him with water.

'Oh, God!' said Walker, gasping.

'You'll have to undress now, won't you, duckie,' said Julie. Walker dropped his wet clothes on the floor and stood there naked, unsure, uncomfortable. 'Oh, you poor thing,' said Julie, 'that was unfair. I'm sorry.'

'Well?' said Julie Snowflake, a little later.

'Well,' said Walker.

'And how was it?' asked Julie.

'I admire your energy,' said Walker.

Julie found cigarettes, put two in her mouth and lit them both, handing one to Walker. Then she said: 'You mind if I make some criticism in the field of Poise and Co-ordination?'

'I suppose not,' said Walker. 'But I'm pretty sensitive.'

'It's just that you're still not a totally relaxed person, and I feel responsible, you know?'

'Can't sag.'

'No, right.'

'You think I could do better?'

'I think better could be done.'

'Oh,' said Walker.

'I'm not complaining. Hell, we're both really bushed. But what does your wife think?'

'She's never expressed dissatisfaction.'

'Well, as you know, I'm a great believer in criticism. And standards. Like those ties you wear. People don't wear such wide ties any more. Why don't you buy some American ties?'

'I thought they were all right.'

'You could look so much neater, you have this messy look. I guess it's the English style, is it?'

'I like to think I add a certain characteristic messiness of my own,' said Walker.

318

'When we get to San Francisco I'm going to take you to a men's store and buy you some good clothes, okay?'

'Yes, fine,' said Walker.

A little later still, when they were lying in bed, Walker said: 'You remember Dr Jochum, from the ship?'

'Yes, I do. Do you see much of him? I was going to call him on the telephone if I'd stayed any longer in Party.'

'He's leaving, he's resigning from his job.'

'Why? I thought he liked it here.'

'Because of me.'

'You?' cried Julie.

'You told me he was at Hillesley. Why did he leave there?'

'I think it was because they couldn't give him the courses he wanted to teach. And then there was some trouble when some Soviet academician came to be awarded an honorary degree. There was this Russian expatriate group that made some kind of objection. But really I don't think that had much to do with his quitting. I think it was the courses mainly. And of course they didn't give him tenure. It was sort of like *Pnin*, did you ever read that novel? It's marvellous.'

'No, I will,' said Walker.

'It's in paperback. But what happened at Benedict Arnold? What did you have to do with it?'

'Well, you know I liked him, I like him. But it was the speech. The one you read about. He got involved with some protest, not against me really, but against the university's support of me, and ran into trouble with the president.'

'He's a marvellous man,' said Julie. 'He has all these crazy ideas, he's so disillusioned, but if what happened to him had happened to me I'd have them too.'

'I know, I feel the same. I feel terrible about the whole thing.'

'But you had to do what you did, didn't you, duckie?'

'I suppose I did. But the truth is I shouldn't have postured at being a hero. I wanted to work in with the wheels of history. And I should have left history alone, passed by on the other side. That's the truth. I'm a people man. The myths of history, these new faiths, they're all myths of dispossession. Take something away from someone and give it to someone else. But I'm for people, people keeping what they've struggled to have. I don't think we can yield up what exists for the possibility of what might. That's my idea of liberalism; kindness to what is, to those who now exist.'

'I don't think you can say that, duckie,' said Julie. 'Isn't the fact about our humanity that whatever we are, there's always a hurt involved? Because you're on that side of the bed, I'm on this. We all take up space, and the space we take up always deprives someone. You want to take up no space at all. Your answer to the parking problem is a car that disappears when it halts. But that doesn't happen, you see. You don't live without hurting.'

'What about love?' asked Walker. 'What we have now?'

'You think there's no hurting *there*? You think this is a pure situation? I'm here; your wife isn't. I'd say deprivation was going on here right now. There are no isolated cabins in the mountains. The threads go right back. You don't stop Europe existing when you cross the sea. A room of people doesn't stop functioning when you leave it.'

'But leaving at least takes away the complication of your presence. People are quickly not missed.'

'Is that why we drove out of Party so fast last night? Oh boy, Mr Walker, you're a strange man. You want to be a shadow. And you can't be.'

'Can't I?' said Walker, looking up at the ceiling.

Next day they drove on to Salt Lake City, where the main streets are wide enough for a wagon team to turn in; they spent the night in a downtown hotel and in the morning they visited the Tabernacle and the other Mormon sights. Then they drove on, past the lake, and through the salt flats and then the Nevada desert, to Reno, stopping here in cabins on the outside of town. They visited the tourist traps and the gambling clubs. The following day they drove up into the Sierras, past the dark blue of Lake Tahoe, and in the late afternoon reached the Pacific ocean north of San Francisco. The ocean broke on the beaches and Walker looked west to the east. Here was the furthest point he had reached; to go on was to go back. The sea was grey and stirring; Walker stirred with it. They spent this night in some sea-coast cabins and the next day drove south, through Muir Woods, where the prehistoric redwood trees reached vastly into the sky, across the Golden Gate Bridge and into San Francisco.

Julie had friends who were studying at Berkeley. So after they had parked in the city, and Julie had bought him two ties, two Oxford button-down shirts and a madras jacket at a men's store near Union Square, they drove through complicated flyovers and across the long Bay Bridge, past Treasure Island, into the campus country of Berkeley. Julie's friends had gone, but had left them the keys of their apartment; Walker fixed the heating and carried out garbage while Julie set up temporary house. 'This is a great place,' said Julie, 'I guess it's the freest place in the States.' The University of California campanile on the hill sounded out the hours, in deeper tones than Benedict Arnold's. They shopped in the supermarkets, replacing the stores that had been eaten at picnic tables in the mountains and in the long stretches of desert that had terrified Walker with its solitude and loneliness. But here were people again, and in the evening they drove back into San Francisco to eat a Chinese meal and hear jazz. 'We ought to live here,' said Julie. 'Isn't this something?' But Walker, drawn to the city, was drawn even more to the motion of the last few days; to pause even for two nights, as they planned, was to slow down the pace. The city, on its hills, crowned the bay, and when they got back to Berkeley they stood and looked back on it, its lights shining, its bay waters glinting. Shipping moved through the harbour, and the lines of traffic over the bridges were ceaseless.

Back in the apartment, while Julie made up the divan, Walker tried on his madras jacket. The colours, blue, red, and yellow, turned him into a harlequin. The mirror showed him a stranger. 'I think maybe we'll rescue you, after all,' said Julie when he strutted before her. Walker thought of the days through the desert, and the sight of the Pacific, and the Christmas crowds in San Francisco, where Santa Clauses rang bells on the streets, and knew that something was happening. Julie undressed, showered, got into bed, and read again through the letters she had picked up from General Delivery in San Francisco. But for Walker communication backward had stopped. His letters were piling up in Party, but he had left no directions. Christmas letters must be flowing in, but he would not see them; perhaps he would never see them, for he could not believe now that he would ever go back to Party again. His business there was finished. He was a disciple of solitude and love. He had reached, beyond politics and the working of factions, the ideal city, its population numbering two, its location mobile. Julie looked up; she wore glasses for reading and she peered at him through them. 'I wish this apartment was ours,' she said. 'Why don't we live like this? I guess we could.'

'Perhaps we could,' said Walker.

'Anyway we could stay here the rest of the vacation. The kids don't come back for ten days. Or we could go on, see LA and go down to Mexico. Which do you want?'

'Which do you want?' asked Walker.

'Oh, I'm easy,' said Julie. 'Have we arrived yet or haven't we?'

Walker thought a moment and said, 'No, I think we still have to go on a little way.'

They piled the luggage in the car the next day and drove down the coastal road to Carmel. They had looked at the Spanish customs house in Monterey and now, here, was an old mission church, where they looked around. They had booked in at a hotel close to the sea, and after they had eaten in the dining-room they went out in the darkness on to the cliffs. They crossed the golf course that occupied the cliff top and as they did so the sprinklers started working, throwing up water in the darkness. The fine spray blew in the air and they had to find their way carefully amid the high spurts of water. 'It's like walking in a minefield,' said Julie. The water rattled on the wind-blown trees. Then they looked down on the sea again, breaking below them. There were lights out in the bay.

'You know what this is?' asked Julie.

'What?' asked Walker.

'This day,' said Julie. 'It's Christmas Eve. How do you celebrate these things when you're not home? Maybe we should have a tree in the car.'

'We could decorate one of these pine trees,' said Walker.

'Yes,' said Julie. 'I'll put my bracelet on it. It's only a Woolworth bracelet. All Hillesley girls have Woolworth bracelets. It's anti-conspicuous consumption.'

After Julie had put her bracelet on the tree, they walked along the cliff. The misty spray from the golf course still blew over them, and once Walker went too close to one of the sprinklers and got soaked, as he seemed to have been getting soaked ever since he had reached America. 'Hark,' said Julie, 'I thought I heard a seal bark.' And there were noises down below the cliff. 'You know,' said Julie, when they got back to the hotel, and Walker had changed his clothes, 'I think this is one of the best Christmas Eves I ever spent. We ought to come back next year and see if the bracelet is still there.'

On Christmas morning they drove off early, heading south. The coast lost its cliffs and ridges and turned to flat plain and sandy beaches, and before they came to Los Angeles they reached the section where the oil rigs stand up and the air is full of fumes. They avoided most of Los Angeles – 'It's the world's worst city,' said Julie – and it took about an hour to race through and come out the other side. They stopped once, to buy Christmas presents; Julie asked for a pocket tape-recorder, Walker had some bongo drums. In the afternoon they found a coastal motel on the south of the city, and before they had Christmas dinner in the flowery dining-room, they took their first swim in the sea. The next day they again drove out early and headed for the border. By eleven they had passed through San Diego, crossing the ferry, and had reached the checkpoint. Walker worried about his visa, but the American immigration men volunteered to take him back in. Across the border they were assailed by salesmen, men holding up tea services, pottery cows, coloured blankets. 'Take a present for your neighbours, señores,' they shouted into the car. Julie stopped to buy a one-day car insurance from the office just through the Mexican checkpoint, and then they drove on to Tijuana. Striped donkeys stood in the streets, evidently painted, advertising souvenir shops. These shops lined all the main streets, and the Mexican vendors stood outside shouting at the car. When they stopped, small boys surrounded them. They had dark faces and implacable expressions, and they made Walker nervous. Mexico was conducive to insecurity altogether. The streets were ill-marked, and shawled men sat on the pavements. They went inside one of the stores, laid out with blankets, pottery, embroidery. Julie picked out a blanket and Walker asked the price. The reply the salesman gave was preposterous.

'It's too much,' said Julie.

'Give me an offer,' said the man. 'You are beautiful girl, I let you have it real cheap.'

'No, you tell me a price,' said Julie. The man reduced his price by half. 'I can get it for less than that down the street,' said Julie.

'You just got out of car,' said the man, 'this is the first shop you try.'

'I know, but I can still get it for less,' said Julie.

'Okay,' said the man, and he cut his price by half again. Walker paid and they came out with the blanket.

'That was fun,' said Julie.

'I hate that kind of bargaining,' said Walker.

'That's because you're afraid of losing,' said Julie. They had stopped outside another shop, which had a notice outside saying 'Use a piece of dead cow at moderate prices'. A boy came out and offered them another blanket; he asked less money than Walker had paid.

'You see,' said Walker.

'What do I care?' asked Julie, 'I enjoyed buying the blanket.'

'Hello, honey,' said two young Mexicans, stopping and looking at Julie with evident pleasure. 'Welcome to Mexico.'

'Thank you,' said Julie. The two men laughed and looked her up and down, taken with her neat bermuda shorts and sweater.

'You want to walk with us?' said one of them.

'No, I have a man to walk with, ' said Julie.

'Oh, this man? Leave him,' said the man.

'I love him,' said Julie.

'Oh, okay, you make love with him then. Good-bye, honey.'

'Good-bye, gracias,' said Julie.

Walker kicked a tuft of grass in the sidewalk and said, 'Well, let's get out of this place.'

'Why?' asked Julie.

'I don't like it. The whole sad place makes me uncomfortable. The way everyone stares; and all these people wanting to sell you things.'

'They're good direct people.'

'They're direct all right,' said Walker. 'They want my money and your body. They've got it all worked out.'

A sign outside an office said WED AND DIVORCE. 'Simple and to the point, look,' said Walker.

'Oh, quit beefing,' said Julie.

'I'm sorry.'

'No, I apologize for that, but enjoy it, duckie, come on.' A small Mexican boy was sitting in a doorway; Julie stopped and took a photograph.

'Dime, dime,' said the boy.

'Give him a dime,' said Julie.

'Oh, all right,' said Walker resignedly, handing over a coin.

'Come on, let's find a place to eat,' said Julie. The only place they could find immediately was a bare, dingy café with a sign saying 'Welcome Turistos'. The one Mexican dish Julie knew was chile con carne, and they both had that. It was hot and astringent. 'Let's go on a way,' said Julie. 'Maybe it's less touristy out of town.' They went back to the car and got in. They found their way through the town and on to a rough road that led beyond it, past a big sports arena, into the countryside. The land was poorly cultivated, the road rutted and poor. Walker sat in the passenger seat and looked disappointed.

Finally Julie stopped the car. 'I guess you've really made your mind up not to enjoy this, haven't you?' she said.

'I'm sorry, I can't help it. It makes me depressed and nervous and insecure. It just feels to me like a hostile place. I have no grip on it.'

'You wanted to come here.'

'I know, and now I want to go. I was wrong, we came too far.'

'Okay, I'll turn around.' She started the car and turned it round over the rough rutted track. 'You know,' she said, driving back toward Tijuana, 'Mexico is a dreamland for lots of Americans. They come here for truth, you know. But maybe the real Mexico is way down. This bit does look kind of sad. Hey, you hear anything?'

'What?'

'I thought I heard a kind of clanging noise in the car. That would really do it, a breakdown.' They came into Tijuana again; and there, in the middle of a junction on the main street, the car stopped. 'I can't get my gears,' said Julie, 'I guess something's happened to the transmission.'

'Oh, no,' said Walker. A policeman began to wave at the car.

'Come on,' said Julie, 'we'll have to push. Oh, boy, I just remembered something. A friend of mine had a flat tyre here and they put him in jail for two weeks for some reason.'

They got out; Walker pushed the car from the back and Julie pushed on the front door pillar, holding the driving wheel. A crowd of men lined the sidewalks, walking beside them and whistling at Julie's shorts and bare legs. 'Don't just look, push,' shouted Julie. The crowd laughed and clapped. 'Garage, garage?' Julie asked them, 'Service?' The crowd laughed again; some of them waved them onward. Walker plodded dejectedly on at the back as this display went on, pushing hard. They went on like this for a block, accompanied by the crowd, until they saw a garage on a corner. Julie turned the car in and they stopped. Walker sat down on the rear fender and tried to regain his breath. Flies landed on his sweating face. The Mexican serving petrol finally came over. 'Breakdown,' said Julie. The man apparently didn't speak English; he went inside and returned with another Mexican, with a bushy moustache, who was covered in oil.

'I think it's the transmission,' said Julie.

'No can fix,' said the man.

'Oh God,' said Walker, despairing, on his fender.

'But how can I get it fixed? Can anyone in Tijuana fix it?'

'Non,' said the man.

'Won't you please look at it, then?' The man brought out some tools and looked underneath and inside the car. 'Help me to talk to them, Mr Walker,' said Julie, coming round the back.

'I'm sorry,' said Walker, standing up, and noticing with horror that there were tears in Julie's eyes, 'I was exhausted.'

'You can sit,' said the man, waving them inside the garage. There was an old Ford under repair, with the engine out; they got inside the back seat. 'I never had a breakdown before,' said Julie.

'And I never had a car before,' said Walker.

'And here of all places,' said Julie. 'Why couldn't it happen across the border? It's only a few miles.'

The mechanic with the moustache came back to them after a while and said, 'You pay plenty money, I send boy to San Diego for part. Only way to fix.'

'All right,' said Julie, 'I'll do that.'

'You show me money,' said the man. Julie took out her wallet from her purse and showed a hundred-dollar note.

'Okay, I send boy,' said the man.

'How long will it take?' asked Walker.

'Oh, three hours for part. You pay extra, I work at night. Maybe fix by midnight.'

'Shall we do that?' asked Julie.

'It'll be cheaper than taking a hotel here. And I don't know that I'd like to do that,' said Walker.

'Okay,' said Julie.

They sat in the car and watched the life of Tijuana quiet down. The sun faded and darkness spread in the street. The mechanic had gone. 'What a day,' said Walker. Julie said nothing. 'Are you angry?' asked Walker. Julie, lying back on the seat, looking up at the torn roof of the Ford, nodded.

'With me?'

'Among other things, yes.'

'Why?'

'Guess,' said Julie. 'I don't think I much want to talk about it.'

'I see,' said Walker. He put his head back too. After a while, he put his hand on her knee. Julie left it there. The embarrassing piece of his cold flesh was without contact, and after a while he removed it. 'I'm sorry if I disappointed you,' he said.

'You did, Mr Walker, you did.'

'But I don't know quite what I did.'

'Oh, well, if you don't know. . . . '

Walker got out of the car and went over to the wounded Volkswagen. He found some cup cakes and the stove and a jar of instant coffee. He started up the stove in the corner of the dirty garage and made two cups of coffee. He took them back into the car. 'It tastes of oil,' said Julie.

'It's called Offee.'

'Where did you get the water from?'

'There's a tap in the corner.'

'Okay, so we die of typhoid as well. Who cares?'

'Want me to cook anything clsc? There's a can of beans.'

'I don't think I can face beans right now,' said Julie. 'Oh, Mr Walker, you know what you did? You gave in. You lost style. You let it beat you. There were two of us and you acted like there was only one.'

'Yes,' said Walker.

'I thought you'd grown up, I'd thought we'd rescued you from all that. But no. You let me do all the talking. You rode on my back. You looked away when I needed a little help. I thought you'd have taken to your feet and run away across the border, except I guess you thought it was too far.'

'I never thought of it,' said Walker.

'Technology scares you, primitive people you hate. You look like a coward to me.'

'That's unfair.'

'Well, anyway,' said Julie, 'there comes a time when a girl needs a man for other purposes than the one you seem most interested in.'

'You're being unfair.'

'Oh, I know it. But I'm trying to tell you something. I'm trying to tell you that you don't impress me so much any more. I think you're a leaver. I think you don't hold on. The offers you make don't last.'

'I think that's unfair too.'

'I'll tell you something, Mr Walker. I love you. I'd marry you if you asked me, right here, right now. But what I know about you is that you won't.'

'Why won't I?'

'Oh, you'll find a reason,' said Julie. 'But you can prove me wrong.'

'Why does marriage matter so much to you?'

'I suppose because it's you. I suppose because I want to know how far your belief in the one good, which you said was love, really goes. Because I wonder what that means, when you say it.'

'Oh,' said Walker. 'How to lose friends and isolate people. That's the book I should write.'

'I expect you will,' said Julie. 'Hey, is there a can anywhere around here?'

'I think there's a kind of place on the forecourt. Not that I'd recommend it.'

'Well, you wouldn't recommend anything around here, would you?'

When Julie had gone, Walker sat in the back of the Ford and put his head on his knees. The day, with its sun and its depression, had given him a headache. He couldn't get access to his sentiments, which seemed bottled up within him. His sense of suffering had driven him only into solitude. He wanted to break out, to engage, to say 'yes' to Julie, but all that he found ready to hand was the emotion of despair. There was no volition in him now; it had been there, but the last sad day of the journey had exhausted it. It had disappointed Walker in himself; it had questioned all that, in the last week, had taken place around him and within him. The drab, primitive, poverty-stricken town, corrupt, defeated, and senseless, was a place to escape as quickly as possible. Its insecurity and its vulgarity sent him back again in his thoughts to England. And its harsh light and its cruel questions had left him with nothing. The relationship with Julie, even, was not free of intrusion, and today the intrusion had been made. He looked out of the broken car at the shattered wooden frame of the garage, and heard, outside, hungry dogs barking in the back streets of the town. Julie stumbled in the entrance, coming back. He reached over the front seat and looked for the lights of the car, flicking switches on the dashboard panel. But nothing was working. 'I think I sprained my goddam ankle,' said Julie. He got out and made his way through the darkness, over a floor covered with oil patches and parts, to the doorway. Julie was leaning against it, holding her foot. 'What else needs to happen in this place?' she said.

'Does it hurt? Can you walk on it?'

'I can get to the car if you'll lend me your shoulder to lean on,' she said.

'Hold on, isn't there a torch in your car? I'll get it.'

'A flashlight? Yeah.'

Using the flashlight, they made their way to the Ford. Julie took off her shoe; the foot was puffy, and Walker said, 'Do you think I should try to find a doctor?'

'Hell, he'll only say he has to send to San Diego for a bandage,' said Julie. 'No, we'll just sit this thing out. What time is it?'

'About eight,' said Walker, flashing the torch on to his watch.

'That boy should be back now,' said Julie.

They heard his motorcycle drive up about an hour later. Then he drove off again. 'He'll be going to fetch the mechanic,' said Walker.

'I'll believe that when I see him.'

'How's the foot?'

'It's all puffed up. I just hope I can still drive when they get this goddam thing fixed. Oh, why aren't you a driver, Mr Walker?'

'I don't know,' said Walker, 'I seem to be short on all the skills.'

'Oh no, duckie, I didn't mean that. I'm sorry, really I am, Mr Walker, about all those things I said. But you must admit

330

we just don't work out, you and I. It's been a great experience and I'll always love you and never forget you, but I think it's all wrong. What do you think? Honestly and truly? Blessing the truth, being sincere?'

'I don't know,' said Walker, 'I think perhaps you got an inflated view of me, or came somehow to expect too much of me, and I'll go on being a disappointment to you.'

'But what about me? What are your feelings for me? That's something you never say.'

'Well,' said Walker, 'I'm proud to be in your company, and you attract me more, you're more beautiful and human, than anyone I ever met. I can't use the word "love" because it's been queered for me, but among all my ambitions for myself, staying in your company counts highest.'

'But for how long?'

'Now that I don't know. When the other parts of life come in, when the world starts pushing, then I'm lost. Like today.'

'What you mean is I'm an idyll?'

'I suppose so.'

'Well, what happens when we leave here?'

'I don't know,' said Walker, 'but I think I go home.'

'To England?'

'Yes.'

'To your wife?'

'Yes.'

'You're not even going back to Party?'

'Not if I can get a passage home.'

'Yes, well, I should have guessed,' said Julie.

'No, you couldn't, I didn't know before.'

'I suppose I did, I knew from when I met you on the ship. And the way you behaved to that sad kooky English girl. What was the name?'

'Miss Marrow.'

'Yes, that was it,' said Julie. 'That red hair and those funny clothes all hanging off her. She was about your level.'

'She was a nice girl,' said Walker.

'Oh, I believe it. And she didn't ask you for a thing. And that's what you like. You're a passive man; there isn't a

decision in you. You can't stand the questions. You're an intellectual but the questions make you shiver. Isn't that right?'

'I try to stand the questions.'

'Oh, you have the ambition, duckie, but the problem is,
you're too kind. You carry too many woes. You get thrown all
the time. There's everything waiting, if you chase it, but you
stop on the way and then say that the world doesn't give people
what it used to. I don't believe that. I believe you can have
everything, if you just know you're free. But you, Mr Walker,
you think you are, but really you're fixed. It's all those
coronations and all that changing the guard. They hooked
you, and you can't get loose.'

'Not a knight of infinity?'

'No, sir,' said Julie, 'you're more a knight of finity. I guess
that's something, or we wouldn't have had this great week.
But there it ends, I think; don't you?'

'No future?'

'Well, future's something you can't see but can believe in. I
miss the belief, Mr Walker. You haven't any hope.'

'Yes, I miss it too,' said Walker.

'Hey,' said Julie, 'look, here comes the mechanic. We
should be out of here soon. Back in motion, duckie.'

'Yes,' said Walker, 'back in motion.'

Back, back, back. The highway flicked under the wheels, the
blank and hopeless desert of the west rolled by, and Walker, in
his bright madras jacket, looked sadly and sullenly out through
the green sunshielded window from the height of a Greyhound
bus. Indian dwellings of corrugated iron and tar paper formed
small mounds in the desert sand. Bcyond on the horizon were
red ferocious hills. The thin strip of road wound across the
sand, marked out by the lines of telegraph poles, and going the
other way, going west, were cars with canvas water-bags
hanging on their fenders. Walker put his head on the high seat
rest and dozed remotely. Back, back to the family, back to the
safe compound where freedom was held in by obligation,
where the fire burned with connubial coal, where a daughter
played eternally with a panda on the hearthrug. 'I've been too

far off for too long,' he had written to Elaine in the quick note that was all he had had time for during the rest stop at Flagstaff. 'I wanted to be free but you were right; there isn't enough there to make free with. I'll come home like Tom Jones to be the good squire, and hope you'll want me.'

But going home to be the good squire, he could not forget the days on the road. Security already present in his heart, protected already by those green sunshield windows and the Greyhound driver – 'Safe, reliable, courteous', said the legend over his head – Walker was going home like a sacrifice. The wandering wilful self he had spent these last months upon was already starving to death in him from lack of sustenance. And Walker was sorry, very sorry, for he knew already that it was pleasanter by far to be that man. He patted his pocket where his steamship ticket lay; a travel agent in San Francisco had been able to advance his booking by seven months. The eastward journey was well in motion; after five days of day-and-night travel, he had only one afternoon in New York before he took his ship. America was only the things that lay behind him: Jochum getting ready to wander sadly out of Party, Julie lying in bed in the borrowed apartment in San Francisco and saying, 'I don't want you to write me any letters, Mr Walker. I told you how to be cool and that wouldn't be.' He had forgone all those ties by misunderstanding them; they were wrecked on the reefs, part of the barren voyage that had seemed to be going so well and so far. For this voyage Walker had no mythology; he refused to grant it any order or design. The country he was crossing had stopped making sense, and he was pleased; this was an anti-journey, a journey away from meaning. It was touched with illogicalities; sometimes the other buses, travelling in convoy, would appear in front of them, at others behind them, without any visible overtaking. Sometimes the scenicruiser would turn back on itself after leaving a stop and go in the direction it had come. Walker accepted this as a fact of other people's designs for journeys. Every now and then he had to count days and stops in order to understand where he was and how far he had come. Today it was January the first, the day teaching began again in Party; it was the day everyone would know he had taken an incomplete in his course, refused to come back.

So only casually he watched the infertile desert slip past. Cactus spikes stood up in the red sand. The bus overtook an old truck, the back laden with junk and Indians. A sign beside a shanty said NAVAJO RUGS. Then he saw something curious: a large round object passed by the side of the bus and disappeared in front of it. A moment later the driver picked up the microphone and said: 'Howdy, folks. I'm just lookin' through my windshield here and I seen one of my wheels go by and head out for the sagebrush. Ain't no need to panic, it's off the rear someplace and we got plenty more back there, but I'm going to have to pull off the highway and put that maverick right back on there where it belongs. 'Pologize for the delay. And oh, this desert sun's kind of hot, so if you folks get out there don't stay long with your heads uncovered or you'll get sick.' After a while the driver came back rolling the wheel. 'Beep, beep,' he said to the crowd, 'I'm a train.' The heat beat into the stationary coach. Walker tried to sleep in his seat, but the scorch from above was too intense. After about half an hour the driver came and stood at the front of the aisle, looking up the coach. He was a stout elderly westerner, in grey uniform, his cap pushed back. 'I'm having some trouble with this godderned wheel, folks, and I guess I'll have to wait for the other bus to come by to get a message to the depot,' he said. 'Now, I'm worried about all you good people gettin' heatstroke out here, so I got to ask you, for your safety would you mind steppin' out and lyin' under this bus out of the sun? Otherwise I can't take responsibility for you all.' The passengers murmured and then began to file out. They got, one by one, under the coach, in the shade, lying full-length with their faces close to the bus's underbelly. They laughed a lot and someone passed around a bottle of Coca-Cola. They didn't seem uneasy, but Walker, lying in the sand in his harlequin jacket, sweating profusely, grew privately distraught. Deserts he feared; places of breakdown were places of misfortune. He saw his evil chance at work again. He thought of rattlesnakes and of running out of water; such disasters must be run-of-the-mill news, small print, in this big country where planes were always falling from the sky and car pile-ups were so common that they played carols early for the Christmas automobile casualties. He thought of cold desert nights and coyotes. He listened to the desperate clatter of the driver as he worked on the wheel. What was the question to ask in the desert when, going the wrong way, an admitted failure, he was arrested even in that progress? It was clear that the desert said what Jochum said it said: nothingness is here, the world is bland. Desert and New York said the same in different guises: Out of Visions; this is what you have made; there is no you.

And then gradually into his mind there seeped the further disturbing thought: it was that time was running out. The escape route was closing. He had only eight hours spare between the arrival time of the Greyhound in New York and the hour he had to present himself at the West Side pier where his ship would sail. If it sailed away without him, he had little money. It might be weeks before another passage would come his way. So New York, that urban desert, would claim him as it nearly had before. He would lodge in some cheap hotel, without a job, with no way out, unadopted by England, un- wanted by America. He would wander the city, peering hopelessly through the glass at the blueberry pies in the Horn and Hardhart automats. He would turn back and forth, back and forth, in a narrowing American circle, in perpetual loneliness, unable to reclaim his job in Party, unable to reach his wife and his home. His spirit would surely give out; it had little left to thrive on. Buffoon and plaything to the end, governed by his gift for misfortune, the final exhaustion of hope would come; the vision of no vision. That was the con- sistency that governed his life; it lay in the way the world had elected to disappoint him. Terror seized his bowels. Jochum had said, 'You keep asking the universe "How ought I to live?" But it can't answer.' Julie had said: 'You're a passive man. There isn't a decision in you.' But it had answered; he had given himself over to the fates who govern journeys, and they, fates of misfortune and not of fortune, had turned his journeys into nonsense. He had taken his clues from the universe, and it had told lies; but lies were an answer, How, though, had it known it could treat him as plaything? How had it known he was weak? When would the comic muse, whose literary friend he had tried so often to be, shower her famed, final good fortune upon him?

'It's fixed,' said the driver.

The bus reached Albuquerque three hours late, and was taken out of service. The replacement was a sadder, older Greyhound, with an unconfident expression about its front, as if too much were being demanded of it. Porters changed the luggage over and stowed it beneath the replacement vehicle; Walker's face peered forth until he saw his two cases, his typewriter, and his bongo drums safely brought across. The new driver, too, was a sadder, older man, depressed at the impossible task of making up his schedule. And as the hours went by, and the bus pressed onward across central America, it slipped more and more behind time. Walker sat in his seat, hot with tension. He watched the middle west unfold beyond the windows – corn and hogs. Then they penetrated into the rougher, rolling land of the eastern states and upward toward New York. The great conurbations appeared; the post-houses grew more sophisticated; the other passengers, who changed from time to time, were less friendly. The world was returning to the spirit of the old New York malaise. Two youths sitting behind Walker, drinking from a bottle, began to fight in their seats; the driver stopped the bus. 'Get off or quit,' said the driver, 'I don't move until you decide.' 'Oh, get on, get on,' cried Walker in his heart. In the night a soldier slept on Walker's shoulder, and toward morning vomited between his feet; Walker didn't sleep at all.

Once through the tunnel on to Manhattan, they found traffic packed on streets dirty with snow. Garbage cans overflowed in gutters. On one of the Avenues they came upon a vast road-building operation; the street was dug out to half its width for repair, and surrounded by barriers – DIG WE MUST – FOR A GROWING NEW YORK. The bus moved forward in short spurts, and it was over an hour before they reached midtown. 'We're really snarled up here today,' said the driver. 'The Penn Railroad is on strike and that's why all the traffic is out this way.' Then they reached the terminal. Walker pushed down to the front of the car to be out of it early; then he had to wait until the redcaps unlocked the luggage compartment and unloaded his goods. Suitcases, typewriter, bongo drums. Walker hung them about him and fled through the terminal crowds. He reached the door and saw the clock above it. He was due on his ship five minutes ago.

What was left, then, was despair and sorrow and defeat. He was a stranded man; there was no rescue. He walked outside and stood in the cold street, his luggage strung about him, while along the sidewalk by the bus depot the bums of New York watched him amiably, the world's ignoble, the little version of man, ready to claim him. Before the bus had stopped, he had counted his money; forty-five dollars was his worldly wealth, and of wealth spiritual there was none.

A yellow cab drew up by the kerbside and the driver pushed open the door. 'Where ya goin', mac?' he shouted. Whimsical hope butted Walker; he got in with his luggage, and gave the number of the pier. 'Take me one hour minimum in this snarl-up,' said the driver.

'Is there no way of getting there fast? My ship is sailing just about now.' Walker, saying this, imagined the vessel, easing out past the Battery and the Statue of Liberty into the peace of the ocean, the *Welcome Aboard* banners flapping in the bar where the Get-Together Dance would be held.

'Yeah,' said the driver, 'buy a helicopter. Odderwise you take one hour minimum.'

'One hour,' said Walker.

'You wanna go or doncha?' asked the driver.

'Yes, I'll go,' said Walker, 'I'll give myself over to fate.'

'Yeah, why not?' said the driver.

'You should see my fate,' said Walker.

'Take a look at any guy's,' said the driver. 'Take me, I oughta have gone to college. Business school. Now I drive a beat-up cab.' Walker sweated in the cold back seat, the unfortunate traveller.

'One automobile too many and this island stops, you know that?' said the cabbie, inching forward in the blockage. 'We live on the edge of chaos here.'

They moved slowly onward through tenemented streets, past the abattoir. They stopped again, waiting to cross the Riverside Expressway. Hunting along the piers, where the ships stood, Walker saw his own vessel, still at the dock.

They reached the water's edge and Walker leapt out. He grabbed suitcases, typewriter, bongo drums. 'I want to be on that ship,' he said to a longshoreman, paying the cabdriver.

'Not a chance,' said the longshoreman, hostilely, 'they already took up the gangplank.' Walker took up all his luggage and rushed in through the entrance. 'Okay, mac,' said the longshoreman, suddenly redeemed, no longer what he was and had been since Walker's last time here, 'we take a chance.' He seized the two suitcases and ran with them up the staircase. Walker flapped behind, in his harlequin jacket, typewriter in one hand, drums in the other.

The immigration men were talking round a desk, but one looked up at Walker and took his papers. 'You quitting already?' he said. 'Your visa gives you another six months.'

'I've got to go home,' said Walker.

A siren sounded on the ship. He ran along the pier, fat, flabby, trapped in being Walker, while the wooden timbers rebounded beneath his feet. The sweat ran down the blubbery flesh in which he was imprisoned, in spite of the winter cold and the breeze blowing hard off the Hudson. He prayed to Chance: For once, just once, be kind. And then he felt an old familiar sensation growing in his nose. It was a snuffle; he was starting with a cold. For the first time in his life he had gone through half a winter without a chill; the American climate had evidently suited him. He was brown, his health was better, his dandruff seemed to have gone. But one only had to think about England and one was swabbing away at a cold. No time to stop; he dipped in his pocket as he ran and brought out a rather dirty handkerchief. 'Achoo, achoo, achoo,' he cried into the high, echoing, empty building. And suddenly confidence overwhelmed him and he knew that he was going home.

There was no gangplank, now, but at the far end of the dock a small rope-and-metal ladder led up to the ship's high side. The longshoreman reached it first. 'Guy here wants to come aboard. Passenger got caught in the traffic snarl-up,' he shouted. Walker reached in his pocket and felt the final forty dollars. Two stewards emerged at the head of the ladder and came down toward him. Walker took the notes and gave them out; twenty for the longshoreman, ten each for the stewards. The stewards took the cases and the typewriter. Walker held on to the drums, all that he was going back with. He looked up at the steep side he had to climb. Then, above him, he heard a cry. Over the rail, high in the air, a gauzy scarf waved. 'Hello there, Mr Bigears,' screamed a voice. Walker groaned, and sneezed, and applied himself to the ladder.

Epilogue

The committee meeting convened to appoint next year's creative writing fellow took place in the Administration Building over a lunch hour one day toward the end of March. When they arrived, one of President Coolidge's many secretaries was setting up the tape-recorder: 'Come right in,' she said, 'and talk good.' They gathered round the shiny conference table; there were several members of the English Department; there was Dean French; there was Selena May Sugar from Physical Education. They spread out their lunches on the table and looked through the window at the snow outside. There was no sign of spring yet; Party and the campus of Benedict Arnold were still locked in ice. The campanile began to ring out one o'clock and on its last stroke President Coolidge came in. He sat down at the head of the table and called the meeting to order with his special Phi Beta Kappa key. The campanile began a rendering of 'There Is Nothing Like a Dame'. 'Okay,' he said. 'Well, this meeting's to consider about next year's writing fellowship in this U. I got several apologies for absence and other absences. Dr Wink's away on sabbatical; I had a card from him from Perugia and he wants you all to know he's having a great time and that the Italians are going crazy for business administration. I think that's an honour for all of us. Harris, well, Harris isn't too well right now and he felt he couldn't make it. We usually have the present writer here, but this year, I guess some of you, most of you, know, the man we brought out here was suddenly called away in the middle of last semester and, to be frank, we haven't heard a word out of him since. You might like to know he only took his salary up to the day he quit this campus. Now just a minimal point before we hand over to the Head of the English Department:

341

I always say this, but remember if you don't talk good and loud into that tape-recorder Alison down in the pool ain't going to hear a single goddam word. Well, okay, right, I'll hand over to the new English Department Chairman. Okay, Bern?'

'Right, thank you, President,' said Bernard Froelich. 'I ought to start out by saying how sorry I am that Harris isn't here. As you all know, Harris did a hell of a lot for the writing fellowship and in a way it's hard not to associate it with him. He really worked it up to what it is now.' Froelich spoke with ease and comfort; the role of chairman sat on him well, and had done, from the day he had been elected by the department after Harris Bourbon had resigned. 'Of course,' said Froelich, 'it meant so much to him that, as I believe most of you know, it was the issue on which he resigned the Chairmanship. I think we mustn't forget that in our discussion of it.'

'Well, yes, that's right, Bern,' said President Coolidge. 'It was a very unfortunate matter, but Harris came out of it right well. He had his ethics and he stuck by his ethics and I'm always impressed by a man who knows his own principles. Now we all know that Harris boobed a bit in not making enough inquiries at the start, and letting our writer last year get way out of line, but I think that just shows how openhearted and liberal Harris has always been and still is, I guess.'

'Well, suppose we all read that situation differently,' said Froelich. 'But that's all the more reason for being especially careful in our appointment this year. If we want to make an appointment, that is. Because I remember last year Harris – I wish he was here – Harris raised the question of whether the fellowship should continue, whether it contributed enough to the university. I expect we'll all want to talk about that, especially when I tell you that we've already had difficulties in our approaches this year.'

'I thought you were really rooting for it last year, Dr Froelich,' said Selena May Sugar.

'Well, I was, Selena,' said Froelich, 'but my view is that a fellowship like this can only exist where the writer in question isn't under pressure. Now, as we all know, and all deplore, a writer at this university is still under pressure. That's why Mr Walker's not sitting in that chair right there. . . . '

'Oh, I don't think you can say that, Bern,' said President Coolidge. 'I think everyone has to admit that if Mr Walker had wanted to stay on this campus he could have stayed. No, I don't see any blame on this U for what happened to Mr Walker.'

'Yes, well, it's a contentious point, and I'll drop it right now,' said Froelich. 'Now that I've put it on record. But I'd just like to make one proposal to this meeting. I don't know whether this is possible under the terms of the funds, but I'd like to suggest that we accept the fact that the writing-fellowships have been less than successful, and we put the money into a literary quarterly edited from this campus by the staff of the English Department.'

Having exploded his bombshell, Froelich sat back. He felt pleased with himself and a little impressed at this handling of this situation. 'Aren't you writing a book this year, Bernard?' asked Selena May Sugar. Froelich, a man unused to blushing, did slightly blush. His book on Plight had now been refused by four publishers, a fact unknown to his department, and now that he had attained the status he had long ago intended to attain there seemed little need to sail in the difficult waters of publishing any longer. One published only to become what he already was. Froelich's sense of mission remained urgent with him, but he saw it being served in new ways. A magazine would raise his voice high over the prairies, and it would not betray, as writers could betray. Magazines did not, like Walkers, run away, or fear for what they had said, or turn the look of distrust on to their benefactor. The discussion went on, in the dark March light, and Froelich added his word here and there. President Coolidge pointed out that the fund was specifically for a writer; Froelich pointed out that the donor of the fund was still alive, and could be approached. 'In fact,' he said, 'I went to see him a couple of weeks ago, and he wouldn't have any objection, if that clears things up at all.'

'I don't think you ought to have done that, Bern,' said President Coolidge.

'I know how busy you are, President,' said Froelich. 'I thought if the matter was to be discussed at the meeting we'd better find out the lay of the terrain.'

'Well, there's something in that, Bernie,' said Coolidge. 'All right, let's put this one out on the prairie and see if the coyotes grab it.'

Froelich looked around the table and could see success ahead. He looked at an empty chair and had a wish come to him: it was the wish that James Walker were sitting in it to see all this achievement. He often thought of Walker. He knew he had left town, sneaking off into the night, because he believed that to provide this success was all he had been in Party for. He had gone believing himself a manipulated man, and believing too that he, Bernard Froelich, was puppeteer of the whole marionette show. His cryptic letter of resignation, written from San Francisco as he hared eastward for the home-bound boat, had said as much. Froelich had read it in suffering; it was the first thing he had plucked from Harris's files when he took over the chairmanship. 'Please accept my formal resignation from the Creative Writing Fellowship,' it said. 'You may cut off my salary from the point I left. I regret the embarrassment this may cause you; though I save most of my regret for the embarrassment I have brought to Dr Jochum. I hope my action may even facilitate his return to Benedict Arnold, though that is probably too much to hope. For my whole presence I apologize. My one thought – it is not a consolation – is that my short stay probably helped Dr Froelich's book a bit. If I didn't have any Plight when I arrived, he certainly did all he could to provide me with some.' At first reading – he had looked at it many times since – Froelich had sat down, shivering, in his chair. A mistake had been made! For what it overlooked was that Froelich had *cared*. What Walker had never understood, then (though surely there were moments when he came near to it), was that Froelich had loved the man. In fact, the letter was spoken out of that same lack of self-knowledge from which Froelich had attempted to redeem him. We recognize the nature of things, the process of history, or we perish, retire into hopeless provinciality. The lesson was an urgent one and the only one that could have saved Walker; but the pupil had gone, cut class, returned home. The truth was that Walker, this subjective pessimist, this believer in personal relationships (and a conspicuously bad performer in what he believed in), could never have succeeded. Without Froelich he would have done worse.

The odd thing was that it was Froelich, whom Walker castigated as objective, inhuman, who was left with the disquiet. From it all, it was Walker who sailed away most intact, wrapped in his prejudices, confirmed in his doubts, bundled up in his old self – able, of course, to pick up a spare life at the point where he had left it on his departure from England. Behind him, indeed, the world had reshaped; a man had resigned, a man had become department head. This was a natural product, since, eventually, it was inevitable that the world favoured those who had self-knowledge, who understood history, who had ends in view. But that was all Walker could see in it, and there was more. For Walker, morality and humanity were, it seemed, only on the side of those who lost. What happy confirmation he must find in the fact that Froelich had gone forward, and he, Walker, had, well, gone back. The truth was that there were no special injustices involved; that, finally, was what Froelich wanted to show Walker. Even now, the President was slapping his file of papers on the table, and accepting Froelich's proposal to eliminate future Walkers, and already thinking of the meeting of the Committee for Examining Student Ethics that he had now to move on to. From the point of view of the chubby Englishman that must seem all that had happened. But Froelich munched his hamburger and watched the tape flip off the reel and he did not rejoice. Rather he was missing James Walker, missing him really very much.

Waldorf

James Goldman

As an artist, Waldorf felt he had to mature – before he became too old.

So he ran away. He left his unloving wife and over-loving mother and went to Puerto Crisco – where a painter he admired had found success.

But Waldorf was followed there. And the people – the dangerous, dedicated people – who followed Waldorf were followed there. And Waldorf of the thinning hair and thickening stomach suddenly started being seduced by beautiful women.

In fact, a lot of funny things happened to Waldorf. Like finding himself mixed up in the mad and deadly world of agents and double-agents, of the C.I.A., the C.I.C., the F.B.I. not to mention the Chinese, the Russians and M.I.5. But by then he wasn't in the mood to laugh . . .

Not for sale in the U.S.A. or Canada

A Long Way to Shiloh

Lionel Davidson

The message of the Scroll is baffling, fragmented –
and sensational! Buried somewhere in Israel is the
True Menorah, the great golden symbol of Judaism
lost for two thousand years.

The Israelis have a copy, the Jordanians have a copy
and both want the Menorah. The Jordanians have
their infiltrators and their strong-arm men. The Israelis
have Casper Laing – a brilliant young Professor of
Semitics with a genius for hunches and a most
unprofessorial libido . . .

His cracking of the code is just about the most
fascinating piece of detection you've ever read. And the
ending? Let's just call it unguessable.

Not for sale in the U.S.A.

The Rose of Tibet

Lionel Davidson

A selection of comments on Lionel Davidson's novel of straight adventure is printed below:

'I hadn't realized how much I had missed the genuine Adventure story – not thriller, not detective, without social significance – until I read *The Rose of Tibet*' – Graham Greene

'Has all the excitement and wonder of Rider Haggard plus a great deal more. Combines the breathless, keep-you-reading techniques of Haggard with his own modern brand of realism, horror, and irony . . . this is the kind of book you have been waiting for' – Robert Pitman in the *Sunday Express*

'Even experienced readers will find themselves . . . eager for the book to go on longer' – *The Times Literary Supplement*

'Calls forth a deeper, more ancient response than the fashionable novel. A first-class piece of story-telling, well plotted, convincing, suspenseful. Can this book fail to be a best seller? – *Sunday Telegraph*

'He wears the mantle of Buchan, Rider Haggard, Oppenheim. Adventure fiction in the grandest of grand manners, exquisitely written, consistently entertaining. The author is that rare, despised, badly needed type of artist whom critics have shoved upstairs with a contemptuous kick and a superior sniff – the superbly accomplished teller of tales' – *John O'London's*

'An excellent, imaginative and entirely satisfactory adventure story' – *Observer*

Not for sale in the U.S.A.

The Night of Wenceslas

Lionel Davidson

On the strength of this first novel Lionel Davidson's
work has been compared with that of John Buchan,
Graham Greene, Eric Ambler, and even Kingsley
Amis. Certainly this thrilling story, so reminiscent
of *The Third Man*, is told in the idiom of today with all
the imagination and uninhibited will of the true
story-teller.

Young man-about-town Nicolas Whistler, whose
father had once had an interest in a Bohemian
glassworks, really had no choice when he was suddenly
'invited' to make a business trip to Prague. Happily
there was said to be no danger in the journey: Nicolas
was no hero. But as he becomes more and more
deeply engulfed in the seamy underworld of power
politics, the reader is bound to go the whole way with
this reluctant spy – as if to discover his own fate.
'Fast-moving, exciting, often extraordinarily funny.
The freshest first for months' – *Sunday Times*

'Don't miss it. Brilliant' – *Observer*

Night of Wenceslas was chosen by the British Crime
Writers' Association as the Best Crime Novel of 1960
and awarded the Silver Quill by the Authors' Club
as the Most Promising First Novel.

Not for sale in the U.S.A.

La Chamade

Françoise Sagan

Four people. A woman who has not known the
passionate turmoil of love for ten years; who suddenly
encounters the need for no other life. A man with
devotion enough to let her go. A younger man with
desire enough to keep her too close. A woman who
watches, tautly aware that impossible indifference must
hide the hurt within her.

Four people, jaggedly emerging from the superficial
gloss of the Paris social set, each drawn out by
Mademoiselle Sagan's impressive insight into real
life and real love. La Chamade? The roll on a drum to
announce defeat. But whose is the victory?

Also available

Aimez-vous Brahms . . .

Bonjour Tristesse

A Certain Smile

Those Without Shadows

Not for sale in the U.S.A. or Canada

Night and Silence Who is Here?

Pamela Hansford Johnson

Matthew Pryar wasn't really the type to shove nice old men down staircases, or so everyone agreed, except the nice old man in question, which nearly ruined Matthew's chances at the nice American University that allowed him to potter about to his heart's content while pretending to write a thesis about Dotty Merlin's poetry.

Pamela Hansford Johnson's second Dotty Merlin book sees the oh-so-English Matthew Pryar facing up to the Americans, scoring lots of points and winning the biggest prize of all in the end.

Also available
Cork Street Next to the Hatters
The Unspeakable Skipton
An Error of Judgement
The Last Resort

Not for sale in the U.S.A.